AGENT OF THE CONFEDERATION

BOOK 1

I0553219

SOLDIER

Colonel Jonathan P. Brazee
USMC (Ret)

Acknowledgements:

I want to thank all those who took the time to offer advice as I wrote
this book, and the list is lengthy. Thanks first goes to Micky Cocker,
James Caplan, and Kelly O'Donnell for their editing. Then, thanks has
to go to the beta readers who read the book in its rawest form and
helped me decide to release it. I took many of their comments on how
to fix the book to heart. I have to thank, in no particular order: David
Withe, Michael Frederick, Jim McNeil, Robert Gunter, George Hadley,
Michael Fox, Ed Vaisbort, Fraser Butterworth, Randall Reynolds, CB
Glover, Major Frank Anderson, USMC (Ret), Timothy Zeiger, Brent
Spurrell, Master Sergeant Thomas Chitwood, USMC (Ret), Master
Gunnery Sergeant Jim Brown, USMC (Ret), Craig Moody, Colonel
James Mathews, Army National Guard, John McGuire, Armando "Abe"
Abrams, David Kysar, Robert Burnham, Kelly Roche, Chad Downing,
Sherry Bacon Graves, Michael Nordstrand, John McGuire, James
Ellsworth, Michael Graves, and Keith Hickson. Without your help and
advice, this book would never have been published.

Cover by Jude Beers

DEDICATION

SMSGT Gary Koske, USAF (Ret)
1946-1917

AUTHOR'S NOTE

Full disclosure:

Soldier came into being when a young new writer asked, through an editing group, to write in my United Federation Marine Corps universe. I asked my mailing list for suggestions, and the name of a minor character that sparked the most interest was Titus Pohlmeyer, the Confederation of Free States agent who assisted both Ryck Lysander and his twins, Esther and Noah.

I decided to go ahead with the project, writing out a detailed, 12,000-word outline of the first book and sent it through the editing group to my co-writer, coincidently named Jon. To be honest, while I knew I would have to spend an inordinate amount of time on rewrites, I never knew just how much it would actually entail. After six or seven rounds on the first six chapters, I finally thought we had something acceptable pending my final rewrite, and I thought we had a meeting of minds and were on a roll. However, the next chapters were a regression instead of a progression, with weaker writing and unbelievable diversions from my original outline. They were beyond the scope of a heavy edit to fix. I tried one more time to bring the novel in line with my concept, but, to be blunt, the rest was unusable. I could not, in all due conscience, release the book, even under a pen name.

With the concurrence of the editing staff that was managing Jon, I ended up buying him out, and I completely rewrote the rest of the book except for two chapters that I partially used. I was still willing to give Jon co-author credit, but he demurred, telling the editors he only wanted the paycheck. I never even got his last name.

I was still hesitant to release the book, but I sent it out to several dozen beta readers, and all but one told me to release it, so here it is.

I hope you enjoy it.

Jonathan Brazee
North Las Vegas
September 2018

BELLEVIUE

Chapter 1

"This is it, our chance to make a quick end to this revolt and bring honor to the Iron Bastards. As Captain Anand briefed us, the bulk of the Publicas' forces are currently pressing an offensive toward Melmuani, with most of their heavy artillery, armor, and infantry committed, leaving their northern lines exposed for the moment. Alpha and Charlie Companies will be pushing across the river here at Hobson's Ford with a surprise assault on their headquarters." Major Yamin told the assembled soldiers, wielding his laser-pointer like a weapon. "We'll cut off the head of the snake and be home by Founders' Day."

Private Second Class Titus Pohlmeyer, Confederation Army, standing in the back of the CP with the other junior enlisted, listened intently. Not much of what the major was saying pertained to him, but this was going to be his first taste of action, and he was both excited and apprehensive at the same time. The infantry companies would be seeing most, if not all, of the action, and that was where he knew he should be: at the front line, defending the Confederation of Free States with glory and honor, fighting toe to toe with whichever enemy they happened to be fighting. Not in a support role a long way from the front. Still, even in the rear with the gear, this was technically going to be combat.

He had a hard time focusing on what the major was saying, however, and not just because much of this either didn't affect him or went over his head. It was a hot day, and without AC in the temporary command post, the sheer number of bodies crammed into the briefing made it feel like a sauna.

Focus, Titus. This is the real deal.

He was surprised that he and the rest of the lower-rank enlisted soldiers were even there in the first place. Normally, they'd never be at an operations brief, but in a surprisingly egalitarian decision, the CO decided this was going to be a "teaching moment." Or, as Sergeant Bates said, maybe the commander just wanted more people to witness his military genius.

The major pointed a laser dot at the holographic display of the valley where the Publicas had set their CP--according to intelligence reports anyway. The position was at the V in a fork of the river, which provided a natural defense against any unaided infantry advance. The situation reminded him of something, and it took Titus a moment to remember what it was. Titus had never been a big jock in school, preferring gaming, and the Major's map and disposition of forces was a dead ringer for one of the battlefields in *Dante's Armageddon III.*

Titus's forces had been wiped out both times he'd played that particular battle, and he leaned forward, interest piqued. Maybe he'd learn here just what he'd done wrong.

"The commander's intent is to take out the Publica HQ, thereby leaving their forces headless. This is the enemy's center of gravity. Engage any enemy along your axis of advance, but do not seek them out. Do not get bogged down."

He waved his hand, and the battle symbols appeared, arrows indicating the infantry companies' axes of advance.

That's about what I did the first time I played, and Hiram wiped me out.

The major started going through his overview, and the more Titus watched, the more he became concerned. Yes, he'd only played a game, but those games were based on reality, or so the makers claimed. And as with many gamers, Titus was a history buff, always trying to discover an advantage he could use in the next game.

"Before we dive into the details, are there any questions so far?"

Titus looked around to see if anyone else was going to mention the obvious problem with the major's plan. A captain in the front row raised a hand, and Titus felt relieved, but the captain only wanted a clarification on the ROE.

"Anything else?" the major asked.

Titus kept expecting someone to speak up. He was just a PSC, a nobody, but it was glaringly obvious that the major had missed something important. Titus had always been intelligent, one of the smartest in his classes. He might not be a physical stud, but he sometimes compensated by being a know-it-all, speaking up when he thought others were wrong. It didn't make him many friends at school.

Don't do it, Titus. Just sit and play invisible.

But he couldn't. Almost beyond his control, his traitorous arm raised on its own, and he took half a step forward. It took the major a few moments to see it and pause in his briefing.

"Yes, Private?" he asked, clearly surprised any of the enlisted soldiers, much less a private, actually had a question.

Titus stood, the stink of boot camp still so strong that he reverted to form and snapped to attention. "Sir, Private Second Class Titus Pohlmeyer. The private wonders . . ." he started, instinctively reverting to the boot camp form of a recruit addressing a DI before remembering he was in the real Army now. "I was wondering, sir. There's that ridgeline between Alpha and Charlie Companies' axes of advance for about five hundred meters. That high ground would be easily defended, and they could pretty easily rain fire down on Alpha and Charlie Companies. Sir."

That's what Hiram had done to my attacking forces, at least.

The major seemed to resist the urge to roll his eyes, and for a moment, Titus thought he was going to ignore him, but he turned toward one of the other officers present at the briefing. "Would you like to take this one, Captain?"

Captain Anand, a tall man with a bulge already edging over his belt, grunted as he took to his feet. Unlike most front-line infantry officers, he didn't have any ribbons on his chest, only the crossed daggers of the Army Intelligence Corps, or AIC.

"Major, as I briefed in the Enemy Situation, we've been monitoring the Publicas' chatter extensively, and everything points to the all available troops are being sent forward to reinforce their push to the city. Overhead surveillance confirms this. Stretched as they are, no troops would have been left to defend that ridgeline, particularly as they have no idea that we have bypassed their lines and are in a position to attack. That's our conclusion, supported by our up-to-date satellite imaging of their AOA."

Yamin turned back to Titus. "Does that answer your question, Private?" he asked, his tone evident that he was humoring him.

Titus understood social graces, but that never seemed to stop him before. He knew he shouldn't be questioning an officer, but he also had a burning drive to make his points known. It was an annoying habit, but sometimes he couldn't help himself.

Here it goes! he thought, taking a deep breath before jumping into the deep end.

"Sir, even a squad could effectively hold that ridgeline against an assault. It seems unlikely, even if their forces are stretched as thin as the captain says, that they'll just leave their HQ with a such a massive blind spot in their defense."

And it's also pretty stupid to assume that we haven't been spotted. They'd got drones, just like we have, he thought, not that he was going to risk calling an officer "stupid."

"Force Intel reports that all Publicas troops are heading toward the front, *Private*." The major made a point to emphasize the last word, driving the chain of command down firmly. "Unless you have intelligence that suggests otherwise?"

Titus's pale face turned a shade of dark red. "Sir, no, sir!"

"Then I think we can proceed as planned. Unless there are any further questions?"

The devil on his shoulder wanted him to argue, but a PSC did not debate majors. He shut up and faded back.

"Shut the fuck up, boot," Sergeant Bates whispered into his ear. "Who do you think you are, Dellingham?"

It doesn't take a Marshall Dellingham to see the vulnerability, he thought, but for once, keeping that to himself, he kept his eyes locked to the front.

"Excellent, then we can proceed with the Concept of Operations . . .

Titus kept staring at the holo while the major droned on. The major seemed to be using all the correct terminology, right out of the military textbooks, but he seemed to be missing a glaring reality. Was Titus the only one to see the vulnerability in the plan?

Still, he was just a private second class and they were the experts, so maybe he was wrong and they were right.

He hoped.

Chapter 2

"So, we got out to the dock, you know? We were both drunk, so the moment she sees the moonlight, she's got the hots for me. We start going at it, her hands all over me, and—hey, you listening, man?"

Titus snapped his head around, adjusting his angle on the bridge's pillar. "Oh yeah. Hands all over you. I get it." He hadn't been listening, just catching the last few words, but he assumed that Fraser had been recounting one of his many high school conquests.

Fraser and Titus had been all but inseparable during boot camp. An odd thing too, since they were virtually nothing alike. Fraser had been a jock in his teen years, playing Crescent Rules Football until he graduated. Unlike Titus, whose stature could only be described as average at best, Fraser was a hulk of a man, standing a full head taller than him, with the broad shoulders and thick arms that came with hours in the gym. He'd done well at boot camp, but due to a knee injury that had never fully healed, he'd been relegated to the Engineering Corps alongside Titus. Both were bitter about it, which only reinforced the bond that the two had formed at boot camp.

"Anyway, we're going at it, hot and heavy, and then she pushes me away, looking all seductive-like, you know, and I'm thinking she's gonna start stripping for me. But then, the fucking worst thing happens."

"It turns out that she's a part of some pagan cult, and she starts carving your heart out with her bare hands while chanting in a dead language?"

"What? No. No, man. What's wrong with you? No, she turns around and pukes all the beer into the lake. She then sits down, mumbles something about me being the best she's ever had, and then falls asleep. On the dock."

"Not the worst thing that could ever happen, then," Titus said, setting a charge on the pillar and pressing the button to pull his line up until he was level with Fraser again. "How did we get to talking about this again?"

"You asked me what was the worst sex I'd ever had."

"Right. Does it count if you never actually got her clothes off, though?"

"You guys know this is the squad alternate net, not the P2P, right?" Sergeant Bates, their squad leader, broke in.

Shit. Who else was listening in?

Fraser coughed and sputtered, sending himself into a gentle spin as he disengaged from the pillar on which he'd been descending. "Oh, uh, sorry, Sergeant."

"Don't apologize to me, Private. Apologize to the rest of the squad for making them listen to your poor-ass bullshit."

"I could stand to hear a bit more," PFC Nuar, passed over the squad net.

"Shut it," Bates said. "You two finished setting those charges yet?"

"Uh, roger that, Sergeant," Titus said. "Setting the last one now." He placed one last pack of explosives onto the pillar of the bridge, applied the sealant, and poked the detonator into the package. "Done."

The cables from which they hung suspended jerked into motion and started pulling them back up to the top of the bridge. They could hear the rattle of the cables as they were reeled in, but that was quickly drowned out by the sounds of distant gunfire and explosions. There was chatter on the platoon net, but Titus declined to listen in. Glory and honor were being had elsewhere. He was just here to make sure that none of the enemy missed out on it.

Their seat reached the top with a clunk, and Titus and Fraser scrambled over the edge and rejoined the rest of their squad on the near side of the bridge.

"I still think this is bullshit," Titus muttered to Fraser. "If Alpha Company gets cut off, this bridge is the only way for them to retreat."

"You really think they'll need it?" Fraser asked.

"You never know," Titus said, then shutting up when he saw that the sergeant had been listening, and he didn't look happy.

"Intel says there's not gonna be anyone there. You all but got a reaming from the major the last time you brought this up. It'd better be the last anybody hears of this, got it?"

"Yes, Sergeant," Titus said, nodding his head.

"Echo-One, give me a SITREP," a voice passed over the net.

The transmission confused Titus for a moment. He was a member of First Squad, Third Engineer Platoon, and it took him a moment to remember that the infantry usually gave all engineers an "echo" designation, as if they couldn't bother to use the official call-signs. He blinked up his helmet display, and saw it was someone in the S3 operations shop.

"This is Echo-One Actual—" Sergeant Bates started before being cut-off.

"Has the bridge been neutralized, over?"

"That's a negative. Awaiting orders to detonate the charges, over."

"Belay those orders, Echo-One. The situation on the ground has changed. Charlie and Alpha have taken heavy losses and need a way back. Alpha needs that bridge. You need to deactivate your charges and stand by for further orders, over."

"Roger that. I'll need to see the alteration sequence on my display, over."

"Sequence en route. Three-Tango, out."

The line went dead, and Bates's scanned the passcodes sent to authorize the change in plans. The code must have checked out as he passed, "OK, let's move people. I need three men deactivating those charges ASAP. We have friendlies on the way who need this bridge intact. Let's get at it!"

The squad jumped into action, with Fraser and Nuar being assigned the duty of going back down to deactivate the charges. The rest manned the hoists that would lower them. The ideal was always to have two men on each hoist, but time seemed to be of the essence.

"Echo-One, this is EITS-Two. Come in."

Titus instinctively craned his head to look up. EITS, or Eye-In-the-Sky, was one of the teams manning surveillance drones to monitor the assault.

"This is Echo One," Bates answered.

"I'm picking up multiple hostiles headed your way. Scans show they're probably armed with needling tech. You need to neutralize them before they come into range of your charges."

"Roger that," Bates said, looking around to the troops manning the hoists. "Pohlmeyer, Corporal Basu listen up. We've got hackers on the way. If they get within needling range of those charges, we're boned. Weapons check, then get a move on. You're holding the other side of that bridge."

Titus gulped and nodded. Bates didn't seem to mind the lack of protocol as he ran a weapons check of his own, and within seconds, he and Corporal Basu were jogging to the other side of the bridge. Titus could feel the adrenaline in his body spike as he slipped the rifle sling over his head and tapped the safety off of his Mark 37 Infantry Assault Rifle, the IAR-37. Stocky and thick, it was a heavy weapon, far heavier than the Army's main assault rifle, the IAR-42. The newer weapon was individualized to each soldier, both in the stock, cheek weld, and targeting cone. Most were matched to the bearer's combat armor, with the crosshairs superimposed onto their helmet. Engineers and other support troops were not expected to be engaged in combat, and in another cost-saving measure, they didn't get the more expensive tech but were issued the veritable 37's, which were state of the art . . . 60 years ago. The engineers were not even given the same weapon each time. They drew whichever IAR-37 was next in the rack. Like most Confed standard equipment, it was cheap, sturdy, and could survive rough handling intact and ready to fire. Heavier than Titus would have liked, it wasn't a bad weapon, and it fired the same 8mm round as the IAR-42 fired. Once the round struck, it made no difference to the bad guy whether it was fired from a 37 or 42—the difference was that with the 42, it was much easier to hit the damned target.

Titus peered down the road, trying to spot the enemy. His fingers were tingling, hands shaking as he gripped the weapon tighter, trying to hide the panic and excitement, both at the same time, that were threatening to take over.

Basu watched him closely. "It's okay, kid. Once Alpha gets close enough, the hackers will take off. We probably won't even see them—" His sentence was cut short as he was spun around, a hole punched into his shoulder.

"Get down!" Basu yelled, pushing Titus, and both of them hit the dirt just shy of the far side of the bridge, crawling desperately as the ground around them came alive with rounds ricocheting on the bridge's pavement. Titus could hear the reports a half-second after their payloads arrived. Using the simple rule-of-thumb taught at boot camp, Titus knew that the rifle fire was coming from about half a kilometer away, which accounted for the poor aim.

"Fuck, fuck, fuck, fuck," Titus muttered as he crawled alongside Basu to get to some cover on the far side of the bridge. The corporal reached it a few seconds before him and then spun around to his back to finger the torn fatigues where he'd been hit.

"No blood," Basu said, an odd smile visible from behind his facemask. "Hurts like a son-of-a-bitch, but I think it bounced off my armor. Lucky shot."

He laughed and scrunched lower behind the meter-high pile of sandbags that was their only cover. Titus could hear more rounds whizzing by like angry hornets.

"Sergeant, we've got company," the corporal passed over the net.

"How many and where?"

The corporal took a few deep breaths, then popped up for a moment before dropping back down.

"At least a squad, maybe more. They're coming up the runoff ditch."

"We're not done yet. You've got to hold them off."

"Roger that," the corporal said, before muttering to Titus, "With just the two of us. Hell, not asking too much, is he?"

He paused a moment as Titus waited for the corporal to tell him what to do.

"As long as they stick to the ditch, it's canalizing them, like a trench would. If I can get in there, I think I can hold them up a bit."

"Like Horatio at the Bridge?"

"Who the fuck is Horatio?" the corporal asked.

"Nobody. Forget it," Titus said.

"Whatever. Look, I need you to cover me while I make a dash for the ditch," he said, then when Titus didn't respond, "Hey! You with me, soldier?"

"I've got your back, Corporal," he said, running another quick check over his 37.

"OK, man. Keep your head in the game. On my mark, you get up and pour fire on them. Full auto. Make them hug the bottom of that ditch. Understood?"

"Yeah, I've got it. I'm ready."

"OK, then. On three." He shifted to get his feet under him, then said, "One . . . two . . . THREE!"

The corporal bolted from their position beside the last bridge stanchion while Titus stood up to fire. He caught a glimpse of a couple of heads in the drainage ditch, and he sprayed the general area. On full auto, he emptied his magazine in seconds, but that was enough time for the corporal to get to the other side of road and into the ditch.

He dropped the mag and pulled out another, his hands shaking as he tried to seat it. It took three tries before he seated it and chambered the first round.

"Should I come over?" Titus asked.

"Just give me cover. I'm going to hit them, then it's going to be asses and elbows when I come back."

Titus switched his 37 to three-round-burst mode, which was far better than auto in keeping rounds on target. He took a quick look back. The rest of the squad was still working on removing the charges. Until they were done, he and the corporal couldn't retreat back to the rest of the squad.

Don't worry about them. Cover the corporal, Titus!

He turned back to his task at hand. Twice over the next 30 seconds, he saw heads get too high, and he snapped off shots. He knew he hadn't hit them, but it made them duck.

After a long two minutes, there was a flurry of gunfire and at least two grenade blasts. Titus craned his neck, spotting a small cloud of dust rising from the ditch, maybe 75 meters away.

"Corporal, you still with me?" he asked over the P2P. "Corporal Basu?"

Silence.

"Basu!" Sergeant Bates yelled over the squad net. "The charges are going live! We've got about half of them deactivated, but the rest could still leave this bridge a smoking heap. Tell me you got those sparking hackers!"

"Corporal Basu," Titus yelled out. "You OK?"

Nothing.

"Sergeant, I think Corporal Basu might have gotten hit," he passed.

"Then you'd better take care of the hackers, Pohlmeyer. Keep them out of range and off our asses for another two minutes at least."

With the rest of the squad on the charges, if the hacker managed to set off one, then the bridge would go, and more important to him, take out the entire squad.

"Fuck," Titus growled, climbing up over the edge of the embankment and bolting to the other side of the road and into the plasticrete-lined ditch. The drainage ditch paralleled the road all the way to the bridge, giving the hackers an easy, semi-covered route up to the bridgehead. Not that they had to reach the bridge to take it down. Titus didn't know the range of their needlers, maybe 50 meters, which meant all they had to do was close within 25 meters of this end of it. They weren't there yet, or the bridge—and his squad—would already be gone. And it was now Titus's job to make sure they never got that close.

Just do it!

He flipped the 37 back to auto and charged down the ditch, weapon at the ready. He wanted to yell out, but that would alert them and make him an easy target. The ditch curved slightly to the left as it followed the road, and as he came around it, he saw the bodies. Five Publicas were down, two badly blown apart from the corporal's grenade. Slumped closer to Titus was Corporal Basu, his faceshield smashed, blood spreading out over his fatigue blouse.

Except at a few funerals, Titus had never seen a dead body before, he faltered a moment. The smell of death hit him hard—blood, urine, feces, and something else he couldn't quite identify.

Staring at Basu in shock, it took him a moment to realize that there was someone alive in the ditch. A Publica soldier was hunched over a needler, tapping and cursing softly before he spun around at Titus's approach. Titus's eyes opened wide as he pointed his rifle at the hacker and yanked on the trigger, a cardinal sin as that pulled his muzzle up and emptied his magazine uselessly into the sky.

The hacker dropped the needler and ducked, his hands scrambling for the rifle leaning against the side of the trench. Titus dropped his 37 and pulled his sidearm from his hip holster, a .44 cal Glazier, designed to defeat body armor at close distances.

Time slowed as the rifle in the hacker's hands seemed to inch toward him. He willed more speed into his arms as he pulled the handgun clear, flicking off the safety. His ears were ringing, the smell of the caseless propellant filling the air as the Publica fired twice. Titus felt the mule kick his chest as he fell backward, desperately jerking the trigger of his Glazier over and over. A Glazier wasn't very accurate, but at three meters away, he couldn't miss. One of his rounds hit the soldier square in the chest, which blasted a hole in the young man's substandard body armor, dropping him like a sack of flour.

Titus watched, sucking in air like it was cheap beer for a few moments before he remembered he'd been shot. He dropped the Glazier and released the medkit from his belt, fingers fumbling with the pressure patch. Time was of essence, and panic set in when he couldn't find the entry wound. His chest hurt, each breath stabbing him with pain, but his armor was still intact. It took him a moment to realize that the round had not penetrated. His armor had saved him.

Get ahold of yourself.

He picked up his Glazier, then his IAR-37, slamming home a new magazine before stepping over two bodies to check the needler. It looked inconspicuous, like a holo remote. He carefully picked it up between his thumb and forefinger, wondering how to turn it off.

"The charges are disarmed," Sergeant Bates passed, his voice sounding as if coming over a vast distance. "Get your ass back here. Any news on Basu?"

Titus looked over to where Basu was slumped in a heap.

"I'm here. Corporal Basu is KIA," Titus heard himself say. "The hackers are KIA, too."

Chapter 3

Titus held up the restraining pin, twisting it in the light, looking for any propellant residue. He was supposed to have turned in his weapons an hour ago, but with the camp in an uproar, he didn't think anyone would complain.

He hoped anyway.

Titus was sitting on a stool in front of his cot, where he had the pieces of his Glazier spread out over the cot. He was taking the time to clean and oil every screw, bolt, and piece of that weapon like his life depended on it. His grease-stained hands rubbed a rough cloth over the various pieces, going over each one two, three, sometimes four times. Always compulsive, he could hear his dad whispering through the door to his mother when they thought he was asleep. He needed therapy. Medication. Something.

Yeah, well you've never shot a Free States citizen, Dad, so maybe this is a little bit beyond your level of experience.

He put the firing actuator down, picked up the magazine assist, and attacked it with the rag. It was clean, he knew, but he couldn't stop. He couldn't reassemble the weapon yet. The Glazier was finished, but he wasn't finished with it. His hand picked up the grip again. It was too small for his hand, and he wondered if there was a way to address that next time. The grip could have cost him his life. Of the seven shots he'd fired, he'd missed with six. True, he wasn't much of a marksman, but the hacker had been less than two meters away. He should have been able to hit the kid with a damn crowbar.

The too-young soldier had looked shocked when he'd grabbed his rifle and fired at him, and Titus had reacted instinctively. Bam, bam, bam, and one of the .44 caliber rounds had ripped through him, crushing ribs, heart, lungs . . .

Adrenaline warred with shock, keeping his mind muddled as he hoisted Corporal Basu's body over his shoulders and scrambled out of the ditch and made his way back to the others. Half an hour later, the squad joined the retreating Alpha join up with the rest of the battalion to set up defensive positions, and that had kept his mind occupied. Now, however, as he cleaned his Glazier, every detail flashed across his mind. The look of fear, the round hitting him, the kick of his Glazier as he panic-fired. The sound of the round hitting, and piercing the kid's cheap armor, like thunking a watermelon. The smell of death. His mind worried the details like a terrier on a rat, refusing to let go.

He'd been a kid. Younger than Titus, or looked it anyway. He'd probably never even pressed a shaver to his face. Gaunt. Hungry. Publicas had all sorts of people joining them, and as much as Titus's officers refused to admit it, a lot of them had legitimate reasons, too.

A kid was dead because they'd both followed orders. The kid who'd probably never picked up a weapon before was dead because he'd been issued substandard armor. Titus was alive because he'd been lucky. So was Fraser, and the rest of his squad, all due to blind luck and the fickleness of the gods of war.

Titus had wanted infantry, to prove himself. But now that war had touched him, now that he'd taken another life, he wasn't sure it mattered. A soldier was a soldier, and the reality wasn't as glorious as his naive mind had imagined.

The sound of someone clearing their throat to his left made him jump up, dropping the obsessively cleaned barrel back on the bed. The first thing he saw was the flash of the bright neon lights over them, glinting off the two silver olive branches on each collar. His right hand shot up in a salute.

"Colonel Sai, sir!"

Lieutenant Colonel Sai, the battalion CO, had commissioned officer written all over him. From the hair, greying at the temples, trimmed down to precisely the regulation three centimeters, the perfectly ironed dress uniform that set off a trim, fit body, to the impressive collection of ribbons that adorned his chest, his very being screamed "soldier." His cover was tucked neatly under his arm. Dark eyes studied the private in front of him, then the disassembled weapon on the bed.

"At ease, son," Sai said, returning the salute sharply. "Long day?"

Titus followed the lieutenant colonel's eyes and dropped his hand to his side, remaining rigidly at attention. "Just cleaning my sidearm before returning it to the armory, sir."

"There's no rush. The armory's a bit preoccupied at the moment, Private . . . Pohlmeyer, yes?"

"Yes, sir."

"I just had a couple questions for you. The staff sergeant told me that I could find you here."

"Sir, I have nothing to add to my report."

"No, no, not about the after-action report, although I read that, and that was a very brave thing you did."

Titus struggled to keep the turmoil in his mind off of his features. "Thank you, sir."

"I spoke with Major Yamin, and he told me that while he was giving the ops order, you made some . . . very pointed questions about the operation."

"Sir—"

"Let me finish. As it turns out, the predictions you made were . . . quite accurate. The Publicas forces had reinforced that ridgeline to defend against just such an assault as we planned."

"Understood, sir," he said, wondering what was next. A lieutenant colonel didn't come seeking out a private just to give him a battle report. He knew he should wait, but he couldn't. "Was there a question you wanted to ask?"

"Yes." Sai dragged a calloused hand across his square jawline. "How did you know? I assume you didn't read any intel reports, so how could you tell that the Publicas had chosen to reinforce that particular position?"

Titus didn't want to tell the colonel that he'd guessed it from playing *Dante's Armageddon III.* He shouldn't have to. It should have been painfully obvious to any competent soldier that they would have that high-ground covered.

Titus paused, clearing his suddenly dry throat before answering," Sir . . . I . . . well, logically speaking, I thought that even with their impending advance toward Melumani, they wouldn't want to leave their HQ completely undefended. If we were going to push forward to hit their CP from the east, our forces would have to pass by that ridgeline at some point. It wouldn't take much to put some troops up there. And below, with almost no cover, our troops would either have to retreat or take heavy losses to keep advancing. Armor would have helped. We could have scrambled some drones, but I'm assuming—"

"They would have been shot down within seconds." Sai nodded, his head dipping down to stare at the floor. "They have a pretty solid anti-air defense AI in place. That's very interesting. Very good thinking, Private."

"Thank you, sir. How . . . how many troops did we lose?"

Sai looked up, his face unreadable. "Too many, Private. And if it's up to me, we won't be losing anymore. Well, hindsight's twenty-twenty, as they say. The battalion can't afford to lose any more men, so we've been ordered to cease all offensive operations until we can get some reinforcements. In the meantime, we dig in and set up a defense. We might see action, though, since it looks like there could be a Publica brigade heading our way."

"I'm assuming that I didn't hear that from you, sir."

"Correct. Major Yamin made a mistake in not listening to you, or at least taking the time to let you explain your theory, so I want you to keep putting your mind to problems like this, Pohlmeyer. In the interest of saving lives in the future, I'll make sure that your future opinions are considered."

"I . . . thank you, sir."

Sai nodded, replacing the brown cap on his head. "I look forward to talking to you again soon, Private." He gave a sharp salute and, not waiting for Titus to return it, turned and walked away. Titus, shocked that a colonel had saluted him first, returned the salute anyway.

Gods, he even walks like a commissioned officer.

Titus looked back at the bed, studying the pieces of the Glazier.

"Fuck," he growled to himself, sitting back down and putting the pistol back together.

Chapter 4

The tension was palpable. The temp building where the brief was to be given did not look too "temp." It had hardened walls, for one thing, bright LED lights, for another, and the seating was solid folding chairs rather than the cheap plastic stackable ones. A stage had been erected, making it easy for all present to hear and see what was being said or displayed on the massive monitor. Oh, and the air conditioning. Blessed air conditioning that, at full blast, was banishing the oppressive heat from the outside, at least for the moment.

Titus felt more and more out of place. His uniform and body were stained with sweat, mud, and prefab dust. Since before sunrise, he'd been outside the battalion's camp lines, erecting cover and setting up defensive positions for artillery and crew-served fire. The intent was to thoroughly cover every point of ingress and force any attacking forces into kill zones. Since the Arganton Act ten years ago had banned the use of mines in conventional warfare, the options for effectively funneling the Publica forces had consisted solely of long-distance artillery fire and ground obstacles.

The rest of the men present in the room were all officers, the principals being majors or higher, and their Military Assistants, lieutenants, master sergeants, and a few captains. Bravo uniforms—no field fatigues for most of them—were freshly pressed, ribbons proudly displayed, and everyone sported a regulation haircut. Everyone had a reason for being there. Junior officers were furiously tapping on their PAs. The more senior officers were calmly chatting between themselves as they sipped from ceramic mugs of coffee. All Titus could think to do was stand calmly in the rear of the room, hands tucked behind his back, and try not to attract any attention. He wasn't doing a great job at it—he'd been the target of more than a few glances, some with curiosity, some with outright disdain.

The lights dimmed, and everyone made their way to their seats, with Titus holding his position at the back firmly. Nobody seemed to care. Lieutenant Colonel Sai made his way to the podium and cleared his throat.

"Thank you all for coming. I'll get right to it. As we all know, the situation is less-than-desirable at the moment. Since the offensive failed and our position was exposed to the Publica forces, they dispatched a large, brigade-level force in our direction. Sat images reveal artillery, assault vehicles, APCs, and at least two heavy infantry companies heading our way. Defenses are being built around the clock, but our orders are to stand our ground and hold off the assault. There's no easy way to put this: we're in it deep and for the long haul."

Rumbles of discontent rose from the gathered soldiers. They'd been on their own, dealing with the constant pressure of Publica drones and probes with little to no help from division. It didn't take a clairvoyant to know that the Publicas were preparing for an assault. They remained just outside the first ring of the defense Titus had helped build, positioning themselves to maximize their strengths. Morale, already low from the initial defeat, had plunged even deeper. The losses were mounting, and now they were told by higher headquarters to suck it up and hold their position.

"Intel says that the attack on Melumani was only a feint, with Tehri ap Nowl now deemed as the primary objective. As such, we are the first line of defense to the capital, and so we hold. Those are our orders." Sai looked down at his clipboard and cleared his throat.

"Before I turn it over to Major Yamin for the brief, I'd like to introduce someone. Private Second Class Titus Pohlmeyer? Where are you, son?"

Titus snapped to attention and gave a quick salute. "Sir, here, sir!"

"Make your way to the podium, Private."

Titus's eyes went wide, but he followed his orders, walking between the lines of chairs, trying to ignore the fact that every eye in the room seemed to be directed at him. His heart pounded, and he could feel his face flush. He mounted the steps quickly and stood next to the colonel.

"Some of you may know Private Pohlmeyer as the one who accurately predicted that our assault on the Publicas HQ was, in fact, a trap. If our staff had paid heed and at least double-checked the surveillance data, we wouldn't be in this predicament and have lost a lot of good men in the process."

Thanks, Titus thought. *Not only have you made a major resent a private, but now you've made the rest of the officers in this battalion hate me. No, that won't make my career as an engineer impossible moving forward at all.*

"Private, what do you think of the Publicas movements up until this point?"

Titus cleared his throat and nodded, trying to get his brain into gear. He'd been thinking about what had gone wrong in the fight while he was building the defensive positions. It has all seemed to clear then, but now, facing the battalion's staff and officers, pulling those thoughts together in a presentable form seemed like a herculean task.

"Ah, sir . . . the Publicas have moved most of their ground forces across the river at this point and, despite having more troops and a better position, they haven't pressed the attack. It seems that they're preparing an assault on this battalion not as a singular operation, but as the first stage of an assault on the city itself."

There were a lot of blank faces in the audience. Well, not blank as such but with lots of questions that weren't being asked. He assumed that the first and foremost was along the lines of, *Why the fuck am I listening to a private at a briefing?*

Titus cleared his throat again. "As most of you know, the late-Twentieth and early-to-mid-Twenty-first century, Old Reckoning was marked by the great powers fighting against smaller, dispersed terrorist groups that usually fought for a cause, not a single nation."

He paused to look out over the officers. Some had antagonistic looks on their faces while others eyes were glazing over.

Don't try to talk like some uni grad, Titus. You're not fooling anyone. Just say it plain and simple.

"The problem was getting divisions and battalions to fight an inferior enemy who refused to meet them, force on force, in the field of battle.

"During one of the initial wars, the United States of America, joined by many other nations, launched Operation Desert Storm against Iraq."

He'd played *Desert Storm III* a dozen times, both as a "Coalition of the Willing" and as the Iraqi Republican Guard. This was one war that he knew inside and out.

"This was a two-part operation, the first being an intensive bombardment of the Iraqi forces. The bombardment was mostly air, and it was intended to take out Iraqi military hardware and to destroy the Iraqi morale and will to fight. The second—"

Captain Anand, sitting in the front row, interrupted with, "Your point, Private?"

Titus felt his cheek twitch at being interrupted but nodded, not wanting to cause a scene here, of all places. "Sir, I think we can expect the Publicas to hit us hard with artillery over the next few hours, followed by a heavy infantry assault on the battalion itself as the assault vehicles and APCs surround us. If the infantry can't overwhelm our defenses, their point of main effort will shift to their armor. With us defeated, they'll have a clear shot to Tehri. Just like the coalition forces in Desert Storm had a clear shot to Baghdad. That is my point. Sir."

Anand took to his feet, tugging his uniform over the bulge around his waist. "That was educational, Private. But I'd like to remind the colonel that the head of this revolution is Rajesh Acharya. As we all know, he has no military background. He was a history and sociology professor at the University of Melumani. Most of the so-called Publica troops consist of the man's former students at the university. As such, while they've put up an admirable effort thus far, once these undergrads find themselves covered in their friends' blood as we assert our forces, I think you'll find that they'll lose their stomach for battle with amazing speed."

"Sir, I—"

"The captain makes a good point," Lieutenant Colonel Sai said from beside Titus, and the man's hand on his shoulder told him to shut up better than any words could. "There's a reason why command is reluctant to engage larger numbers against the Publicas. They're a summer revolution, and winter isn't too far off."

"I still think—"

"Thank you for your thoughts, Private," the colonel said quietly. "They will be taken into consideration. Go ahead and take your seat."

Then to the gathered staff and officers, "I imagine the rest of you are wondering why I brought a Private Second Class to lecture you." Most of the gathered men nodded, many frowning. "My point was to get you to think outside the box. We went into our last fight over-confident and without a full analysis of the situation. We knew what we were going to do even before we started the planning process.

"I didn't want to put Private Pohlmeyer on the spot, asking him to tell all of us what was going to happen next, but I wanted to make a point. If I'm going to listen to what a mere private has to say, then all of you can certainly take into account what your subordinates think. It is an ineffective leader who does not make use of all his assets. Remember this lesson as we move forward."

Titus ground his teeth. He wasn't a soothsayer. He couldn't tell how many lives would be lost over the next few days and why. But he couldn't shake the nagging feeling, the kind that told him that he was the one who was going to be covered in his comrades' blood when the fighting started, not the officers, and certainly not their brightly-colored ribbons.

And now he knew why the CO called him forward to give his opinion. It wasn't because the colonel thought he knew anything. He'd merely been a tool, a lesson for the staff. And now that the point was made, it was time for the children to leave and let the adults do the actual planning. But the ironic thing was that the CO was ignoring his own point. He wasn't about to really listen to a private.

Maybe the lesson would help, however. He doubted the officer and staff would start asking privates for their inputs, but maybe a few sergeants? Stranger things have happened.

He looked over at Major Yanin as he left. The man was smoldering. The CO might not have mentioned him by name, but everyone knew that "staff" meant him. It was possible that the colonel's little lesson would have some effect, but he had the feeling it was going to make his life hell.

Chapter 5

"Incoming!"

Titus couldn't tell who had called the warning, but he ducked down behind the prefab wall and covered his head. The last part wasn't strictly necessary of course, more instinct than anything else. A second later, the whistle of an incoming artillery round ended with a ground-shaking, ear-splitting explosion that his helmet did a bad job of filtering out. He had never imagined just how loud combat would be, and he swore he'd get his ears checked as soon as he made it out of this.

A hail of bullets thudded against the absorbent material of the prefab, and Titus stayed as low as he could. He checked the ammo in his IAR-37 for what felt like the hundredth time. The enemy had been laying down harassment fire for hours now, enough to interrupt their preparations. Titus's squad had been ordered to link up with two other squads, forming an ad hoc platoon, to hold the right flank of the artillery battery against a potential infantry assault. There had been nothing so far except for the enemy artillery and small arms harassment. No one had been hit, but the fire had been enough to remind them that they were in combat.

He peeked out from behind cover when this round of shooting stopped. He could make out movement in the far distance, but even at max magnification, his helmet display didn't give him much in the way of details. For all he knew, the Publicas could be preparing for an assault or a massive retreat. They were beyond his 37's max effective range, but he let off a quick burst to let them know that there were soldiers waiting for them if they came. He ducked back down as Fraser joined him.

"Well, this is sparking fantastic," Titus growled.

Fraser smiled. Titus had never used "sparking" back home on Kyne—he never swore much at all, but after nine months in the Army, the last three with a field unit, he'd been corrupted, and Fraser had done much of the corrupting.

He pulled out a CalBar from his cargo pocket, took a bite, and passed it to Titus. The bar was covered with pocket-lint, but Titus didn't bother trying to brush it clean. He took a big bite and handed the rest back to his friend. Another thing he'd learned in his short time in a field unit was to eat whenever he could.

"We've got movement!" Sergeant Bates passed over the squad freq. "Stand by."

Titus peeked over the edge of their position, and out beyond 900 meters or so, those bodies he'd spotted before were moving forward with intent.

"We've got bad guys!" Titus told Fraser. "Nine hundred meters out."

"About *sparking* time," Fraser said, with emphasis on the "sparking." "I'm about fed up with their patty-cake, long-distance shit."

"Weapons ready!" Bates passed. "Wait until I hit them up with a 40 mike-mike, then light the bastards up."

In the infantry, the 40mm grenade would be fired by the assistant team leader in a fire team. Theirs was an ad hoc squad, however, and the sergeant had pulled rank to draw the launcher, now attached below the barrel of his IAR-37. It was ancient tech, but it could still kill. He opened the breach, slid in the anti-personnel round, propped his weapon on the edge of their position, and waited. The 40 mike-mike could already range the enemy, but they were still beyond the max effective range of the squads' 37s.

Come on, Sergeant. Any time now, Titus thought as he watched his squad leader. Like Fraser, he was anxious to finally engage the enemy instead of just being targets.

Finally, the Publicas were close enough, and the sergeant adjusted his aim, took a deep breath before letting half of it out, and fired. Propelled by a mag-ring, there was only a slight hum and the grenade arched out towards the oncoming Publicas.

Titus waited for the round to hit, his finger hovering over the trigger. He took four deep breaths, then popped up his head, acquiring targets about 600 meters out, just within his 37's range. An explosion erupted right in the middle of the advancing forces. Two Publica fighters were blown apart as the squad opened fire on the rest. The Publicas moved into squad rushes, one group running forward ten or 20 meters while the rest gave covering fire. Titus shifted his aim to a group of four fighters, firing just as they went prone. Another group jumped up, and Titus engaged them. He managed to get out four three-round bursts before heavy automatic fire made him duck back down again. He waited a few seconds, then popped up and fired another two bursts.

"Fuck, I didn't sign up for this. I didn't sign up for this, damn it." Nuar said, his 37 slipping from his hands.

Fraser caught his eye, and Titus shrugged before he fired off another three-round burst. His target went down, but Titus couldn't tell if he was hit or just taking cover.

Fraser turned back to the Nuar, gripping him by the shoulder. "Grow a pair, Nuar."

"I joined the Army to learn a trade, man," he said, "Not this stuff, and I can't do it. First the bridge, and now this? They're Free States citizens, fog God's sake."

'You are learning a trade. Killing the enemy. So, start putting rounds downrange."

"Give me some fire!" Sergeant Bates yelled out, bypassing his comms.

Titus fired again, dropped his mag, and slammed another one home. "Fraser . . ." he said before commencing fire again.

"Come on, Nuar. I know you. You're not a coward. What would Yana say?" Fraser asked as he fired four measured rounds.

Titus didn't know Nuar well, but Yana was his bride of two months.

"She'd say get the hell out of here and come home," he said.

"Bullshit. She'd be ashamed. She married a man, not a rabbit. And we need you, bud." Fraser said and he fired two more times.

Nuar picked up his 37 and hugged it to his chest, eyes closed. He looked like he was about to throw up, but he started to mutter, "I . . . I've got this. I can do it."

"Don't tell me, show me!" Fraser said. "Engineers, hooah!"

Nuar's face was white, but he thumped his chest three times, working up anger. He took three deep breaths, and popped up, shouting "Hooah, motherfuckers," and fired and un-aimed burst before dropping back down, his breath coming in gasps.

"That's it, Nuar! Get some!" Fraser shouted.

Nuar suddenly stood up and opened fire. "Get some, you pig fuckers! Get some! Get—"

There was a hollow thwock sound that cut him off, and the soldier dropped to the dusty ground with a thud, his head gone, the remnants splattered across the helmets and armor of his comrades. Titus recoiled and tried to wipe off brain matter that had splattered him.

What the hell can take off a head like that?

"Shit," Fraser growled, rising up to fire another burst.

Titus stared for a second in shock. Nuar, who'd been there beside them one moment, was now a hunk of meat, his head gone. A growing stain of urine spread over the body's crotch. Images of Corporal Basu flashed through his mind. Titus shook his head as if to banish the sight and smell that overtook him. He pulled himself away and popped up, firing a burst, and saw the answer to his question on what could have taken off Nuar's helmeted head.

"Get out!" Titus shouted. "Clear the prefab now!"

Lumbering toward them was a Gentry-made PTY Armored Combat Vehicle, a "Patty." It might not be a United Federation Davis or a Brotherhood Scimitar—true tanks—but against infantry, its 60 mm smooth bore cannon looking huge and deadly. It was going to roll right over them. Their position was designed to absorb hundreds of rounds, but a 60 mm round from the AV? Not a chance.

"Come on—" he shouted as he scrambled clear of their position.

The Hand of God slammed into him and threw him clear. He could feel his organs press against his spine as he hit the ground, rolling and scraping across the dirt. His ears were ringing, and hot blood poured from his nose and into his mouth, the coppery taste bitter. He could feel his heart thudding as his eyes cleared. Their firing position was obliterated, a pile of twisted plastic and ceramic. Fraser had managed to avoid the impact, but the other two hadn't. What was left of them was scattered in pieces through the ruined fighting position. Titus coughed and rolled over onto his stomach, trying to crawl but his body refused to cooperate. Even breathing was a struggle.

"We need to get rid of that fucking Patty!" Bates called over the net.

Titus was getting angry. Two days of this. Two days of this hiding and shooting from cover. Two days of the brass alternating between telling them to stand strong and that transports were on the way to evacuate them. Two days of engineers fighting alongside infantry as the numbers of both had dwindled. Ammo and supplies were getting dangerously low.

He couldn't help but feel that the Publicas were toying with them at this point. Playing with them, teasing them to come out from behind their defenses, just to see what would happen.

Fraser was beside him, already on his feet. Those jock reflexes had been an advantage, and he'd been a good three meters farther from the prefab before it had gone up in the blast from the Patty.

"You okay, Titus?" Fraser asked, squatting down next to him and running a scan on his vitals.

"Yeah," Titus growled, nodding. "Just need a sec."

"We don't have a sec," Bates shouted, kneeling next to them. "We have the Pickard here. Anyone fire one of them before? Who's the best shot?"

In an infantry squad, every soldier would have a Pickard, but with the engineers, they'd been given only one of the man-packed anti-armor missiles, almost as an afterthought.

Fraser immediately said, "That'd be me, sergeant. I fired it at boot."

"Good. That's better than nothing. The rest of you, give him some cover fire."

Titus looked around. He'd lost his rifle in the blast.

He groaned, reaching down to pull out his sidearm when Fraser stopped him. "Sit back. I've got this. Seriously."

Titus glared up at him, trying to shrug the man's hand off his shoulder and failing miserably. With a cocky grin, Fraser took the missile from the sergeant and deployed by extending the launch tube.

A Pickard was a relatively low-tech weapon with minimal guidance. It was fire-and-forget in the same way a rifle was. Fraser would have to acquire the Patty in the sight funnel before firing, or the little guidance cell would never lock on the AV. From a frontal aspect, Titus wasn't even sure that the Pickard would penetrate the Patty's armor.

"Hurry up, Fraser," Corporal Bell shouted as the rumbling of the big armored vehicle got louder.

As if to punctuate the urgency, a huge chunk of the prefab disappeared in a cloud of dust and pieces. Titus ducked back down and hugged the ground as he was showered with debris.

His Glazier felt puny in his hand, and he scanned the ground for his rifle. Fraser had laid his on the ground in order to deploy the Pickard, so Titus picked it up.

Fraser saw him and chuckled. "Better get that thing back to me in perfect condition. It's got extreme sentimental value."

Titus nodded, and unable to come up with anything clever as a retort, so he just grunted out, "Will do."

"Ready Private?" Bates asked, and Fraser nodded.

Titus plugged the IAR to his combat suit's little AI, and as Fraser rose to take a shot, he rose as well, firing off an un-aimed burst of three rounds. Even the suppressed recoil sent stabs of pain through his battered body, but he ignored it, firing several more bursts until his magazine was empty. He dropped back down and looked to Fraser, but his friend hadn't fired the Pickard.

"I need another angle. The armor's too thick from the front," Fraser said, sliding back down.

"You'll be shredded before you can get a lock," Bates said. "We need it taken out now."

"I'll draw the fire," Titus piped up, "Long enough for a lock."

Bates looked at him doubtfully. "No offense, but . . ." He broke off as another 60mm round hit what little was left of the prefab, showering them all with more debris. "It's a plan! Go!"

Titus pushed himself to his feet. He could feel adrenaline starting to pump through his system now.

Push through the pain.

He wasn't particularly fast off the mark, but he managed not to get shot—probably because nobody expected him to pull a stunt like this. A thunderous impact shook the ground as the Patty's gunner traversed the cannon to engage him. Unlike a Federation Davis, the Patty's big gun was manually operated, and the gunner was just too slow. The gunner should have switched to the .30 cal co-ax, but Titus was not about to remind him of that.

Running downhill gave him extra speed, even if the footing was unstable. As he ran, his body protested, but he knew the Patty's gunner wouldn't miss a second time, and that gave him all the impetus he needed to keep moving. He glanced back to see the big gun traversing ever closer to having him in its sights

Turning to look back was a bad move. Just as he found the massive vehicle, the huge barrel looming large, he lost his footing and tumbled to the ground. He scrambled to his back, trying to spot the Patty, knowing it was his death about to come a'calling. He aimed Fraser's 37 at the AV as if he could hold it off with the rifle.

But the big gun was traversing away from him. The gunner finally realized—or was told by the AV commander— that he wasn't a threat. He started to stand when a round bounced off his torso armor. He may not be a threat to the Patty, but he was a target to the dismounted infantry.

And there was Fraser, right in his line-of-sight. He was kneeling in the open, Pickard on his shoulder. He *was* a threat, and the Patty gunner knew that. In a few moments, the gunner would fire.

"Over here, assholes!" Titus screamed as loud as he could, firing Fraser's 37. The AV itself wasn't hard to miss, but the rounds bounced off the armor like they were made of rubber. The cannon kept swiveling.

"NO! AT ME! AT ME!" He called helplessly, pulling at the trigger. Dirt erupted around him as the Publica infantry took Fraser under fire. Titus spun around to engage them when the battlefield exploded in a massive white light. His helmet display caught it just in time and darkened, but he still couldn't see much until the white had turned to yellow, and the blazing heat became a pillar of smoke.

The Patty was a smoking heap, a catastrophic kill. That was too much for a little Pickard, but the missile must have penetrated the ammo locker, setting off a secondary explosion. Titus could see Fraser and Bates both beating a hasty retreat to an intact prefab. Titus took their lead, groaning as he pushed himself to his feet, and running back while keeping as low as possible.

He kept expecting to catch a round in the back, but he somehow made it, collapsing behind the prefab wall, breathing hard. "That was . . . a sparking nice shot. I thought you were toast for a second there."

Fraser winked. "Told you I had this. Practiced on the simulators with one of these bad boys back in boot a couple of times—"

"Wait," Sergeant Bates said. "You only fired one on a simulator? Not a live round?"

"I hit the damned thing, right Sergeant?"

Bates slapped him across the shoulder and said, "I guess you're right at that!"

"Grenade!"

Titus caught a brief glimpse as the grenade arched down to hit the ground not two meters behind him. A red LED flashed, indicating an active fuze. Game over. He couldn't get to it in time. The Publica soldier who'd thrown it should have been set the detonator for impact, but it didn't matter. The grenade was close enough to turn every man behind the wall into ground meat.

Titus turned away and closed his eyes.

A second passed. Two. He heard a muted blast, and he winced, expecting to feel bullet-sized shrapnel tearing through his body any moment now.

Three.

Four.

Titus opened his eyes again as a silence seemed to fall over the battlefield. Beside him, a body lay, curled in the fetal position. A body he recognized.

"No!" he shouted, reaching to over to pull on Fraser's shoulder

His friend, or what had been his friend, flopped over, hands gone at the wrist and a bloody mess of what had been his stomach.

"Titus," Bates growled warningly. Titus ignored him.

"No! No fucking way, Fraser. No—"

"Pohlmeyer, get a grip." Titus felt a hand on his numb shoulder. He shoved it away. It came back again. He swung at it with the barrel of Fraser's 37. All the pain in his body was gone. Well, not gone, but dwarfed by the sudden burning that had engulfed him.

Titus jumped to his feet. He wanted blood. He needed it. The 37 was empty, so he dropped it beside Fraser and pulled his Glazier. Heedless of the danger, he jumped up and ran around the edge of the prefab wall and came face to face with another helmet, the helmet of a Publica soldier who looked . . . excited? . . . as if to see who he'd bagged with his grenade. At least, that was Titus' take on it.

"Surprise, asshole!" Titus screamed, grabbing the Publica soldier by the collar and dragging him closer, close enough to see the shocked look on the man's face.

Titus planted the barrel of his pistol to the man's forehead and pulled the trigger once, twice, three times. The soldier's faceshield disintegrated into bloody shards. Titus let the body fall, but not before he grabbed the man's Weimer. His combat suit could not integrate into a Weimer A-4, but he didn't need it. The three other soldiers were too close to miss, and they'd been focusing to the front and firing at the prefab wall. That gave Titus the split second he needed to fire first. He dropped the nearest fighter, taking out one of the soldier's un-armored legs.

They may have had their attention on the wall, but they were soldiers, after all, in combat. Two spun around to engage him with rounds that were pulled high. Titus barely registered that so focused was he on them.

A roar erupted from his very soul as he pulled the trigger, feeling the kick, watching one of them go down, three rounds easily punching through his body armor. Titus pivoted, finding his second target, and pulled the trigger. Down he went. The third one, the guy he'd shot in the leg, was down, but not out. He was raising his Weimer when Titus shot him twice in the face.

He spun around, looking for more soldiers to engage. He wanted more. He *needed* more.

Motherfuckers killed Fraser. Gotta kill them all. Gotta send him some company.

He felt like superman, but that was all in his mind. He was still human, something he was reminded of as the first round hammered his chest, piercing his abused body armor and sending him staggering back as he tried to find who was shooting at him. A second and third round tagged him, one to the shoulder the other to his stomach, the last one doubling him over and finally downing him as he fell on his back, coughing. Blood sprayed the inside of his helmet, blocking the view of his helmet display's bio readouts. He was hurt bad, but he didn't know how bad. If the pain in his belly was any indication, he was pretty far gone. Surprisingly, he didn't care much. Either he'd given up, or his medbots had filled him up with happy juice. He wasn't sure how long he lay there, and it might have been a dream, but through the blood on the inside of helmet display, he caught a glimpse of a massive gunship, rocket pods, and chain guns firing furiously. And a Confederation of Free States flag on the side.

"Get some," he coughed out as the battle, and everything else, faded from view.

Chapter 6

Titus's eyes fluttered open. His lungs were working, at least partially. He could have sworn that the first round had punctured at least one. He tried moving his hands. The feeling was there, but they only responded with a twitch of his fingers. He blinked a few times, trying to get his eyes to focus. He turned his head to the right, letting him see the rest of the room. There were other beds. Hospital beds. Empty though. He would have expected to see them full.

"Private Pohlmeyer?"

He turned his head, making out a young man. Late thirties, his hair longer than regulation and greying at his temples. His uniform was clean pressed. He had no ribbons on his chest but had a major's single olive branch on one collar and a crossed daggers on the other: AIC. Army Intelligence Corps.

"I'm—" His voice was dry, so what came out was less words and more a squeak. He cleared his throat and tried again. "I'm afraid I can't salute, sir."

"I think we can do away with formalities for the moment, Titus. Can I call you Titus?"

"Yes sir. Who are you?"

"Major Jaeger."

It was an odd name, even for planets that had been populated by Federation colonists.

"I'd like to have a few moments with you, if I can."

You're a major. I'm a PSC. You can talk to whoever you want.

"I'm here to debrief survivors of your battalion, trying to glean whatever information wasn't included in your after actions reports."

"I haven't made mine, sir."

"Of course. And to be honest, with the casualties, I doubt anyone will ask you for it."

"How many . . ."

"It was heavy. At least two hundred KIA beyond resurrection. The CP was hit. Colonel Sai was killed, along with Captain Anand, which is a big reason why I am here now. He was AIC, you know," the major said needlessly.

Titus may only be a PSC, but he knew Intel officers were all AIC.

"But you did delay the Publicas long enough for the divisions to pivot and face them. The capital is safe."

Titus really didn't give much of a shit about the capital at the moment. Sure, he was loyal to the government, and that was its planetary seat, but he fought for Fraser and the rest, and he'd lost his best friend.

"I don't really know much of what went on, sir. I don't know how I can help you."

"Well, there's the thing. I'm not here to grill you on the operation. I'm here about something else. Captain Anand forwarded some reports about you."

Shit. And now I have to pay for a dead man's accusations? This is getting petty.

"He said you were smart, number one, but that you also stood up to high-ranking officers."

What? He's saying that like it's a good thing.

"He said you have potential."

I thought the captain hated me.

"What potential, sir? I mean, I was just doing my job."

Jaeger waved his hand in dismissal. "You are an engineer. Your mission was to build fighting positions, blow up bridges, neutralize bunkers. The fact that not only were you able to take in information and develop intel but had the balls to question your superiors were all above and beyond what you signed up for . . . and what we can normally expect from a junior enlisted soldier."

"You here to give me an attaboy or something?" he asked, surprised that he was so flippant with a major

"No, better than that. I'm here to offer you a job."

Titus waved his hand feebly at his bed-ridden body. "I think I'm set for a while here."

"A couple of months in regen, a couple weeks in physical therapy, and you'll be good as new. After that, you could put in for your discharge or go back to the engineers. Or you could keep serving the Free States, but more effectively than you ever could as an engineer."

"What do you mean?"

None of this was making any sense. For the first time, he wondered if he was dreaming all of this. No, he decided as he looked around him. It was all too clear, too real.

"AIC, son. You have the brains and the guts for it. You spent the past couple of weeks showing that you do. I saw the operations reports. I saw what your officers had to say about you and what you said. You've got a mind for what I do. Well, not exactly what I do, but something similar."

"Why would I do that? If you're to be believed, I can get an early discharge because of my wounds."

He didn't buy that, though. Go home to Kyne? And do what? He was only nineteen, for Pete's sake. No, this major was playing him like a trout at Pichola Reservoir.

"I've read your psych profile. You didn't join the army for the easy life."

Titus scowled at him. He felt like the major had mapped out every moment of this conversation, and it was all proceeding according to plan.

"Your friend," Jaeger had to consult some notes to recall the name, "Fraser Butterworth. PSC, like you. Joined around the same time. Inseparable, your drill sergeant said in his report. He was killed in the fighting."

"What about it?" Titus growled through gritted teeth. He couldn't keep the image of Fraser's body from his mind. Fraser, who'd taken the grenade to save him.

"He died because of faulty intel and arrogant officers. I guarantee that there are a lot more like you and Fraser scattered across the Free State's military. Soldiers that'll die because of mistakes, mistakes that could have been avoided. You can save them. Keep this kind of shit-show from happening again."

Titus didn't answer, fighting back tears as he stared at the pristine white covers that wrapped him from the stomach down. Jaeger didn't speak, but after a few moments, he came closer to Titus's cot and placed a card on the bed under Titus's eyes.

"If you decide Intel is your thing, give me a call. I'll pull some strings, and you'll be enrolled in the Intel school in New Mumbai once you're up and about again."

And with that, he was gone. Titus picked the card up, trying to read it through his watering eyes. *Major Ajun Jaeger, AIC, CFS Army.* Titus stared at the card for a moment, trying to make sense of what the major had said.

I could help avoid shitstorms like what we just went through? That killed Fraser?

The thought brought back a wave of grief, and he leaned back, almost crying out from the hole in his heart and the pain that washed over him. He slipped the card under his pillow and pushed the call button for a nurse.

He wasn't sure if he wanted the nurse to up his pain meds or numb his mind.

NEW MUMBAI

Chapter 7
Six months Later

Graduations were always such formal affairs. A celebration of transitioning from one spot in the military to another should be celebrated with what the graduates would be missing out on when they were deployed. Booze, games, potential hook-ups, and the occasional brawl. Well, they'd be seeing plenty of the latter, but again, in a less formal setting.

Titus felt uncomfortable in his parade uniform, constantly adjusting the pure white gloves and tugging at the collar that always had to be ironed and form-fitted to his neck. The purple cap that was supposedly tailor-made for him never sat right on his head despite his hair being back to the standard three centimeters. He had to keep his head perfectly straight, or it would slide off to one side or the other, making the whole ensemble look lopsided. Which made sense, he supposed. Soldiers in parade uniform were held to ridiculously perfect standards, so lolling one's head to one side or another wasn't permitted.

They'd marched out onto the tarmac where the ceremony was being held. All of the graduates, some sixty of them, held their antique rifles in a ready position as speech after speech was made by officers of differing rank, but all above major. And there, they were supposed to stand, under the blistering New Mumbai sun, expected not to sweat or otherwise ruin their perfect lines. Toy soldiers, all standing in a line while senior officers who didn't care about them and never would expressed pride and admiration.

Keeping cool under the collar, literally and metaphorically, bordered on the impossible at this point.

"And now the graduates," Colonel Herram said, finally allowed a few minutes on the podium once the rest of the officers had finished. "We'll be starting with the honor roll. Graduates who showed exceptional skill in the tasks presented to them and are graduating with honors. We look forward to the bright futures you will have while serving in the Army Intelligence Corps. Please step forward, Second Lieutenant Aarav Pusapati." There was a pause as people in the audience clapped politely as Aarav marched onto the podium to have a pin placed on his lapel. "Second Lieutenant Arushi Kothapalli . . . Second Lieutenant Alisha Montgomery. . . "

Six names had made the list. The idea of diversity was becoming wildly popular in government circles, but the army had always been a bit slow to pick up. Most of the graduates all had parents in the higher caste system—a social system that was officially frowned upon but never quite left by the wayside, no matter how much their civilization advanced—with the handful of non-Indian graduates that had shown themselves to be worthy. Not unlike him. Most were graduates from OCS before coming here.

Not me, though.

"Private First Class Titus Pohlmeyer."

There wasn't any applause from the audience, but as he ascended the steps, he saw that his classmates had all started clapping for him. Despite their upbringing and culture telling them that they were a league above the private who would be an Intel soldier, a kind of respect and even friendship had developed between them. They were all in this together. No need for snobbishness when you would be fighting in the same metaphorical foxholes, as it were. Titus held himself to a small smile and a nod in thanks as the pin was attached to his lapel. His own parents didn't have the money to make it to New Mumbai for the graduation, so it was nice to have some support.

Chapter 8

"Pahtar hits the ball and runs for the other side, but he trips and falls. He's rolling around on the pitch, wheezing and groaning, claiming that the other batter hit him with his bat when they crossed paths. I mean, it's like these guys don't know that the umpires can just watch a replay and know that the *payu* is full of shit."

Titus nodded and sipped at his beer. "So, did the other batter hit him?"

"No, the umpire looked at the replay and saw that he just slipped on a rough patch of turf. He was ejected from the game, and the Solas went on to win the match five to three."

Titus nodded again. Fives had never been popular on his home planet, with more settlers from the European states than Asia, but over his time in New Mumbai, he slowly started picking up on the details of the game. It was a crude evolution of the ancient game of cricket, he'd realized, but with more violence and drama. Despite having been here for the past twelve weeks, however, the subtleties of the game still eluded him.

Still, nothing like talking a bit of sports to wind down after the graduation. His cap had been stowed away where he wouldn't lose it when it inevitably fell off, but he hadn't bothered to change out of his uniform. Total babe magnet, his fellow graduates had assured him. But the pristine purple was no longer pristine, the gloves were gone, and they'd all undone the blouse buttons before heading out to celebrate. Still, the gleaming crossed daggers on his right collar shouted that he was IC.

The class would be given their assignments the following morning, so a night of rough partying was off the table. Some drinks with the guys, on the other hand . . .

"I bet Titus here still thinks we should all play this *football* where they use their hands to play with an egg," Rodra said with a light punch to his shoulder.

Titus grinned and shook his head. "I said you should watch—note, watch—not play. It's easy to follow, and who doesn't like watching a bunch of big bruisers hurt each other instead of me? It's like wrestling, but with less acting, and actual, you know, rules. But don't ever play it. You'd all be collectively turned into one of those," he made a flat motion with his hands, "those pancakes that you guys make here."

"Chapatis?"

"That's the one. The moment you get the ball—"

"Egg."

"*Ball*. Chapatis, each and every one of you."

Silence descended as each of the six graduates sipped their drinks. Sports wasn't what was on their minds, not really. Of the group, Titus was the only one that had actually seen action, but they'd heard stories. In Intel, fighting on the front lines wasn't likely to happen, but other kinds of violence could be encountered by a select few. A shadowy side to the war, a long way from the front lines.

Looking around at the others, Titus wondered who would be following which track. The Free States Army Intel was essentially an umbrella over two different branches. One was the open military intel, like Captain Anand, who took the intel and presented it to the ground commander, or the analysts at the HQ level who took the initial collected information on a tactical level and made some sense of it. This was simple staffing, and it was normally a fairly safe career. Captain Anand getting killed in an arty strike was a rarity.

The other, sometimes more shadowy branch, was the gathering side, the ones who pulled in the information that the analysts turned into usable intel. Much of this was done by passive or active surveillance, electronic or otherwise, by Intel folks remote to the source. But that also included operators on the ground, soldiers who put themselves into harm's way to ferret out what needed to be found. These shadow-operators were held in high esteem, but their work was more dangerous than even infantry grunts. A distressing number of them were killed in action, their names engraved on an ever-growing plaque back at the AIC Hall of Honor at Army HQ.

Titus was sure that Major Jaeger, the man who'd recruited him, was part of the covert side of AIC. And that gave Titus hope that he'd be part of that as well. He'd lost his sense of glory in battle the moment Fraser had been killed, but part of him still wanted to prove to himself that he was something special, that he was one of the few.

Titus was not alone in wondering about their future assignments.

"Where do you all think you'll be transferred tomorrow?" Aarav finally asked, putting his cider down.

"My father said that he's pulled some strings," Rodra said. "I'll be sitting at a desk in G2 at Army HQ. Back home in New Mumbai with a cushy job with a quick ladder climb. Promotion almost guaranteed in the next six months." It was difficult to say if he sounded relieved or disappointed.

"As close to the fighting as I can get," Titus said softly, playing with the empty bottle in his hands. "Those guys need someone watching their backs. Wish I'd had that when I was there."

"I'll drink to that," Locklear, one of the older graduates, said raising his bottle. The rest did the same. Smatterings of conversation failed to lift the moods of the graduates, and one by one, they left the dive, either to find somewhere a little more upbeat or back to the barracks and their bunks to try for some sleep.

INDUS

Chapter 9

Back at the bar after graduation, when he said that he wanted to be on the front lines, this hadn't been exactly what he'd meant. It wasn't the front lines, but it wasn't a staff job, either. Call it a hybrid position. He'd wanted to be in direct support of the troops when he'd called Major Jaeger to take him up on his offer. While at school, he'd been more than a little enraptured with the idea of being a ground asset, "pooping and snooping" to gather information. What he hadn't expected was that he'd be staring at a handful of monitors, keeping an ear on communications

He probably felt more at home here than with the engineers, digging trenches, but not by much.

The war was basically won. After their assault on Tehri ending in disaster, the Publicas had tried to withdraw, reassembling their troops for another offensive. The Free States military didn't allow them any respite, however, keeping up the pressure and forcing them to withdraw from first one, then the second of the three planets on which they'd been fighting. With much of their forces attrited, they had little offensive power, and however gifted their commanders had been at offensive operations, they were simply not organized for nor skilled in defensive ops.

Titus had caught the last of the operations on Wayward, the second planet taken back from the Publicas. Initially, he'd been far behind the line, going over after-action report after after-action report. It seemed mindless to him. He hadn't even been given any concrete instructions, just to "note anything that caught his attention." He dutifully filed his reports, getting no feedback. It took him a while to realize that no one expected him to discover the key to victory. It was all part of the "whole man" concept in Intel. An Intel soldier had to have a broad understanding of the strategic and tactical situation in order to piece together usable intel from the vast amounts of data being gathered. A drone capture of a small movement from River A to Town B could indicate entirely different things, from enemy troops deserting to an impending all-out assault. The correct analysis could only be made in context of the larger situation.

After four weeks, he'd been transferred to a support battalion command post in the rear area of one of the areas of operations where he was spun up managing the stream of data being collected by the Drone Surveillance Platoon. He wasn't the primary analyst—those were the staff weenies back in the rear with the gear, up in orbit or back at AHQ. He did pull out time-sensitive data from the 248 feeds and route them to the battalion S2 for further dissemination to the infantry battalion commanders. He was sure some of that had helped the infantry, and he thought he'd saved soldiers' lives. He hoped so, at least. But even so, it was mostly routine, a daily 18-hour grind and something that he struggled with not to lose perspective. He'd gotten to the point where he'd almost forgotten that he was on a battlefield.

Almost. The daily KIA report reminded him that even with the Publicas on the run, Free States soldiers were fighting and dying out there, just 30 or 40 klicks away.

After the fall of Wayward, Titus joined the rest of the Army for the assault on Indus, the home planet of the Publicas Revolution. The fighting had been going hot and long there, but they'd finally cornered the leadership and most of their troops in Apras, having seen it turn into a slugfest through the most densely populated metropolis on the planet. As more and more troops arrived to support the Free States assault, more and more Intel personnel were required to coordinate them, and Titus found himself working in positions normally filled by much higher pay grades. More than a few staff and officers seemed surprised to see a private first class where a sergeant would usually be, but no one took issue with it.

Almost. A master sergeant had almost refused to deal with him, asking for his "principal." He seemed to think that Titus was just someone watching the monitors while someone more senior was taking a piss break or something. It had taken Sergeant Ambrose to assure the master sergeant that Titus was the man.

"I'm not sure why they thought putting me here would be a good idea, Sergeant," he said as the master sergeant left.

"Me neither, to be honest," the massive man said with a chuckle. "But we're spread thin here, so I'm glad of the help. Just keep an eye on the communications intensity and send out an Eye-in-the-Sky for a looksee if anything looks suspicious. Let me know if you need the big guns, and I'll send in the cavalry and blast the suckers into oblivion."

The AIs were constantly monitoring the transmissions, trying to break the codes. The Publicas could keep the Army from knowing most of what was being passed, but they couldn't hide the transmissions themselves. Increased intensity of transmissions could indicate something was up . . . or it could indicate that it was a spoof and they wanted the Army to *think* something was up. That was where Titus came in, trying to see patterns that the AIs missed, patterns that he might recognize after reading all the reports. Modern AIs could do many things better than humans, but they sadly lacked in effective intuition.

Titus had initially been surprised that as a mere PFC, newly promoted at that, he could control the EITSs. But as Sergeant Ambrose had said, he was sitting in the seat, so he had the authority. He couldn't send up calls for fire himself. That took the sergeant. But he'd assured Titus that was only a formality. It would be Titus's call.

Sergeant Ambrose was a decent enough boss, who took no issue with Titus's rank, but the guy was positively bloodthirsty. He reveled in the possibility to send in the "cavalry," which might be naval gunfire, arty, drone, or air strikes, depending on the mission. He hadn't put in a call for naval gunfire in his career yet, and he yearned to have the big gunboat in orbit above them fire its death and destruction. Not that he'd ever really called for fire. They were Intel, after all, not forward observers. But the commanders and fire control personnel would take their targeting and analysis to approve any calls for fire,

So, even if Titus would never actually pull a trigger, so-to-speak, that decision rested on his ability to send up accurate intel. It was a heavy responsibility that sometimes gave him pause.

Titus nodded, slipping on the headset. "What if I send it up the chain, cavalry comes and levels the place, and turns out, it's civilians?"

The sergeant shrugged. "Regrettable, sure, but these guys have been hosting the Publicas leadership for the past three years. They'll have had to see this coming, right?"

"Right," Titus said, unsure.

The transmissions scrolled across one monitor, with a handful of EITS feeds covering the other. For the longest time as he stared at the monitors, all he could see were letters and numbers. Titus dragged his hand across his face, taking a deep breath and leaning in closer, focusing. Numbers became IP addresses, letters became encrypted transmissions. Not all were encrypted. Many seemed to be normal calls and messages sent between civilians, discussing the conflict, looking for loved ones. He ran them through decryption software anyway. Publicas were known for using low-tech cryptography to hide their transmissions in plain sight, or so his instructor in his previous station had told him. None of them were in enough numbers to warrant a follow-up.

His AI gave a low-level alert. He pulled up the numbers. The intensity at a single location at the western edge of Waterton had jumped over the last five minutes.

"Whiskey-Three-Alpha, I'm getting a lot of chatter from an IP address at coordinates to follow: Golf-Delta-One-Niner-Six, Zulu-Bravo-Three-Three-Two." He pushed the coordinates, the primary method, but the Army loved redundancy, and the AIs would make sure that what he said matched what he entered into the system. "Can you give me a flyby?"

"Roger that, scrambling a bird now to Golf-Delta One-Niner-Six, Zulu-Bravo-Three-Three-Two. It's a Thirty-four-Bravo. Serial One-Eight-Four-Niner-Two."

The 34B was one not as capable as the Delta model, but it should do. Titus entered the serial number, and the tiny feed that had been on the left of his display moved to the center and expanded to full size. He could see it sweep to the left, then a red target circle appeared in the distance. He zoomed in to observe a fifteen-story, non-descript building. It looked nothing out of the ordinary.

"Doesn't look like much," his counterpart in the drone platoon said. "What're you looking for?"

Titus could walk the other soldier through it, but it was easier for him to take over, especially as he wasn't sure what he was looking for.

"I'm taking over the sensor suite, Whiskey-Three. Keep the bird at one-thousand meters."

"Roger that. You've got the suite, Two-Sierra-Nine. Happy hunting, and let me know when you're reverting."

Titus had given the other soldier his credentials when he'd come on duty, so the transition was smooth. His screen lit up with the sensor suite icons.

He studied the visuals for a moment, then switched to the Echo-Three, a general life-form scanner. With vermin and anything the size of a small dog or less screened out, nothing showed up, to his minor surprise. An intact building of that size should be occupied.

After a moment, he switched to thermal scan. Color gradients took over his display. Most of the building was the purple of the ambient temperature, but the fifteenth floor was a vibrant yellow.

"What do you think that is?" the drone platoon communicator asked.

"Don't know. It's at eighty-five degrees C."

"What, did somebody leave the heating on and then left?"

"I doubt it. The weather's been fine, and it's way too hot for that. Could be a server or repeater that the Publicas are using to bounce their signal."

He ran through the suite, using each of the Bravo's six sensors. The high-freq sensor showed some increased activity, but the rest revealed nothing. It looked like a comms repeater, not an actual command or communications cell. He logged in the Intrep and bounced it up the chain. He could ask the sergeant to order a fire mission, but the threat and surety level didn't justify him to take that action. Let the task force G2 folks make that decision.

Hours passed with more of the same. Nothing concrete, just bits of information that would become intel once higher headquarters analyzed it. After graduating, he'd wanted to be on the gathering side, not the analysis, but this was pretty boring, a far cry from the holovids of secret agents and spies. His eyes were gritty, the lids heavy, but all he could do was rub them and stretch to keep the blood flowing before ducking down into the job again. It wasn't quite tedium that he felt. He could follow the progression in the battle, and he knew the Free States infantry was approaching the Parliament building, and the fighting was getting intense. But he wasn't in the thick of things. He was back in the rear, watching the readouts and AI alerts, trying to contribute to the cause. The main forces were retreating for what looked to be a final stand around Parliament, but there were Publica cells scattered around the city, doing what they could to impede the Free State progress, and it was Titus's job to find them. The thing was, he wasn't finding much.

After a few more hours, his head was pounding, and he turned into auto-mode. Look at each AI alert. Study the number of transmissions stemming from a single address. Put the transmissions through the decryption suite. It was all basically useless, a victim of the speed of the battle. There were hundreds of transmissions being sent per minute, and depending on what kind of effort had gone into the encryption, the decryption AI would spit out a decrypted message between minutes and hours after it had been fed in. That didn't matter much, though. The decrypted messages would be kept for AIC to analyze once the fighting was over. And it would be over soon. The battle was all but won.

Come to think of it, I'm probably going to be one of the guys sifting through all those messages. It's not like they'll have anything better for a PFC to do once these command posts are shut down.

His AI pinged for his attention. He pulled up the alert. There was a surge of activity in the Delta bands, but the combat geosynch was having problems coordinating an exact location.

"Hey, Whiskey-Three-Alpha, I've got another one. I don't have an exact location, but it's in the Larimore neighborhood, location Golf-Delta-One-Eight, Zulu-Bravo-Three-Four. Can you give me a closer look?"

The coordinates covered an area 100 meters by 100 meters—not ideal, but the drone should be able to get some better data.

"Roger that. Scrambling now. I'm giving you the Delta for this, serial Delta-Four-Seven-Seven-Six."

His counterpart had a New Mumbai accent. He wasn't sure what rank would be handling the platoon's comms. For all he knew, the guy was a lieutenant . . . or snuffy like him. The drone jockeys thought much of themselves, and despite working hand-in-glove with them during the operation, he'd never met any face-to-face.

Whoever he was, Titus was glad he was scrambling the 34D, with its much more capable suite. He entered the serial and watched as the drone banked hard, a too-large red circle indicating the target area.

"We've got plenty of people there," his counterpart said needlessly.

The area was full of hits, to include a platoon-sized Free States unit just to the north. Titus could pull them up to see who they were, but he ignored them for the moment. If he needed them to check something out, he could send up that request. Right now, he had to narrow the Delta's search parameters.

"Got that," he acknowledged as he ran his eyes over the IP addresses. "This might take a bit. I'm getting fifteen different addresses a minute here. Seems excessive for a residential area. That's why I tagged you. Let's switch to thermal first and try to match up bodies with heat. If we can find the servers, we can figure out what's going on, and they'd need to have their servers running hot to bounce the signals around that much."

"Roger, that. How about this one?" he asked, putting a cursor over a building. "I'm seeing fifty-two bodies and a big hotspot on the ground floor."

Titus considered it for a moment

"Could be. Let's run the Gamma Vector."

Titus could have taken control, but he was not as versed in the Delta, so it made sense to let the Whiskey-Three handle that while he tried to make sense.

"Roger that."

There was a quick flicker as his display switched to the amber of the gamma screen. Immediately, his AI squawked.

"Bingo!" Titus said as a list of weapons appeared, including six Gentry-made Wandas.

"Damn," Whiskey-Three said. "I guess we found some shit."

The weapons were powered down and shielded, so a 34B wouldn't have picked them up. The people, yes. The heat of the servers, yes. But not the weapons. And definitely not the Wandas. Those powerful missiles had the punch to take out any of the Free States armor . . . or the Task Force forward CP, for that matter.

"You calling for a strike?" Whiskey-Three asked.

The drone platoon was surveillance, and their drones were not armed, unlike the combat drones. Titus could hear the excitement in his voice.

"We need to do a complete scan for civilians, first. Give me readouts on numbers and distances from the weapons. And the heat signatures."

He ran his cursor over the Free State platoon and sent the enquiry. It was an engineer platoon from Fourth Battalion. Probably moving forward to help breach the Parliament building if it came to that. If it was infantry, he might request they be diverted to clear his target building, but even out of the engineers, they still impacted his fight. He snorted and brought his cursor back to his target.

"I've got the fifty-two on the bottom two floors. Lots of sidearms. I can't get much more," Whiskey-Three said.

Titus studied the readouts. Either they were Publica soldiers or armed civilians. Most of them, at least.

"Can't you get body mass readings with a Delta?" he asked.

"Yeah, normally, but there's too much interference going on. Some are smaller than the others, but by how much, I'm not sure. Let me ask Sergeant Uchida."

Whiskey-Three had just violated protocol by passing a real name over the net, even if their transmissions were encrypted. Not that Titus was going to do anything about it.

A full minute later, Whiskey-Three came back on and said, "He can't tell, either. And if he can't, no one can. He's been at this for twenty-two years."

Which meant Sergeant Uchida was probably a sergeant first class at least. And if he couldn't read it, Titus certainly could not. But Titus needed that information. If he could get body mass readings, he could better tell if some of them were children. The bodies were different sizes, that was discernable. But the smaller bodies could be female fighters.

Or just women taking refuge, as with the larger bodies.

The weapons readings didn't lie, though. That much was for certain.

"Do you see that? One of the Wandas is powering up," Whiskey-Three shouted into his mic.

Titus did see that. But was that because it was being prepped to fire, or was it simply part of the maintenance cycle? Wandas couldn't be kept in standby for long, and they were shut down to be periodically powered up for a few minutes. The problem was that it was impossible to discern between the two.

He ran a quick query on the Wanda, and he was correct. Both cases were one and the same.

He couldn't take the chance.

"I'm passing it up, Cat Bravo," he said. "Keep the Delta on station."

"Roger that," Whiskey-Three-Alpha said, sounding disappointed.

"Sergeant Ambrose," he said. "We might have something. Weapons, to include six Wandas. I'm passing it up and cc'ing you."

"Wandas? No shit! They can reach us no problem. Had them hit us at Vanu once. Not fun. You want me to initiate a fire mission?"

Titus hesitated, then said, "We don't know if there are civilians there. I hope G2 can get one of our guardian angels to take a look first."

"You think just because they're in orbit, the Navy can see what your drones can't?" he said as he looked at the report. "You had a Delta on station."

"Better safe than sorry."

"You'll be sorry if you catch a Wanda up the ass," he said, but left it at that.

Titus reduced the feed, and brought up the general display, but his eyes kept drifting to the now smaller feed from the Delta, wondering if he'd made a mistake.

"Two-Sierra-Niner, this is Juliette-Three-Foxtrot," interrupted his thoughts.

Titus snapped to full focus. "Juliette-Three" was the task force operations center. "Foxtrot" was the fire support coordination center, the FSCC. The fact that someone there was contacting him directly meant this was hot.

"This is Two-Sierra-Niner," he asked, his heart jumping.

"You submitted Intrep Twenty-three-dot-three-six-four for weapons at Golf-Delta-One-Eight-One, Zulu-Bravo-Three-Four-Two."

Titus checked the Intrep number despite knowing exactly which one it was.

"Roger that. Weapons and probable server."

"We cannot pull up the drone feed. Please relay the serial number."

"Roger that," he said again, this time punching forward the serial number of the Delta, then opening the feed to Whisky-Three-Alpha.

The FSCC would see he'd done that, but no one objected, and Titus wanted to be ready. He wasn't sure why the FSCC could not pull up the feed, though. It was clear on his display.

"Two-Sierra-Niner, we are being jammed and cannot pull the feed. You reported six Wandas? Confirm."

"Roger that," he said for the third time. "And personal weapons as well as a probable server."

"What is the situation of the target. We have it as a twenty-story office and apartment."

Titus didn't know what the configuration was inside, but it was 20 stories high.

"Roger on that. Twenty stories."

"Are there civilians in the building?"

His heart sank. This was the crux of the matter, and he didn't know the answer to that.

"I am not sure. We've got fifty-two signatures, all on the bottom two floors. Maybe half of them are armed. We could not get body mass readings."

"Wait one," the FSCC rep said, and the line went dead.

"What's going on?" Whiskey-Three asked.

"That's the FSCC. They want to know if there are civilians in the building."

"Holy shit. They're going to run a strike on it," he said excitedly. "What did you say?"

"I said I don't know."

"Shit. You know. They're all armed, and they're all down with the weapons. No one up higher."

"That doesn't mean they are all Publicas. They could have human shields."

"Not our fault if they do."

"Two-Sierra-Niner, this is the "Juliette-Three-Actual," a voice came over his comms. "I need your eyes."

The "actual" was the task force operations officer, a brigadier general. Titus had never talked to a flag before, and he sat up straighter in his seat.

"Yes, sir," he said, even if "sir' was not used in comms.

"Son, we're blind up here. Something powerful is jamming the area around that building. We're working to break that, but at the moment, you're the one with the eyes on the target."

How can they be jammed and not us with just a little Delta? And how can they be talking with me if we're being jammed?

"I need to know if there are civilians in that building, son."

"I . . . I can't tell, sir."

"Think," he said quietly, but with steel in his voice. "This is important. We've got Intel that . . . well, it's vital that we find and take out any Wandas in the AO. Extremely vital. But the ROEs, you know how they limit us."

Titus was not stupid. Naive, inexperienced, but not stupid. The Wandas were a poor man's missile, able to take out armor or any number of targets. That would not normally concern the J-level staff. But they could also carry tactical nukes, both "dirty" and "clean." The general didn't say it, but that's what had to be going on.

The ROEs, however, approved by the president himself, was that civilian pockets could not be targeted. These were Free States citizens, and even if they supported the lost cause of the Publicas, they needed to be brought back into the fold. Wholesale killing of them would not win the peace.

The general wanted clearance to fire. Hell, he needed clearance. And with whatever was happening up there, his decision was going to be based on what one junior private first class said.

It wasn't fair.

"Well, son?" he asked again.

Whiskey-Three-Alpha sent over a text message that simply said, "Give the all clear."

"You can't send in infantry to clear it, sir? There are only fifty-two Publica fighters there."

"So, you called them fighters," the general pounced. "Not civilians. But to answer you, I'm rerouting a line company now, but time could be of an essence. I need to know now!"

This time, all the "son" and niceties were gone. He was demanding an answer.

If those Wandas were armed with nukes, they wouldn't change the course of the battle, but many more Free States soldiers would die. More civilians would die, too. In fact, they might be targeted, a last gasp from the Publicas to raise anger against the government.

He took a last look at the display. At least half of them had sidearms on them, and there were enough personal weapons stacked to arm each one of them. They had to be soldiers,

Right?

"Private First Class, I need to know—"

"Soldiers, sir, they're combatants!" he blurted out.

The risk was just too great, to both his fellow soldiers and the local populace.

"Say that again."

"They are combatants. No sign of civilians."

"Understood. You did right, son," he said before the line cut out.

"My God," Whiskey-Three-Alpha said in a rush, as if he'd been holding his breath. "They're going to do it."

"How can they if they're getting jammed?"

"They don't need anything to drop a rock on them."

That was true. A "rock" was an inert tungsten tube, dropped from orbit. Even a 500kg rock would smash through the 20 floors and obliterate the entire building.

"I'm going to record this," Whiskey-Three said.

"Hey, who are you?" Titus asked, regardless of protocol.

"First Lieutenant Angus Banerjee, at your service. And you are?"

"Private First Class Titus Pohlmeyer, sir."

"A PFC? No shit? Well, I owe you a beer when all this is over."

"Yes, sir," he said, but not feeling the moment. He had a sinking feeling that he'd made a mistake. But there really wasn't anything else he could have done.

"Look at that," Lieutenant Banerjee said after a few minutes. "Three of the Wandas are powering up."

It was true. Three of them were powered up, which could be a portent that something was about to happen. Titus wondered if they were too late. He kept looking at the building, waiting for the hand of God to strike.

When it did strike, it took him by surprise. One moment, the building was standing tall. The next, there was a flash of brilliant light that whited out the Delta's pick-up until the compensators could kick in. A column of smoke rose into the air, and underneath it was only flames and rubble. The building was gone. And with it, 52 souls.

Titus hoped they were all soldiers.

Chapter 10

Even with the weapons and server taken out (Titus kept focusing on the hardware in his mind instead of the soldiers he'd killed), the battle was far from over. Titus still had a job to do. The hours kept dragging until Titus had a hard time remembering when his ass wasn't stuck in a field chair in his trailer and there weren't lines of communications scrolling in front of his eyes. What felt like a lifetime later, a welcomed message came over all frequencies.

"To all forces of the Confederation of Free States. This is General Almualim. At zero-four-thirty-five hours this morning, Free States troops breached the Parliament Building and captured the revolutionary council. They have issued orders to all Publica forces to unconditionally surrender. Publica forces are turning in their weapons and surrendering to our brave troops across the city. No Publica fighters are to be harmed unless they keep fighting.

"The war is over. You all can be proud of yourselves for a job well done. Stand by for more from your local commanders."

When the communication cut off, Titus expected to hear a collective cheer from the rest of the AIC operatives that occupied the twenty or so cubicles on either side of him. The actual action was far more subdued.

Some of them took off their headsets and leaned back in their seats, closing their eyes. A handful more didn't bother taking their headsets off, simply placing their heads on their desks. The rest looked at the others and nodded. A job well done was the unspoken consensus. No words were exchanged. The battle was over, but there was still a lot to be done. After a few minutes of congratulatory rest, they just . . . went back to work.

****

The battle had been etched across the city like an artist's brush across a canvas. In some places, it barely showed. The vehicles were mostly intact, and the buildings too. Some shops were even open, with people coming out of their homes to walk in the sunlight for the first time in what must have felt like a decade. There was a heavier than usual coat of dust across the whole scene, but other than that, it looked like business as usual.

The same could not be said about the whole city, however, especially near the center and the Parliament building, where the fighting had been the heaviest. Whole buildings had collapsed. Fires were burning, and rubble and glass filled the roads, making navigating difficult. Here and there were bodies, some covered by black tarps, others that hadn't been attended to yet. The level of destruction of three weeks of fighting was stunning.

Titus rubbed his eyes. He'd discovered that he'd been at his desk in the support command post for over twenty hours without a break. A bathroom break, a quick meal, and four hours of sleep later, he was back at it. Instead of being assigned to run through all of the decrypted messages as he'd assumed, he was instead assigned to scour the city, making an on-the-ground evaluation of locations on which he'd sent up intreps. He was supposed to note what was there to compare with his intreps and incorporate where they converged or diverged on his after-action report.

He'd been joined by Sergeant Ambrose, and together, they'd hit each of their locations. The sergeant had NCO written into his DNA, and if he weren't here, Titus could imagine him berating recruits for any number of infractions, real or imagined. Out here in the city, he seemed in his element. Despite having worked just as many hard hours as Titus, if not more, he seemed in a chipper mood, commenting over what had likely happened here, offering old anecdotes there. Titus tuned most of it out and focused on driving their AMROC Combat Utility Vehicle through the scattered debris. Not easy work, considering the thing was a broad, flat-headed thing that looked like a toad, which was the unofficial name for it. It could ram pretty much anything out of the way with the massive grates at the front, but it made for slow going.

"I gotta tell you, I never liked this city. Too crowded. Too many people. It kind of breeds a sort of self-importance. 'Oh yeah, I'm putting numbers into a communicator for six hours a day. I make seventeen figures. That makes me more important than you, despite the fact that I couldn't change the oil in my overpriced hover if I tried.'

"You know, I dated a girl from Apras once. She liked to talk. She smoked, so she'd make me come out of my house in the dead of goddamn winter to talk about how we should be taking the time to study plant life on the terra-formed planets, let them evolve naturally rather than settling them right away. I mean, she might have had a point or two there, but talking about it when my nipples can literally cut glass doesn't make me very happy to agree with you, know what I mean?"

"Sparking fantastic," Titus mumbled under his breath.

"What was that, Pohlmeyer?"

"Ah, she must have been hot for you to take that, though."

When occupied with his own job during the battle, the sergeant had been a supportive non-factor, letting Titus do his job. Now, as a passenger, it was as if he had three weeks of pent-up conversation he had to unload. It wasn't to the level of annoying, but not much he said was interesting, and all of it was distracting as Titus guided the Toad.

"Oh yeah. Hot, but she was nuts too. She tried putting a tracking device in my boot when I shipped out once. It showed up on the sensors when I was boarding the carruca, and they had us all strip down and wait until they'd found it. Got a lashing from my CO. Broke things off with her after that. You know what they say: never stick your prick in crazy, am I right?

"OK, the next one is yours, just up ahead on the left here. That's your big attaboy," he said without pause, then returned to, "But we never learn. Always need that hook-up. Did I tell you about the threesome me and Nick Delbert had on Prisana?"

Titus's heart dropped. He knew that was one of his targets, but the Toad's little nav system didn't use the standard geo-coordinates, and what with guiding the ungainly vehicle and the sergeant's chatter, he hadn't put two and two together yet. Up there, he'd killed 52 people. He might not have dropped the rock, but he'd been the one to give the OK. He had no desire to see his handiwork.

"I mean, I couldn't believe it. She was hot as shit, tiny as a mouse, but she had a dick bigger than mine. Nick says why the hell not, so . . . Watch it! Get out of the fucking way!" he shouted to the woman and child who were walking down the middle of the road.

The woman slowly turned and looked at them with a glare that could melt plastisteel

"Christ, you'd think we'd just sold them all into slavery or something," the sergeant said with a chuckle.

"Yeah, or killed their loved ones," Titus muttered as he passed the two.

He ignored the sergeant's recounting of whatever he'd done on Prisana, looking ahead as the Toad rounded the corner and the 20-story building—or what was left of it—came into view. It looked out-of-place with the other dust-covered, but intact buildings surrounding it. He had to give the Navy credit. The Rock was a precise, almost surgical weapon. He didn't have a clue as to the science behind the weapon—they didn't have them in the Army, and he'd received no training with them as an engineer—but whatever the science, the thing was obviously effective.

He guided the Toad to the nearest clear area in the road, then shut down the motor. The two soldiers stepped out. Ambrose was armed with a Hammerhead Assault Rifle, which looked like an IAR but had a heavier stock with an attached shotgun beneath the main barrel. It massed a cool 5.4 kilos without ammo, but the man carried it like it was a child's plaything.

Titus slung his 37 over his back and pulled the Hydra out of the pouch on his hip. The Hydra was a small, all-purpose scanner that could be adjusted for five types of scans. Titus flipped the selector to "A," which was the life form scan.

"No beating hearts inside," Titus said. He flipped the selector to "C," then added, "No known booby traps either. I guess we're good to go."

"Roger that," Sergeant Ambrose said, climbing over the first of the rubble. The entire building hadn't been destroyed, as Titus had first thought. A massive support pillar still protruded from the rubble, and attached to it, part of a wall. Titus climbed over the rubble to take a look, carefully watching where he placed his feet. Whether that was to make sure he didn't misstep or if he didn't want to see what else was buried in the rubble, he wasn't quite sure. He couldn't miss a dust-covered, motionless hand, though, that reached out as if trying to trip him

He reached the wall. Right in front of him, at eye-level, was an M88 conduit box, tell-tale fiber-optic cables dangling beneath it. Most commercial servers used flash-links, but those were readily hackable to any sophisticated hacker. The old-fashioned fiber optics, which probably ran the signals to the roof where they were encrypted and transmitted, were virtually hack-proof. Of course, the transmissions could be jammed or detected, which was what Titus had done, after all. "Looks like a server junction, all right," the sergeant said. "Need to take them back to be sure, but I'll bet my right nut that they're Publicas. You know, these pricks had our troops running all over the damn city until we figured out that they were bouncing signals? Yeah, this battle would have been over in a couple days if they didn't keep hiding their shit in civvie buildings."

Titus had to agree. He recorded the box, then snipped some of the cable. He doubted the techies would be able to pull anything from them, but it didn't hurt to be thorough. He turned and looked around for anything else. There was paper scattered everywhere, a sad reminder that people had worked in this building, and lived on the upper floors. Whoever they were, they were refugees now. And the government, who had destroyed their home, would now have to provide them somewhere else to live.

I guess the construction contractors will make out, even if no one else does.

He leaned over and picked up one of the pieces of paper, brushing off the dust. There might be some good information there that the analysts could pull. It was stock paper, not the plastisheets usually used by businesses. Surprisingly intact it was about 30 cm by 40, and on it was what looked to be a child's drawing. The colors were faded, but he could make out a house and a flower. No, the sun, not a flower."

"Some proud parent had this in their cubicle," Titus said, dropping it to the ground. There was not going to be any intel drawn from that.

He stopped to pick up another. Again, it was a child's drawing. This one was of a cat, and a gold star was still affixed to the top, looking almost obscene with how shiny it was.

What the . . .?

He picked up more papers, almost falling into one of the gaps in the rubble. More than a few were pictures, some were messages about upcoming events—children's events. One was the bottom third of a poster that was unmistakably the feet of Bongo Giraffe.

"Hey, Sergeant! I think they had a day-care center here, or maybe a school!" he shouted out.

Ambrose laughed and said, "Ironic, considering that it was you who schooled the Publicas here."

"Yeah," Titus said, thinking on what could have been. At least the Publicas had warning of the Free States assault, and the bulk of the civilians had fled the city. The children who'd drawn the pictures might not have a day-care to which they could return, but they should be safe somewhere.

He found a plastisheet with a series of numbers. It might be important, or it could be someone's Grand Lotto guesses. He slipped it into his evidence bag. He made his way to the edge of the rubble, where he thought there would be a better chance to find something less-damaged.

"You about done here?" the sergeant called across the rubble field.

"Yeah. Not much to see."

Thank goodness.

He'd seen weapons or parts of them, which confirmed that. Nothing he recognized as Wanda parts, but he was sure the tech teams would sift through the rubble more thoroughly. To his relief, there hadn't been as much in the way of bodies. A few intact bodies, obviously dead, and more body parts, but covered with dust. They looked more like mannequins. Titus could ignore them.

Standing on a large slab, he jumped across to an even larger, tilted slab of what looked to be an intact wall. His feet slipped, however, and he slid down the wall on his ass, scrambling for purchase. No such luck. He went past the jagged edge and fell between the two slabs, falling a couple of meters into a small space.

"Mother fuck!" he shouted, wincing in pain.

"Hey, you OK, Pohlmeyer?" Sergeant Ambrose shouted.

Titus looked up and shouted back, "Yeah. I fucked up my side." He reached up to grab the edge of the slab to pull himself up, then gasped. "Uh, I think I might need some help getting out of here."

"Where the hell are you?"

"Just follow my voice. I fell between the two canted slabs."

He looked around him for the first time. The two slabs had fallen against each other, forming an open space, about five meters by three. As his eyes adjusted to the dim light under the main slab, he could make out what looked to be small toy horse, the kind that children rode, and . . .

Titus jumped up and grabbed the slab, pain forgotten. He scrambled up to its apex, then fell on his belly as he vomited out the quick meal he'd eaten before entering the city. His stomach heaved, even when there was nothing left, bile and digestive juices burning his throat and mouth.

"Hey, there, Pohlmeyer," the sergeant said as he jumped on the slab, "I thought you said you needed help. You jumped up here like a kanga-fucking-roo."

Titus heaved again, arching his body, and the sergeant changed his tone and said, "You OK? What happened?"

Titus managed to point his hand behind him, but he didn't turn to look. He couldn't.

"Down there," he managed to get past his vomit-covered lips. "Kids. Maybe six or seven. They weren't evacuated. They were still there!"

The image was burned in his brain. Kids. Toddlers, really. No more than four or five years old. Six of them, probably. Two were caught under the far edge of the slab, half of their little bodies sticking out from under it. The others were by a crushed table. One had a sippy cup on a lanyard around her neck. Orange liquid had slowly seeped out, staining the dust that covered her chest.

In an instant, he knew what had happened. They were too young to understand that there was a battle going on. They were simply in the day-care one moment, having a snack. The next moment, they were gone.

Because Titus had told the general that the building did not have any civilians there.

"No shit? There were kids here?" Sergeant Ambrose said as he carefully, half crawled, half-slid to the edge of the slab.

Titus didn't want to look, but he turned back as the sergeant pointed his Hammerhead into the gap and turned on the weapon's light. he waved the muzzle around, and Titus hoped the man would laugh and tell Titus he'd been dreaming. Too long without enough sleep and all.

"Shit," the sergeant said in a subdued voice, and that last grasp for sanity was shattered.

He turned off the light and edged back up to Titus.

"I killed them," Titus said.

"Hey... hey." The sergeant was obviously unused to this sort of behavior, looking visibly uncomfortable. "It's not your fault."

Titus looked up, suddenly angry. "Not my fault? I told the general that he could fire. I did that. I told him there weren't any civilians there."

"You told him what you knew, that you didn't have any evidence that there were civilians in the building."

"There's my evidence," Titus shouted, pointing back to the gap between the slabs. "Not my fault? I might as well have walked in there with a fucking gun and shot them all myself."

"Not. Your. Fault." Ambrose grabbed him by the shoulder and dragged Titus to his feet. "Look, you wanna blame someone, blame the Publicas assholes. They're the ones that kept hiding their assets in civvie buildings. Hoping we wouldn't attack them because they were using their own people as fucking meat shields. You wanna blame someone, blame them!"

"They didn't kill kids!"

"The fuck they didn't!" Ambrose roared. "They had warning. They were told to evacuate non-combatants. The children. They fucking chose to put them there, with fucking Wandas for Pete's sake! Them, not you! The fucking assholes! I'd . . . I'd . . ."

The sergeant was angry, breathing hard as tears formed in his eyes. That anger somehow broke through Titus's own anger, collapsing it like a balloon. Sergeant Ambrose sat down, shaking his head.

"Not your fault," he said again, but Titus wasn't sure to which one of them he meant.

Titus sat down beside him, eyes drawn to the edge of the gap.

"What happens now?" he asked.

"What do you mean?"

"I made a mistake. A big one. I told the general he could fire."

Fifty-two people were dead, including children. Probably other civilians, too. And he was asking about his future? He felt guilty about that, but he had to know.

"Don't worry about it. We'll file the report, and you'll be asked some questions, and then it'll be forgotten."

"But—"

"But nothing. I was there. I heard the general. I heard how he pressured you."

Titus hadn't known the sergeant had listened in, but he shouldn't be surprised.

"The general needed an excuse. He got it. But he can't use you as a scapegoat, and he knows it. If he does, then everything comes out in the wash. No, you did the best you could have done given the circumstances, and that's how the final report will read.

"Just remember, as they say, shit happens. Never more true than in war."

"But they died. I don't even know how many of them."

"And how many would have died if they fired off the Wandas? How many of our troops? How many civilians. No, this sucks, and it'll be on your conscience for the rest of your life, so for your own sanity, remember how many lives you saved."

What the sergeant said made sense, but he couldn't accept it. Not yet, anyhow.

"I can't do this again," Titus said. "Never again."

"Yes, you can, and you will. Because we're soldiers, and that's what soldiers do," the sergeant said. "And now, let's get going. We've got six more sites to survey before we can file our reports."

Titus was numb. He knew it would take a long time to process what had happened. Whether it was a general who had to find a way to take out the Wandas, or faulty information—or a combination of the two—that resulted in the children's death didn't matter. Dead was dead. But he vowed then and there to make sure his intel was the best it could be in the future.

The two stood and made their way out of the rubble. Titus couldn't look back.

NEW MUMBAI

Chapter 11

Official celebrations had taken over the Free States. Public officials were everywhere congratulating soldiers and touring first efforts at rebuilding. Everyone, it seemed, wanted to cash in on the good press of a war well won. Medals were being tossed around right and left. Even Titus had a shiny new Direct Combat medal for his participation to put alongside his Red Shield—a pair of gladius crossed over in bronze—for being wounded in the line of duty.

It felt empty, somehow. The net was flooded with an outpouring of sympathy for the lives lost on both sides, and he was sure that those who'd extended their sympathies were honest about it. But it still felt like it was coming from a long way away. They wouldn't have to keep remembering the weird sex stories that Fraser was so fond of or the odd way that Nuar seemed interested. They hadn't seen heads blow up and heard the sickening sound and smell of a body soaking up an exploding grenade to save others.

It's not that I don't appreciate the sympathies, Titus thought to himself, taking a pull from the long-neck ale. *I'd just appreciate having my friends back instead.*

He'd gone out with a few of the others after the battalion put a new battle streamer on its colors a couple of hours ago but had since been separated from them. Still in uniform, he sat at a bar, the name of which he hadn't noticed, nursing his drink. It felt good to be alone for once

"Hey, there, soldier boy."

Titus snapped out of his thoughts, almost dropping his ale as he spun around to see who was talking to him. The scent hit him first, an overwhelming musk of peach and roses. Or something like that anyway. An older woman stood there, long gleaming black hair falling over her shoulders, and pale white skin. Facial sculpting couldn't hide her age, however, and the low-neck Bitra blouse currently favored by the teen titans didn't do her any favors. She leaned forward, arm on the bar beside him, unsteady on her feet, yet aware enough to show off her cleavage.

Titus couldn't help but glance down. Her face might be pulled tight by the body sculptors, but she evidently hadn't paid for the entire works. Crow's feet patterned the exposed skin of her cleavage.

Titus jerked his gaze back up, and she was smiling at him before draining her glass, all the time eyes locked on his.

"Uh, do you know me?" he asked.

"No, but I know you," she said with a throaty chuckle that turned into a cough.

What? I just asked you if you knew me, and you said no.

She was drunk, so he let it pass.

"So, I can see you were in combat. Wounded, even," she said, eyes dropping to his chest and the two ribbons. She reached out with her glass, forefinger extended, and touched his Red Shield. She licked her lips in an almost predatory manner.

"Uh . . . yes, ma'am," he managed to stutter out, backing just out of her reach.

"'Ma'am?' How cute," she said with a laugh while sliding into the chair beside him. "I'm not so much older than you."

Titus automatically wanted to correct her. She had to be well into her seventh or eighth decade. Not old, per se, but definitely getting there. Even as socially inept as he could be, however, he knew better than that.

He wasn't sure what she wanted with him. Titus had never been of interest to many women his age, much less one older than him. He'd heard of the war hawks, men and women who sought out soldiers, wanting to hear stories of battles. When most people never served, there was sort of a glamor attributed to those who did. She knew what his Red Shield was, and seemed impressed, but she . . . well, he was sure she was flirting with him.

Really? Or am I just reading into things?

Fraser had a sort of joke he liked to tell about the difference between men and women. If a woman saw a man staring at her, she would wonder if she had a piece of salad stuck in her teeth. If a man saw a woman staring at him, that was because she wanted him. Not entirely true, of course, but that had stuck with him. Maybe she did just want to hear war stories.

She quickly dispelled that when she put her hand on this thigh, gripping it hard as she scooted her bar stool closer. She gave him a squeeze before slowly taking her hand away.

"So, what's your name, soldier boy?"

"Titus, ma'am," he said, the heat of her hand lingering on his thigh.

"What did I say about 'ma'am?' We're the same age, right?

"Hey, bartender! How about getting this young hero a drink. Not that crap ale. A real drink. A GB."

"I'm not a fan of hard—"

"Hard what?" she asked, interrupting him.

"Liquor, hard liquor," he said, feeling his face turn red.

"Oh, I'm rather fond of hard things. But OK, no GB? How about a Wongson, then?"

She raised her hand to signal the robotender. It reached under the bar, opened a cupboard, and brought out a three-quarters full bottle of the pale-yellow liquor. With a slow pour, unlike the usual quick flip, it poured three fingers full into a glass and carried it—not sending it down the bar—to Titus.

The woman—he didn't know her name—flashed her wrist to pay, then lifted her glass, only to realize hers was empty.

"Hey, what about me?" she demanded.

The robotender dutifully rolled back to pour hers, doubling the amount when she shouted that she wanted a double.

"Wait for me, love," she said, putting her hand on his to keep him from drinking.

He froze, extremely conscious of her touch. His mind was a mess of confused thoughts. She was four times his age, and he could see that she had to have been a knock-out when she was young. Not that she was unattractive now, he quickly thought guiltily, as if she could read his thoughts. And her hand burned against his.

He was only nineteen standard years, "full of cum and vinegar," as his grandfather described him. Sometimes, he thought his hormones controlled him. And now, here was a woman, a real, live woman, who for some reason seemed to be interested in him.

"OK, love. Now. Sip slowly," she said, as she released his hand and raised her glass to her lips. "Slow and gentle, to make things last."

He sniffed the glass first. He'd heard of Wongson, of course. Who hadn't? But he'd never thought he'd ever taste it. A bottle supposedly would cost him three months' pay.

Looking at her, he took a sip, and his mind exploded into colors and smells. A look of amazement came over him, and she said, "Pretty good, huh, soldier boy?"

"Yes, ma'am," he said, almost forgetting about her and how close she was to him as he looked at the glass. He raised and drained it, savoring the complex, yet still somehow simple taste.

His head was swimming. He might not have much experience with women, but he knew he could hold his booze, yet three fingers of the stuff had him tipsy. He barely noticed that the robotender had refilled his glass.

More drinks followed, Wongson and some others he'd never heard of, and with liquid courage, he was drinking with his arm intertwined with hers. He even told Fraser's joke, and was rewarded with a trilling laugh.

She isn't that old, he realized. *Damned attractive, in fact.*

Titus had never hooked up before. He'd had his furtive fumbling around with a few girls back in school, so he wasn't a total noob, but nothing like this where someone he'd never met was actually into him. She even laughed at his attempts at humor. He kept looking around at the other dozen or so patrons at the bar, wanting them to see what was happening, but none of them seemed the least bit interested.

After an hour, maybe two—Titus had long ago lost track of time—she leaned in to whisper into his ear, "How about you and me going back to my place?"

"Sure!" he blurted out, spilling some of his current drink in his lap in his eagerness.

"Oh, anxious now, are we?" she said, taking her napkin and blotting it forcefully in his crotch. "Let me get that for you." She made a show of dropping the napkin, said, "Oops," but then kept using her hand.

Titus started to pull back as his erection made its fifth or twentieth appearance, but then he relaxed. This wasn't a shy classmate.

"I like," she said, as she continued to press with her right hand.

"Close out," she said.

The readout in front of her tallied the amount, and despite the placement of her hand, Titus couldn't help but look at it. It was almost three months of his pay. This woman was either crazy or loaded. Or both. Not that it mattered at the moment to him.

She flashed her wrist over the readout, and it flashed a green "Thank you for your patronage."

"OK, soldier boy, let's get you and mama home," she said, struggling to get to her feet, this time pressing painfully against his crotch as she lost her balance.

Titus had to jump up, head spinning, to keep her from falling.

"Oh, my own soldier to the rescue," she said, this time gripping his biceps. "And so strong."

This was so over-the-top. Titus was not a gym rat by any stretch of the imagination. But still, it swelled his ego. He had to restrain himself from flexing.

"Thank you," Titus automatically told the robotender as they stumbled together, the woman draped over him.

The eyeless robot "stared" silently as they made their way past the tables, into the hotel lobby, and out the door. A human doorman, with a uniform far more impressive than Titus's, said, "Have a good evening, Mz. Armitage."

She ignored him, but slurred into Titus's ear, "Drive me home."

He looked at her, confused. Did she have a hover here at the hotel? Did she think he did? He glanced over at the doorman who gave him a wry smile and pointed down the walk to the "AutoCab Pick-Up" sign.

"Mz. Armitage prefers Silk Road," he said.

Evidently, this wasn't something new for "Mz. Armitage." Titus felt the slightest tinge of disappointment, but he managed to push that back. What did he expect?

"Have a good night, *sir*," the doorman said with more than a little sarcasm.

Mz. Armitage's hands openly grabbed at his butt as he mostly carried her to the pick-up sign. She mumbled something incoherently, and when she didn't summon a ride, he found Silk Road. Thirty seconds later, the autocab arrived in a whisper, the doors opening. It took some effort, but he managed to get both of them inside, where his . . . date? . . . put her arms around him and leaned into his side.

As soon as the door closed, the cab AI asked, "Welcome to Silk Road, the finest autocab experience on New Mumbai. As this is your first ride with us, Mr. Pohlmeyer, we are happy to offer you a ten percent discount. Would you like me to take you to 235-33 Warren Gill Avenue? If that is your destination, then you will need a Confederation of Free States ID."

"No, no. Not there," he blurted out, only mildly surprised that the company system knew his barracks address.

"Very well. What is your destination, sir?"

"I . . . uh, Mz. Armitage," he said, wishing he knew her first name. "Where are we going?"

In reply, she lowered herself, face in his lap.

Almost in panic, Titus turned around, wondering who could see. The doorman was still standing there, but not looking in their direction.

But she didn't do anything there. She lay motionless.

"Uh . . . Mz. Armitage? Are you OK?" he asked, giving her a slight shake.

She mumbled something, then snuggled in closer. In seconds, she started to snore.

Titus had to do something. If the cab AI detected enough warning signs of what could be a crime, it would lock down and summon the police.

"Mz. Armitage?" he asked again, giving her another shake.

"What is your destination, Mr. Pohlmeyer?"

He reached for her right wrist and pulled it free, then passed it across the reader on the dash. "Can you take her home?"

"Certainly. Our destination is 21 Morena Place, Elysium Hills, Mz. Mintera Armitage. Would you like to confirm that destination?"

"Yes," he said, hoping it didn't need her voice recognition.

"Thank you. We expect to arrive in eighteen minutes, twenty-two seconds."

The cab filled with bamto-rock, something popular almost seventy years ago, and evidently in Mz. Armitage's—Mintera's—preferred listening account. Titus mentally added a few more years to her age.

The autocab pulled out and slotted itself in traffic. Titus tried to gently push Mz. Armitage out of his lap, but she grabbed him with her free arm and hugged him tight. At least it was the side of her face, not the front, that was pressed into him.

A compartment opened up on the side, with an assortment of drinks. Would you like a refreshment, Mr. Pohlymeyer?" the AI asked.

He definitely didn't need alcohol. His head was swimming as it was. He could use a pick-me-up, though, he decided. He reached in and grabbed an ESX-Gold.

"Thank you. Four-point-seven-three C have been added to your total bill.

"Shit," he shouted, trying to put the energy drink back, but the compartment door had already closed. "I don't want this!"

"I'm sorry, but city Code Five-Zero-Three-Point-Two-Three prohibits the return of consumables once in the customers' possession.

This one stupid drink was ten times the PX cost. He looked down at the lightly snoring woman, wondering, hoping, she would offer to pay for the ride. She was obviously loaded. Maybe if he said it was for her? He decided not to open it.

As the autocab pulled into the Tata Boulevard, Mz. Armitage stirred, raised her head, then lifted a hand to stroke his cheek. She mumbled something unintelligible, then went back to sleep.

Elysium Hills was a gated community, heavily fortified, but the gate opened to allow them in. It must have read the wristtrans she obviously had implanted. Just one more sign that the woman was in the money.

He didn't need the wristtrans to know her financial situation. Elysium Hills was simply stunning. Large homes dotted the road, just enough showing over walls and between huge trees to let him know that he didn't belong here. Not an Army PFC.

At 18 minutes, 22 seconds, the autocab pulled in front of an understated, four-story condo. Small details, though, that even someone from his social class could recognize, was an indication that the understatement was all part of the grand plan.

The autocab door opened, and a liveried doorman approached. Titus doubted he'd seen three human doormen in his life, two of them this evening.

"Ah, Miss Mina, let me help you out," he said, nonplussed, reaching in to gently pull her off Titus.

He turned back, snapped his fingers, and a chair rolled up. Titus jumped out, and between the two of them, they got her into it.

"Will the gentlemen be escorting Miss Mina to her penthouse?" he asked with zero trace of disapproval.

Titus was surprised, though. He'd agreed to go with her because he'd expected something amazing, a wild night. But she was out cold. The doorman could see that, yet he looked at him expectantly.

"Does . . . do men often go up with her?" he asked, afraid he was stepping over some social line.

"It does happen, sir," he said. "Quite often," he added as if taking pity on him.

Part of him, especially the part centered below his belt, wanted to say yes. Standing above her, he had an expansive view of her cleavage. But he knew right from wrong. She was drunk when she invited him, and she was unconscious now. Neither implied consent.

He took a deep breath, then said, "No. I think I'll just go home."

"Very well, sir. I'll make sure to get Miss Mina home. You'll need a code to get past the gate. Key in zero-four-zero-five. That will get you through."

Titus wasn't sure, but he thought a small look of approval flashed across the doorman's eyes as he put the chair in follow mode and walked to the entrance.

"Mr. Pohlmeyer, I see that you are still here. Do you wish to travel to another destination?"

"How about back to base?"

"Certainly, sir." He got back inside, and the AI informed him, "I have already charged your account thirty-two-point-two-naught C."

"What?" he asked, shocked.

The AI repeated the exorbitant amount.

"And how much to my barracks?"

"Approximately forty C, depending on traffic conditions that may develop."

"No, I think I'll find another way."

"Very well, sir. Please consider Silk Road for any future ride needs."

Titus watched the cab roll off, then checked his PA. There wasn't much in the way of public transport here in rich-person's land, but 900 meters past the gate, he could catch the first of three buses back to the base, then a free shuttle to his barracks. Total cost for the buses? Two-point-two C.

He took one last look back at the condo, wondering which penthouse was hers, and wondering what he'd missed. He hitched up his uniform trou, then started walking, none-too-steadily, but feeling good about himself.

Which lasted all of 30 meters before he vomited up some very expensive liquor onto Elysium Hills' very manicured roadside shrubbery.

L5G-21

Chapter 12

Titus wondered if having joined the military while the Free States were in conflict might have altered what he felt was normal for a military situation. Even his time in boot camp had been influenced by the Publica rebellion. There'd been a sense of urgency among the drill sergeants, and that sense had been passed on to the privates. There was a need to be on the front lines, fighting the enemy, preserving the peace. Something always needed doing, always important, no matter if it was sifting through data, building prefabs or just handling the many, many chores that came with maintaining a barracks. It was all for the war effort.

But now, with the war done and dusted and most of the paperwork squared away, Titus couldn't help but feel that every task that was sent his way was busywork. Something to keep the troops sharp and ready for when the next bit of action began.

Which wasn't the point really. Soldiers were supposed to fight for an end to the fighting. But what were soldiers supposed to do when the fighting stopped?

That was the long version. The short version was that he just wasn't feeling his job.

He was a soldier. He was supposed to be defending the Free States from the corporate stooges that called themselves the Federation, not watching them dig up a planet through satellite feeds and drone captures.

The mission was, in theory, simple. A battalion had been sent down to hold onto L5G-21, a planet whose mining rights had been granted to Dhoop, Inc, a New Mumbai-registered company. However, BHP Billiton, a Federation corporation, claimed that since the Free States had ceded from the Federation, the original charter granted to Dhoop was now null and void. The fact that it was 75 years after the initial charter and 73 years since the Confederation of Free States formally split from the Federation evidently meant little. The fact the survey team Dhoop had finally sent to the planet had discovered significant deposits of heavy earths carried more weight, and old court cases were dusted off and brought out into the open again.

With the court cases as justification, BHP Billiton had proceeded to set up a mining operation on the planet, beating Dhoop to the punch. Dhoop immediately reacted, sending their own mining assets to the planet's surface to join the survey team. Afraid that the Federation might send in their hated FCDC, the Federation Civil Defense Corps, colloquially known as the "fuckdicks,", the company appealed to the Free States government to intercede on their behalf. In response, a battalion had been sent to establish a presence alongside the Dhoop workforce meant to scan the planet's resources.

Neither mining operation had extracted much in the way of material, yet. Both of their presences were more to establish legal advantages while the case began to work its way through the United Assembly of Man courts in Brussels.

No hostilities had broken out yet. While on the same deposit, the operations were separated by 112 klicks and a low mountain range. In both locations mining had been ramping up until a UAM-brokered arbitration panel had ordered both mines to cease operations until the legal status of the planet could be determined. A shipload of "settlers," hurriedly dragged out the slums on New Mumbai in an attempt to show civilians living on the planet, had been turned back. That might have worked 73 years before, but not as a blatant ploy after the discovery of the deposits, and the Federation protest had been upheld. Technically, the planet was uninhabited. The question at hand was whether a charter issued to a Federation corporation, by the Federation government, was still valid if the company was now a foreign corporation.

BHP Billiton—and the Federation—held that no, the charter was no longer valid. Nothing had been done to settle the planet, nor had there been any mining. Dhoop claimed that they had spent vast amounts of money, contributing to the still ongoing terraforming process. Only now, they contended, could humans survive without full body suits, and that was why they had waited.

With mining operations ceased and the negotiations left to the diplomats, there was nothing for the Free States Army to do but monitor the situation, and with long hours watching nothing, Titus had time to think, and the more he thought about it, the more he realized that it wasn't so much a righteous battle against the evil corporations that ran the Federation. Rather the Free States military was being used to defend the profits of yet another corporation. That was supposed to be the Federation modus operandi, not that of the Free States.

So, now, instead of watching for enemy combatants on the move, he watched hours of surveillance of the BHP Billiton mine, looking for any hint that they'd renewed the operations. He wasn't sure how he could determine that. A mine's operations were mostly underground, by definition, so unless he could send micro-drones into the mine, he wasn't sure what he could determine. Even faint vibrations could be explained away as normal tectonic activity.

He wasn't even part of a full AIC team. The agreement limited the number of soldiers that the Free States Army could keep on the planet, so the entire surveillance cell was Titus and a sergeant. That meant, 12 hours, on, 12 hours off, in a temporary suite watching excruciatingly boring feeds.

Titus had lost count of how many times he'd fallen asleep on that tiny desk. L5G-21 had an irregular rotation, and the long, 38-hour days played havoc with the Army's biennial clocks, despite the synchshots given each of them. Titus decided to simply keep his small space continually lit. It might not be healthy, but it helped keep him awake.

And the result of all the time he spent on the feeds was that no rare-earth-loaded vehicles were exiting the mine. That's it.

He checked the time. Six more hours? Hell, he was hoping he just had two hours left on duty.

Titus rubbed his bleary eyes, reaching for a mug of PC-20, the military's generic version of Zap. The military swore it was the exact same thing as the commercial version, but there wasn't a soldier alive who believed that. The current trend was that not only wasn't it the same recipe as Zap, it was spiked with a libido-depressant. It did, however, kick like a mule and could keep a full-bodied infantryman on his feet for days. But after two weeks of the stuff, Titus's palate was crying for the taste of real coffee. Or at least the stuff that was made to taste like real coffee. He'd even settle for some chai at this point.

He settled back in his chair, closing his eyes just for a moment . . . and one of his alarms went off. He jerked upright, realizing he'd nodded off again. He shook his head to clear it and shut off the alarm, centering the Navy feed on what had set it off.

Three carrucas had entered the planet's atmosphere, which was not unusual in and of itself. The miners needed supplies, whether they were mining or not. He hadn't known there was a scheduled run, however. After checking the list, he saw whatever the three carrucas were doing, it had not been scheduled.

Not that it had to be. The scheduling was there just to keep things calm, but it was not a requirement. The Navy, in the shape of a single gunboat with a crew of 72, was not squawking, though, so Titus wasn't extremely concerned. He'd like to know who they were, however. Tempted to just contact the Navy, he held off. If they already knew about them, which they had to, by asking, he was putting the Army on notice for not promulgating that information down to him.

He had the AI calculate the carrucas most efficient trajectory down to the surface and the Fed mine. There were a few high-altitude drones along the path. He'd have to ask permission for the Navy-owned drones, but two were Army. He couldn't change their positions on his own, but he could shift their scanners. He switched both to visual, and had them watch along the carrucas' projected flight path.

It was a long three minutes before the first of the images appeared on Titus' screen. He worked quickly to clear some of the clutter to give the images more space, looking at them closely as soon as the scrubber cleaned the images enough for him to make out any details.

Most of the arriving craft had the logos of their companies emblazoned on their sides, making them easy to identify even by visuals. They also had ID transponders, but while the Navy could identify any ship known to man by the transponders, Titus did not have access to the same information without jumping through a million hoops.

That's for the after-action reports, he told himself as he studied the images. Titus had a list of the companies authorized for transit to the surface. That list was not going to help him here. There were no images on the sides of the three carrucas, which he could see were configured for personnel and not supplies, and the sides were blank. No apparent company logos, no clear sign of who they belonged to. Possibly BHP Billiton execs? Investors who didn't want to excite the markets?

The three pulled out of range of the drone, and never got close enough to the second to learn anything more. He wanted to see who would get out of them, though.

"Whiskey-Three-Delta, I'm going to need a closeup of the BHP landing pad. You got anything for me?"

The woman on the other line wasn't the same Whiskey-Three-Delta as on Indus. The "Delta" was coincidence, "Whiskey" was surveillance, and "Three" was ops.

"Easy-peasy, Titus," she said. "Give me a moment, and I'll have something for you on Forty-Three-November."

There were so few soldiers on the planet that it wouldn't have been difficult for her to find out his name, but the breach of protocol bothered him.

He switched the feed and a moment later, he was looking at the BHP landing pad. He checked the descent track of his three carrucas, and unless they did a wave-off or fly-by, they'd be on the ground in a little over six minutes.

"How's that, Titus?"

"Can you get any closer, Whiskey-Three," he asked, refusing to resort to first names.

"That's a negative. We're getting 'stay away' strobes from the base as it is."

The two sides were free to observe the other's locations, but there were no-fly zones buffering each one. Whiskey-Three had pushed the envelope to get the drone this close.

"None of the cargo docks look deployed," Whiskey-Three remarked.

"They're personnel carriers," he said, then wondering why. There wasn't any prohibition against doing so, but AIC culturally tended to keep things close to the vest until they could present actual intel.

"So, they can land anywhere, and not even on the pad," she said.

Military craft didn't need a pad, but commercial shuttles needed loading docks in order to be automatically unloaded. People didn't need them. They could simply walk off a shuttle under their own power.

He didn't reply, waiting for the carrucas to land. A carruca was essentially a space sled, not the luxury shuttles favored by corporate execs, so he doubted his first guess had been on target. He watched with interest as they came in for a neat landing, in almost military precision.

Even on full magnification, the feed was not very clear given the distance and atmospheric divergences. He was tempted to put in an intreq to the Navy for an overhead shot, but once again, they had to have seen the three carrucas, and he didn't want to cause any waves.

Shit. Forget that needing loading docks theory.

As the back doors opened, a small fleet of what had to be cargo mules left the cover of their shelters, and personnel began to unload crates, placing them on the mules. That didn't make sense. Why not use the existing cargo docks? This was a mine, after all, where large amounts of material passed through, not some isolated research station.

He tried to adjust his display for better resolution. He couldn't make out details, but six people were standing off, with what could be weapons in their hands. They had the look of armed guards to them. Or soldiers. Which could also explain their use of manpower to unload the carrucas. Like militaries everywhere, their standards did not always match those of civilians. If those were military carrucas, then they might not be able to marry with the civilian loading docks.

"You getting what you need?" Whiskey-Delta-Three asked.

"You sure you can't get closer?"

"Yeah? And get thrown into the brig for violating orders? Fat chance. You want closer, you call the Navy."

She was right. And he didn't really need it. He knew what was happening. Hell, he was surprised it had taken them this long. The Federation was efficient, if nothing else.

He knew what he had to do next.

"I need to speak with the actual," he said as the S-3 ops comms watch answered his call.

"Sierra-Three-Actual?"

"Negative. The CO."

"Wait one, Two-Sierra-Four."

Titus continued to watch the feed. Whoever that was out there, they'd unloaded a shitload of cargo.

"Two-Sierra-Four, this is Sierra-Three-Actual. Are you sure you need the CO?"

"Yes, I am," he said, leaving it at that.

"He just hit the rack, for the first time in two days. You can't tell me?"

"Protocol Victor, sir."

There was a moment of silence, then, "Understood. Wait one and I'll patch you through."

Almost immediately, Lieutenant Colonel Ives Varand was on the line, gruffly asking, "Who is this?"

"Sierra-Two-Four, sir." There was a moment of silence, so he added, "AIC liaison."

"Hell, son, this had better be important . . . PFC Pohlmeyer," he said, probably just pulling Titus up and mangling his last name

"I believe this is a Protocol Victor," he answered, suddenly wondering if he was wrong.

A Protocol Victor was the second highest alert status, but maybe he could have just passed this to the battalion S3. He was a major, after all, and he could decide what to do with it. Intel provided what they could, but never took action on it.

"Victor? Well, get on with it."

"I don't have all the details yet," he said, second-guessing not requesting Navy confirmation.

"Sir, I believe that armed personnel have landed at the HP mine site."

"Federation Marines?" the CO asked, suddenly sounding hyper-alert.

"I can't tell. But I had visuals on their carrucas. No markings."

"No markings? Not Marines, then," he said, sounding relieved.

Titus understood why. The Federation Marines were probably the finest fighters in human space, but they did not do clandestine work. Wherever they went, they proudly displayed their logo.

"I'm guessing either fuc . . . uh, FCDC or mercenaries," he said. "Maybe company-sized. I believe they're well-supplied, too."

There was silence on the line, and Titus began to get nervous. Had he panicked?

"I could have requested Navy surveillance, but that would take a while, sir, so I thought I should tell you first. Sorry I don't have more details yet."

"No, no, Private Pohlmeyer. You did exactly right. Give me ten minutes and I'll be there so you can show me exactly what you observed. Actual, out."

Titus let out a long sigh of relief. He just hoped the battalion CO would agree with his take on what he saw on the feeds.

****

"They're just flexing. They saw that we brought in a military presence, and they wanted to put up a show of force to scare us off," Major Jones, the battalion operations officer said.

"I'm not entirely convinced. All those crates. That's enough weapons to support an offensive. If they have a trained, battle-hardened crew, they wouldn't have a lot of trouble keeping us off them until the UAM sent in their inquiry team. Three years from now," the CO replied.

Soldier

The office was ordinarily small. Between Titus, the CO, Major Jones, and Lieutenant Gil (the S2), the place seemed to be getting smaller by the minute. The colonel had taken over Titus' seat, the Major stood over him, while the lieutenant and Titus pushed into the corners of his tiny space while the two field grade officers discussed just what the feeds meant.

"If we do anything without provocation, it'll come down on our heads," the major said, clearly growing frustrated.

"If we're forced off the planet by a third party, any inquiry will give the planet to the Federation while the mercenaries are slapped with a fine for their involvement. If that," Varand replied, seemingly unfazed.

"We're not equipped to go—"

"We outnumber them. Five to one. We can handle a company of mercenaries."

"With all due respect sir, we might not."

"Are you telling me that you don't have faith in our soldiers?"

"Most of them are replacement troops, sir. You know that. They were sent so the conscripts from the war effort could go home. Hell, Meyers has more experience in the field than they do."

"Meyers? Who?"

Titus cleared his throat. "I think he means me, sir."

Varand shook his head and said, "Pohlmeyer, Major. PFC Pohlmeyer. But to this point, I'm not going to let a bunch of mercenaries just waltz in here like they own the place."

"They think they do. That's the point of the arbitration, sir."

"Then they think wrong. Look, Derrick. If we allow them to establish themselves, then all of this will be a fait accompli, and I'll be damned if I'm going to let that happen. Get back to your staff and give the contingency plan another look. See how we can improve it. I want to see something by 0600."

"Are we going to assault the BHP mine?" the major asked, sounding defeated.

"I don't know. I'm going to report up to division. But I want to be ready for an immediate course of action, should it come to that."

"Yes, sir," the major said.

"And Lassiter," the CO said, turning to the S2, "What can you tell me about these mercs?"

The lieutenant looked uncomfortable, then stammered out, "Not much, sir. We don't even know their unit. They could still be FCDC, for that matter. That kind of Intel, sir, that's more in his ballpark." He pointed at Titus.

"You're my S2 and you're ceding to a PFC?"

Titus sympathized with the lieutenant. On a battalion level, the S2 took Intel and disseminated it to the CO. He didn't analyze, nor did he gather. Titus, while just a PFC, was part of "The Big I," meaning, he was part of the division-level Intel staff. As such, he had access to far more than the lieutenant despite the disparity in their ranks.

"Sir, I can try to find out more. Between G2 and the Navy, I'm sure these mercs left some breadcrumbs we can track."

The CO shifted his gaze to him, took in what he'd just said, then nodded. "Find out what you can about these mercs. Who they are, how expensive they are, down to who makes their boot lacings. Anything you can. We need to know who we might be fighting."

"Roger that, sir."

"Well, let's get going," he said, clapping his hands.

The lieutenant mouthed a silent "Thanks" as he followed the two senior officers out of the space.

Now, all Titus had to do was make good on his promise.

****

Doing that was easier said than done, especially with the 0600 deadline. He leaned back, closing his eyes for a moment. They felt like he'd used sandpaper on them. He couldn't remember the last time he had slept, but it felt like a damned eternity.

Despite being under higher headquarters, it wasn't as if he could just download the information the CO demanded. The feeds from the EITS just weren't good enough to pull anything. A preliminary search on the personal weapons alone brought up fewer than 33 potential matches, which wasn't going to help narrow down the mercenaries. Too many models that could have more than a dozen different manufacturers, which could, in turn, be made and sold on a horde of different customers.

No, he needed those Navy feeds. But instead of simply requesting them from the *CFS Reliant*, the gunship in orbit above them, he'd had to bump this up to the G2 back in New Mumbai, which sent it to the Navy HQ, which then had to approve the request, which then had to send the directive to the ship, which then . . .

Too many "thens" later, Captain Wallace back at G2-4, and his contact for the intreq, came back on the net.

"The Navy finally got off their asses and forwarded us their feeds. We've got a confirmed hit on the personal weapons. W-25s."

The 25s were heavier, older versions of the 37 Titus had borne as an engineer. All but indestructible, they were common among Federation and Federation-aligned planets, they were not the weapon of choice among top-of-the-line units or security companies. That still left a lot of possibilities, however.

Kalasse, the manufacturer, had manufactured hundreds of millions of them before ceasing production and dumping their remaining stock on a few large Gentry distributors. That still left a lot of possibilities, however.

Titus grunted. He was hoping for something a little more definitive.

"We've also identified the ATVs. Diamondbacks. YT-65's."

Now that was more promising. Diamondbacks were the generic name given to a line of ATVs that had hit the market less than two years ago. They were cheap to produce, almost indestructible, and could climb almost vertical surfaces with their cutting-edge chameleon-tracks. Named for their diamond-shaped profile which lowered their center-of-gravity, they were too inefficient for paved roads, they excelled over rough terrain.

Diamondbacks were manufactured in two locations, one within the Brotherhood and one within the Federation. That, and the short length of time they'd been produced narrowed down the search tremendously, but if Titus was a betting man, he'd bet on these coming from the Federation factory.

"Sir, can we run a search on who's bought Diamondbacks recently, and corelate that with recent or even past purchases of W-25's?" he asked.

"Already done. And I think we've got a good hit. Take a look."

An image flashed on his screen. A Turtle. Titus shook his head, rubbed his eyes, and re-focused. Yes, it was still a turtle. Yellow on a field of black, held in by a simple pentagonal shield. Underneath the words "Ridge Security Consultants" was written in bold type. More details loaded.

"Ridge Security. These guys look like they run corporate security, not mercs, sir."

"What do you think most mercs are?" the captain said with a laugh. "Do you think they run ads as ABC Mercenaries?' Only a few do on the independent worlds or the Alliance, but mercs are technically illegal throughout most of human space, even in the Federation."

Titus felt embarrassed. Of course, most merc units could not register as a mercenary company.

"Roger that," he said. "Anything else on them that I can pass to the ground commander?"

"Officially, they're new, run by a career Legionnaire, ex-*Sergent-chef* Akinyemi. He's run two other 'security' companies, the last one folding the day Ridge Security was established. I'll zap you what we have and past campaigns under his tenure. Stand-by."

The data packet arrived a few moments later. Titus looked at the clock. 0536. Twenty-four minutes until it was due, which wasn't enough time for him to go over it first. He'd have to forward it as is. At least he had a name for the unit that he could forward. He wrote a tagline with a promise of more and sent it on up to the S2. Let the lieutenant handle the brief.

"Anything else you can give me?" he asked.

"That's about it for now. I've got half-a-dozen searches going on with the Jasper, so—"

The captain's transmission cut off.

Shit. I'd like to know what the Jasper can piece together, and this happens now?

The Jasper was a JSPR-4700, a non-AI computer that was essentially a huge numbers cruncher, but one that could recognize patterns when no human or AI could. Titus didn't understand how something so basic was more capable than an AI, but that was science. Might as well be magic, for all he was concerned.

"Captain?" he asked before running a quick diagnostic on the line. A small red triangle appeared on the display with the words "Connection Disconnect" underneath. Titus tried to reconnect, to no avail. Then he powered down the system and booting it back up. Nothing.

He was about to call the comms shop, but he knew they would want to know where the break was, so he ran a system check. His outgoing stopped at the array.

L5G-21 was subject to micro-tremors, not something desired in a mining planet, but it was what it was. It was possible that his array had been knocked out of whack by one, even if he hadn't felt anything. If even a single bolt was now out of alignment, that could have made the software freak out and shut down until repairs were made. Which, in this case, had to be done manually. For all their advances, the Free States military really needed to upgrade their software.

He grabbed the field kit and an acquisition meter, then went to see if he could get the system working again. If not, he'd have to wait for a tech team, and who knew how long that would take.

Due to existing protocol, Titus was in a field shed, which was simply a commercial shipping container converted to a comms suite, probably at an exorbitant cost. It was located 120 meters from the main CP. With the double locks on the hatch, Titus wasn't sure why the precautions. They were all on the same side, after all. But procedures were procedures, and they rarely made sense to those in the field.

He first checked the optical cables inside the suite. His test had shown that the break was at the array, but he didn't want to climb on top of the suite only to find out the problem was inside. His line-meter showed green. He was going to have to go outside.

He eyed his body armor. Technically, he was supposed to don it, but the fit on his wasn't good. He strapped on his environmental hood, then opened the hatch to the outside. Blinking in the bright sunlight, he turned towards the ladder to the roof when something hard pressed in his back.

"Don't move," came the gravelly order.

Couldn't if I wanted to. All Titus could do was nod.

"Close the door nice and gentle-like."

"I thought you told me not to move," Titus answered.

Oh, gods why?

"Smart guys don't survive this kind of situation." The man's voice was punctuated by the jab of a barrel into his back. "Close it and leave your hands on the handle."

"Understood," Titus answered, trying to emulate the man's growl but it came out more like a very dry cough. He closed the suite, door leaving his hands in place. The pressure of the muzzle in his back lessened, and a hand reached around to grab his left wrist. Titus didn't resist as a flip-cuff was slapped around it with a loud snap, or when the hand was jerked behind him.

Where's my support? he wondered.

120 meters over that rise, he knew. Fucking procedures. There wasn't any reason he couldn't be co-located with the ground forces. He thought about calling out, but the barrel in his back was demanding his full attention. If he tried to shout, the man would fire, and Titus's mother would lose her favorite son.

The man reached for Titus's right wrist. With the weapon between them, all the man could reach was his elbow. "Stay still," the man ordered as he shifted his feet, now slightly off balance as he reached for Titus's right right wrist.

Titus could feel him shift his feet, the barrel digging in from a slightly different angle as he moved.

Titus had a strong desire to keep from being restrained. Nothing good was going to come out of it. While the man was slightly off balance, reaching for his right wrist.

Without really thinking about it, Titus reacted, spinning in place, his elbow lashing at where he assumed the man's cheek was. He ended up clipping the crown of the man's head instead, which sent a jolt of pain across his arm as he twisted around. The man was a good deal shorter than Titus had been envisioning. Probably why he'd had trouble reaching.

His spin had pushed the barrel of the W-26 away from him, and Titus grabbed the barrel to keep the man from bringing it back to bear on him. The man may have been shorter than Titus, but he had the physique of a gym rat, stocky and powerful. It took both of Titus's hands to keep the muzzle of the weapon off of him. The man hammered his left hand into Titus's ribs, almost doubling him over and knocking the breath out of him. But Titus didn't let go, hanging on for dear life. The merc all but lifted him, hammering him into the door of the suite, making the muscles in his back spasm, but he held on.

It was a desperate wrestling match for control as the man kept punching Titus in the hopes that it would weaken his grip. It worked, but only because Titus decided that he had no chance of beating the man through brute force. Titus pivoted in place, letting the weapon twist in the direction the man was pushing

The man fired. His ears were ringing, but he'd managed to divert the muzzle just enough, and the merc hadn't reacted quite quickly enough. With the muzzle of the W025 past him, Titus rammed his elbow in the merc's sternum, then pushed off against the suite wall into the man, taking both of them to the ground with Titus on top. He put his weight and left hand on the W-25, trapping it on the ground, and started pounding on the man's face with his right.

He couldn't entirely control the weapon, and it started to slide as the man put all his efforts into bringing it back up. That left his face unprotected, and Titus kept hammering away. He felt the man's nose crush, but still the merc fought. With a heave, the man rolled over, turning his head until it was flat on the ground. Titus connected with the man's temple just as the merc fired.

Agony shot through his leg, but Titus didn't relent, hitting the merc's temple twice more before realizing the man was out cold. He tried to roll off his opponent, but the pain made him cry out. Looking down, blood was staining his fatigues. Gorge started to rise in his throat, and he had to choke it back down.

He'd been shot before, but he'd been in something of a stunned and shocked state of mind, and the pain had been bearable This time was different.

The merc's groan jerked his mind away from his leg. In the Hollybolly vids, people knocked out stayed out, but this was real life. Titus lunged for the man's W-25, pulling it back out of reach. He aimed it at the man, trying to figure out the firing. For someone who was supposed to know enemy capabilities, that didn't extend to how to operate enemy weaponry.

"Don't sparking move," Titus yelled. The man groaned and reached to his head. "I said, don't move. And what the hell were you doing here?"

Titus could see that for himself. The man had a typical hackers kit. He was either hacking into their comms, or as Titus had lost his uplink, blocking them. That was either harassment or a prelude to some sort of action.

But why would he come alone? There had to be more of them.

"Hey," he said, "where's the rest of you?"

"We're right here, Confed. So, why don't you put that twenty-five down before we do something you'd regret."

Titus turned to his right. Six mercs were standing there. All six had their own W-25s. The difference was that they had theirs locked onto Titus's chest.

Titus had somehow managed to overcome the gorilla laying next to him, but this was too much. He slowly lowered the 25, careful to make sure the muzzle didn't come close to pointing at any of them.

He glanced back to the CP. The merc had shot him. He'd fired twice, in fact. Surely someone had heard that and would come investigate.

"Check Velasquez," one of the men said. "The fuckwad let this piece of Confed shit get the better of him."

"Sorry about your hacker," Titus said. "I'm sure he'll be up and about in no time."

The man simply harrumphed.

A woman moved forward, keeping well clear of Titus, which he would have thought comical in any other circumstances. He was out of any fight with a hole in his leg, he probably had broken ribs, and there were still five mercs with their weapons trained on him. What did they expect him to do?

"He'll be fine," the woman said after a quick exam. "Pissed, but fine."

"OK, so what do we do with you?" the leader said.

He'd been asking rhetorically, but Titus couldn't help himself. "You can let me go. I'm wounded," he said, pointing at his leg, which was throbbing unmercifully. "You know, the Harbin Accords."

The leader actually chuckled at that, then raised the muzzle of his W-25.

"Harbin Accords, he says," he said to the others before turning back to Titus. "Well, you uninformed folks have to follow that crap."

"Even mercs have to follow them."

"'Cepting we ain't mercs," he said as the others laughed. "We're private security."

Titus felt his anger rise, and despite the situation, he snapped, "Then what the fuck are you doing here, and why did that asshole shoot me?"

"That was providing security for our client, of course. And you here," he said, waving a hand at Titus's suite, "were trying to spy on company activities."

"Bullshit," Titus said automatically.

Except that was what he was doing. A moment of doubt crossed his mind. His righteous indignation might be misplaced, at least from a legal standpoint. That was all beyond his paygrade, however.

"So, what do we do with this guy?" one of the others asked the leader.

"Check inside. See if Velasquez shut this thing down before he fucked up."

The merc pushed against the door, which swung open. Titus should have secured it the moment he walked outside, but things had gotten out of hand quickly.

"Spirit, cuff him," he said after the other merc disappeared inside the suite.

The woman warily approached Titus and said, "Give me your hand, nice and slow, or so help me, I'll fuck you up good."

Titus almost laughed. She sounded scared while he was weak as a kitten. He wasn't going to argue. He brought both hands together, and she quickly ziptied them.

"Looks like the comms are down," the one with the accent said, sticking his head out of the suite. "Velasquez must have gotten the jammer working before he got beat up."

"Don't think he's living that down anytime soon."

"So, what are we going to do with him?" the woman named Spirit asked.

"Take him with us. That or ghost him so he can't talk."

He saw Titus jump, and he said, "Relax, Confed. If you don't give us cause, you're going to make it through this fine. We like to keep casualties at a minimum here. So long as the rest of your Confed buddies don't fuck with us too much, nobody's getting hurt. Well," he corrected quickly when Titus started looking pointedly at his bandaged knee, "killed anyway. But we can't leave you here to talk, so you're coming with us."

"I don't think I can walk," Titus said, more relieved than he would have guessed.

One of the others stepped up to him and knelt by his leg. He poked it a few times, which sent bolts of agony that Titus had to bite back from screaming.

"It's gonna need surgery," the man said through his heavy accent.

He took out a pressure wrap, immobilized the knee, and gave Titus a pill.

"Come on, boy. Take it. It'll help."

Well, they don't have to poison me to kill me, he rationalized before he took the pill and swallowed.

Almost immediately a wave of lassitude swept over him. His leg still hurt like a son-of-a-bitch. He just didn't care that it did.

"Good, huh?" the man asked.

"Yeah, good."

"You behave like a good little Confed, and we'll let our surgeon fix that knee of yours. Good as new." Titus felt a gloved hand pat him on the cheek.

"Huang? We really need to get going. I'm getting lots of activity," said one of the others, a tall, whipcord woman who'd said nothing so far.

She held up a small scanner for the leader to see.

"Yep, you're right. Hog, you and Spirit take our friend here. Asper, you help Velasquez."

Titus was flying pretty high as the two helped him to his feet. He looked back at his suite as they marched off, wondering when he'd get back to his unit.

****

The trip hadn't been as bad as he'd feared, first because he'd been drugged to the gills, second, because he'd only walked—mostly carried—a klick or so before they reached a high-tech stealth hover. Titus had never seen one like that before, and the Intel side of him tried to make mental notes that he might remember after the drugs wore off.

Within three hours, he was in a hospital ward, inside the mine. He'd been trying to pierce the veil to know what was going on here, and now he was inside. Not that he had discovered much other than this ward was like any other. Several other battalion soldiers and what looked to be a BHP miner were in the ward as well. A company doctor had examined him, determined that the autodoc could handle the surgery, and less than 30 minutes after arrival, he was strapped to the operating table while the robot removed the round and stabilized the knee. The human doc told him he might need more surgery later, but that he would be fine.

This was his second time being shot, and he was starting to think that his initial ambition of earning glory and honor in the Infantry might not have been his best idea. He just wasn't cut out for being on the front lines. Or maybe Jaeger--or Daniels or whatever his name really was--had been right. Maybe he should have retired after the first time, lived off a pension, written memoirs, and gone on talk shows about how terrible war was.

Ten hours after he'd arrived, there was a flurry of activity. No one bothered to keep any of them informed. It wasn't until the next day, when they were shoved to the side for incoming wounded, that they began to find out.

Titus had been taken in what was the preparatory phase of the Federation operation, which was designed to blind the battalion. Instead of raising the alarm, the CO had tried to fix the comms in-house, never dreaming that they'd been taken down instead of falling to maintenance issues. One of the captured captains had bitterly said that the CO had been more concerned with not looking bad to those higher up the chain that he'd refused to report the problem.

The S3 also turned out to be correct in his assessment of the battalion's capabilities. When the numerically inferior "security" forces hit, the battalion had collapsed—and collapsed spectacularly. The only good thing was that the route was so complete that there had been very little loss of life. The battalion had never been at full strength, but with just over 500 soldiers, only 36 had been wounded and 3 killed. Defeated by what was probably fewer than 120 Fed mercs.

These weren't even Federation Marines, which would have been bad enough. But for those results from what were a hodgepodge of military personnel brought together by a *Sergent-chef* who'd been kicked out of the Greater French Foreign Legion was downright pitiful.

The accented guy, a merc that went by the name of Henderson, had been right. Their main objective was to take over the base with as little bloodshed as possible. At the moment of their strike, most of the battalion had been in the mess for lunch, with tactical strikes having taken down the lookout posts. With the jammers keeping any alarm from being raised, the battalion had been defeated by an embarrassingly small number of Feddies. After the "great victory" over the Publicas, the Army had been feeling pretty good about itself. When going against professionals, however, its true capabilities, or lack thereof, had been exposed.

In a word, they sucked.

With the fight over so quickly, things quieted down. For Titus, that meant lying in a cot, still in the BHP mine, with his leg propped up. Others had been treated and taken away, but the ten more seriously wounded lay around with nothing much to do. They weren't technically EPWs as no state of war had been declared. According to BPH, they were trespassers, common criminals, awaiting disposition. Still, they were each interviewed by a rep from the Red Cross just as if they were EPWs protected by the Harbin Accords.

Needless to say, captivity grew old fast. He was going "bat-shit crazy," as Sergeant Sharma, who was in the next cot with burns to his torso, called it. So, two weeks later, when he could hear the sounds of activity, he was chewing at the walls to be able to see what was happening. Voices, movement, footsteps. Were they being evacuated to a Fed base somewhere for a proper incarceration?

One of the mercs who brought them their food entered the ward, a trundle chair following him. A short guy with a bright red beard and hair, came over to his bed, and Titus was almost exploding with questions.

"What's going on?"

The merc didn't answer right away, checking the pad with his patient details before rolling a chair over to the side of the bed.

"Get on," came the grunted order, with the accent that Titus was already getting used to hearing.

"Something's happening. What's going on."

"You're being lifted back to Free State Space. Looks like it's no concentration camps for you, eh?" The merc said with a laugh, scratching his beard. "Come on, I don't want to pick you up, but I friggin' will."

Titus pushed himself to the side of the bed, and with some deft maneuvering and a little help from the man, he managed to seat himself on the chair.

"How come? Federation declaring control of the system?"

"Nah, you Confeds managed to broker a deal which would avoid the UAM getting their fingers in the pie. Something with BHP and Dhoop having an auction over the resources, or some such shit. I don't know the details. But one of the specifics was that there be no military presence from either side on the planet. Which means you get shipped out, and then we get shipped out. Fun times are had by all."

Titus growled, using a bent piece of wire he'd managed to scrounge to reach inside his cast and scratched his ever-present itch. "But you guys had us dead to rights. We didn't have a military presence on the planet anymore. I mean, a combat-ready one."

The man shrugged. "I know. But the UAM talked the CEOs down from pressing their claim. The planet's no good yet anyway. What's the point of fighting over it now?"

Titus didn't know how to take that, so he didn't respond.

He was rolled out of the improvised med bay, taken up the elevator, and out onto the landing pad, the same one he'd observed over two weeks ago, the same one onto which Ridge Securities had landed. This time, there were two shuttles, both with Free States flashes.

"I don't get it," Titus said when his escort stopped the chair. "You mercs—"

"Security consultants."

"Right... security consultants had us down. Even if we had reinforcements on the way, which I don't think we did, they would have had a hard time taking the planet back with nowhere to land."

The man chuckled, scratching his beard. "Hell if I know. Confed—"

"Free States," Titus corrected.

"*Confed* diplomats," Ginger said forcefully. "They did their talking, and now we're doing some walking. It's above my pay grade, and I think it's above yours, too. So, don't ask questions, board your shuttle, and get lost."

The man's tone was softened by a wink as a Free States nurse checked him off his list, then took command of the chair.

"Diplomats did their talking," Titus mumbled to himself, as they approached the shuttle. "Huh."

"What was that?" the nurse asked.

"Nothing. Sorry, just talking to myself."

The problem was that he wasn't quite sure just what he was trying to tell himself.

NEW MUMBAI

Chapter 13

Titus dropped down on the bench, his shirt drenched with sweat. The sun was high in the sky, baking the field. Titus would have preferred the cool, conditioned barracks himself, all things considered. But being out and about again after another couple of weeks of physical therapy was good for his knee. Maybe the brass would figure out that it was time to take him away from the front lines since he was apparently made of some hitherto scientifically impossible magnet for bullets.

He rubbed his knee. The Federation surgeons had only to "touch up" what the BHP autodoc had done, and the reconstruction process had gone without too much of a hitch. The therapist said that there might be some pain, but it would be mostly psychosomatic from this point on. All in his head. Up until now, he'd had his doubts, but after a few hours of running around playing Fives, he'd realized that the pain had mostly faded. It was barely a throb now.

Of course, his knee wasn't the reason why he'd taken a break.

"Sparking sun," Titus said with a grimace, brushing his arm across his forehead and taking a long gulp of icy water from the cooler. It wasn't the sun's fault that he was terrible at this game though. He wanted to say that he would have felt a lot more comfortable on a gridiron field, but that wouldn't have been true either. He'd played chess. And Vertigo. He'd been good at those. Mental acrobatics failed to pass over onto the field though. He'd been giving it his all, but in the end, some coordination was required.

Titus picked up the bat that he'd left on the bench, brushing some of the brown dust from it with his forearm. It was long, with a steel grip and a flat wooden blade. The toe was cut diagonally, allowing it to be held against the ground without letting the ball—small, white and made almost entirely of plasteene and whippet—slip by underneath. It tended to happen anyway when Titus was at bat, but his teammates were forgiving. Mostly.

He spun the bat in a figure-eight to warm up his arms and took up his place at the sticks. The sun was directly above him, so while there was no glare, the heat was getting to him. A slow rivulet had begun to run down from his temple and into his eyes. He brushed it away, but he could still feel it there, pooling above his eyebrow. Distracting.

The opposing player set up across from him. A corporal in the engineer corps by the name of Bilal, Titus recalled that he liked to put the ball forward with speed, not knowing how to put any spin on it. Nobody here was professional, which made it all the more embarrassing when Titus found himself at the bottom of the totem pole.

The ball was bowled, bouncing once across the grass before it collided with Titus' bat. It careened away, out onto the grass. Titus jumped forward, carrying his bat forward with him as he broke for the wickets on the opposite side. His eyes flickered out into the field where he saw one of the outfielders tracking the ball with his eyes and jumping up to catch it before it touched the ground.

"Damn it!" Titus wanted to throw his bat at the ground in frustration, but a sense of decorum held him back. Private Solace, acting as umpire, called the play dead. It was his team's last out, and they all jogged over to the shed that provided some cover and water.

"It's all good, Titus," one of the other PFCs, Viran, said while clapping him on the back. "You just need to learn how to put distance on the ball instead of height."

"I think we should be glad that he's hitting the ball at all," Corporal Weinstein said, a tall, muscled man who had had a chance to play professionally but chose the army instead. By his word, anyway. A couple others chuckled, and Titus nodded.

"He's right." Titus picked up a plastic cup and filled it with water. "At this point, maybe it'd be better to set me up with a less demanding team. Maybe some local under 18s church league," he said facetiously.

"There aren't gonna be many under 18s come next season," Viran said. "Did you see the new conscription bills that Congress is trying to pass? Mandatory military service at seventeen years of age? I have a kid brother who's sixteen now."

There were a few rumblings of assent, but Titus shook his head, taking a sip from his cup before speaking. "They're using that as a red herring for everyone to latch onto. Once they've been 'convinced,'" he used floating air quotes to indicate his sarcasm, "to drop that and a couple other hardline bills, the liberals will be a lot more amenable to the rest of them."

The corporal nodded. "Yeah, yeah. I mean, getting even the Liberty Bell conservatives to accept a bill about adding fucking Federation Marine regimens to the training cycle is gonna be a tough pill to swallow. I hear that they even want to bring in some advisors to help with the transition."

Titus narrowed his eyes, moving to refill his cup. "I thought they were only bringing those in from New Budapest?"

"NB, Feddie Marines, even some from the Brotherhood Host for the Special Forces training."

"Seriously?" Viran asked, a confused but decidedly disgusted look on his face. "I have to think that the *Exploratores* are gonna have a word or two to say about that."

"None of these bills are going to be popular," Titus said, swirling the water in his cup. "It's why they're resorting to all this politicking to get it through. With the past couple of military blunders with the Publicas and the Federation, the public opinion of the military has taken a lot of hits. There are some in the FOS that want to start scaling back military spending, investing more in the Diplomat Corps. Get some trade agreements going."

A few of the others nodded. The bad taste of having Federation "advisors" coming in to train was rampant throughout the military.

"What else do you know?" Bilal asked.

"Hmm?" Titus' head shot up when he realized that he was the one that was being addressed.

"I mean, you're AIC. You gotta know something about this whole shebang."

Titus chuckled. "Seriously? I'm a PFC in the Army Intelligence Corps. I push papers or pencils or envelopes, or whatever the hell else they want me to push. I look for typos in after action reports. Do you really think that they'd tell me anything before all this became official? They haven't even voted on the first set of bills yet. It's going to be months before any of this stuff actually impacts any of us."

"You gotta know about some back-alley deals or the preparations that they're running to push this all through. I mean, shit like this doesn't sit on someone's back burners, and I'm betting that all the quads are in a row so that troops can be mobilizing the moment that pen hits paper."

In truth, Titus did know a thing or two about what was happening. The AIC hadn't seen this kind of action since the Publicas, and there was excitement in the air back at G2. Nobody told him anything official, but memos crossed his hands, conversations were heard, transcripts read. This was cooperation on a scale that hadn't been seen in at least a century, and it was now his job to learn as much as he could about it. But he'd been told to keep everything quiet, and even if he hadn't, a growing sense of caution would have kept his mouth shut. So, he played dumb.

"Seriously. PFC. I can tell you how General Bakresh likes his coffee though. And the answer may surprise you." Titus winked and tossed his cup into a recycling bin nearby.

EARTH

Chapter 14

"Come on, Titus, you've got to give me something."

Titus rubbed his temples. When they'd told him that he was going to have the opportunity to train under the best that the Federation could offer, he really didn't think it would be this. He wasn't sure what it would be, but when he heard "training," he didn't hear small-talk oversight.

Yes, he knew that intel work was more than just staring at screens, but he'd never anticipated being in training for fieldwork. He was a PFC, and while he always told himself that he'd performed above his rank, he'd earned more respect, he wasn't sure if he'd believed it. And now his doubts were starting to grow. A long conversation with a Federation operative about the weather and how it affected interplanetary travel had left him studying his notes, feeling stupid as he'd failed to gather much of anything. His job had always been deciphering data that had already been gathered, never gathering data on his own.

He studied the notes on the conversation again. It was a test of discernment as much as memory. Sure, he could remember every single word uttered during a conversation, but facial expressions, emphasis, or lack thereof--the nuances of the conversation--were a bit more difficult.

Titus looked up at his training officer. He was slight, with a hooked nose and a mouse-like appearance. Titus had originally underestimated the man. It was almost instinctive to think of any Federation citizen as a corporate stooge only capable of speaking in bureaucratic terms. A common joke was that Feds never had one-night-stands because filling out the

ATI-1885-4 form in triplicate required for sexual intercourse was difficult to fill out while drunk.

He'd been wrong. Surprisingly.

The man had a mind like a steel trap and could infer intricate details from the smallest of dropped hints. In most branches of the military, having heard of the exploits of someone fighting for another military was the highest of praise. These were the heroes of holos and vids. In intelligence, the opposite was true. The best were those who remained in the shadows, unknown. Titus had never heard of Agent Greer before, so maybe that meant something. Or maybe not. Still, Titus was somewhat fascinated by this small man.

"We talked about the weather in Pennsylvania. Ummm." Titus looked over some research papers. "Semi-independent commonwealth within the United States. He said that the Appalachians only looked good when they were covered in snow."

"And how would he know that?"

"By having seen them covered in snow?"

"Correct," Greer said, with a small, patient smile. "And any second-grader could tell you that it hasn't snowed on the East Coast of the US since February fourteenth, fifteen years ago. And the time before that was almost 180 years ago."

"Right."

"Which either means that the man you spoke to is over two hundred years old, or he was there fifteen years ago, yes?"

"Or he saw a picture," Titus said.

"He said he'd been there. Note the tone of the conversation. Relaxed, calm. Not bragging. Talking about having been on Earth, where he, as an FSA citizen, wouldn't have been able to set foot for the past 50 years. Which means that he would have had to have been there in an official capacity. Fifteen years ago, the FSA was forced to sign trade concessions over to the Federation by the AOM. Where were these concessions signed?"

Titus sighed. "Pennsylvania. February fourteenth, fifteen years ago."

"Correct. Pay attention. We've got an assassination mock-up planned in fifteen minutes. Get your notes and collective shit together and be in the ballroom."

Greer left the room, leaving Titus leaning back in his seat, looking over those notes. How had he missed that? Snow in Pennsylvania. That was the clue, and he dropped it. He'd been dropping a lot of them lately. He could feel his attention slipping away. This sort of cloak and dagger hidden behind aperitifs and polite smiles didn't suit him. This wasn't his world. But he was one of two Free State AIC representative sent for this course, and the pressure to succeed was getting to him. He couldn't make the Free States look bad. All his mind could do was keep reminding him that this was only training, and it was keeping him from focusing.

He rubbed his eyes, standing from his seat and stretching. If he was honest with himself, he was being unfair about it. The training was interesting, and it was the kind of boondoggle the higher-ups always tried to finagle to get away from G2 while still on Army time. But three weeks of this non-stop, intensive training was starting to weigh on his mind.

It's not like they're ever going to put you in the field, he thought to himself, straightening his clothes. *AIC is going to see this as a valid improvement to one of their assets and just stick me behind a desk again until I make corporal, which will be never, the rate promotions are going. Maybe sometime in the next few decades.*

They'd conducted the assassination mock-up three times over the past three weeks, and never in the same location. There were two teams, one working to find a hole in the security provided by the instructors, from a different branch of school, while the other worked to find the same holes and cover them, all the while trying to identify the assassins. They were provided some of the high-tech spycraft gadgets that Titus had assumed were Hollybolly creations. Each time the teams had struck a sort of stalemate, with the "assassins" failing to breach the security, and the "security" failing to gain any real intel on them. As tests went, it was good for keeping them on their toes, but it did feel rather . . . futile.

Fifteen minutes later, Titus slipped into his pod for the exercise, the contacts sliding him into virtual reality. A moment of darkness was quickly dissipated by a surge of color as the machine kicked in, assessing his various characteristics and feeding them into the matrix. He blinked, and the images cleared. He was in an old building. Chandeliers lit massive rooms coated in swathes of gold and red. Every surface had been polished to a sheen.

An embassy party. The last time had been at a picnic, and the time before had been a debate. Titus sighed, looking over himself. He was a waiter for this exercise. Most of the characters in the room were AI-generated, but extremely high-level avatars. Titus had never picked out the artificials in the previous missions. The two teams in each exercise were broken into aggressors (assassins) and security. Interspaced among them were the instructors. As Titus surveyed the room, a small gold diamond appeared above the head of each of his teammates. At the moment, every avatar was frozen.

He was holding a tray with canapes. He couldn't identify any of them, so he hoped no one would test him. That was a sure way to get nailed. One of the rules of spycraft, however, was that the most unassuming identities had the best chance of remaining undetected.

Of course, all the players in the room knew that as well, so, maybe they would focus on him. Unless they thought of that as well, knowing no one would be in that role. Unless . . .

Get your mind on the game, Titus!

"Nice of you to join us, Pohlmeyer," Reimer Han said, his voice, which was coming from one of the adjacent pods but sounded as if it was through Titus's earbud as he held a tray of canapes. "We were just running through the briefing."

"What'd I miss?"

"Just the basics. Positionings, mission profile, possible targets—you know, the same old, same old, which you would have known had you been here."

Reimer was a Federation agent-in-training and the exercise mission head. He didn't hide the fact that he didn't like having the two Free States classmates. Nor the Juliette Station classmate. Hell, in keeping with the Federation stereotype, he didn't seem to approve of his female Federation classmates.

And it wasn't as if Titus was late. They'd been injected into the exercise one after the other, the control AI calibrating each one before bringing in the next. Titus had no control over when he'd been injected.

"Get yourself caught up," Reimer said.

The information flickered across his (pseudo)vision as if he was at the party, but wearing the display lenses he might have on a mission. Faces, names, and relevant information. The base scenario was that the Federation's XYZ Trust (the good guys) was engaged in a trade war with ABC Corporation (the bad guys), from the fictitious Fraternal Alliance (a slight dig at the Brotherhood? Titus wondered) over the rights to a mineral-rich asteroid belt deep in the black at an unclaimed system. ABC had accused XYZ of attacking their transports in that sector and was calling for the UAM to intervene. The party was a social meet and greet hosted by the secretary general himself (not the real secretary—every character was fictitious) before the actual negotiations commenced the next day.

"Pohlmeyer, Jiminez, and Alil will be on the ground floor of the embassy, mixing with the guests. Lassiter, you're down there too, of course. Keep an eye out for any of the keys, and let me know if you see anything. I want the rest of us on the balconies, watching. Rachelle-June, you come with me. Remember, we're the security here. We're here to react. One-twenty-two will have to show themselves, and that's when we nail them. Understood?"

"Roger," Titus said as the others chimed in.

It wasn't much of a plan, but that wasn't the real purpose of the exercise. It wasn't about winning, despite the obvious note of competition in Reimer's voice. It was about practice tradecraft.

"Exercise commences in five . . . four . . . three . . . two . . . one . . . commence" the AI announced.

Immediately, the room fell into motion. The hubbub of voices was almost deafening. Titus glanced at Reimer, who was in a metallic blue tux, his hand on Rachelle-June Darrow's bare back as if guiding her. Couples also tended to remove suspicion, but for someone who belittled women who'd joined one of the Federation's clandestine branches, he sure seemed to gravitate to the women in the class.

A tiny label appeared over his canapes, much to his relief, and he turned to two gentlemen standing next to him and asked, "Misty Ices? Formin caviar, gentleman?"

"No, thank you," one of the men said, but the other, a short, middle-aged man reached up to take one of the caviar-laden crackers.

"Lower the tray, Pohlmeyer," Agent Greer passed.

Shit. Of course, he thought as he belatedly dipped so the man had an easier time to pick his.

He'd get dinged for that.

He looked around, getting his bearings. Music from a subdued string quartet wafted over the guests. Musicians were generally unnoticed, and Titus gave them the once over while trying not to be obvious about it. If they were anything other than musicians, or at least artificials of musicians, he couldn't tell.

He offered the tray to more guests, wondering what he was supposed to do when he ran out. He shouldn't have worried. As soon as he was down to a third of what he'd had, the tray was magically refilled.

He wished he was tasked as one of the party-goers, not as the hired help. It was difficult to get into any conversations when he was moving from one guest to another. All he could catch were snippets.

"Bullshit, Silvestrie is past his prime. He needs to be traded . . ."

"While you're here, you must let me take you to Mister A's, I insist. Best ceviche on the planet . . ."

"No, I really need to hit the gym. Just not enough time . . ."

". . . you decided your position on the sanctions, or are you open to discussion?"

That last one caught his attention. He slowly turned his head to see two men, a tall, older gentleman with a yellow sash across his chest in conversation with a burly, middle-aged man in an ill-fitting tuxedo, as if he'd had it fitted before age had lowered muscle from his chest to the start of a pot-belly. He wanted to hear more, so he edged behind the two men, asking, "Formin Caviar, madam?" to a tall woman in some sort of brightly-colored robe, a silver chain across her forehead. He knew that signified something, but he was more intent on listening to what the two men were saying.

"I do not consume the unborn, good sir," the woman said, her voice calm, but her eyes flashing.

"What?" Titus asked, mind confused for a moment.

"I am a Castlelight. We believe every soul has the right to life, and those are unborn fish," she said, pointing to his tray.

Oh, hell, that's right.

The Castlelights were a small, but growing sect that were pure vegan, to include not eating eggs. There were some within the Confederation, and he'd never met one, but they'd been included in the file on human religions that he was given on the first day of class.

"I'm sorry madam. My apologies," he stammered out.

"You should really know who the guests are if you intend to keep on with your career choice, good sir," she said before she turned away, presenting her back.

He stood there for a moment, waiting to hear from Greer. His earbud remained silent, but that didn't mean much. His gaffe would have been noted.

" . . . the implications on trade in the quadrant should be enough to make the Assembly think twice. But in the long run, if it keeps them to themselves, that would open the door to, shall we say, more honest corporations a fair shot at the business," the taller of the two men he'd wanted to hear said.

What did I miss?

"I'm pleased to hear you say that, Cardinal Yves. That aligns with our thinking as well."

Titus pulled up "Cardinal Yves." Brotherhood diplomat, current position as Undersecretary of Refugee Affairs in the UAM.

"If I could get a word in with the Secretary Okoye before we officially begin, I think we might be able to nip this in the bud, for the benefit of everyone," the burly man said.

The cardinal seemed to contemplate that for a moment, then turned to look to where the Secretary was holding court, half-a-dozen people surrounding him and laughing at something the worthy had said.

"I think I can manage an introduction, Mr. Khan. Why don't you come with me, and then maybe you can pull him aside and let him know your *unofficial* position."

Titus quickly pulled up Mr. Khan. There were two of them at the party, but only one who was balding and with a potbelly. This was Argon Khan, a representative of the Processors Union on for the Federation. He was one of the good guys.

"I would be most grateful for that, Cardinal. Most grateful."

Mr. Khan gave his trousers a hitch and smoothed out the shirt where it was tucked in under his belly as he followed the cardinal as they made their way through the crowd to the secretary. Titus smiled. These AIs would make a gamer orgasm, they were so sophisticated. Mr. Khan, a simple training avatar, was programmed to be conscious about presenting a good appearance.

Unless he was part of Class 122, of course. He opened a line to Hank Lassiter, and as he offered his tray to another guest, he subvocalized what he'd just overheard to him. Hank was acting as part of the secretary's security team, which was funny in a way. Security playing as security. But then again, sometimes hiding in plain sight was the most effective.

"Got it," Hank responded.

Titus left Khan and Yves to Hank, then looked around for another target. His job was to circulate, gathering specific pieces of information. And if this exercise was like the others, there would be hints dropped among the static. Reimer and most of the rest of the class were taking an overall view, ready to piece together the various fragments into a mosaic that made sense.

This was an assassination exercise, so the obvious target was the secretary. This was spy-school, however, so that was not a given. Titus spotted the Federation ambassador, Admiral Vasiliev, standing off to the side, deep in conversation with a young man. Titus did a slow scan, and an elderly woman, resplendent in a peacock gown that changed colors as she shifted her weight, kept glancing toward the ambassador.

That might rate a closer look, he told himself when the room erupted in a flash of light.

Titus spun around. The secretary general was down, as were half-a-dozen people around him. Hank, his gun drawn, and Mr. Khan stood upright amidst the carnage. Khan smiled and gave Hank a sloppy salute as the lights went dark.

Chapter 15

Titus stepped out of the chamber, and Agent Greer was already there. His face showed no expression, but Titus knew what was coming next, but he wanted to get his thoughts in line first.

His excuses.

He tried to step around the man, but Greer stopped him with a hand pressed against his chest.

"Well?"

"Mr. Khan was a suicide bomber, sir. His target was the secretary general."

What he didn't understand was why the assassin was from the Federation. In real life, sure. There were assassinations within the Federation as with anywhere else. The rumors were that many of them were government-sanctioned. But this was a school exercise, a Federation school. In these exercises, the Federation was always the good guys.

"And why?"

"I don't have a clue," Titus snapped. "You Feddies are always the good guys, right? At least that's what you always push to the public."

He'd failed his part of the exercise, and he'd feel the consequences, but he wasn't going to go down without a fight. It had been a set-up, anyway. The Feddies being the bad guys? A suicide bomber?"

Agent Greer stepped back, dropping his hand from Titus's chest. He stood looking at him for a long moment as his frown slowly deepened.

"Yes, the United Federation are the 'good guys,' as you so rightly put it. We're trying to keep the peace in all of human space. But there are others who would like nothing more than to sow discord among humanity. There are those who would take on the identity of a Federation citizen to point the blame to the Federation citizen."

What . . .? he wondered as a sinking feeling replaced what had been growing indignation.

"In this scenario, the assassin was a Fraternal Alliance agent, bent on killing the secretary general and pinning it on the Federation. He succeeded in that because your team, and specifically you, failed to pick up on the clues he left."

"But—"

"You accessed the guest list and pulled up Mr. Argon Khan. Did you notice that he was listed at 179 centimeters tall and massed 130 kilos?"

"Uh . . . yes, sir. I saw that."

"And did this Mr. Khan fit that description?"

Titus thought back. Whoever from the other class played "Mr. Khan" didn't matter. It was how the AI portrayed the avatar. He pictured Khan standing alongside the taller Yves.

"No, sir," he admitted.

How did I miss that?

"That's correct. He did not. You simply compared his ID to the other Khan, and since the other was tall and thin, you didn't bother to dive closer into the details.

"And did you notice that Khan's tux didn't fit properly? As if something . . . say, a suicide belt . . . was now under the clothing? To make matters worse, Agent-in-Training Wysoki made the mistake of adjusting the belt right in front of you, and that didn't ring any warning bells?"

Titus had simply admired the AI's attention to detail, but Greer was right. He'd been given more than enough information to stop the assassination, and he'd blown it.

Several of his class stood by, watching as Titus got his ass handed to him. Reimer looked relieved. He'd led a team that failed, but if he could blame that on a Confed PFC, that would help.

"As clumsy and ineffective as your team was, and there is more than enough blame to go around, you performed the worst. I'd say that I'm surprised that you were the weakest link on your team, but then I'd be lying. You have the brains for this training course, Pohlmeyer, but you lack the drive or even the interest in the world around you. You've been unfocused ever since you got here."

Titus nodded. "I guess I'm just not cut out for this, sir."

"Nobody's cut out for this, Pohlmeyer, not at first. Application and dedication to learning a skill set that's foreign to most in the human race are what's required. You have it. I've seen that, but you haven't shown it, and frankly, I don't want to waste any more Federation resources on you."

"Am I being canned, sir?"

"Yes and no. Yes, you are done with the training. No, because we are not officially dropping you. You are here as a guest of the Federation, and to be blunt, you are not worth a diplomatic row, even as innocuous as this might be. You were scheduled for two more weeks, so you'll be sent back then as originally planned."

Titus was bitter, but at least he wasn't being sent home in disgrace. "So, what do I do until then?"

"We're giving you a Freedom Pass and a credit account. Use it to see something of Earth. See how we live. Just be back here by midnight of the 23rd for your flight home."

Titus looked up at the rest of the class, none of whom had left the room. He couldn't read their expressions. There wasn't much he could say to Agent Greer. Things were taken out of his hands. He might as well take the pass and do as the agent said.

"Thank you, sir, for not officially failing me. I'm sorry I didn't do better."

Agent Greer put his hand on Titus's shoulder, his expression softening, and said, "You're young, Pohlmeyer, too young for this course. Your government should have let you grow more, to understand more, before they sent you. But take what you've learned here, and look through life with that in mind. I don't know if you have what it takes to ever become part of the covert community, but you can serve your government in more than one way.

"So, go relax. See the planet. The cherry blossoms are in bloom in Tokyo, and that's worth a trip."

Titus had seen holos of the Cherry Blossom Festival, and it looked interesting. WonderWorld, "The Largest Theme-Park in the Galaxy," however, seemed like more of a must-see for him.

"Thank you, sir. For everything."

Ignoring his ex-classmates, he walked out the door.

NEW MUMBAI

Chapter 16

Truth be told, getting kicked out of the course and having a two-week vacation on Earth wasn't the worst punishment in the universe. With the Freedom Pass, he'd managed both the Cherry Blossom Festival *and* WonderWorld—and quite a bit else. In the Confederation of Free States, the Federation, the granddaddy of a transnational humanity, was considered long past its prime, heart beating on life support only to keep the multi-galaxals making their money. Titus had known that much of this was hyperbole, but he never actually embraced that until this trip. The Federation had issues, big ones, but the people were just like Free States citizens.

Titus was royally pissed at himself. He'd failed, and he didn't take that lightly. And the failure was on him. He hadn't really put his full attention on the task. The experience had lived up to his expectations, but at the same time, having his every move monitored and judged by the Federation school staff had been trying at best, oppressive at worst. One of his biggest problems was that he hadn't bought into the system. Yes, some of what he was taught was uber-cool. But much of it didn't seem pertinent to the present day. Three assassination-based exercises? How often in the galaxy today was that an issue? Covert death squads, citizens "disappearing," that happened in some places. But with modern technology, smuggling in a suicide belt to assassinate the secretary general of the UAM? Wasn't going to happen. It seemed to him that much of the training was speculative, based on the past several centuries. If it weren't for the other people in the class, he'd have suspected that the Free States was being given a taste of the appetizers, not the full buffet. He still should have done his best, but except for the black mark on his records, he wasn't too upset with the way things turned out for him.

His superiors hadn't been happy with him. While he hadn't been officially dropped from the course, Major Buroker, the other Free States student, had reported that he'd disappeared for the last two weeks of the course. Upon his return to New Mumbai, he'd been debriefed, and he'd held nothing back. His label of wunderkind had been irrevocably lost, and he was immediately given a transfer to Humber, an underpopulated planet on the rim of Free States space. The planet mostly served as a military outpost to keep an eye on trade routes in the region. As whenever the military established a foothold, the civilians followed, springing forth like mold. A wide variety of shopkeepers, restauranteurs, entertainers, distributors, and a hundred other professions formed a small town outside the post. A few farmers tried their hand at scratching out crops in the poor soil, but the resource-scarce planet kept anyone from penetrating far from the post.

In a fortunate turn of events, Titus had no direct supervision. Administratively attached to the post, he was operationally attached to the Sector HQ. Major Washington-Aspic, his detachment commander, had yet to even visit Humber since taking over the command.

After his outgoing brief at G2, he'd assumed that his mission would be to ferret out smuggling, and he'd anticipated most of his time would be spent going over reports, looking for discrepancies, and inspecting cargo. As it turned out, this was pretty much the job of the entire garrison, so the major had told him to watch the watchers. In other words, he was to make sure the soldiers weren't getting involved. Corruption was not rampant in the Army, but there were always individuals who would turn a blind eye to an incorrect manifest for a little—or not so little—bump in their personal accounts.

That meant that he was not the most popular soldier on the base. He was AIC and an outsider. He was generally OK with that as a trade-off for a job a little more interesting than expected. He didn't hope that his fellow soldiers were doing something shady, but the cat-and-mouse aspect was more exciting than the grunt paperwork he'd expected to be doing.

After initially checking in, a curt sergeant had shown him to his small office, which looked like a converted supply closet. He had his weblink console, a secure comms link to the AIC office at Sector HQ, and files upon files that had been awaiting his arrival. At first, the massive number of files seemed daunting, but he found, to his surprise, that he rather enjoyed going through them. They offered little windows into the souls of those at the post with him, and he found that fascinating. And as IC, he had access into all of them, even the CO. It gave him a feeling of power.

Not that they were all interesting in their own right or pertained to his mission. But even the most mundane still helped him flesh out those around him. The sergeant major's wife was on another bender, and he was trying to get her to check herself into rehab. Corporal Hortense broke up with his fiancé. Sergeant First Class Theodore, after multiple attempts, was now going to be the father of twins. First Lieutenant Abbat had his Hyundai Aster repossessed.

All of this was information, at this point, but analyzed and collated together, it became intel. His mission was to develop the intel to protect the integrity of the post's mission—by catching the corrupt among them.

Spy? Probably so. But he could live with that.

And it was all on "normal" time. He worked ten-hour days, no more, getting all the sleep he'd missed since transferring from the engineers. He could be woken at any hour. His ST-AI went over every message being sent or received within the post, flagging those with over a 245 pertinency score and forwarding them to him, but that had yet to happen.

To be more accurate, however, his daily schedule was for ten hours. Often, though, he found it hard to tear himself away from his desk. Working was certainly better than going back to the cold, empty room that served as a home.

After two weeks, Titus realized there was a gap in his coverage. Humber was considered an unaccompanied hardship post, but some of the soldiers, enlisted and officer alike, had brought their families along, finding quarters off-base. As an unaccompanied tour, the Army didn't pay for that, so it stretched the wallets of the junior enlisted and officers. Civilian jobs were difficult to come by for most of the dependents, and at least two wives were working as "social girls," the term for the hostesses in the various bars that served the crewmen and women who kept commerce moving. This wasn't illegal, but certainly exposed both the dependents and the soldiers to a less savory type of character. Couple that with the financial hardship, and the potential was there for a temptation too great to ignore.

Living off-post also meant that communications were not going through his ST-AI. That left a gap, and Titus prepared a report to that effect, bypassing the post command and sending it directly up to G2. The next day, he'd received authorization to capture those communications as well, along with written strict limitations as to what he was allowed to do with such information.

Sometimes, he couldn't help himself with regard to the scope of the messages. Young soldiers, like young people anywhere, had high levels of hormones coursing through their bodies, so much of the communications, were sexually charged. Not just the young soldiers—the CO himself had a predilection for being "punished" by his wife for being a bad "baby."

He also had access to the vids and holos being sent. Many of them were graphic. Sergeant Sear, well, he was . . . perhaps the best the best way to describe it was that the sergeant would make a stallion jealous. The guy was huge, and he sent holos of his cock, usually erect, to his coterie of no fewer than 17 women and three men in his personal web, professing love to each and every one of them, that they were the "only" one for him.

The responses were even more graphic. In a way, it was like a hover wreck. He didn't want to look, but he couldn't help himself.

And all of this made it very clear that he was particularly naïve with regards to sex—not that he needed that reminder.

This insight made it awkward when Titus passed other soldiers in the corridor or sat next to them at chow.

"Hey, sir, are you ready for that spanking?"

"Sergeant Sear, is Penny even big enough for her to take that massive thing in?"

As a result, Titus was keeping more and more to himself. The soldiers on base knew what his mission was, and they knew what he was doing. Most had to feel that it was an invasion of their privacy, they knew that he was only doing his job. But job or not, that didn't change the fact that he knew everything they said or wrote and sent off.

The truth was that he didn't know everything, but they had to assume that nothing they said was a secret. Which wasn't really a good situation if he was supposed to catch corruption. While he doubted anyone was simply going to be open about being paid off by smugglers, if he did his job correctly, he could find the warning signs and have his ST-AI try to work out patterns in codes. While foreign adversaries had very sophisticated encryption capabilities, the average Joe either used their personal AI to encrypt messages (which would raise all sorts of warning flags) or they relied on stupidly simple code words.

Titus checked the time. He was 45 minutes into his free time. He could go back to his quarters, but to do what? He shrugged his shoulders and brought up the next batch of ten message trains. These were all mid-level pertinency scores, so he didn't expect to find much with them.

The first two messages didn't reveal much, and Titus filed them. The third, however, piqued his interest. It was sent five weeks ago from Palaver Inc., a travel agency that specialized in passenger delivery to remote locations such as Humber, to Captain Farran, the post S4. The message asked for Farran's eye-scan to approve the payment. There was nothing suspicious about that. He could have been bringing a friend to come visit, paying for the ticket, and the travel agency would want to make sure the payment was authorized. But the added line in the captain's message instructed the travel agency that all future correspondences be routed to a different, off-base terminal

Captain Farran was married, his wife back on Harper Void. The travel agency was on New Mumbai, where the captain had last been stationed. It could be something as simple as Captain Farran bringing in a lover and not wanting his wife to find out. Not illegal, but Titus checked, and the captain had not registered an off-post residence.

This was a violation of the regs, but that didn't mean there was anything else but the captain's desire for privacy. Still, he couldn't ignore it simply because the captain was an officer.

Titus checked the ship ID, then ran it through the system. The ship had left Gentry, made two hops before reaching New Mumbai, then three more before arriving at Humber. He narrowed his eyes, flagging the message before moving away. Farran's last furlough had been four months ago, but he couldn't find any records of where the man had gone for his two-week leave. The contract showed that the transport had departed originally from Gentry, engaged in a series of planet hops where the cargo had switched transports twice before landing on Humber.

Gentry always raised the eyebrows of those in law enforcement, but once again, this proved nothing. Titus sat looking at his display, wondering if there was anything there. On a whim, he looked up the local office of the agency on Gentry. As with most larger companies, it offered round-the-clock service in order to serve a humanity that lived in various time zones.

Humber had only one quantum node, which handled the comms throughout human space. Titus had access to the military line, and within moments, his call went through cloned node to cloned node to probably more cloned nodes until it reached Gentry and was transferred to the local comms system. The technology behind quantum communications was one of the miracles of the modern age—without it, there could be no instantaneous communications—but like most people, Titus took it for granted. Unlike most people, however, Titus could mask his IP, selecting a New Mumbai address.

"Palaver Incorporated, your traveling needs met with style and efficiency. Every time," came a soft female voice after a few minutes. "My name is Natasha, how may I be of service?"

What a mouthful. Does she have to say that every time?

"Hi, Natasha, this is Beri Mahan from Transport Authority, New Mumbai office. I've got a flag on a transport that passed between Gentry and Pashta. Passenger transport, KID number 45778-32ia. Upon entry into New States Space, the cargo was listed as "passengers," but the entry documents were never filled out."

"There must be some mistake. I'll check it again."

Titus tapped his fingers on the arm of his chair as he waited.

"There's no error. The transport is listed as passenger transport."

Titus's eyes ran over the manifest details. "I'm not seeing any visa applications attached to the document."

"It's based on a work contract. I'm sorry, but shouldn't all this have been handled at the port of entry?"

"Indeed, it should have. I guess I'll have to check with them. Thank you for your time."

Titus cut the connection as he turned his chair back around to his screen. There wasn't a work contract associated with Captain Farran's name, which would have been necessary if he was bringing in a maid or any other kind of labor-related personnel to Humber (which in itself would have been an odd thing for an Army captain to do).

There was a work contract attached to the transport manifest, but even so, all this was highly irregular. Could it be human trafficking? This was a rough planet, and prostitution was a factor. But an Army captain getting involved with that?

There was enough here for Titus to forward what he found so that if deemed necessary, they could bring their far greater reach to figure out what was going in. Titus didn't want to call in the cavalry if this was simply the captain getting it on with his lover and trying to keep it on the down-low.

Titus pulled up the captain's admin record, which was open to all.

Shit. Should have looked at this first.

Four weeks ago, the captain had been on leave. His leave address was on Harper Void. With a growing sense of certainty, he was sure that the good captain had not actually gone to visit his family.

There was something else he could do. Gentry was a free trade planet, and as such, all official contracts were in the public domain, and the manifest was a contract. He did a quick search and a moment later, he was looking at the eye-scanned copy of the one the captain had verified.

It didn't match the one on the original request. Someone had altered it after the fact.

Titus leaned back and stared at the ceiling for a long minute before he sighed and sat back up. He didn't have a choice. He just wished he had something solid to pass up the chain.

He typed in the address, leaned in for his own eye-scan, and with a simple command, the curious case of Captain Alamanzo Farran was out of his hands for the time being.

HUMBER

Chapter 17

Two days later, Titus was standing outside of Captain Farran's quarters. He didn't have to be there. He'd been advised against it, in fact, but he sort-of (no, flat out lied) that he was ordered by the G2 himself to be at the scene. The G2 actual had signed his Letter of Commendation that had arrived that morning, along with a note to advise the G2-A (the G2's administrative office) when all was completed. The post Provost Marshall, a boot lieutenant, obviously didn't believe Titus, but he didn't have the cojones to contact the G2 and possibly question a lieutenant general's orders, so he'd permitted Titus to accompany Staff Sergeant Yancy Livingston and Sergeant Uriah Glory to the Highest.

Titus hung back while the staff sergeant ignored the bell and knocked on the captain's door. He waited fifteen seconds, then knocked again. Finally, a voice asked, "Who is it?"

"Staff Sergeant Livingston, sir. If you would open the hatch?"

There was a long pause. There were two commands at the post: the detachment, which were the operators, the ones performing the mission, and the post command, those who kept the post running. The captain was part of the detachment. The MPs were members of the post command. (There were a few cats-and-dogs on the post, to include a Navy engineer inspection team, a IV-level comms team, and Titus, among others, who reported to higher-level headquarters.) The fact that two MPs were at his door could not be sloughed off as routine.

The captain finally opened the door and peered out. He had on in his uniform trou and a white T-shirt, and he still clutched a beer in his hand.

This was the first time that Titus has seen the man, other than in passing around the post. But he now knew quite a bit about him. A mustang, someone who'd risen through the ranks, he was a capable logistician who'd rubbed his seniors the wrong way, hence his exile to this armpit of the Free States. He'd never attended any of the "proper" universities which belched out perfect little officers from their assembly line. Those from outside the normal sources usually had a more difficult time advancing in their career, but it wasn't a death knell. Titus's own ultimate boss, Lieutenant General Pace was a mustang. An officer could overcome an unfortunate background by being both capable and having a personality that demanded respect from others. Captain Farran was capable, but he didn't have that personality. Far from it.

The captain had been a hardass DI, and that impressed his officers enough that they put him in for a commission. He'd completed his required schooling from an online program, then was ordered to OCS where he finished near the top of his class. He'd been assigned as a logistics officer, and after follow-on training, he'd hit the ground running.

Hard.

To him, he'd achieved success by being a . . . well, asshole, to be blunt. So, to continue that success, he'd kept up the same modus operandi. As his first battalion commander placed in his fitness report, he'd "never left the drill field." He harangued rather than led. Threatened rather than inspired. He pushed his soldiers well beyond the bounds of reason when there was no need. Instead of increasing their productivity, it declined.

Titus had counted no fewer than six formal counseling sessions where he'd said he understood and would change, but from all the evidence, he never did. He left his first battalion, probably frustrated that his command hadn't realized what a superb soldier he was. From all evidence, he doubled down as a junior officer in J4-32, division, responsible for coordinating the movement of supplies and equipment to where it was needed.

Once again, he'd shown a knack for the job itself. And once again, he'd shown a decided lack of social skills, not just with his subordinates, but with his peers, who he considered less-than-adequate soldiers. He was the one that maxed out the Army Fitness Test. He was the one with the perfect uniforms.

He must have burned with righteous indignation when he was ranked last among the lieutenants by the J4-32 director.

Finally, he was taken out of contact with subordinates and assigned as a liaison for transportation hubs, both within and without the Free States, to include Gentry. He did well enough to be promoted to captain (which was almost a given), but he had to have realized that his chances of making major were slim to none. In four more years, he'd be kicked out of the Army—not retired, but dismissed, without a pension or benefits.

Titus wondered if that was why the man had chosen the path he took. Was he simply lashing out, or was he trying to set up his own nest egg?

The "why" didn't matter in the long run. What mattered was what he'd done. It was bad enough when scum did this shit, but for an Army officer? Titus had almost been beside himself when he received the word, and that was why he insisted that he had to be there when it all went down.

All three soldiers saluted him. He half-raised the beer to his forehead in a bastardized return salute.

"What do you want. I'm off-duty for the day."

There was a hitch in his throat. Titus caught that, and the tic in his right eye. The guy was about to shit bricks. Maybe some of the training on Earth had stuck with him after all.

"Sir, if you can get dressed and come with us?"

"I'll be at my office tomorrow morning, 0700 sharp. You can speak to me then."

Nice try, Captain, but that won't wash.

"I'm afraid this can't wait, sir," the sergeant responded politely, but firmly.

Titus could see the wave of defeat wash over him. The man sagged, as if being deflated.

"Let me get dressed," he said, and started to close the door.

Staff Sergeant Livingston stuck his foot forward, blocking the door. "I'm sorry sir, but we need to come in while you dress."

"Why? You think I can't dress myself?" he asked with a forced tone of bravado.

Sergeant Glory to the Highest had already told Titus that they could not leave the captain alone. They didn't fear the man somehow destroying evidence. They had all they needed. But they didn't want him to kill himself before he could give up the others.

No one would mourn his loss, Titus had thought at the time, and nothing since then had changed his mind on that.

He shrugged and opened the door, making an exaggerated sweep with an arm in a fake welcome. "Are you going to watch me take a shit, too?"

"Sergeant Glory to the Highest will, sir, if you need to use the latrine."

"And who is this?" he asked, looking at Titus for the first time. "A PFC? What . . ." he started until he noticed the crossed quills on his collar that designated Intelligence Corps. "Ah, I bet you're the one who set me up. Enlisted pukes like you are all pussies," he said, real bravado slipping back into his voice as he sneered at Titus. "Not like when I was enlisted. We almost got our asses kicked by the Publicas, and what do we do? We call in the fucking Feds, the Brotherhood, the NPA, for fuck's sake. All that touchy-feely shit. 'You can't hurt the little private's feeling, Captain!' Shit, we're turning into pansies, and that's going to cost us, you mark my words."

The captain had let his voice elevate. He was railing at them, railing at the system that held him back. There was almost a messianic aura to him.

Which meant jack shit.

Titus was supposed to stay quiet, but he couldn't help himself. "No one cares how you treat your men, *sir*," he said, every ounce of scorn layered onto the honorific. "It's what you do to civilians."

The righteous anger faded, replaced by fear. He'd let himself be sidetracked for a moment, using his pent-up anger to fuel himself.

"What . . . what do you mean," he squeaked, barely getting the words out.

Titus had no doubt that the man knew exactly what he meant.

"You're being charged with—"

"Private Pohlmeyer!" the staff sergeant cut him off.

Titus bit back what he was going to say. It wasn't his position to state the charges.

"So, if I'm being charged with something, then what is it?" the captain asked, his voice wavering.

Titus knew the staff sergeant would rather have the provost marshal read the charges, but the man had the right to know. And if First Lieutenant Park had thought it important, then he should have come along. More likely, he was afraid of getting some of Farran's shit splashed on him, and wanted their interaction done behind closed doors and limited in scope. Get the captain on a transport and off the post as quickly as possible.

"Captain Farran, you are to be held in custody pending formal charges of a violation of UCMJ, Article 56.01, Conduct Unbecoming an Officer," the staff sergeant said.

That seemed to take him aback, and he asked, "Conduct Unbecoming? That's it?"

Titus could see the gears turning in his brain, hope forming where there had been none just a minute before.

The staff sergeant could have left it at that, but he said, "That is a placeholder, sir. You will be charged with 59.02, Crimes Against Humanity. For Human Trafficking. And, as you must know, that could entail a DD & TCA. We are in the process of working through that."

Whatever hope he'd started to fan was snuffed out. A Dishonorable Discharge and Transfer to Civilian Authorities meant his ass was grass. It wouldn't be to the Free States judiciary, but the UAM Tribunal for Human Trafficking. The

Army liked to keep things in house with criminals, but some things were beyond their control—mostly.

"Look, it doesn't have to be like this," he said with a rush. "I've . . . well, I've had *arrangements* in the past with others. You know, sharing the wealth. I can pay you if you just give me a couple of hours. I can pay a lot. Just say I wasn't in, and then come back again."

Staff Sergeant Livingston stared at the man for a moment, who shifted his weight back and forth as if he had to piss. He looked at the other two soldiers and seemed to contemplate the offer.

What the fuck? You can't be considering this shit!

"And, if we decided to take you up on this, how much are we talking about?"

"I can get you twenty-grand right now. Twenty."

That was a lot of money, more than Titus made in six months. Human trafficking must pay well. He started to protest, but the staff sergeant silenced him with a raised palm, all the time watching the captain.

"Twenty apiece?"

"Ah, I don't know if I can get that."

"Twenty apiece."

"Ah . . . OK, sure. Twenty apiece. Just let me get my terminal." He raised his eyebrows, pointing behind him. The staff sergeant nodded.

Titus didn't know what was going on. He sure the hell wasn't going to accept a bribe, but he held his tongue. He'd let this play out before he took any action.

If I even can, he told himself, looking at Sergeant Glory to the Highest. The man was massive.

The captain opened a small safe and pulled out a commercial terminal. He brought it back and showed it to them.

"OK, you've got to realize that I can't just zap you over the credits. That's too easily traced. You'll get caught. So, we've got a very sophisticated little scheme here," he said, sounding as if he was proud of it. "Not even the spooks can follow it."

Titus looked on with more than feigned interest. Something might come out of this after all.

"It starts with a delta order, you know, like in a river delta," he said, spreading out fingers on one hand. Only this is a reverse delta, going from little to big. The program makes twenty innocuous orders for normal goods . . . well, for sixty-kay, it'll have to be fifty or so. Anyway, these orders go to a fulfillment house on Daros Station, triggering the orders, only, you see, nothing gets shipped. Instead, a record of the shipment is made, all the way to delivery. After a day or two, the 'buyers' decided to return the shipments, triggering refunds, which are then entered into accounts. But still, those credits have to get to you, right?"

The man was getting excited. Titus wondered if he'd developed it himself. He was a transport expert, despite his moral failings.

"So, the refunds go into a dozen ghost accounts our insider at CAA creates, ready credits. You will have access to those accounts with the codes I'm giving you. You can buy things, transfer funds, anything you want, all invisible—well, except if you transfer any funds into your own personal accounts, of course. So, go light on that, if you're smart. Don't trigger any of the net worms. Keep it below three-hundred credits, and you should be OK."

Titus wasn't an expert in the vast web of the credit system. He just used his code and bought what he needed. But what the captain had so proudly described might indeed work. He wondered for a moment why he hadn't used the same system for the human trafficking that had tripped him up, but then he realized that all of that system took place in the ethersphere. Human trafficking took place in the real world.

"And this is all untraceable?" the staff sergeant asked.

"Completely. Been using this baby for five years now. You'd be surprised at how many in the military have done very well with this, you know, making their lives a little better. It's not like we don't deserve it, am I right? I mean, they pay us shit for what we do. And besides, no one really gets hurt."

Except the people you traffic, you asshole!

"So, do we have to give you our account numbers?" the staff sergeant asked.

"No, don't you see?" the captain said, sneering as if Livingston was dense. "I don't know your accounts. No one knows them. You take the codes I give you, and that is how you access the credits. Unless you do a direct transfer, there will never be a connection between the credits and your account."

Staff Sergeant Livingston looked at Sergeant Glory to the Highest and Titus one more time, then told the captain, "Do it."

"And I get five hours, right?"

"Two hours. Take it or leave it."

Titus kept his face passive. Two hours was enough for him to report this bullshit, then get orders on how to stop it all.

"Fuck. OK, two hours," the captain said before tapping on the manual keypad. He waited a moment, and then using a pen and plastisheet, scribbled down three alphanumeric strings. "Take these. Memorize them if you can. But if you lose them, the credits are gone. There's no way to recover them."

"So, it's done?"

"Signed, sealed, and delivered."

"Very well. If you'll turn around, sir?"

"What? Why?"

"Why? Because I need to ziptie your wrists before we bring you in."

"What? I paid you already. Really. The credits are there. I'm not trying to fuck you over."

"I believe you. But you are still under arrest."

"You said you'd give me two hours," he said, almost crying.

"I lied. Now turn around, sir."

Titus felt a huge wave of relief sweep over him. Staff Sergeant Livingston wasn't about to go rogue. He'd just collected another charge to throw on top of the pile.

"No, no, you don't understand," the captain cried out. "I can't get arrested."

"Looks like you're wrong, sir. I can certainly arrest you. Here's the warrant," he said, flashing his PA. "Sergeant Glory, restrain the captain."

The sergeant stepped forward, turned the unresisting captain around, then ziptied his wrists together.

"No, I mean you can, but I'll be killed. There are some very big people involved with this. Very big. They won't let me live. I'll tell you all about it."

"Sir, you are not required to tell us anything without a lawyer present, and even then, you can remain silent."

"I'll talk! I've got names, names you'll want. Vice-minis—"

"Stop!" Titus shouted, stepping in.

All three of the others turned to look at him.

"You will not say another word. Staff Sergeant, if you can step outside for a moment?"

Staff Sergeant Livingston furrowed his eyebrows, and then said, "You're just here as an observer, Private Pohlmeyer. I think I'll remain with my prisoner, if that's OK with you."

Glory to the Highest snorted his amusement.

"No, Staff Sergeant, you'll step outside as I asked. I'm invoking Charly-forty-eight."

The staff sergeant started to argue, but he stopped, mouth gaping open as what Titus had said sunk in. C-48 was the AO-5700, Processing and Treatment of Prisoners and Enemy Combatants, paragraph that authorized the AIC taking control of a detainee. It wasn't invoked often, and most soldiers had probably never heard of it, but the staff sergeant, being an MP, would have. He had no choice but to comply despite the disparity in their ranks.

"OK, Private, you've got him. But if you let him get away . . ."

If I let him get away, nothing. And I'll do it if I think it's for the best. But hell, I'd better be right about this. I'm out on my ass if I've overstepped my bounds.

"Go ahead and secure him to the chair there, then please just step outside and wait."

The staff sergeant nodded to Sergeant Glory to the Highest who took out another set of zipties and attached the first set to the chair. The captain could still run, but he'd have to carry a 20-kg chair with him.

"He's scum, Private," the sergeant said quietly as he passed back by Titus. "Don't you go playing spook-shit and let him off, or I'll come find you."

Titus ignored him. He didn't have time to see who could piss the highest.

"Sir," he started once the two left and closed the door behind him. "I assume you know who I am, or rather, what I represent?"

"Yes, I know you. You're AIC," he said, nodding at Titus's insignia. "Look, I know stuff that you can use to bust some pretty high up people. I can tell you all of it. Just don't put me in the brig. I'm serious. I won't survive a day."

Should have thought of that before you turned rogue.

"I can start now. Vice-Minister Pa—"

"I don't want to hear," Titus said, cutting him off.

"But—"

"Oh, someone will hear, but not me."

"But you'll keep me out of the brig? You can do that?"

"No, I can't," he said as the captain's face fell, "but there are others who can."

Titus pulled out his small secured PA, then routed a call through to the AIC sector det commander, coded for his eyes only. A moment later, the major came on the line.

"What do you have, Pohlmeyer?" the major asked, ignoring the social niceties.

"Case number Foxtrot-hotel-six-six-eight-four-three-niner-dash-eight-two. The subject has expressed a desire to cooperate, stating that this is much more than the subject offense. He has implicated a vice-minister-level official and fears being killed if he is in our brig."

There was a moment of silence, then, "Who is he implicating?"

"I don't know. I'm not ITT-qualed, so I shut him up, sir."

"I'll tell you now. Let me speak to your boss," the captain said, listening to Titus's side of the transmission.

Titus waved him silent.

There was a long pause, then the major asked, "What do you think? Is he telling the truth?"

Titus looked at the captain. The man was sweating profusely despite the strong AC. His lower jaw was trembling, and all trace of bravado had vanished.

Oh, shit, put up or shut up, Titus.

"Yes, sir, I think there might be something there."

"Very well. Do what you need to do, and I'll authorize transport here. I want him ready at 0930 Standard Time. I'll let Sergeant G have a crack at him before I decide on sending him back to New Mumbai."

"Sergeant G" was Master Sergeant Gulczynski, a trained interrogator. The major wanted to see if Captain Farran really had anything of value before he sent him up the chain. Smart for him, and Titus would do the same if he could, but unfortunately, he didn't have a Sergeant G with him at the post. If he'd overreacted, it was on his head.

"Roger that, sir," Titus said, mentally doing the time conversion. He had four hours to kill.

"Twenty years at hard labor is the minimum sentence for human trafficking. You'd better hope that any information you give up is good enough to get you out of a very hard life," he told the captain.

"It will be. What now?" he asked, becoming calmer.

"Now, we wait. I'm going to bring in the two MPs, so don't open your mouth again. Sir," he added belatedly.

He just hoped that whatever the captain offered up would justify the action he was taking.

****

It was.

Farran had opened up to Sergeant G, and instead of sending him back to New Mumbai, where his presence might alert targets, an additional team was sent to wring the man dry. According to him, the captain had not only been a part of the smuggling operation run by Palaver while he'd been on Humber but also during his previous billet in J4 on New Mumbai. His travel and government clearance, coupled with his intimate knowledge of transport, had made him an ideal candidate for the smuggling ring, which was fronted by JSP

Distribution, Inc, a small, but moderately successful company. Moderately successful from the outside. On the inside, it was extremely successful, and laundering their ill-gotten gains had been a major task, one that Captain Farran had helped develop.

But it wasn't just human trafficking. There was too much illegal potential in the galaxy to limit to just one enterprise. Business school 101 taught diversification, and JSP was on its way to become major player in illicit trade.

Titus followed what he could, but much of it was being kept closely guarded. The name of the vice-minister, for example, was not revealed. Titus had idly spent time going over the list of Free State vice ministers to see if anything stood out, but he didn't find it.

From what he did hear, the times, dates, and shipping lines seemed to match up. That, and the fact that he hadn't been called and berated for overreacting led him to believe the captain was being forthcoming, selling out his compatriots to save his own skin.

Luckily, Farran could back up his claims since there was going to be a physical meeting with his contacts. They were looking to expand their operations in the sector and even set up a base of operations on Humber.

Titus worked with what he had for a day, trying to learn more, but he just didn't have the resources nor experience to do much. He gave up and went back to his routine, but the titillating messages had lost their allure. He'd been instrumental in bringing down something big, and he wanted more of the same. He couldn't have expected to be part of it anymore. He'd received his Letter of Commendation, and that was enough. Others, more experienced and senior, would get the glory when all of this came to light.

That was before he'd received a message to meet in a non-descript office in the post annex. He arrived to find Staff Sergeant Livingston, Sergeant Glory to the Highest, and a sergeant he'd never met. It became quickly clear that the "sergeant" was anything but. He told the three that they were to go out on the town, spending credits like water. They were not to speak of anything, especially Captain Farran, but they were to celebrate.

Telling soldiers to go out and get drunk and do whatever they wished on the government's dime was a dream come true. Not exactly the government's dime, however. They'd simply left the captain's bribe in place, figuring that the bad guys could have eyes on them. They were told to meet at the barracks at 1700 local, then go out and live it up before the other two were dismissed.

With just Titus, the "sergeant" became an AIC lieutenant colonel. Titus was going to have to play a role if they were going to get corroboration on what Captain Farran had provided. The captain had been about to attend a meeting of JSP operatives interested in expanding their reach to Humber. Under tight supervision of the ITT team, he'd contacted the operatives, told them the heat had turned up on him personally, so he'd skipped the planet for a few weeks. He'd given them Titus's assumed name as a contact, and the fact that he and the other two had accepted the kings' gold. The fear was that the operatives would smell something fishy and pull out, but they agreed to the change of plans. Evidently, they thought that anyone could be bought.

Titus was given a supply corps collar device, which he used to replace his AIC one, and corporal's chevrons. That was a little risky, given that he could have been seen going to help arrest the captain, but that was determined to be an acceptable risk to make his field more likely to be of use.

He was also the best choice given that even if he hadn't graduated, he'd gone through at least one "spy" course. He'd been trained on clandestine operations.

The first part of the operation lasted two nights, and it was a whirlwind of long nights. The three were ordered to party hard, and party hard they did. They drank expensive booze, ate real food, not manufactured, and enjoyed the company of multiple entertainment professionals. Multiple for Staff Sergeant Livingston, at least. The man was a satyr, pure and simple. Even Sergeant Glory to the Highest enjoyed the company of one, which surprised Titus. He'd assumed that the Torritites were all conservative. As the sergeant told him, however, while they couldn't take the Lords' name in vain, almost anything else goes.

During work hours, Titus was stashed in a warehouse. He looked at the shelves of gear, and he contemplated faking busy-work, but the head-ache from over-indulging and lack of knowledge on just what a supply soldier did resulted in him simply sitting, watching old holos on his PA, and waiting for the call from the JSP criminals on the PA given to him by the AIC lieutenant colonel.

The call came on the third afternoon. He was told to meet at a transport packaging material supplier, which would provide cover for both the operatives and Titus.

"I believe you have some samples to show me?" Titus said as he walked up to the counter at the supplier's warehouse.

She looked at his name tag. "Corporal Vikander, so glad you could make it," the young woman said, smiling pleasantly. "And yes, if you will follow me, I'll take you to the showroom."

He was sweating, excessively so, and he expected her to notice and sound the alarm. But she ushered him to an elevator, then joined him inside, announcing "Fourth Floor." The door slid shut, the elevator started to rise.

A few moments of silence followed until she spoke. "So how long have you been stationed here? I read that you were sent here after a stint on—"

"Ma'am, I understand that this sort of small talk is part of your regular job description. But I'd appreciate if we could keep the conversation to a minimum while I'm here."

He'd been given a fake background, knowing that they would have checked him out. The lieutenant colonel had advised him to say as little as possible to avoid being tripped up if they decided to quiz him on something.

"Of course. Sir. Yes, that's me, a blabbermouth. Couldn't stop talking if my life depended on it." Titus fixed her with a pointed glare, causing her to stop and clear her throat. "Right." She made a gesture of zipping her mouth shut and throwing away the key.

Titus aimed his gaze at the reflective surface of the elevator doors, which opened again a few moments later. Again, Titus forced himself out his own personal comfort zone by taking the lead, stepping forward in front of her and making her move faster than her absurdly high heels allowed comfortably. She escorted him into the showroom, which was little more than any other conference room replete with a dozen chairs and an oblong fake wood table.

"Is there anything you need while you wait?"

"No, thank you."

He watched the woman leave, her butt swaying alluringly, and he realized that he'd never asked her name. If they were watching him—and they almost assuredly were—they'd probably dangled her as bait. And he'd ignored her, the sign of someone afraid or on a mission. He quickly stuck his head out the door, watched her intently until she got into the elevator, then leaned back in while he pursed his lips and shook his hand in a "mama mia" gesture.

OK, if you're watching, I'm a normal guy. Got it?

It was almost ten minutes later before two women and a man came in, hands out to shake. Titus knew better from his courses, but he expected people more, well, who looked more like criminals. These three wouldn't look out of place at any local Chamber of Commerce meeting. They were so ordinary.

Introductions were made, and the man apologized before running a wand over Titus. He tried to look relaxed. He was not transmitting anything—but he was recording. He had a small "stealth" recorder, which mechanically "felt" the vibrations of sound and let tiny micro-beads fall into slots. No electricity, no energy. Nothing to be picked up by a wand. Very, very high tech, but using what was an absurdly simple concept. Also, very classified. The concept had been written about in various journals, but the fact that the Jesuit labs had managed to put it into practice was not well-known.

"He's clean, Melinda," the man said.

"Well, then we can begin. We've had a long and mutually beneficial relationship with Alamanzo Farran," Mz. Yorba-Manuel, "Melinda," said. "We were surprised when he said he was indisposed and for us to work through you. He wasn't too forthcoming, but can you tell us just what the issue was?"

"Certainly, ma'am. The captain screwed up, big time."

All three of them tensed up and exchanged concerned glances.

"He neglected to renew his contraceptive implant, and he got a young woman pregnant. He promised to pay child support, and all was well and good until he missed some payments. Said young woman complained, and the brass reacted. He's going to get NJP—"

"NJP?"

"Non-judicial punishment. Not a felony, but he could end up in the brig for a month or two. The Army takes a pretty dim view of this kind of thing, especially from the officers."

"I've told him to keep his dick in his pants," the other woman, Mz. King, said.

"We knew that when we started with him. But with what he makes through us, to forget a fucking child support payment? Idiot!"

"He deserves jail if he's going to let his kids suffer," the man said. "I hope he gets raped there."

Sergeant G and the others had asked the captain what was bad enough for him to be indisposed, believable enough for the bad guys to buy it, but not in an area that would raise suspicion. He'd immediately said the child-support scenario, and it seemed as if he was right.

Titus almost laughed. Here were human traffickers who smuggled drugs and weapons, and they were mortified that someone missed child-support payments. Oh, well, as Agent Greer had said, even criminals had their own set of moral standards.

After a few more moments of bashing the captain, Melinda turned back to Titus.

"Alamanzo recommended you. From what we know, you were only recently joined up with him."

"You mean, he only recently bribed me. Me, Glory to the Highest, and Livingston."

The slightest tic of her eyebrow was revealed that he was right. The question had been a trap.

"Well, then why should we trust you?"

"The money's good, and I want more."

He knew this was something they could understand, but that wasn't enough. There was the elephant in the room.

"OK, granted. But Alamanzo was a captain. You're a corporal. No insult intended, but what can you offer us? We've got all the goon-backs we need."

"No insult intended, but I don't believe you understand the Army. The captain, sure he had more power to flash around. Sure, he's got a mind for the overall picture. But the Army is run by the NCOs. We hold the real power. You want something done, you go to an NCO. You want details, you go to an NCO.

"Say, you want to get a license to open a distribution center here on Humber."

He could almost feel the hook sink in. This was their primary goal at the moment.

"You have your interview with the post commander. He doesn't like it, and he recommends no go to that. A lowly admin clerk had to type that up. If the CO's opinion somehow is changed to an approval before it's given to the clerk, what gets passed up? If another monthly report from one of your rivals somehow gets adjusted, then how will that make your case look? If there is a need for a small space in a container coming from Gentry, then what better way to have that container military, and not subject to the port inspectors?"

That's enough. Don't go overboard.

But he could see that he'd set the hook. They'd decided right then and there that this supply corporal was a better partner than the child-support-avoider Farran would be.

Melinda didn't even look to the others, but said, "I see your point. And I'm willing to give this a try. So, let's go over a few of our operations, just in a general sense at this time, and I want to know how you can be of assistance."

"And I get . . . ?"

"Oh, you'll be well-compensated."

"No offense meant, Mz. Yorba-Manuel, but as an enlisted soldier, I know what vague promises are worth, which is shit-nothing. I'd like to know exactly what 'well-compensated' means."

She smiled. "How about fifteen-kay a month to start, then we'll see how much more you will be worth."

Titus widened his eyes and gulped, hoping it looked real. "Fifteen kay? I think you've got a deal," he said, reaching across the table to shake.

She looked satisfied as she shook, but she kept ahold of his hand for a moment, and said, "But cool off on the extravagance. You're making a spectacle of yourself every night. We don't like our partners to be noticeable. You and your two friends, too. Deal?"

"Deal for me. But they're not my friends, and I don't control them."

"Well, if they don't, Melinda, I can make sure they disappear," the man said.

"If it comes to that."

Titus kept the smile on his face, but he'd have to get word to the other two. That, or make sure they were suddenly transferred off-planet.

"So, then, let me start earning my pay. You said you wanted to know how I can help. Tell me what you want, and I'll answer you."

The four sat back down and got to work.

Chapter 18

He leaned back in his seat, making a soft creaking sound as the old office chair was forced to work its hinges. It seemed like most meetings like this ended up with him being talked over and forgotten as people more important than he got into arguments about how things were supposed to be done.

"We've got more than enough corroboration, as well as details we didn't have before," Lieutenant Colonel Jalben, the "sergeant" who was the AIC point man on the planet, said. A lean, muscular if a bit short man, he impressed Titus with his piercing intellect, always asking the right questions.

Titus had met with the unholy trio, as Jalben referred to them, four more times before they left the planet. Each time, they'd revealed more and more of their overall operation. They had enough to crush the human trafficking ring, but there were hints of other operations that needed to be investigated. No mention was made of a Free States vice-minister, and Titus had not pushed for that. The AIC lead team would have been told the identity by Farran, but no one had mentioned the name to Titus.

"You know, we're going to have to cooperate with the DSI on this," the third man said.

Despite the relatively short time since then. Colonel Jaeger looked older than when he'd recruited Titus back at the hospital ward, with more wrinkles and more gray. The thought brought a twinge of pain to his healed-shoulder, and he absentmindedly rubbed it.

"We've been dealing with a smuggling ring in this sector for a long time," Jaeger continued, sitting comfortably in his own chair, a mug of tea in his hands. "We can act now and bust the human trafficking, the drugs, some of the weapons, but that's only within our own space. As for the rest . . .?"

"As for the rest, we request our allies to act. This isn't a Free States issue. Go to the damned UAM, sir."

"Sure, and what about our little internal problem in the ministries? Do we act now, or do we let things play out?"

"Yeah, about that. That's why you colonels and generals get the big credits. What does the director think?"

The "director" in this case was the head of G2, which made him the head of the entire Army Intelligence Corps. He answered to the Director of State Intelligence, and was on an even level with the Director of Naval Intelligence, the Director of the Internal Security Agency, and the Director of External Surveillance. Each leg of the DSI "chair" tended to be jealous of the others, and they hated to cooperate and share information. But with a vice-minister in the crosshairs, this was above mere Army concerns.

"This is a sophisticated operation, and we can't let them get away with it because of internal squabbling within the community.

"So sophisticated that a private was able to unravel it by looking through some errant communications?" Jalben asked with a soft chuckle.

"Corporal," Jaeger corrected. "That collar device is for real now."

Titus hadn't expected to make corporal this next month, but the letter of commendations, first for discovering the discrepancy in the manifests and then for his undercover work, had bumped his cutting score just high enough to get the promotion.

"Corporal then," Jalben. "And congrats on that, Pohlmeyer."

"Thank you, sir."

"Just because an operation is sophisticated, doesn't mean that they're immune to incompetent personnel," Jaeger continued.

"I'm not giving up on this," Jalben said after a few moments of thought. "I'm not letting these useless pricks off with a slap on the wrist just for covering their asses by giving up someone else."

"You won't have to," Jaeger said, pausing to blow into his tea and take a sip. "The information that Pohlmeyer gathered mainly went to corroborate what we already had, so whatever they might give up now isn't as valuable as it might be."

"And if the weapons get off-planet? Who's going to take the fall for that? You?"

"We still don't know for sure they're here. Data forensics are going over all shipping docs as we speak. Let's focus on trying to ferret out that. Increase the pressure to make them stumble."

One of the reasons the JPR wanted a presence on the planet was so they could use the military presence to help mask the shipment of weapons out into the Far Reaches. That had been mentioned to Titus almost in passing, but with no details. The forensic techs back on new Mumbai, armed with this Intel, were now trying to pierce the veil of records to determine just where those weapons came from and where they were. They'd found some sources and hints that some were on Hurum

Jalben sighed. "Fine. What do you suggest?"

"If I could?" Titus broke in. The other two didn't look overly surprised, and Jaeger nodded for him to continue. "Whoever is running this particular show, you can be sure that they're going to be feeling uncomfortable under the kind of scrutiny that they've been getting over the past week or so. They'll be looking to either cash in on what they have in this sector or abandon what they have. Pull back, and make them feel safe again. We've got other fish to fry here on the planet. Bust them, then make a big deal with the media. Let JPR think that whoever we bust was always our target to explain the increased activity."

"And what does that do for us, Corporal?" Jaeger asked.

"It gives us time. Look, sir, they trust me. Let me get in deeper. Give me a shipment of weapons I can give up."

"So, you want to give them more?" Jalben asked, his expression proof of what he thought of the idea.

"Yes, sir. But, we can put trackers on the weapons and then follow them to where the rest are."

"All weapons have trackers. The smugglers know this and deactivate them."

"Leave the standard ones there. But when I was on Earth, I was told that there are some trackers that are virtually undetectable without a cloned scanner. No way for anyone else to detect them."

Colonel Jaeger nodded, but said, "Expensive, though. And they're not micro. Easy to spot visually."

"Put a few in M223's."

"Why M223's?" Jalben asked.

"Sir, with all due respect, you officers don't have to lug the Fat Boy. They're heavy and a bitch to clean. They're knuckle-breakers."

"So?"

Titus wanted to sigh, but that would get Jalben, in particular, pissed. He kept his voice calm and steady.

"No one wants to clean them, sir. You get smashed hands and fingers, especially trying to open the chamber housing lock. If we put a couple of these inside the chamber housing, I'm betting no one will disassemble them enough to find the tracker."

"And if they try to fire one to test it?"

"The Fat Boy will still fire. Might crush the tracker, so that's why we put in several.

"Let me go undercover again. I can give them the good lead on the Fat Boys, then we make sure they can hijack them. Track them until we know more. Even if they don't have any of the missing weapons here on the planet, knowing their methodology should be worthwhile."

Jaeger tilted his head, taking another sip from his tea as Jalben stood up and paced back and forth several times.

"It's not a bad idea," Jalben finally said. "But you aren't really a field operative. We used you because of circumstances."

"And because of that, I'm already known to them," Titus countered.

"I think he's right," Colonel Jaeger said.

"Even without the training? He's just a private, after all."

"Corporal," Titus and the colonel said in unison.

"Right, sorry. But even as a corporal? This isn't going to some meeting in a warehouse. This is the real deal, and the guys on this end play for keeps."

"I think we should do it. But, it's your call. You're the mission chief, not me."

"Right, but who's the one with the ear of the director? You are."

Titus was not fully embedded on the political side of the AIC, but he had the feeling that Colonel Jaeger carried a lot more weight than most colonels would.

"Still your call."

"Screw it. But we need to build a better backstory that'll stand more scrutiny. We can't have you hiding out in your warehouse every day. And you'll need to have access to weapons information."

"We can bring in some engineers to make an offsite weapons depot. We'll have Titus here assigned as their liaison, bringing in supplies and such as needed. That will give him the opportunity to know about these lightly guarded M223's," Colonel Jaeger said.

"Sir? I was an engineer. Someone might recognize me."

"I doubt it, and we can screen any platoon we send. But I'll talk to my counterpart with the Navy. I can get the Navy to send in some seabees to construct the depot. Maybe that's better. Less security than soldiers would give."

"That should work," Jalben said. "Let's go with that."

"You did well before Corporal Pohlmeyer, but this is at a whole new level. Don't let us down this time."

Titus wasn't going to make a promise that he couldn't keep, so he left it at, "You won't regret this, sir."

Chapter 19

Three weeks later, Titus was 56 klicks from the post, out in the middle of nowhere, in a tent camp with the Seabees. Life with the Seabees was not the same as life with the engineers. They had a certain degree of pride that he'd observed with the infantry, but unlike the Army combat engineers, they didn't just blow things up or put in bridges, they built things. They could put in a shuttle port on any planet in 20 hours, they liked to brag, and from what he'd seen, that might be true.

After two days, the weapons depot was taking shape. But it wasn't just erecting walls. There were power generators, waste disposal, food fabrication, machine shops, and everything else to enable up to 25 soldiers to run the place. Titus spent most of his time working out the supply requests— as the Navy was providing the work-force, the Army had to provide everything he needed. Titus had no experience with requisitions, so he simply sent lists back to the sector S2 where they shanghaied someone to do his work for him.

That gave him time to meet the sailors, something he'd never done before. And he discovered that sailors were just like soldiers. They simply spent more time in space.

What surprised him was that they filled a void. He missed the comradery he'd felt in the engineers, and as the AIC liaison on the post, he was almost persona non grata. Here, he was accepted, even as a "doggie."

And with the extra time, his engineer training kicked in, and he offered to help out. No sane military person would ever turn down help, so he was adopted by the others, who were amazed that a paper-pusher supply guy actually seemed to know his way about a wrench.

Today, he was helping Petty Officer Three Waylon Sukiko lay the sewer line from the quarters to the recycler. That consisted of running the badger a meter deep underground, then feeding in the plasteen sections. Each section had to be tested for weld integrity.

"Can't you Army pukes get us Wylamer sections? They report the welds, not like this."

"I told you, we don't have Wylamer as a supplier. You'll have to make due with G&S. We're not the Navy with all that money to spend."

"Not my fault the people love the Navy," he said.

Titus rolled his eyes, but there was more than a little truth to that. The Navy got the glory, and they'd never been close to losing to the Publicas. Every time they took down a pirate, that was a media hit.

"Is that why you picked the Navy? For all the girls who throw themselves at you?" Titus asked as he sent in the mole to check the latest weld.

"I wish. I was married for most of my time," Waylon said.

"Was?"

"Yeah. Was. Divorce came through. She was a Rim widow."

"A what?"

"A Rim widow. You know, husband on a ship out in the Rim for nine months."

"Ah, I get it," Titus said.

"So, she's a Rim widow, but I guess lonely. I find out that she's shacking up with some guy out in the ville, so I filed for divorce."

"Oh, shit. Sorry, man. When did that happen?"

"Divorce came through two months ago. You know the worse thing? She gets custody of our little girl. I'm not a suitable father, you know. Always gone."

"So, you gonna get out when your enlistment is up?" Titus asked.

"No. No use for that. Besides, I need the job. I'm paying child support. I'm glad to do that, of course," he said hurriedly. "But I need to make the money to do that."

"That sucks, brother," Titus said.

Yeah, we're all the same, Navy and Army, with all the same stories.

****

Two hours later, they were just finishing the junction with the recycler when a civilian version of the military dragon-wagon, the eight-wheeled all-purpose supply truck came lumbering up into the depot.

"You expecting a supply shipment?" Waylon asked.

"No, nothing," Titus said, his heart skipping a few beats. He knew damned well what was in the dragon-wagon.

By the time they trundled their badger back, the Seabee lieutenant was arguing with the civilian driver, telling him to take back the shipment of weapons as the armory was not yet finished. The driver was just as adamant, refusing to stop the crane arm from unloading. Titus and Waylon stopped to watch as the lieutenant fought a losing battle. As soon as the last crate was unloaded, the driver took off back to civilization.

"Well, fuck it all. Chief, let's get these in the machine shop for now. That's up at least."

"Security, sir?"

The lieutenant looked at the stack of crates, then around at the gathered sailors, who all avoided his gaze. It was Saturday afternoon, and they were all looking forward to getting a ride into town for the rest of the weekend.

"Lock the door and get the duty watch section to put a man there," he said. "If something happens, it's their fault, not ours."

There were sighs of relief from sailors whose plans had not been changed.

"Damn! I was afraid he'd put on two watch sections. We'd better get changed on the bus before he changes his mind."

"Roger that, my squidly friend," he said as they hurried for the field showers.

The next phase of their plan was about to begin.

Chapter 20

Titus sat sipping a cider in a nondescript bar far from the hustle and bustle of the Zone, the area that catered to off-duty soldiers, and tonight, about a hundred Seabees. He'd ditched Waylon, signaled his contacts, and waited.

After two hours, he wondered if the request had made it up the chain, or if it had, if the JSP suspect something.

"Corporal, can I buy you a drink? A Lansing?" an older gentleman asked.

Titus sighed with relief. He accepted the drink, and after the robotender delivered it, the man said, "We didn't expect to hear from you for another two weeks. How's life out in the boonies?"

"Interesting, and full of potential."

"Really?" the old man asked quietly. "And how so?"

"We're building a weapons depot, as I told you. And today, the fuck-ups at some higher headquarters sent a load of weapons. M88s. M223s. AA12's."

There was a tiny flicker of interest in the old man's eyes, but he asked, "And why is that news? You are building a weapons depot, after all."

"Because the armory isn't finished, that's why. We're not ready for it. The lieutenant just put them in the machine shop. Locked the doors and put a single watch-stander on the front door."

"And?" he prompted.

"And? And so, if someone unlocked the back door, then it would be easy to remove said weapons, and none would be the wiser. The machine shop is backed up against what will be the fence, right alongside the road out."

"And what makes you think we'd be interested in these weapons?" the man asked. "We've been dealing in other goods and services."

Bullshit, Titus thought. He could see he'd already hooked this fish.

"I assumed you were businessmen, and businessmen do business. These are worth a shitload of credits. The AA12's? Hell, I can find buyers for those without you?"

"Then why not do it yourself?"

"Because I value my mother's favorite son's ass, that's why. Some of them might just as soon zero me out instead of paying. These are AA12's, after all. I trust you to keep me healthy so I can continue to provide good services."

"This is interesting. I'll have to check in, of course. If we do this, when?"

"The armory will be finished next week. So, I'd do it tonight or tomorrow night, before most of the liberty hounds return to the depot."

The man handed Titus a small PA and said, "Keep this on you. I'll be calling."

Titus pocketed it and watched the man pay the bill for the drinks, then leave. He leaned back, ordered a Coke, and waited. Two hours later, the PA buzzed for attention.

"Yes?"

"Eleven-fifteen tomorrow night. Have the back door unlocked."

Phase two was about to start.

Chapter 22

At 13:00 the next day, Titus approached Seaman Ellen Wymer, the watch-stander on the machine-shop door.

"I thought you'd be on liberty," she said. "Who did you piss off?"

"I made the mistake of calling in about our shipment. Now they want me to inventory them."

"That was stupid. Never volunteer anything, even just information," she said.

"So, I need to get in."

"Sure thing." She waved a key wand over the door, and it clicked open. "Need any help?"

"Nah, you just relax," he said as he entered the large shop.

The machines hadn't been delivered yet, so the only things in the building were the 20 cases of weapons. Titus walked behind them to the rear door, and unlocked it. He pushed it open a crack. No alarm sounded, not that he'd expected any. None of the alarms had been delivered yet, as per the plan.

He came back to the cases and opened each one, more to make sure he timed himself to make his "inventory" believable. The AA12's, a cheap but effective anti-air missile, were not live. Each case of four missile had a "Deadlined" tag inside. While the other two weapon types were operational, the brass couldn't risk 12 missiles getting into the wrong hands.

When he opened the M223s he wondered which ones had the trackers. All of this effort was to get those into the smugglers' hands. A lot was riding on his shoulders, and he hoped the plan would work.

He spent another ten minutes inside, then opened the door.

"You going back into town?" Ellen asked.

"Nah. I think I'll catch a few holos and get some sleep."

"Hell, I thought you doggies had more stamina than that. So disappointing."

Jonathan P. Brazee

Titus gave her the finger and wandered over to the tents. He could have gone back into town, and that had been the original plan. But he wanted to see this thing through. He pulled out his PA and opened Season Three of "The Bastard," intending on binge-watching the entire season, but he couldn't concentrate. After rewinding and watching a key section three times, he gave up and simply decided to wait it out. He got more and more nervous the closer it got to 23:15. At 23:30, he stepped out as if stretching his legs. From the vantage of the recycling station, he had a line-of-sight to the back of the machine shop. He could barely make out figures carrying cases out and into the darkness. After another ten minutes, the activity stopped.

They'd taken the bait.

At 0430, an hour-and-a-half before reveille, a military dragon wagon pulled up with papers to remove the weapons. The lieutenant had not yet returned from liberty, but after reading the documents, Chief Roulade gave the OK. A sergeant first class who looked amazingly like Lieutenant Colonel Jalben relieved the watch-stander, telling him he might as well try to catch a few z's before morning formation. Titus watched as they backed the dragon-wagon right to the door, effectively blocking the view. Titus watched and the men disappeared inside. Twenty minutes later, the truck pulled in front of the CP where the SFC got out with a scan pad for Chief Roulade to certify. Within moments, the dragon-wagon left the camp.

Two days later, all construction at the depot ceased. Rumor was that some equipment had turned up missing.

****

Three weeks after the sting, the Free States Army, in conjunction with the ISA, announced the capture of a major smuggling ring and the seizure of over 22-million credits of weapons on the planet of Humber, culminating two years of investigation. Eighteen people were captured, including the vice-president of JSR Distributors.

Two days before the raid, Titus was given orders off planet. Two days after the raid, he received a vaguely-worded Letter of Commendation, citing his hard work—without any details.

GULWAD

Chapter 23

With his unacknowledged/unofficial success behind his belt, Titus begged Colonel Jaeger to put him back in the field. He'd felt a surge of excitement in the hunt and capture not only of the horrendous human trafficking ring, but of the larger organization. This was something worth doing, and he felt he had an affinity for it, Agent Greer be damned.

The colonel told him he had other plans but agreed to put them on hold. Another case had come up, and Titus might be the soldier to check it out.

The Army was expanding its foothold on Gulwad, which was out on the rim and within spitting distance of the nearest Federation system. The Confederation of Free States and the United Federation had a complicated relationship. With the Feddies' recent spat with Greater France, the Free States Council had determined that a show of force might be enough to inhibit any Feddie encroachment into Free States space.

Gulwad might be a Rim planet, but it had a population of a billion or so, located on three major continents, and a full division plus spread out across four bases. One of the bases had been abandoned 20 years prior when priorities were toward the inner worlds, and now, with five-thousand soldiers reestablished at Fort Chowdhury, the straining infrastructure was falling apart. Enter the engineers, trained for combat, but now thrust into maintenance.

With the influx of soldiers and gear, the confusion alone made theft of gear easier, and there was a potent black market ready to snap up anything it could get its hands on. A billion people took a lot of support, and out here in the Rim, far from

New Mumbai, the civilians' distribution was not as regular, and what arrived was over-priced.

Titus, with a new identity, was sent to the 34th Combat Engineer Battalion, which had a history of a lack of supervision. The previous battalion commander and sergeant major had been relieved only a week before Titus arrived.

Assigned to waste disposal, Titus had spent the first two weeks on site fixing sewer lines and recycling stations, just as when he was with the Seabees. He wondered at the perversity of the gods of war. What he hadn't caught wind of was of any theft or smuggling ring. His back story was of a corporal who'd been a sergeant but busted down for punching his First Sergeant, and now was in financial straits.

Titus had left the engineers, and he couldn't say that he'd missed this sort of work, not that he'd ever done construction while an engineer. But underlying it all was the knowledge that he was a hunter, looking for prey. That helped with dealing with the drudgery of working sewer lines. The banter of soldiers also helped, but he did wish he could share that banter from the comfort of an office instead of in a hazmat suit, looking for why this particular line was plugged.

"No amount of money is worth this." Sergeant Hank Valdez, growled as he slipped inside the access pod, which was simply an enlarged section of the line where. "Cleaning gunk with cheap suits and second-rate tools, the Army way."

Titus heard him splash into the muck at the bottom of the pod.

"Remember," Titus said, "You're clearing sewer blockages in a Rim Base for the glory of the Confederation of Free States. If the smell knocks you out, you can apply for a Red Guard medal."

"Yeah, fuck you, too. You've got the next one, my friend." Then, "Oh, wait, I think I see it. Looks like twelve meters further in."

They both had three-meter-long extendable arms, but three did not equal twelve.

"How do we reach it?" Titus asked, fearing the answer.

"What the hell kind of engineer are you? We crawl. So, come on down."

"I'm a combat engineer," Titus muttered.

"Welcome to the peacetime Army, my lad. Ours is but to do or die."

"I think I will die if I go in there. I swear I can smell this shit even through my suit," Titus said, peering up the meter-and-a-half-wide pipe. "Hey, if the blockage is on the other side, what happens when we break through?"

"You hang on for dear life or you're going to be surfing the brown wave."

"Sparking wonderful. Just what I wanted to do today."

"That's the Army for you." Valdez said, "This is going to be a bitch, so let's take five."

"Sounds good to me. I'll delay going in there for as long as I can."

So, what'd you do to get sentenced to this fresh new hell-hole, Petros?"

Titus's new identity was that of Corporal Bilda Petros, called Bil by his friends. He'd spent a day memorizing the details of his life, and he'd been quizzed on it by an older, disapproving woman. He must have passed, because the next day, he was on his way to the Gulwad

"I was told that this was a hardship post, and I'd get the extra pay. I need the money to keep up with the alimony payments."

"You were married?"

"No, that's why I'm divorced," he snapped. "Fuck, sorry. I'm still kind of raw about all of it. Yeah, I was married. It all came down during a six-month pump on Terminus Three.

"No, shit? What was that like?"

"It's an airless moon. What do you think it's like? So anyway, I'm on Terminus Three when I get an early leave, and I catch a hop back to surprise my wife back on Kyne, where we lived. I surprised her, all right. And she surprised me. Surprised Gast Nuncy, too. I don't think he expected me to walk in on him and my wife."

"Shit, man,"

"I filed for divorce immediately, but since I'm always away . . . you know, putting my life on the line, she gets our 5-year-old girl, and I have to pay her on top of that." Titus shook his head.

As performances went, it wasn't the most nuanced, but he hoped that wouldn't be noticed through the hazmat hood.

"That sucks some heavy balls, my friend."

Titus looked around to the man, tilting his head to the pile of shit on his shovel. "You don't say? I'm here shoveling crap for a living while she gets a forty percent of every credit I make. Oh yeah, the rent for her apartment? The one I never use? I pay half."

"And was that when you punched your first sergeant?"

"Yeah. The son-of-a-bitch was on my ass about something, and I just lost it. Knocked the sucker out."

"And you got busted for it."

"Yes, siree. Busted, fined three months' pay. So, less money to pay off the bitch. I don't mind supporting my little girl, but not her."

"Been there, my friend," Valdez said. "Not the first sergeant. But with women."

"Divorced too?"

"Nah, still married. My wife is a traditionalist though and sees that men should do all the work while the women stay home and do nothing. Except go through every check I send her on three or four shopping sprees per week."

"Do you have kids?"

"Nope. Dodged that particular bullet before getting married." Valdez said, pointing at his crotch.

"Surgery?"

"Yep. Snip, snip."

"And what does your wife think about it?"

"Doesn't know. She just thinks that we need to keep trying more. I'm taking this deployment to rest up for when I get home."

"That's a dangerous way to live, man." Titus said.

"Is there any other way to live?"

"None worth mentioning."

"Well, let's get going. That shit's not going to get cleared with us sitting here gabbing like this."

Titus waded through the ankle-deep muck and peered into the pipe. "We're really going to have to go in there?"

"No."

"Thank God. Then how are we going to fix this thing."

"*We're* not going in. *You* are. Not enough room for two to make a difference."

Titus turned and looked at the sergeant, who shrugged.

"You are junior, after all. If it makes you feel better, I'll be tending your line."

"Oh, yeah, that makes me feel a whole lot better," Titus said. "Lots better. I can't tell you how much better."

"Here, let me get you attached," the sergeant said, pulling out a line from a reel on his utility belt and clipping the end onto Titus's belt. "Just crawl ahead until you see the fatberg and—"

"Fatberg?"

"Yeah, fatberg. Where the hell have you been, Petros?"

"Not in the sewers."

"A fatberg's a mass of shit, lard, and debris that congeals together. First, it hangs like putrid stalactites, but then they grow until it blocks the line. In the big public sewers, they can get huge. This here's just a baby."

"And you know this how? I mean that this is a fatberg thing?"

"Don't know, but probably. These older pipes are prone to them, especially when they've been out of commission for a while. Whatever was in there hardens, then when the new shit comes in, it gets caught like on a grate. A new fatberg is born."

"And I just have to poke at it?"

"You might have to dig a bit. But like I said, this one's just a baby. So, go get it."

"Just great," he mumbled, getting down on his hands and knees. A small amount of sewage was getting past the "fatberg," and his hands disappeared beneath the dark sludge. He knew his hazmat suit was protecting him, but his thinking brain couldn't get past his animal brain that shouted at him to get out. He imagined all sorts of bacteria and pathogens coursing into his body."

His hood torch lit up the pipe, and up ahead, he saw the blockage. The fatberg. It wasn't brown, as he'd expected. More of a whiteish, tannish, sick-looking color.

"I've found it," he told Sergeant Valdez, extending his multi-arm. He gave the fatberg a poke. It was hard and didn't give. This wasn't going to be easy.

With a twist of the handle selector, a bright, half-meter-long blade extended from the body of the arm. He gave the fatberg another poke, and this time, the blade sunk in. Not easily, but it did penetrate.

This is going to suck big time.

The sewer pipe was only a meter-and-a-half in diameter, so he couldn't stand to get leverage. The best he could do was to crouch, then lean into his arm as he started stabbing the mass. That didn't seem to be doing much, so he switched to slicing off chunks from the near side.

"How's it going?" the sergeant asked.

"Sparking fine. I'm having a good time. Wish you were here to enjoy it, though."

I'm not even an engineer anymore. Why the hell am I stuck doing this shit? This is above and beyond.

It was slow going. The awkward position was murder on his back and arms, and he knew he could back out to take a break. The sergeant would probably take over. But in his disgust, he turned that to anger, anger directed at the fatberg. A "baby" fatberg at that. He was not going to let it defeat him, and he attacked it with greater fervor.

He'd focused his efforts on left side, right in the middle, digging out a hole. When it was a meter deep, he shifted his angle, and when he plunged the blade into the fatberg, a small stream of putrid, black liquid shot out.

"Hell, yeah!" he shouted as the stream hit his chest. "I've got you!"

He turned from slicing to digging, plunging the blade into the area around from which the stream had appeared, over and over.

He should have thought it through. Behind the fatberg was a mass of sewage building up, liters and liters of it. It was backing up all the toilets and the galley, some of which were over 300 meters away. That meant there was a lot of shit.

Just as with a break in the dam, all that mass of shit, piss, and garbage pushed forward, demolishing the weakened fatberg that had blocked its way. A wave of shit washed over Titus, sending him backwards, ass over head. He tried to scramble to his feet, but the flood was too much for him. He banged against the side of the pipes until he emerged in the pod, where Sergeant Valdez grabbed him and helped him stand up as the flood tried to sweep his feet out from under him again.

Clutching each other and hugging the side of the pod, they managed to keep from being swept away in the first shit-tsunami. After a long few moments, the flood started to recede to a more manageable flow.

"Damn, Petros. You could have given me fair warning."

"I didn't have any. The fatberg just gave way," he said.

The flow was now knee level but moving steadily instead of in a mad rush. The two separated, and Sergeant Valdes started to laugh.

"What's so sparking funny?"

"You, man. You're covered. There's not a centimeter of hazmat that shows through the shit."

"Oh, eat me. You're not looking so clean yourself."

The two waited until the flow abated some more, then the sergeant waded to the opening and looked inside. "We've got to check it." Titus sighed and started moving forward, but the sergeant said, "No, this one's on me."

He disappeared into the pipe. Two minutes later, he reappeared and said, "You got most of it. We'll send down a trundlebot to check the entire line, and it should be able to jet out what's left of the fatberg."

"So, we're done?"

"Yeah, I'm calling it. Let's go get cleaned up."

The two clambered out of the access hatch and started back. Other soldiers saw them and quickly gave them a wide berth.

"You playing in the shit again, Valdez?" someone shouted.

The sergeant gave him the finger. They reached the motor pool decon station, which was used to clean vehicles that were to be taken off-planet—no one wanted a contagion to move from one planet to another. In this case, the high-pressure hoses would clean off the sewer-gunk better than anything else.

The spent five minutes under the jets while a disgusted-looking PFC ran through the cycles. With a final salute, the two took off their hoods and stepped off to return the suits. Titus took a tentative sniff. He couldn't smell a whiff of shit.

"Hey, you, know, I've been thinking," Sergeant Valdez said. "About your financial situation and all. If you're interested, I think I may know a way for you to get on top of that."

Titus turned back to him, eyes narrowed. With the sewer mission, he'd almost forgotten why he was there. "I wish I could say that I didn't need it, but if you need some help and are willing to pay for it, I'd be more than happy to—"

"No, no. Nothing like that. It's just the locals like to keep the boys on base happy, and they're more than willing to put some coin in our pocket in exchange for a few small favors. Nothing major, and it'll mostly just be ale money, at least to start."

Titus nodded, taking a moment to pretend to think it over. "Favors?"

"Yeah. Blind eyes, some small equipment management, shit like that. Nothing serious. If you're interested, I think I could arrange for some deals to be made."

Titus nodded, and after a moment shrugged. "Hey, like I said, it's not like I have much of a choice. Let me know what you can set up, and I'll be happy to get paid for it."

"Cool jewels. I'll check with some people, and I'll let you know."

Chapter 24

The rest of the morning went quickly. He ran simple checks on the detonators, all over 40 years old, but still indicating green. That was gratifying to his engineer side, but his AIC side was gratified that the numbers worked out. If there was gear theft going on in the battalion, then it wasn't with the detonators, which had multiple civilian uses.

He was just finishing up when he felt a presence and spun around to see Valdez standing there.

"Hey," Titus said. "I'm just heading to get chow. Want to come with?"

"I'm going, but I think you might want to put that off for the moment."

"How do you mean?"

"Remember what we talked about, you know, helping you out with your alimony problem?"

Titus nodded. "Yeah."

"Well, one of the owners of a bar out in the ville burnt out his generator, and he put in an order for a new one months ago. Still nothing. He said he'd be very generous to anybody who'd help him out."

"You mean, like a G-20?" Titus asked, naming the standard Army 20KW generator.

"That, or a G40."

The story didn't pass the smell test. Yes, Gulwad was at the end of a long logistical tail, but generators were everyday items, not something that had to be ordered. Having an off-the-record generator might be valuable for someone running an off-the-grid smuggling operation, and a G40 was a great piece of gear, but this was more likely a test. A generator was not a controlled item, and it might not seem to be putting the Army at risk, but it was still theft, and the consequences were significant. If he did steal one and sell it, he was tying himself to the criminal operation, for better or worse.

"Look, it's an opportunity for a few credits. We've got some deadlined. Get a good one, substitute a deadlined one in its place, and no one will ever find out. The best thing is that if you pull this off, there might be more opportunities for you in the future."

"What about security?"

"Hell, we're engineers. We always need generators. No one is going to give you a second look. And the deadlined pool isn't secured. Check out a good one, then before you turn it in, switch it for a junk one. Those end up getting auctioned off anyway. Slam, bam, thank you ma'am, and those'll be the easiest credits you'll ever make."

There was no doubt that Titus was going to do it. That's why he was here. But he couldn't seem too eager.

"What if I get caught?"

"Shit, Petros, are you a pussy? You won't get caught. I'd do it, but I'm just trying to help a buddy out."

Titus paused as if he was thinking things through.

"Look, they busted you down a rank, took your money, too? What do you owe them?

"Fuck yeah. You're right. OK; I'm in."

"Sweet." Valdez patted him on the shoulder. "I can get the staff sergeant to assign you to something that'll need the generator this afternoon. Make the switch and meet me after evening chow at the dozer pool."

Chapter 25

Titus had been somewhat nervous about getting the generator, despite Valdez's assurances that it would be easy. Valdez had been right. Maybe when the brass kept screaming that they had to up-grade the Army's training, they had a point after all.

Even on a base this remote, Titus had expected to find at least a modicum of security. Deadlined or not, some of the equipment was far more valuable than a generator. Salvage for some of what was in the warehouse could run to the tens of thousands of credits, if not the hundreds of thousands.

Titus had chosen to steal a G20. Valdez had hinted at a G40, as it was worth more, but it was also a little larger, and a G20 could be carried concealed in this engineer kit. He needn't have worried about it.

When he walked into the warehouse, no one was at the front desk. With no one there, he didn't bother to sign in, but walked into the warehouse proper. A sergeant and three troopers were loading equipment onto a sled. The sergeant was noting each item loaded, but he never checked for serial numbers to match against the inventory. None of them even looked up at him.

Sloppy, he told himself, his time as a fake supply NCO having an effect on his outlook. I wonder if this is by chance or on purpose. Sure makes it easier to smuggle stuff off-post.

The warehouse was huge, but only half-full of pallets of gear, seemingly placed without rhyme or reason. He started wandering, trying to find the generators. A soldier was busy with an artillery range-finder. The one on the pallet had been taken apart, and he looked to be working on another that was on a hover-cart. Salvaging one part to keep another working, the Army way. A few others were scattered around, probably doing the same thing.

"Hey, what're you doing?" a soldier shouted to him, clad in his fatigue trou and a T-shirt.

Titus jumped, then stammered out, "I need a part for a G20."

"What a G20?"

"A generator."

"Ah, OK." he said, then shouted out even louder, "Hey, Sergeant Bocatti! Where are the generators?"

The staff sergeant who was supervising the loading didn't turn around, but he said. "L-31."

The blouseless soldier turned back to Titus and said, "Four down to the L row, then left to 31."

"Thanks," Titus said, but the soldier simply waved an impact wrench and went back to his task.

Titus walked down to L, then left to space 31. Piled high on a pallet were about 30 generators. That seemed like an awful lot for a post that had only recently been re-commissioned. Generators tended to be sturdy and foolproof.

He found the G20s and put his kit beside the pallet before pulling one of them off and onto the warehouse floor. He knelt, took out his star wrench, and opened the fly housing. He took what he hoped was a surreptitious look around, but no one was looking at him. Still, he made a show of removing a part and stowing it in his kit. His supposed part retrieved, he picked the generator back up to return it, but instead of placing it on the pallet, he placed it inside his kit. He expected someone to shout out, but there was nothing.

As he knelt to close his kit, a flash of orange caught his eye on another of the generators. It wasn't much, just a smudge, but it tickled his sense that something was amiss. Curious, he pulled the generator out. It looked a little beat up, but on a hunch, he powered up the display. He wasn't surprised when it lit up. The display was solar powered, but it's draw was minuscule, and it could work even if the generator itself did not.

Titus was an engineer, however, and he had his kit with him. He pulled out his scancheck, plugged it into the data port, and turned it on. The results were not only green, but well into it. There were still a few reasons why a scancheck would show green for a broken generator. Titus had to know for sure. He looked around to see if anyone was watching, then powered up. A hum filled the air and the generator came online, ready to provide its rated capacity of 20 KW. He quickly turned it off.

Son-of-a-bitch! They're sending good equipment out for public auction. The orange mark is the sign for which ones are still good. Whoever buys it has a record and now owns a working generator at salvage prices.

He looked at more of them. Five had the same, seemingly random orange mark.

If this is how they do it, why did Valdez want me to steal one?

He thought about it for a moment, and he figured that either Valdez was working with another ring or they wanted to test him to see if he'd physically steal one.

****

"Run into any trouble?" Valdez asked when they met in the dozer pool after dinner.

Titus shook his head and pulled the G20 out of his backpack.

"You couldn't have gotten one of the G40s??"

"I needed to hide it in my engineer kit. But they'll still pay for this one, right?"

Valdez chuckled and said, "Yeah, they will. Nice work, Petros."

"Call me Bil."

"Bil it is. I'll get this over to our bar-owning friend, with your compliments. Give me your PA."

Titus handed it over, and Valdez tapped his to it before handing it back. The display showed a transfer of 80 Universal Credits."

"You would have gotten a hundred for a G40, but it's a start, and there's lots more where those came from. Stay frosty, and we'll see if you can't make a little more."

Chapter 26

A little more was right. Over the next two weeks, Titus found himself paying visits to the deadlined warehouse three more times, first for another generator, then for parts to military vehicles. Valdez had given up on his bar owner in need story by now, and having proven himself reliable, the sergeant had asked him to make a pickup, then get the product off the post.

As soon as the unnamed soldier handed Titus the package, he knew he'd just stepped up to another level. The soldier faded away into the night, leaving him holding a PAAM 3, the big brother of the Pickard Anti-Armor missile, the one Fraser had used back on Belleviue to take out the Patty. This was getting serious, and it gave Titus pause.

As an AIC operative, Titus had leeway to do what he felt he needed, to include the use of non-judicial lethal force. This was different, however. Innocent citizens could be put at risk if the missile got into the wrong hands, and Titus wasn't willing to make that decision. He stashed the missile, then went back to his quarters and made the call to Lieutenant Colonel Jalben. After a long discussion between the two, the colonel authorized turning it over to his still unseen bosses.

Time was of an essence, and this time, instead of turning over the goods to Valdez, he had to get it off the post, and it was too big to slip into his overnight bag. He changed into his PT gear, but with his environmental hood on and carrying his backpack.

Some hard-charging soldiers had taken to running with hoods and full packs. Titus thought they were high. Running was hard enough without all of that. But they gave him some cover. He went back to where he'd stashed the missile, then carefully disassembled it. With it in parts, he could just fit the pieces into his backpack. The body was a little long, and it forced his pack out of shape, but he didn't think it was too noticeable.

He hefted the pack to his back, then started jogging. After only a hundred meters, he *knew* those who did this were high.

No question about it. The hood made heavy breathing difficult, and the pack was bouncing into his back with every step.

Titus headed for the Charlie gate. Masochistic soldiers took this gate to run up the hills in back of the post. He tried to look relaxed as he approached the gate, which was difficult as he was about to puke up his lunch. The gate guard held up his hand to stop him and ask for his ID. Titus hadn't realized that they checked going out. He gave his ID to the guard who scanned it before giving it back.

"And your pack?" he asked.

Titus's heart fell. He'd seen the running freaks run all over with their packs and hoods, but he'd never considered that the gate guards would check the packs. Stupid.

He slowly started to take off his pack, considering his options. He could make a break for it, but laden as he was, he was sure the guard could run him down. He could request to talk to the post commander, and have him contact Lieutenant Colonel Jelan, but even if that worked, his cover was probably blown.

He refused to consider the last option, the use of lethal force. The guard was simply doing his job.

"Knowles, the sergeant major," another soldier said after opening a window on the guardshack.

The guard stepped away from Titus and looked past the gate where a solider in a hood and carrying a pack was pelting down the last stretch to the gate. He stepped up and pushed the gate release to give the sergeant major an open entry, no need to slow down.

Titus took the opportunity to run out. The guard didn't stop him."

"Hooah, soldier!" the sergeant major shouted as he passed Titus. "Another great Army day!"

Titus gave his own weak hooah, muffled by his hood. The gate guard greeted the sergeant major with his hooah and got one in return.

Hooah, hooah, hooah. But it got me through the sparking gate.

He struggled up the hill, trying to keep the pace up until he hit the top of the first rise. The moment he started down the other side, he left the path and slowed to a walk. He was about to puke, so he took off the hood and dry-heaved, with only some spit making a long rope as it hung from his lip.

When he'd finally felt human again, he hiked down to a wash that ran under the road to Blue Water, a small mountain town 20 klicks away. He stashed the missile parts, then hiked back up the hill. Just before coming into view of the guard post, he put some rocks in his pack and redonned the hood. Slowly, he jogged down to the gate, every step a symphony of agony.

Yes, those who did this for fun were off their sparking rockers.

****

Three hours later, after a delivering the missile to the drop-off point, Titus slid into the seat across from Valdez, then poured himself a cold one from the half-empty pitcher. He took a long draught, and not entirely for show. His heart was still beating wildly.

"Everything go OK?" the sergeant asked.

"Yeah. Barely. I almost got caught."

"Almost means you didn't. And you'll be happy with our bonus for the effort."

"Effort? I did all the work. What did you do?"

"I'm the contact. I know the buyer," Valdez said.

"While I take the risk."

The sergeant shrugged, then took a sip from his beer.

"This isn't going to work," Titus said.

"Now don't you be talking like that. You're already in. You can't just pull chocks when you want to."

"I don't want to pull chocks. I mean this penny-ante shit. If I'm going to risk getting my ass caught, it ain't gonna be for a generator, or for a freaking anti-armor missile. No, I want it to be worth my while."

"What's worth your while?" Valdez asked, leaning closer.

"My sparking life turned upside down when I caught my wife sucking off my friend. I was a good soldier, with a good career ahead of me. All gung ho. Hooah and all, you know."

"Until you decided to drop your first sergeant."

"Yeah, until then. And I found out the Army doesn't give a flying fuck about us. I've got fourteen months left on this enlistment, then I'm out on my ass. With my court martial, I'm not eligible for re-enlistment."

"And so? What does that have to do with us? That's fourteen months from now."

"I've gotta look out for myself. When I was stuck in the brig for three months, I had this dream. Find a one-time job to set me up for life. Either stash it until I'm kicked to the curb, or just desert. Go to one of the indie planets, live a life of luxury. Or at least comfortable, and never give my ex another credit."

"What about your daughter?"

"Collateral damage. Make the bitch work for a living," Titus said with fervor before calming down and saying, "Well maybe set up a fund for her, one her mother can't touch. But I need to make enough to make it all worthwhile. Not these onesies and twosies. All that's gonna do is get my ass caught, and they'll put me away for a lot longer than three months this time. I need the big score."

He took another sip of his beer, trying not to look at Valdez to read his reaction. He knew he couldn't force the issue. Valdez had to think it was his idea.

He only had to wait twenty seconds.

"You know, our client would probably be amenable to that if you could pull something together. Opportunities like tonight won't drop in our laps very often, but I'm not sure what's in the warehouse of the dead that could be enough. Is there anything in there that might work?"

"What? The deadlined stuff?" He acted like he was thinking it over. "Yeah, in bulk. The indie planets pay a shitload for their goods. If we could get enough out and into the Far Reaches, we could make a boatload."

"On generators?"

"No, that wouldn't work, I guess. We'd need containers full, and there's only two pallets in the warehouse now. Most of them don't even work, and if we tried to switch that many out, even the dumb shits we work for would figure something was up.

"Then what?" Valdez asked.

Titus shrugged as if he hadn't been planning this conversation for weeks. "I don't know. The power diggers, maybe? Not from the warehouse. The battalion's prepositioning stores. They're just sitting there all bundled up and waiting for the next war. We've got fifteen, and there isn't any security on them. I don't know what they cost the Army, but I bet we could get a cool million for them in the right market. I could live on that."

"Except you won't get a million. Unless you have the customers in your PA. And unless you can convince our *partners* that they don't deserve their cut. Anything else?"

"Well . . ."

Time to put the bait in the water.

"Well . . . there're the old clankers," he said, meaning the Shieldlight 12 combat units, out-of-date infantry mech, energy hogs that couldn't stand up to anything a potential military adversary might have, but it could be potentially useful against local police or security. Titus wasn't serious about them. They were relatively available on the black market and were bulky to transport. He was just chumming the water.

"Oh, and the IAR-37s. We've got a ton of them."

Sergeant Valdez perked up at that. The IAR-37, the same weapon Titus had used as an engineer, had been a well-regarded infantry weapon 60 years ago. They were still in use by various militaries throughout human space. The Confederation Army, in its present modernization spasm, had phased the weapon out over the last two years, issuing every soldier and ground sailors the newer IAR-42. As a consequence, they had hundreds of thousands of the weapons awaiting disposal. Fifty-thousand had been sold to Highwater at a fraction of their purchase cost, but that still left more stored in armories at posts like Fort Chowdhury.

The best thing about them for Titus' purposes was that they'd been so ubiquitous during their manufacture that there was a huge and ready market for them. They might as well be universal credits.

Valdez leaned back in his seat. "Huh. Why do you think they haven't asked us to pull those out yet?"

Titus shrugged. "Maybe they don't have the pull to move that much stuff off-planet. Or maybe they'd rather not unless they can guarantee a buyer, so it doesn't stay on their hands for too long. They are weapons, after all, not generators. Much bigger penalty if they're caught."

"So was today's package."

"Yeah, I guess you're right."

Slowly now, reel him in, Titus.

"Well, maybe they think it would be too hard for us to get them out."

"And it probably is. Those are in the armory, not the deadlined warehouse," Valdez said, but Titus knew the sergeant wanted him to disagree.

No use disappointing the man. "I'm not so sure. I've got a few ideas. I bet I can get a case of them."

"How? I mean, this is some serious shit."

"Serious shit brings in serious money, my friend. If I want a big kill, I need to provide something worthwhile to our friends."

"But really, how're you going to do it?"

"Let me work out the details. But I don't want to be spinning my wheels for nothing. There's risk even checking this out. You talk to our friends and find out if they're interested. If they are, I'll get them twenty as a test run, 500 C apiece. You hook me up, that's all. No risk. And you'll get 150 per for your time."

"Bullshit. We're partners. Fifty-fifty."

"But you're not taking any risk. If I get caught, I'll get thirty years," Titus protested.

"Shit, Bil, you don't know these fuckers. They play for keeps. If I tell them you're delivering, and you don't, it's my ass on the line."

Titus acted as if was wavering and said, "I didn't think of that. OK, tell you what, sixty-forty. But this is just a test run. If it all goes down right moxie, then I want a commitment for five thousand."

"Holy shit! Five thousand of them. Where the hell are you going to get that many. Five thousand and five hundred C? Hell, that's . . . uh . . . that's a quarter mil!"

"Two-point-five, Sergeant. Not a quarter mil. And your take would be a cool million."

Sergeant Valdez whistled, then sat stunned. "I guess you weren't shitting when you said you wanted a one-time score." He gave Titus a closer look, then said, "Something tells me this isn't just something you thought of now over our beer."

Titus shrugged, suddenly worried that he'd gone in too strong. "Well, I'd be lying if I said I hadn't had this burbling around my brain-housing group for a while. But, wouldn't you rather be doing business with someone who was looking at all the risks . . . and benefits?"

The sergeant stared at him for another few seconds, then topped off their beer glasses. "Yeah, I think I would. If you say you can do this, I'm in. Let me go see if my contacts are interested, and if they're too pussy for this, I'll find someone who is. Deal?" he asked, glass held out.

"Deal," Titus said, clinking the glass before the two sealed it by draining the beer in one long swallow.

Chapter 27

Getting the IAR-37's had been easy, not that he'd let Valdez know that. A simple request to Colonel Jalben, and a case, labeled "Line Check Kit," was staged behind Warehouse 102. He picked it up with a mule and carried it to Motor Pool Delta where Sergeant Valdez waited with an MPV-30, just two engineers out to check the emergency power lines that hooked to the civilian grid.

That was Valdez's idea, and it was better than anything Titus had come up with to get the weapons off post. They were waived through the gate with only a cursory check, and off they went cross country, well off the main roads. Except their contacts had off-road transport as well. They married up under the cover of some tall trees, too tall to have grown naturally in the amount of time humans had been on the planet. There were four of them, two obviously "muscle," who stood seemingly relaxed, but to Titus's military eyes, ready to jump into action at the slightest provocation. A stern-looking middle-aged man checked the weapons, then told the third person, a 30-something, slight man with unnaturally red hair that they were acceptable. The two were searched, PAs taken, and then loaded into their cargo bay with the weapons case and blindfolded. Titus felt a twinge of anxiety, one he had to push back down.

Titus had expected them to leave the PAs in their MPV-30. There were too many ways to convert a PA into a recording unit. Their otherwise thorough search hadn't revealed that the third button on his shirt was a highly sophisticated scanner, straight from the Brotherhood. It worked on the same basics as the Jesuit scanner Titus had used before. Unpowered and made from organics, it picked up vibrations and recorded those vibrations by rearranging nano-particles. It was easily jammed with frequency scramblers, but that supposed its use was was suspected by the target. This technology was so new that Titus didn't think the black-marketers would think to deploy defenses against it.

He hoped.

Titus grunted as the truck hit another big bump. These guys were going at it the cheap way with wheeled trucks instead of hovers or ground effect vehicles. Either they were a fly-by-night operation, or they wanted to look like one. They'd refused to pay 500 C for the weapons, bringing the price down to 425 apiece. That meant they were either simply driving a hard bargain, or they didn't have the wherewithal to swing the bigger deal. Titus hoped the former. He'd bust whoever they were, but he didn't just want a stuffed head to mount on his wall, he wanted a trophy catch. That was why the 5,000 IAR-37 offer. Use a big hook for a big fish.

They'd been driving for at least thirty minutes, but despite how the heroes in the holos could tell where they were by the twists and turns, Titus was lost. They'd left the back-country and were traveling on roads, and there were more sounds from normal traffic, but that was all he could tell.

"They're going to fucking kill us," Valdez whispered beside him.

"Doubt it," Titus whispered. "We're back in civilization. If they'd wanted to do that, they'd have left us with our MPV and done it there. We wouldn't be driving this far, and back into town, if they didn't want to talk. Besides, we've been making these people money. No sense in killing the goose that lays the golden eggs."

"Not quite."

"What aren't you telling me?"

"These aren't the people I've been working with. Those guys were minnows. I had to, you know, climb up the food chain to the sharks."

"Fuck. Glad you decided to tell me sometime."

On the one hand, that was good. He was hunting larger game. On the other hand, there wasn't the trust he'd built up with their former clients. It was too late now, however, to do much about it. That train had left the station the moment they'd turned over the weapons.

The truck finally came to a stop. Hands removed the blindfolds, and an older man motioned for them to get off. The two soldiers hopped down into what looked to be a maintenance facility. Men and women were in teams, working on trucks and hovers. None looked up as a trundlebot picked up the case of weapons and took them deeper into the facility. Maybe they were just there as cover, repairing vehicles. Maybe they were part of the criminal operations. Maybe both. Two soldiers being escorted, along with a military case, was evidently nothing noteworthy.

The slight, redhead man, led them to an office that would not look out of place in any shop throughout human space. Windows looked out into the shop floor. Through the windows, Titus could see a rough-looking, broad-shouldered man talking on a phone set. His temples were just starting to show gray, a sign that he didn't care about looking younger. Standing in front of a wall display was an older woman, her hair completely gone gray.

With the ease of coloring hair, Titus wondered why neither bothered. Maybe it was their corporate culture? Then the redhead man knocked on the door, blowing that theory out of the water.

The man opened the door, then nodded at the case. The redhead man opened it, and the man leaned in and grabbed one of the IAR-37s. He worked the action, sighted at the ceiling, then replaced it without saying a word. He waved his hand for the two soldiers to enter the office, then pointed at a couch for them to be seated. Pulling up a chair, he sat down, still saying nothing.

Trying to make us nervous? Not going to work.

Except, it was working.

Valdez broke before Titus. "So, do we have a deal, sir?" he asked the man, who merely grunted in reply. The sergeant gave Titus a worried glance.

"Yes, we have a deal," the woman said, turning from the display and taking a seat beside the man. "For this shipment, at least."

"Who are you?" Valdez asked shifting his attention from the woman to the man to the woman again.

"Oh, come on, now. You don't need to know that. I know who you are, though, Sergeant Hank Valdez. You, too, Corporal Bil Petros. Grigori Tester vouched for you, and that's why you got in the door. As to the rest of your offer . . ." she said, trailing off.

"But . . ." Valdez said, looking back to the man again.

Oh, come on you sparking idiot. She's in charge, not him.

"Thank you, ma'am, for giving us the opportunity. You won't regret it," Titus said.

"I hope not, Corporal. And I'm not a 'ma'am.' Never was."

"Then how do I address you? 'Hey you?'" he snapped out, immediately regretting his tendency to be flippant. This was neither the time nor place for it.

The man started to stand, and the woman's eyes grew larger and her mouth dropped open for an instant until she broke out into a deep belly laugh. The man looked at her before settling back in his chair.

"I've been called worse, young man. Much worse. But you've got a point. You can call me Mantis, if you need something."

Valdez still looked confused, but finally, it started to sink in. "So, you're in charge here? Not what I expected."

"That's what everyone else says, right before I slit their throats and leave them for the rats," Mantis said softly, pouring tea from the kettle into a ceramic mug. "Would you like some tea?"

Valdez shook his head.

"I'll pass," Titus said, clearing his throat.

The woman chuckled. "So little trust between us. It's to be expected, I guess."

Shit. I just didn't want tea, and now I've pissed her off.

"On second thought, maybe I can use some. You know, to cut the dust from riding in your truck."

She laughed again, poured a cup from the small side table and handed it to him. Titus looked her in the eye and took a long sip. It wasn't bad.

"So, social niceties done, you've made an extraordinary offer to us. What makes you think you can get your hands on 5,000 rifles?"

"I think we proved that with the case outside."

"So naïve," she said, speaking to the still silent man before turning back to Titus. "A case of 20 is a nice appetizer, but that's a far cry from 5,000. That's 250 cases. 50 truckloads. Forgive an old woman if I wonder how you'll pull it off."

"That's our problem," Valdez said. "All you have to do is have the credits to pay for them."

"I want to hear from him," she said, tilting her head at Titus.

"We can't do it all at once, ma'a . . . Mantis. Every three days, 17 cases."

"Seventeen? Interesting number. You're moving them with a Dragon Wagon. Sixteen inside, one in the basket."

"That's the plan."

She's done this before. She probably knows what every vehicle can move, better than any transport sergeant.

"And how will you . . . acquire said cases?"

"Well, you know we're moving them under the Arms Transfer Program. We just sent—"

"Wayward of Juliette Station. Tell me what I don't know," she snapped, breaking her grandmotherly façade for a moment. Now she was the woman who was running a major smuggling ring.

Titus gulped, not entirely for show. "What you might not know is that five thousand . . . well, four thousand, nine-hundred and eighty now, have been transferred to the prepositioning stocks. There's a problem with that, though. With the new IAR-42s, there's no room in any of the armories. So, they're being stashed in the old ammo dump."

"And you have access to the dump?" she asked, raising an eyebrow.

"I have a friend who does. A very good friend."

"Who?" Valdez blurted out. "And how much of a cut are we giving him?"

Titus held out his hand, palm outward, to cut him off.

"I want to echo what Sergeant Valdez just asked. I don't know your 'friend,' and I don't like working with people I haven't met."

"He's, well, he's nervous. He watched "The Operation," you know."

Mantis scowled. "The Operation" was a long-running holo series that dealt with both sides of a criminal organization.

While the cops were not shown to be the paragons of virtue, the criminals were depicted as bloodthirsty thugs who killed on a whim . . . even their partners and associates.

"No way to run a business," she muttered. "We don't off our associates."

Was there the slightest lifting of the eyebrows from the still unnamed man? Titus couldn't tell.

"So, if we don't meet this person, then how will I know he can be trusted?"

"He's addicted to one-up, and he's not a good player. He's big time in debt, and he's running out of time. He's scared. He'll come through."

"And after he's paid off his debts?" she asked.

"Who cares? He's weak, spineless. He'll gamble more and get in debt again. But you'll have the IARs, and the only contact he has is me. You're in the clear."

"I like the way you think, Corporal. But how long will I have to move the product? I can't help but think that even the Army will take issue when five thousand rifles disappear."

"That's what's so sparking great about this, Mantis. Unless there's a war and the reserves are called up, no one's going to know."

She was facing Titus, but her eyes lost focus and she thought about his offer. With a slight nod, she reached out to shake his hand. "I think we can proceed with your plan. Payment to be made within 30 hours of receipt."

"Well, there's one more thing," he said as Valdez gasped and elbowed him.

Her eyes narrowed, and her hand dropped several centimeters. "And that is?" she asked.

Titus could hear the steel in her voice, a force of will that had enabled her to create a large, successful, criminal enterprise.

"Upon the last payment, I want help getting off-planet. Out of the Free States, to one of the independent worlds. And I want a new identity."

"I don't like changes in an agreement, Corporal. But in this case, I can see why. I agree, and I won't even charge you for those services."

Titus mentally sighed with relief. He had hesitated with that last request, but he thought it would cement the role he was playing. He took her hand and shook. He was now in, for better or worse.

Chapter 28

"This is it, man," Valdez said as they drove the Dragon Wagon out to the rendezvous. "We're about to earn a hundred-and-fifty-grand."

"One-forty-four, five hundred," Titus said. "Minus ten percent for my contact and a grand for the gate guard."

Valdez wasn't going to be denied his excitement, however. His share came out to just over 50k, and that was probably more money than he'd ever seen in his life.

Not that he'd ever see it, of course. His military career as a free man was about to come crashing to the ground.

Four hours earlier, the two had loaded the cases into the Dragon Wagon. There was minimal surveillance in the old ammo dump, and Lieutenant Colonel Jalben had assured him it would be cut off. Titus would rather have had a hand in it, but as the MPs hadn't come out to investigate, it was all good. Valdez had been nervous as they waited, sure something would go wrong, but Titus had placated the man, telling him that their gate guard wasn't on his post yet. Titus didn't know the soldier on the east gate, and he was feeling a little nervous as they drove up, but the soldier simply waved them through.

Once off post, Valdez switched from nervous to excited. Titus was excited, too, but it was the excitement of the hunt. Not that they would spring the trap today. Colonel Jaeger wanted to map out Mantis's operation, and that meant tracking the weapons, seeing where they went, how they were shipped, and which hands touched them. The arrests would be made during the second delivery.

They weren't taking any chances, though. There was a platoon *of Exploratores,* the Army's special ops troops, supposedly on the planet for training, but there as a reaction force in case things went south. Several drones were high in the sky, tracking the delivery, from pick-up at the ammo dump all the way until they were loaded for off-planet. After that, tracking would be left to higher headquarters.

Titus patted the Glazier at his thigh. He didn't want to rely on others, and he felt being armed still fit the role he was playing. If the spec ops troops had to react, Titus needed to be able to survive long enough for them to get to the scene.

Aside from the obvious Glazier, he also had a snub-nose Scorpion Micro 2 dart-thrower attached to his ankle. Made of exotic organics, is should be invisible to most scanners.

He settled in for the ride. Two hours ago, the delivery point had been changed to the outskirts of Wasted, a small town of fewer than 2,000 people. That had surprised Titus, who had assumed they'd use the same spot as last time for the test run. But it made sense. Fewer people meant fewer chances of observation. And if Mantis was still suspicious, it would give her team time to see if they were being followed.

Shifting the Exploratores had been easy. They were in the field conducting training ops, and in the three hours it would take Titus and Valdez to reach Wasted, the spec ops guys would be in place to where they could react.

Titus settled in for the ride, as the Dragon Wagon made its way along the selected route. Valdez stuck in his ear bud and was soon slapping his thigh along with the music. Titus was not going to be distracted, like that. He was going to be alert.

Which was why he was surprised when he jerked his head up after nodding off. He checked the time. He'd been out only five minutes or so, but he vowed to stay alert from here on out.

They'd been told to avoid traffic as much as possible, so the navigator had picked out a somewhat convoluted path down secondary and tertiary roads. Not all deserved the title of "roads," Titus thought as the Dragon Wagon turned off the main road to take an unpaved path that would strain a civilian personal hover, but that the big wagon took with ease. Not comfort—ease. Titus lifted his feet and jammed them against the dash to brace himself.

He'd just settled in when the wagon lurched to a stop. Blocking the road were two commercial off-road trucks. Titus's heart jumped through his throat, thinking that they were being hijacked, but then he recognized some of Mantis's men.

He opened the door, leaned out, and asked, "What's up?"

"Change of plans," the middle-aged man who'd picked up their first shipment said. "Too much activity in Wasted today, so the boss told us to stop and just take the delivery here."

"Hell, good deal. Saves my ass from getting pounded," Valdez said as he opened his door and hopped to the ground. He stretched, then walked up to meet the group of four men.

Titus swung down and joined them. "We've only got the rail loader," he told them. "Unless you've got something, we're going to have to load them by hand."

"That's why I brought my team. And you two, of course."

Titus shrugged. It would have been better at a warehouse, but he wasn't going to object about a little work. He was a soldier, after all.

An hour and thirty minutes later, he was beat, soldier or not. The side rail was only designed to move cargo within the bed, then lower it to the ground. The cases were heavy, and unlike the first time, there were 17 of them. His arms were burning, his lower back complaining, as they horsed the last of the cases into the second truck.

He accepted a bag of water, activating the cooler, and gulped it down.

"So, we're copacetic now? You all set?" Titus asked.

"Well, the boss wants to see you," the man said, then drained the last of his bag.

"I can't bring the Dragon Wagon into town. Too conspicuous."

"No problem. She's here."

Titus was surprised, and he looked around for her.

"You know, we can't let you pack when she's here. Personal security and all," he said, pointing at the holstered sidearms on each soldier's thigh.

Titus didn't want to give up his Glazier, but he didn't have much choice. He kept a smile plastered on his face, handed it over, and resisted the urge to look up to where the drones were observing them.

He hoped.

While they'd probably scanned them, they didn't physically search the two for any other weapons, which was a big mistake, something no soldier or cop would do. The little

Scorpion might not have much of a range, but he felt much better with it on his ankle.

While he snapped his empty holster shut, he touched the second of two innocuous buttons on the belt. The first was a red alert, come in with guns blazing. The second was a stand by for possible trouble. Its clones with Lieutenant Colonel Jalben and with the Exploratores commander repeated the action. Since they were quantum-cloned, there was no way for anyone else to detect the action.

"Is the Mantis here?" Valdez asked looking around.

"We're clear," the man passed into his throat mic. "And now we wait. You want any more water? Something stronger?"

"Yeah, I can use something," Valdez said, his voice breaking from the nerves.

The man nodded at one of the others, a young, if husky, man who looked like he was still in his teens. The man handed over a bag to Valdez, who took a swig, then started coughing.

"Woah! That's more like it!"

He took one more swig, then held it out to Titus, who refused it.

"Suit yourself," he said, taking a third swallow before handing it back to the young man.

One of the men hopped up into the cab of the first truck, and a moment later, the sounds of thunder-pop had the others nodding their heads to the beat. Titus found himself doing the same when the next song came up and Winter Tulane started singing her hit "This is How it's Gonna Be."

They'd listened to four songs before a small cross-country pulled up, settling with nary a whisper, and Mantis stepped out. She might be using low tech transport for the goods, but the Bighorn cross-country was a super-sweet ride.

She strode right to the back of the first truck and looked inside.

"All accounted for?"

"Yes, boss. Checked each case."

"So, you delivered as you promised," she said, turning to Titus.

"Yes, Mantis," Valdez said, pushing in front of him. "I told you, I always deliver."

"I wasn't sure you actually would," she said, looking past Valdez to him.

"You had my word," Valdez said, again stepping into her line of sight.

She scrunched up her face and said, "You know, I'm getting a little tired of you when the adults are talking. Var, now."

Something was wrong, and Titus reached to push the first button when there was a bang, and the left side of the sergeant's head exploded in a fountain of blood and brains. Arms grabbed Titus just as his finger grazed the button. He didn't think he depressed it.

He tried to pull away, but he was held fast. "Why did you do that? We delivered, and there's more still coming, he said."

"Still playing the part, Corporal Petros?" Mantis said, stepping over Valdez's body and walking up to him. Except, we know that's not really your name, right? Because Corporal Bil Petros died in a training accident two months ago."

"What?" Titus blurted out.

Did AIC screw me over?

"Oh, you did a good job. The record tree was sound. But you forgot to scrub social media. There were two references to the dear departed Bil from the furry community. Or "Tail," as they called him."

Titus's heart fell to the pit of his stomach. As part of his persona, he'd been told that one of his usernames was "Tail." Evidently, that was a nickname as well.

That tiny detail had escaped the mighty AIC, and that was going to cost him his life.

He wasn't going to beg. He could see a glint of cruelty in Mantis's eyes, and he knew she wanted him to.

"And that's why you changed the location," he said.

"Got it in one. See, I know how you ISA work. Or is it AIC? Doesn't matter. You were going to give me this shipment, then try and bust me later. You almost assuredly have eyes on at the Wasted site, and right now, there's a pretty good mock-up of a Dragon Wagon making its way there for any eyes-in-the-sky you have watching.

"So, we nail this shipment, get rid of any tracking devices, and call it a day."

"And we don't have to pay you, doggie," Var, the middle-aged man said. "Precious."

"Now Var, no need to gloat," she said.

"Except you are," Titus snapped.

"Oh, we still have some bark now, don't we? Well, I deserve to gloat, young man."

"Now what?" Titus asked.

"Oh, we kill you, of course. You know that. Got to keep things tidy, you know. But, while I hate to be such a drama queen, and I hate the tropes, it can go two ways: hard or easy. Tell me what I want to know, and Var here will put a slug from your own weapon into you. Resist, well, I think the rest of the boys would like to have some fun with you."

"I guess that depends on what you want to know?" he asked.

"Who are you? All I know is that you're not Petros."

"Well, I am from Kyne," Titus said. "Corporal Titus Pohlmeyer, Free States Army."

"ISA or AIC?" she prompted.

He thought back to his training. His name and branch were a matter of public record, and in keeping the subservient position of the military to the population, he was required to give that information up to anyone. No mention was made if that somehow didn't pertain to criminals.

He shrugged, then said, "AIC."

"See, that wasn't too hard," she said pleasantly before her tone changed to hint at the ruthlessness she must have shown to rise to the top of her organization. "Now, I want to know what you reported up your chain. All of it."

This was something he couldn't do. Things were going to be getting nasty, and he hoped he'd be able to hold out until they pushed too far and killed him.

He knew he should be concerned about his own skin. He should be trying to find a way out of this, of living. But all he could think of was to resist telling the bitch anything.

He shook his head, and she turned to one of the men holding him and said, "Soften him up, Rob."

The man holding his right arm let go, stepped in front of him, and with a smile on his face, buried his fist into Titus's solar plexus, driving all the air out of his body. He would have fallen in agony if the other man hadn't been holding him up.

I can do this! Push through the pain!

Rob looked to Mantis expectantly.

She waved a dismissive hand at him and said, "I'm not going to stand out here in the sun. Var, come with me and go over how you're going to sweep these. Rob, give him five more minutes, then drag him over to me. We'll see if he talks then."

"Yes, boss," Rob said, his smile getting bigger. "Can I cut him?"

"Do what you want. Just don't kill him. Yet."

She started to walk back to her Bighorn while Rob pulled up his shirt to reveal a small, eight-centimeter long blade. In the holos, the torturers went for big and flashy blades. Rob knew, however that an artist could inflict much more pain with a small blade.

Also, in the holos, the hero could turn the blade against the torturer, defeat the assistants in combat, and get away. But Titus was being held fast. He had his little Scorpion on his ankle, but it was just out of reach. If the man on him would just let him fall to the ground, he could try and shoot his way out. Highly improbable that he could, but going the quick way and not revealing information sure sounded like his best option. If he could take one of them with him, then all the better.

He forced himself to straighten up so the man on him wasn't supporting his weight. Now, as Rob stepped up to him, he had to decide when to make his move.

The little knife looked huge as it approached his face, and the fear he'd been able to suppress before came roaring back. His plans evaporated as the flight instinct took over. He pulled back.

"Hold him steady, Ming," Rob said, laughing. "He can't be squirming around."

Titus wasn't even aware of the man called Ming. All he could see was the blade moving up to his eyes, the leering face of Rob as he leaned in.

And a red rose appeared just under Rob's right eye. He dropped like a rock, falling against Titus and Ming.

"What . . . ?" Ming started to say, instinctively reaching out for his partner-in-crime.

That was all Titus needed. Without thinking, he dropped, pulled out his Scorpion, and shot Ming in the throat, the small dart expanding on impact. With the fins deployed, it tore through both carotids, blood trying to force its way out of the tiny entry would, spraying out like a fountain.

Titus didn't watch. He pushed himself away from Rob and fired four darts at Mantis, who was just turning around to see what was happening. At twenty meters, she was at the max range for a Scorpion, but two of the darts found their mark, one in her upper arm, and the kill shot in her left orbit. At twenty meters, the darts might not have enough left to penetrate a skull, but she fell with the boneless flop of the dead, something anyone who'd ever seen it before would recognize.

Rounds hit the dirt beside him. Var had his Glazier and was shooting at him. The Glazier was a very personalized weapon, and while it didn't have a bio-lock, it would be pure chance if the Williams sights would be accurate for anyone else. He should have jettisoned the Williams and used cold iron sights.

Titus fired one more dart, missing him, then got to his feet and bolted to the other side of the truck.

Where's the other guy?

He had only one dart left. One dart for two men. This wasn't going to be a shootout at the OK Corral. That left running. He sprinted for the bushes alongside the road. They wouldn't stop rounds, but they could give him cover. He reached them, then on his hands and knees, moved deeper into their embrace. Back on the road, Var was yelling something at the other man, but Titus couldn't make out the words.

He lay there, trying to catch his breath without sounding like a bellows, when he remembered his belt. He frantically pushed at the summons button to call in the cavalry. He just hoped they were close by and not up near Wasted.

"You can't hide from us, soldier boy," Var shouted.

Titus remained silent. From the sound of the voice, they were only separated by 10 or 15 meters. If he tried to crawl away farther, he was sure the noise would betray his position.

"I should thank you. Now, with Mantis out of the way, I can step up."

There was slight rustle off to the left. That would be the other man, trying to flank him. Titus slowly shifted his Scorpion so that he was pointing it in the direction. If the man came for him, he had to make sure to make his last dart count, then hope he could evade Var.

"Come on, soldier-boy. We don't need to be doing this. You let us go, and we'll let you go. Hell, if I get back in one piece with the goods, I'll still honor the payment."

The last person to call him soldier-boy had wanted to screw him. So did Var, but metaphorically.

A high-pitched whisper reached him, and for a moment, he wondered what Var was doing, but them a brief flurry of shots rang out, some shouting—one of which was cut off. The whisper became louder, then air whipped around him as a ventijet flared in for a landing.

Titus slowly stood, hand in the air.

"Freeze!" a soldier in full combat gear shouted.

"Look. My name is Corporal Titus Pohlmeyer. I'm with AIC—"

"Shut it and step out into the road."

Two more soldiers debarked. The first one kept his weapon on Titus while the other two did a sweep of the area.

"I'm the one who called you in."

"I said shut it."

"I can prove it."

"You can prove it by getting on your knees, hands locked behind your head. Now."

Titus knelt while a UX-5 flared in for a landing. The UX-5 didn't have the stealth capabilities of the venitjet, but it could carry far more pax. Twenty Exploratores jumped out and secured the LZ.

These were the good guys, and Titus started trembling as he realized how close he'd been to getting killed. He'd just have to wait until they were done and he could prove who he was.

It only took a few minutes before a captain came up and asked, "Are you Pohlmeyer?"

"Yes, sir," he said, still with his hands clasped behind his head.

The captain waved off the other soldier, and Titus tentatively lowered his hands.

"Well, that didn't go as planned," he said, the understatement of the year. "What happened to Sergeant Valdez?"

"They knew it was a setup. Knew I wasn't Corporal Petros."

"And so, they killed the one who really was a criminal? Ironic that," the captain said.

The captain seemed to be missing the bigger point. How did Mantis know he was a plant? The more he thought about it, the more he wasn't sure he bought the social media angle.

"Captain, all KIA. The woman and two of the men are unrecoverable."

The captain, followed by Titus, walked over to where Mantis was laying on her back. He asked, "Was she the Mantis?"

"Yes, sir," Titus said as the captain leaned forward and stuck his finger over the little entry wound just at the edge of her eye.

"Shit, did you have to use a dart? We can't recover anything in a mess like that."

"I didn't have much of a choice, sir."

The captain looked around and the carnage, then said, "Yeah, I guess you didn't."

"What now, sir?"

"This mission, at least for us, is over. We'll hold our position until a clean-up crew can examine the scene. With those guys?" he said to where the bodies of Var and Ming were being placed into stasis bags. "We'll pack them back to see if they can be resurrected. Try to get some intel out of it all."

"And me?"

"I'd suggest you make yourself comfortable and stick around with us for now. Your people are going to want to debrief you as soon as they get a hold of you."

****

Ten hours later, Titus had had about enough of his debrief. He still had to do a formal write-up, but the questioning had been relentless. Titus leaned back in his chair and rubbed his eyes. All he wanted was to take a shower and hit the rack, but he was waiting for the next debriefer to come in. Titus was surprised when that person turned out to be a civilian in a four-piece suit.

The bald man took a seat across from him, pulled out his PA, and studied it for a moment. The man hadn't said anything yet, but something about him screamed DIS.

"I'm Mr. Donagan, Corporal, and I thought it might be appropriate to give you an update on what's transpired."

"I'm sorry it all came down early," Titus said. "I know we wanted to try and track the shipments."

"Eh, don't worry about that. This was only one tip of the investigation. There were many more operations going on."

"What? Sir," he added belatedly.

"This was just one piece of the puzzle, albeit a big piece. But it was only one piece of an operation that's been going on since the end of the war. You even had a part in it before?"

"I did, sir?"

"Sure. On Humber. That was part of it."

Titus had to digest that. He'd been torn about the operation. While he'd survived, Valdez had been killed. He'd been a criminal, of course, but Titus had gotten to know him. He hadn't deserved to die.

"So, this was just a little piece of the pie. You didn't need me?"

"No. Far from it. From your initial reports, we were able to connect far more dots. And what looks like the major ring here on Gulwad was crushed. I'd call that a win.

"In the big picture, we've been able to develop more intel, but we've now got something actionable to push for sanctions on Gentry."

"Gentry is in on this?" Titus asked, surprised.

"Probably not. Oh, some officials have got dirty fingers. But we want the Gentry government to stamp down on the smuggling and arms dealing. Make it harder for them."

"And Mantis? Who was she?" he asked.

"We've done a DNA search. Born Elizabeth Carrol, on Earth. We're seeing some interesting linkages already that promise to be helpful. It would have been more helpful if you didn't have to shoot her in the head."

Mr. Donagan was the fourth person who had told him that. He got the message after the first.

"I didn't have much of a choice."

"I understand. I also understand that you were not supposed to bring a concealed weapon."

Titus smiled and said, "I had a feeling that our side would be a little tardy in saving my ass. On Kyne, we learned to defend ourselves."

"Touché. Don't worry about it" Donagan said with a smile. "Anyway, it all worked out for the best, or not the worst, at least. As for you, we'll get you some chow here, but you'll be restricted to this room until we've got transport for you back to New Mumbai for a full briefing."

"And Corporal Petros?"

"I think it's time for the good corporal to die a second death. This time for good. He was killed along with Valdez when they happened upon a smuggling transaction occurring. As far as how it affects you? It would probably be best if you don't show your face around here for the next couple of years. Personal advice."

Titus nodded. "I'll take it."

KYNE

Chapter 29

Titus spent five days undergoing debriefing, first by the worker bees for the G2, then from higher-ups. He didn't know many of the ones higher on the food chain. Most wore civilian clothes, even those who would be screaming Army while naked. There were some others, though, from ISA, ESA, NIA, and a few other agencies. He'd been put through a repressed memory session, but he'd been so drugged up that he didn't remember a thing about that.

When he'd asked about that session, Colonel Jaeger had assured him he'd done nothing wrong. It was just SOP when trying to pull every piece of information hidden in each crevice of his memory. After the last person had wrung him dry, he was given two weeks leave. Titus was ready to jump back into the fray. They'd broken the biggest ring on Humber, but there were more bad guys out there. But the colonel insisted, promising him that he'd be plenty busy upon his return.

Not that the Army would pay for his ticket if he wanted to go home, and two weeks was not enough time if he tried to fly Space Available on Navy Ships. Kyne was not a major military stop to have transports pulling into orbit. So, his choices were to hang out at the transient barracks at Army HQ or go home. With some trepidation, he forked out a month-and-a-half's pay for a commercial ticket and boarded the next day. He couldn't help but think of the credits deposited into "his" account for the gear he'd stolen. That would have been more than enough for a hundred tickets. But the Army had confiscated the account.

As was right. But he couldn't help but think that for a few weeks, he'd been a very well-off man.

Should have partied more when I had it.

But no, he'd had to present the image of a conservative, careful criminal to hook Mantis and her crew.

He hadn't been too enthused about visiting home. He wondered if he'd still fit in. But when he stepped off the shuttle that brought him to the surface, his heart started racing. He was excited. The smell of the refineries hit him first, dredging up memories. He'd hated the smell growing up, fearful of what it might be doing to his body. Now, it was somehow comforting.

Like many Rim planets, Kyne was settled for mining. Originally terraformed by the United Federation, the people owed a huge transition fee when the Confederation of Free States declared themselves independent. For the next 40 years, almost all of the planet's output went to bare subsistence and paying their debt. Infrastructure other than those for the mines suffered, and life was hard. Titus's childhood was rough, with little in the way of human comforts. Not that he was alone in that—83% of the population lived below the UAM poverty level. Still, there were good memories, and to his surprise, he was happy to be back for the first time since he left to join the Army and find glory.

But that was almost four standard years ago. He'd seen so much, he'd changed so much, and he no longer felt combat was the path for him. The allure of glory had faded. But he was proud of what he was doing for the Free States.

He'd told his parents he was arriving and begged off from them picking him up at the shuttle port. He wanted time to adjust again. He took the tram to Rarington, the barrio where his parents lived, then walked around the little market where people tried to make a few credits selling whatever they had. Business did not look to be booming, but no one seemed too concerned. Children shrieked with laughter as they dodged through the stalls while their parents chatted. He picked up a bottle of Scottish Glen at an amazingly low price—which meant it was undoubtedly counterfeit. It didn't matter. It would be expected, and no one would probably know the difference.

His parents lived on the fifth floor of a walkup, right off McGregor Boulevard. As he reached the floor, the smells of home cooking reached out to him, a siren call, and his mouth started watering. He'd been introduced to a wide variety of food since enlisting, food from every corner of the galaxy, but this was home. He knocked on the door, and his mother opened it, rubbing her hands on her apron before reaching up to give her son a hug, almost squeezing the life out of him. When she finally released him, his father stepped forward, for his hug.

I'm glad I'm home.

His uncle was there, Mr. Know-it-all (his mother said Titus was just like him, to which Titus vehemently disagreed). He relieved Titus of the Scottish Glen, poured himself a glass, then kept going on about how he'd had it before, and how a person could tell the real quality from the rotgut normally sold on the planet. Titus didn't correct him. Let him prattle on. In truth, Titus was grateful—if a little guilty--that his uncle assumed he would only bring the real thing. His oldest sister and her family were there as well, and the four kids, only two who'd he met, were seemingly in awe about their soldier uncle.

His mother had outdone herself. The meal was fab ham, but she'd bought some real herbs to rub it before roasting. Titus had grown up on fabricated food, so while it was considered lesser quality, he was used to the flavor. Heck, 90% of what the Army served him was fab as well.

After the meal, Titus sat with his uncle, sister and brother-in-law in the tiny living room to watch a football game. It was an odd tradition, he realized, that a colony made up mostly of people of Irish and German descent had adopted a sport that was traditionally from the United States. The game had changed over the centuries. More civilized, or so people said.

Doesn't look too civilized to me, Titus thought, taking a long pull from his ale. With a full belly and more than a little alcohol in his system, his eyes drifted shut before the whistle blew for halftime.

Chapter 30

He was going stir crazy.

For the past four years, he'd lived a structured life, being pushed and prodded one way or another. It hadn't always been pleasant—usually wasn't, to be honest. But it wasn't boring. There was always something for him to do, whether he wanted to do it or not.

And now he was doing nothing. The first couple of days had been fine, but that was about all he could take. He was going stir crazy. He tried to look up a few of his friends. Gunter was in jail, convicted of breaking and entering—while drunk, of course—so he was out of the picture, but the rest all had jobs in the mines, and they just didn't have time for him after work. John Coddinton had promised to meet on Sunday, but that was still four days away.

Salvation arrived in the form of his younger sister. Melody was the smart one in the family, and was enrolled into one of the technical schools, sponsored by one of the mines. They were paying for her education in return for her accepting a five-year contract upon graduation. She'd come home for the weekend, and she had less patience with their parents than Titus did.

"Come on, Titus. I'm taking you out for drinks at the Mackerel," she said after only 30 minutes of the obligatory visit with their mother. "I've got a few friends who want to meet you."

Titus tried not to look too excited. He needed to get out of the house. Meeting up with Melody's friends over drinks was as good an excuse as any.

Melody took his arm as they walked, chatting about her classes. Titus just listened. He and Melody were only two years apart, and he'd spent most of his childhood with her.

The Mackerel was a decidedly low-brow Irish pub, the kind of place that used bachelor parties and brawls to keep the clientele entertained when there wasn't a game on. But with a galaxy's worth of planets colonized by humankind, there was always something on. The management had never been too concerned as to who patronized the pub, so it had been the first place where Titus had a beer outside of the home. He'd barely been 14, but his money was as good as anyone else's. Once he'd hit legal age, he'd gravitated to some nicer bars, but he'd always had a fondness for the dark and run-down place

Lots of memories in this place. Pity I can't really remember them all.

"There he is!" was all the warning he'd gotten before he was enveloped by massive, smelly arms. Knuckles rubbed into his scalp, and he was pounded on his back.

It took him a moment to realize that he was not here to meet Melody's friends. She'd arranged this party for him.

He mouthed "Thank you" as he was dragged to the third booth, roundly considered the prime table because the seats were almost intact.

"Get the man your finest ale!" Caleb Mattieu shouted into the tablecom.

He had to yell. The tablecoms had to be over a century old, and they'd never been replaced. If you didn't yell, it was hard to guess what you might be served.

"Hey, so what's it feel like being a war hero," Bakar Nui asked. "Your da said you got a medal."

"Give him time to catch his breath," Melody said.

"And get a drink," Titus added.

Before he'd left, he would have thought he'd revel in telling his friends about life as a soldier, but surprisingly, he wasn't so anxious now. It was because they weren't soldiers, he realized, and they couldn't comprehend just what it meant.

But military duty was still paid at least some lip service in on Kyne. Once others realized that he was a soldier home on leave, he never paid for a drink, and not just from his friends. Strangers paid for rounds, including one old drunk who said something about serving in the Navy, but even though Titus understood every word, the man arranged them in an unusual combination that left Titus nodding and not understand what the man was saying

Caleb Mattieu. Bakar Nui. Vera Coral. Bernhard Malloy. Rack de Montri. Mike O'Shay. Names from his past. While

Caleb had been a close friend for a couple of years, before he became a jock, Bakar had never been one. He'd bullied Titus, in fact, something he seemed to have forgotten, regaling time-after-time that the two of them had adventures. The thing was, Titus remembered none of them. Bakar had been an A-lister at school, and now he seemed to revel creating a relationship with a soldier come home. Titus didn't know if Bakar was making things up or if he was confusing Titus with someone else.

And he realized that while he was happy to see Caleb and Vera, he'd bypassed the others. He'd left and created a new Titus Pohlmeyer while they were wallowing in past glories.

"Really, tell us about combat," Bakar said. "Did you kill anyone?"

"Come on, Bak. That's not appropriate to ask," Melody said with a laugh.

"Why not? I mean, he fought against the fucking Publicas, right?"

"You fought the Publicas?" a voice said from the next table. "On Pashtar?"

Titus looked over. The man who'd spoken looked vaguely familiar.

"No, Bellaviue," Titus said.

"I heard him say you got a medal," the man said, pointing at Bakar.

"Look, friend, I'm just out catching up. I'd rather not talk about the war. Here, let me refill that pitcher."

The man was sitting with three others: two men and a woman who looked familiar as well. One of the other two men's eyes lit up, and he picked up the empty pitcher, but the first man pushed it back down.

"What's the matter? You ashamed of something? Were you a coward?"

"Titus, Franz is drunk. Just ignore him."

Franz. Franz Serister. Asshole then, and I see nothing's changed.

Franz Serister was three years older than Titus. He'd lived in the next quad, so Titus hadn't as much contact with him as other younger kids did, but he hadn't escaped unscathed. At least half-a-dozen times, Titus had been the target of the older boy's attention, and never for the good. With all the other bullies, though, Franz was just part of the wildlife, like living with lions. Try to avoid them while going on with life. When Titus was in his last year in school, Franz had disappeared for a while, and rumor was that he was in prison. Titus hadn't thought about him even once since he enlisted.

He looked rather worse for wear. If he had gone to prison, it hadn't treated him well. He was still a big man, but he looked soft, someone whose muscles had gone to fat. His nose was red and bumpy with broken capillaries.

"Did you see anyone killed. Get their head blown right off?" he asked, taking his hands to the side of his head, then "exploding" them outward.

Titus closed his eyes. He saw Fraser, heard the sickening sound of the grenade going off.

His stomach churned and he thought he was going to vomit.

"I gotta go," he managed to get passed his compressed lips as he stood up. "Thanks for the evening."

"Tite . . ." Melody called after him, but he was heading for the door.

"Hey, I was talking with you," Franz said, standing and blocking Titus's way.

"I'm sorry. I've gotta go," he said, trying to step around the man.

"So, you were a coward. I knew it."

"Franz, let it go," one of his friends said.

"No, this fucking coward comes in here all high and mighty. People buying him drinks. But they don't know he was a coward. Didn't even join the infantry, the cotton-ass. In the rear with the gear. Isn't that what they say? No fucking honor, but now he walks around like God's gift to the Free States, when others really fought. Fought and died."

Yeah, you fucking asshole. Fraser died. Nuar died. And what did you do? His nausea disappeared, replaced with anger.

"Franz Fucking Serister," Titus said, stepping into the bigger man's chest. "You know, I hear you talk about honor, but I didn't see you enlisting now, did I? Oh, yeah, I forgot, how can you serve when you're in jail. Don't you lecture me about honor. I had the balls to serve. Can you say the same?"

Both tables had emptied, to stand around the two. Franz's face turned from flushed red to enraged purple. The man stepped forward, bunched his shoulders and threw a haymaker.

Titus had assumed a lot of things when he'd signed up, and one of them had been that the military would teach him how to be an expert hand-to-hand fighter. From the looks of his friends, they expected him to make short work of Franz. He'd been disabused of that notion quickly in boot camp. Sergeant Winston, his hand-to-hand combat DI, had told them that the moment that a soldier started using fists in a fight, he'd already failed. The Army gave them weapons and trained them on their use because even the toughest Federation SEAL or Brotherhood Wings, all experts in martials arts, couldn't stand up to a single .462 round fired by the wimpiest limp-dick in the Army. Yes, he'd spent three long and miserable days getting the shit kicked out of him while he tried to do the same to others, but he was not an expert by any stretch of the imagination. What he had learned, though, was that aggression often carried the day when skill could not.

Franz was drunk, and his punch was telegraphed. Titus jumped back, even as he realized the punch never would have reached him. The moment Franz's momentum carried his body around, Titus reversed and dove into the bigger man, knocking him over while delivering several solid punches to his side. Franz grunted, then pushed himself upright, shoving Titus aside.

Drunk or not, he was as strong as an ox. Titus did not want to get into a grappling match.

"You son-of-a-bitch. I'll crush your balls," Franz yelled, bull-rushing forward.

Titus jumped to the side, giving Franz a shot that bounced off his shoulder and hit the side of his head.

Fuck, that hurts! he thought, shaking his hand.

"Never hit a man in the face with a closed fist. That's a quick way to break your hand. Use your elbows in closed spaces. They're less fragile than your wrist and knuckles. They're easier to strike with and do a hell of a lot more damage," Sergeant Winston had told them.

He danced back, shaking his hand. He'd be doing better if he hadn't been drinking, but he was in better shape than Franz. He tried to bring up the class, to remember what he'd been taught.

"Don't get tangled with a larger opponent. Close the distance, do your damage, and back away. Or get them to back away."

Great. How do I do that?

Titus was less than an inch shorter than his opponent, but the other man had a lot more muscle to his arms and torso, and his shoulders were broader. Even with him drunk, Titus would lose if they started grappling. He took a step back, waiting for Franz to get untangled from the chair he'd hit. As the man stood up, Titus danced in, elbows ready, when Franz almost felled him with a blow to the chest. He grabbed the edge of Franz's table to keep him upright.

"Yeah, now you'll pay, you chicken shit, no-honor asswipe."

Titus was dazed, and he knew now he'd made a mistake. He'd tried to analyze the fight instead of simply brawling. He needed to be the aggressive one, not wait to counterstrike. His hand closed on their empty pitcher, and as Franz grabbed his shoulder to spin him around, Titus let him, bringing the pitcher around in a roundhouse swing that connected with Franz's left temple. The big man collapsed in a heap on the floor. Titus swung again, the pitcher making a hollow thwock as it connected. He wound up to hit him again when arms grabbed at him.

"That's enough, man," Caleb said. "Don't kill him."

He fought with Caleb a moment, but the man was much stronger than him, even when fueled by anger. But it was Melody's voice that broke through.

"I'm OK," he told Caleb. "Let me go."

"You're not going to kill him, are you?"

"No, I'm fine"

As soon as Caleb released him, he put the pitcher back on the table. "Get a refill, on me," he told the slack-jawed friend.

The woman looked at Titus and said, "You didn't have to do that. You're a soldier, for God's sake," before rushing to Franz's side.

Ah, Laresha Tripili, he thought as he recognized the woman. *You still with this asshole? Despite the fact that he's never had a milligram of fidelity? Serves you right.*

Time had not been kind to her, either. She looked rode hard and put up wet, and what was she? Maybe 22 or 23? Too young to have deteriorated like that.

"Did you see that? He murdered Franz," Bakar said from behind him. "Did anyone get that on cam?"

Franz groaned and opened his eyes. Laresha turned to him, putting her hand against his cheek, asking, "You OK, baby?"

"What . . . ?"

Disgust warred with anger, and anger won. Titus leaned forward, pushing Laresha out of the way and glared at Franz.

"You don't know the first thing about honor, about bravery," he said, spittle flying from his mouth. "You never did. I've lost friends, good men. I've seen children blown apart by naval gunfire. I've killed people, people like you and me. I've bled for the Free States, and I've given more than you. Any of you." He pointed out the rest, who had fallen silent at the sight of the little geek who'd changed so much.

Melody called out after him as he turned. He hadn't felt this angry in a long time . . . and it felt good. He felt powerful. Blood pumped in his veins, he relished the sight of a man he'd detested since he was a child, coughing and bleeding on the ground at his feet. It made him feel good and sick all at the same time. He brushed his mouth clean with his sleeve, glaring, daring anybody to follow him as he tucked his hands into his pockets and stalked out into the night.

NEW MUMBAI

Chapter 31

The managed chaos of New Mumbai's Gandhi shuttleport was in stark contrast with Kyne's. He took a deep breath. The air had that ozone hint, injected by the scrubbers to increase productivity.

Home, he thought, then stopped dead in his tracks, making someone dodge around him, muttering about "tourists."

Is this my home now? What about Kyne?

The thought was both exciting and disquieting.

He waited for his lone suitcase, then made his way to the military liaison desk to check in. He had to wait in line for fifteen minutes before he could present his ID, which the Navy petty officer on duty scanned, officially checking him in from leave.

"Checking in early, huh?" the petty officer said. "Problems?"

Not unless you call getting taken in by the cops, lectured by the night-judge, and released with a firm warning and the suggestion that I cut my leave short, a suggestion I was more than happy to follow.

"No, just got bored."

"Tell me about it. I'm from Roritora. We just got our first PattyMart. You've never seen such a dead place in your life."

PattyMart was one of the largest physical chain stores in the Federation, the Free States, and probably half of humankind. They prided themselves on being the biggest game in town for mid-to-low-level populations centers, so if the petty officer's home planet just got its first PattyMart, then it really had to be small.

"Nothing like New Mumbai, right?"

"You got that right, amigo," the petty officer said, fist out for a bump.

"Well, I need transport to Camp Uray."

"Not according to this. It says you're to report back to Army HQ. G2-30."

"The head shed? No, I'm at Uray."

Titus had been to Army Headquarters, which comprised one wing of the Pyramid, the Free States military headquarters, more than a few times, but that was the domain of colonels, generals, master sergeants and sergeants major. G2 was the Army Intel general staff, and those who were stationed there advised the Chief of Staff, interacted with the other general staffs, and worked with the J2, the Joint Service Intel. The bulk of the AIC was located at Camp Uray, ten klicks from HQ and a universe apart. Uray was where most of the grunt work in turning information to Intel was done, to be disseminated over to G2 or the operational units as needed.

"Well, I can get you on the next bus to Uray, but they're just going to send you on to Army HQ to check in, he said, swinging the display around. The petty officer was right. He was to report to G2-30, whatever that was.

"But I'll still live at Uray, right?" he asked as the petty officer shrugged. "So, can I just go there?"

"I've already checked you in from leave. You've got to go to the Pyramid, check in there, and then go to Uray for quarters."

"But—"

"Welcome to the military, Corporal. But you should know how it works by now, right?"

"How about you two cut the gabbing," someone said from behind Titus. "I'm Major Lash, and I need to check in."

"I'm sorry, sir," the petty officer said. "But there seems to be a problem with this corporal, and I have to address them as they come in. You understand, right, sir?"

"Bullshit, Petty Officer. I don't know how you work it in the Navy, but in the Army, being an officer means something."

"It means something in the Navy, too, sir. But it was probably a major who set up my SOP here, sir, and I can't go against them. If you like, though, I can contact the duty colonel at Army HQ to ask if I can do something for you?"

The major looked like he was going to argue, but with a resigned expression, he closed his mouth and glared at them.

"Now, Corporal Pohlmeyer, where were we," the petty officer said, winking at Titus. "As I see it here, you need to go to the Pyramid first, check in, then once checked in, you'll catch a ride to Camp Uray. Do you know where the transport liaison is at the Pyramid?"

Titus made a show of concentration, then said, "Oh, yes, on the D-level."

The major might be Army, but the petty officer was the same as an NCO, and no matter the service, they stuck together. Besides, wasn't it one of their duties to train officers? Even majors?

The petty officer gave a few more unnecessary instructions before he stopped, his point made. He handed Titus his gate assignment for the ground transport, then a file bud.

"What's this?" Titus asked, pocketing the bud.

"Oh, haven't you heard? The Army's changing the names of your units. I've got to give every soldier the file as they pass through."

He wanted to ask more, but the major was about ready to breathe fire, and while majors were nothing at any of the headquarters, a corporal was more of a nothing.

The bus gates were right outside, and his was there waiting. He stowed his luggage underneath, then found an empty seat and took out the bud, tapping his PA with it.

What he read made no sense. The Army was renaming units. Not the number designations, but the terms for units. There were to be no more battalions, but rather "cohorts." No more companies, but "centuries." And so on.

Why?

He looked around. A sergeant major was sitting across from him, reading a novel on his PA. He shouldn't interrupt the man, but he was more than a little confused.

"Sergeant Major, what all of this about cohorts and such?"

The sergeant major looked up from his PA, then rolled his eyes. "Our grand government leaders decided that the Army needed a makeover."

"But we've been doing that. I mean, we're getting retrained by all the foreign services. new weapons systems, too."

"Not enough. Some policy wog getting paid the big bucks thought we needed a mental reboot, and our President bought into that shit. And since here on New Mumbai, you know they love all things Romans, and since the Roman legions were the best in the world at the time . . . "

"Sparking hell. We're adopting Roman units?"

"You got it in one."

Titus thought about it for a moment, then asked, "A rifle company's got about 180 soldiers. A 'century' means a hundred, right? Are we going to change the size of a company?"

"No. All that stays the same. This is just to instill some bullshit pride into us, like we need it," he said, visibly getting upset now.

"Damn. This is going to take some getting used to."

"Not for me, Corporal. Thirty-two days and a wake-up, and I'm out of the Big A. No fucking Roman shit for me."

Just like civilians, thinking they know better and can just make big changes for asinine reasons. Why do they have to get their fingers into our shit?

Titus leaned back as the bus backed out of the gate and started off. He almost closed the file, but with a sigh, he started studying it. He had some new terms to learn.

Chapter 32

It soon became evident that the new names for Army units were only window dressing. The mission and daily grind remained the same. Even with his new assignment within Counterintelligence, not much had changed from his previous billets.

G2-30 was a small office in the bowels of the Pyramid with a colonel, three majors, four senior enlisted, and him. There were no quarters at the Pyramid, so he was back at Uray in the barracks. Every day at 0630, he took one of the shuttles that left every ten minutes during the rush hour. At 0700, he was supposed to be at his desk. He had an hour for lunch, where he could either eat at one of the enlisted messes or work out at the PAC, the Pyramid Athletic Club, either skipping lunch or grabbing a hotdog to eat back at his desk. At 1630, he quit work to catch a shuttle back to Uray.

His job consisted of reviewing AI captures, rating them as high potential, low potential, or ignore.

He knew that more than a few of his rank-peers within the community would love to take the steady hours, with no watch-standing, but Titus had tasted the adrenaline of fieldwork, and this was just dull pencil sharpening by comparison.

Captured communications could be interesting, but only if something of interest was being communicated. And so far, little to nothing had been shared. He'd spent the last ten days staring at his screen going over messages, rating them, sending almost all to storage, but sending a precious few up the ladder for further disposition. He didn't even know if the ones he sent up had anything to them. There was no feedback. He had the protocols taped to wall beside his display, and it wasn't a difficult job. It was one that needed doing, he knew, but gods in Hades...

Once in a while, the colonel would ask him for clarification over some message, and it depressed him that those occasions were the highlights of his day. He remembered talking to a captain back Bellaviue, and how eager the man had seemed to help him. Titus assumed that it had been because the man was just very good at this job. He now realized that it had been to stave off the boredom.

Makes a guy wish someone was spying on us, just to have something helpful and productive to do other than pushing memos up the chain.

He looked around guiltily, as if someone could read his thoughts. Of course, he didn't want anyone to spy on the Free States just so he wouldn't be bored.

But still . . .

Chapter 33

"You want to what?"

Titus shrugged. "Ever since I've come back from leave, they've slapped me with desk duty. I'm bored out of my mind. I was chasing smugglers on the outer rim. I was working on the front lines when we were at war. I can't—it's just not me."

Ex-Sergeant Rodra Thomas shook his head. "But re-enlisting with the Infantry? That's not just regular crazy talk." The man raised his pint glass. "That's lager crazy talk."

"Still hating on my lager?"

"Always and forever. I'm just looking out for you, Titus."

Titus and Rodra had served together on Wayward, and they'd stayed in touch since then, even after Rodra had reached his EOE and joined DAT, Inc, one of the local military contractors who snapped up Army personnel, keeping the cycle churning. Most of these corporations hired officers, but DAT hired Intel enlisted as well. Rodra was essentially doing the same job he'd done in the Army, but at a much higher salary. These employees were supposed to keep their contacts with those on active duty, and the companies gave them an expense account to entertain and maintain their relationships. Titus was in the middle of enjoying some of the expense money at that moment.

"I know, man," Titus said, sticking to the tall glass of amber that his friend loved to hate and taking a sip.

"I'm not just talking about your rotten taste in ales, my man."

"I know."

"I mean, re-enlisting? You want to go back to the front lines, but there's no front line anymore. All you'd be doing is the same, but living in the mud with all the creepy-crawlies. Do you really want that for yourself?"

Titus shrugged. "It's got to be better than this. I mean, I've been at this for less than two months, and I'm already bored out of my mind. I've put on a kilo and a half of muscle just from all the anxiety-induced working out I've been doing."

"Guns for huns, my man," he said, flexing his less-than-impressive biceps. "You must be hooking up like mad now."

Titus didn't want to admit that he wasn't hooking up. And that hadn't been his point.

"That's like saying you've lost weight because of a tapeworm. It's a symptom of something bad. And I don't think working as an analyst for DAT would be any better."

"The hours are regular, the starting salary is far, far better than what you'd get as a sergeant, and it has a legitimate career path for someone like you. You're sharp, Titus, and you've got what it takes to run that path like a boss."

"I don't want a job that's defined on when I get off work for the day. I want work that means something. Makes a difference."

"And I want three high-end hookers who have a tendency to forget to charge their customers."

Titus lifted his glass to clink Rodra's. He'd been flippant, but he had a point. He could "want" all he could, and that wouldn't matter. It was up to him to make something of his life.

Titus remembered the last time someone had told him he had what it took for a career change. He'd been in an infirmary bed, grieving the loss of Fraser and high on painkillers when he'd made that decision. A change had been needed then. Titus wasn't sure if changes weren't needed now as well. Maybe he'd gotten so used to the action that stewing in a cubicle was just too dull for him. The problem was that he didn't know if that need for speed was a good thing or not.

I've got the painkillers nailed at least, he mused, taking a sip of what was his third beer of the night. With Rodra paying, he could afford to go for some of the imported stuff.

"Tell me you'll at least think about it. You've got two weeks before your time is up. That's plenty of time to be bored enough to think about it."

Titus laughed. "I'll do it, but only if you promise to stop talking about it. I'm worried about my life enough as-is. . . . And you have to try this Amber Killjoy. That'll change your mind about lagers."

"Why would I abuse my body like that? Why would you abuse me like that, Titus? I thought we were friends."

"Look, I'll drink a pint of that dark shit you're drinking."

"Frothy Amenodan Ale was not developed over the centuries by monks dedicated to creating the most the most refined and elegant of fermented delicacies just to be called 'dark shit.'"

"Fine, I'll have a pint of Frothy Amenodan Ale."

"Centennial Edition," Rodra added.

"Hell, you're paying. Well, DAT is paying, so OK, I'll try the Centennial. But if I'm going to try it, then you have to try the Killjoy. Deal?"

"I'll make this sacrifice," Rodra said, donning a somber face and formal tone. "But remember how I put your taste buds over mine."

Titus tried to keep a straight face, but he lost it as Rodra waved for a waitress to join them. Besides, that Amenodan Ale didn't look half bad.

Chapter 34

In Rodra's defense, the Frothy Amenodan Ale, Centennial Edition, was in fact, pretty damned good (not that Titus would have admitted it to him). It went down smooth, it was nutty, fruity, and bitter all in one stroke. With double the alcohol content of the lager he'd been drinking, it snuck up on him quickly, giving him a welcomed buzz. Titus could almost taste it again as he burped, which he'd been doing all morning at work.

In hindsight, drinking three of the supersized glasses probably had been a bad idea, however. He'd woken up with a hell of a headache, but he took a Hang Away and within 15 minutes, he was as good as new. But he'd pay for it later when the pill wore off.

Maybe it was already wearing off. His head was beginning to complain again as he stared at his screen, rubbing his eyes and trying to make sense of the amassed data being displayed. Working counterintel, his job was basically studying captured information packets that had been flagged by the AIs and looking for signs of potential espionage. The AIs were good, but the bad guys kept upping their game, so it took a human to pull any flagged messages and send them up the chain.

He wasn't sure why the last message had been flagged. There weren't any of the telltales that he'd been taught to spot. He sent it to records, to join the billions of messages already being stored for . . . for what? He sure didn't know.

Titus brought up the next message. Two people chatting about sports. Whatever excitement he'd had about reading insights into people's lives had long ago faded, but he dutifully read on. The AI had keyed on the scores of a Five match, a match that hadn't occurred yet. Titus studied the message. It was awkwardly written, but that could be attributed to the voice-to-print AI as it transcribed the sender's spoken words.

This would be a hell of a lot easier if it was a voice message, where Titus could hear the inflection, but when compressed, a message like this took up a few kilobytes of data and cost just a few micro-credits, whereas voice comms through the relays were much, much bigger packets.

Titus was just about to banish it to the records when something held his hand. He wasn't sure what it was, but the more he stared at it, the harder it became to point out just what had tickled his subconscious. His poor, hung-over brain was moving in slow motion.

"Run decryption key Charlie," he ordered.

Charlie was not as reliable as the AI's prime code. It was built upon a chaos theory-based matrix, and sometimes, it could pull things together that other programs missed.

The messages split into two, and a moment later, the right version blurred, then reappeared with several sections highlighted in blue. The relevancy score was 12%.

So, what's bothering you about it? Hell, my messages home probably have a relevancy score worse than that.

"Pull up any messages between these two individuals," he ordered. "And I want bios."

Twenty-two messages popped up, all within the last three weeks, which wasn't many given the familiarity exhibited by the message he'd just read. Possible, though. Maybe they'd just met.

Aaron Palaver was a 46-year-old Free States citizen working as an analyst in the Ministry of Commerce's annex office. He was hired by the MOC right out of the university, and he'd risen to GC-11, which put him in the middle of the government scale. His ID image looked like a billion others, a somber-faced, middle-aged man. Nothing to make him stand out in a crowd. Divorced ten years ago, his only relative his mother.

Winston Ting was an Alliance citizen, living on Woomoora where he was a janitor for a bank. Divorced, 29 years old. Parents deceased. No siblings. Titus ran through the schools, jobs, and one run-in with the local police for drunk-and-disorderly. Unlike Aaron's ID image, Winston sported a blue-dyed mohawk, and one lip was raised in a half-sneer. He would stand out in a crowd.

Which meant absolutely nothing.

New Mumbai was a long way from Woomoora, across half of the galaxy, so Titus ordered, "Give me travel records for Palaver and Ting."

Two windows appeared, showing minimal off-planet travel for Palaver, all conducted over the last three years, and no travel for Ting.

So, they never met in person, he thought.

Which wasn't that odd. Human space was large, and people didn't have to meet in person to become friends. Social apps were among the most popular use of bandwidth.

Nothing jumped out at Titus, so he took a look at the messages. They looked innocuous to him. None of them had triggered a flag. They seemed to be normal chitchat, with a heavy interest in sports. The two seemed to be betting on Five and basketball, crowing when they beat the other, trash-talking when they lost.

His timer dinged. Titus had a lot of files to check, so he gave himself ten minutes max on each one. If he hadn't found a reason to send a message on up within that limit, it was trash-it-to-records-time. He raised his hand to hit next, when he stopped, hand frozen.

"Remove timer," he said. "And give me a record of financial transactions between subject Ting and Palaver."

To his disappointment, there was a record of payments, coinciding with each bet.

I'm wasting time with these. Just let it go.

But he didn't. His gut was keeping him latched onto the message—he just wished his gut would tell him why.

"Give me a bio-check on Laeti Palaver, mother of subject Palaver."

The AI pulled up a normal-looking record, one that revealed no smoking gun no matter how hard he tried to find one. He could do a deeper dive into her record, but he was pretty sure he wouldn't find anything.

One last chance.

"Give me a bio-check on Stephanie Coff, ex-wife of subject Ting."

The bio popped up. Titus knew the woman probably hated the ID image. Like her ex-husband's, this one did her no favors. She looked angry at life. But he didn't care about the image. He started to scroll down, and it was . . . decidedly lacking. For a 42-year-old woman, there wasn't much there. Sure, there were her parents, her residences, her schools, her jobs. There were the organizations to which she belonged. There were her marriage and divorce. But not much else, no run ins with the law, no promotions or demotions at work. No images of her other than the ID.

Nothing about what he saw was wrong, but there just wasn't the depth that he would have expected from a woman her age.

"Pull all social media originated by subject Coff."

Titus frowned at the number of messages that popped up. Over 400,000 of them. That might be a little light, but well within reason.

"Run Multi-scan," he said, feeling like he was chasing rabbits.

His display flickered twice before the results popped up. For the Bradbury-Sloan test, the results made his heart skip a beat. *Probability of machine origination at 83.3%.*

Bingo!

Titus still didn't know what had caught his attention, but he'd just hit paydirt. One of the things he'd pulled out of the Federation course on Earth was that people get lazy, even criminals or agents. It took time and effort to completely populate a web of fake identities. While Ting and Palaver, and Palaver's mother, for that matter, had records that got past his scans, whoever had created the identities had not put the effort into Stephanie Coff's. Someone had taken a short-cut, and that had tripped them up.

There could be reasons for Coff's records that had nothing to do with counterintel. She could be under witness protection. She could be working for the government. She could be many things. But in his heart, he was sure that Stephanie Coff, ex-wife of Winston Ting, was nothing more than an electronic construct. And if she was a construct, then what about Palaver and Ting? Who were they?

He leaned back in his chair, headache forgotten. He had something there—he just didn't know what. The question facing him was just what was he going to do with it?

Chapter 35

"Sir, do you have a moment?"

"Come in, Corporal," Major Aja said. "What do you have?"

Titus didn't know how to handle the major, his immediate superior. The man was a career soldier, a mustang who'd climbed the ranks and who'd been working intel as long as Titus had been alive. Evidently, he'd somehow gleaned that Titus was an Army experiment, seeing how junior soldiers would fare in Intel, but who had not performed well, bouncing around from position to position. That last part was true. He was bouncing around, but not because he couldn't find a home. It was the nature of his missions. But the details of those missions were in classified files, not his RES, his Record of Enlisted Service. The major didn't seem to hold his opinions against Titus, but it was obvious that he didn't take him seriously.

Titus sat down in the office chair opposite Aja and handed him a file wand "Sir, I found a packet that has some discrepancies."

"So, why didn't you just forward them up?"

"I wanted to discuss this with you. The initial message tree didn't reach a fifty—"

"You know the parameters, Corporal. We're not interested in anything that doesn't hit fifty percent," the major said, cutting him off.

"Yes, sir. But something was wrong. I couldn't tell what, so I did some digging. And on some secondary data, well I hit an eighty-three-point-three."

The major's eyebrows raised at that. "An eighty-three-point-three? From the Bravo Scan?"

"No, sir," he said. "I did a Prime on a message, and it came back an eighty-three-point-three for machine language."

"You know the Bradbury-Sloan is hardly reliable," the major said, picking up the wand and making the file transfer. He spent a few moments studying it before asking, "I don't see

Jonathan P. Brazee

anything here. The initial screening flagged it with a twenty-nine-four. You ran a Charlie and came up with a twelve. Where's the Bradbury-Sloan's numbers? I don't see them here."

"I ran it on Ting's ex-wife."

The major frowned as he switched to results for her. "Why? She's no longer in the picture." He studied it for 20 seconds, then wiped it from his display. "That could simply be the way she talks."

"I ran it because her bio is too simple. It's a half-assed job, sir."

Frowning even more, he swiped her data screen again. "Nothing out of the ordinary. Some people just live simple lives"

"Sir, don't you think this warrants a closer look? Palaver works for Commerce, and he and Ting have some sort of connection. He could be a plant."

"And just what do you think is happening here?"

Which was a question to which he had no answer. He just knew something was wrong.

"It's MOC, sir. It could be economic espionage. It could be data gathering."

"Look at his job, Corporal. Who wants to steal information on algae for the fabricators? No, this doesn't pass the sniff test."

Lots of people, you dip.

The fabricators that fed the masses needed organics, and the companies kept their strains secret. Espionage was not only government against government, but business against business.

"Sir, I wanted to bring this directly to your attention instead of passing it up the chain."

"Which you did. Now, I'm sending it to records."

"But—"

"But nothing, Corporal. Look, I understand you've had a rough time since being transferred to G2, and you want to get that big catch. But Intel is not what you see in the Hollybolly flicks. We aren't spies, hiding in the shadows. All we do is look at the information and develop Intel.   Nothing glamorous."

Except that Titus had been in the field, being a "spy"—sort of.   He wanted to tell the major that, he ached to see the expression on his face.   Instead, he had to accept what the major, six months from retirement, decided.

"Can I at least put an Alpha-track on these two, sir?"

"No.   I've made my decision.   And even if there was something there, and I don't think there is, we are AIC, Army Intelligence, not MOC.   They've got their own people for that. No, this isn't anything for us.

"Is there anything else?" he asked, already moving to his next file.

"No, sir.   Thank you for your time, sir."

He came to attention and performed a drill field about face, then marched off in defiance.   An act wasted.   The major never bothered to look up to see it.

The major was wrong. There was something there, but no one would find out unless it was investigated.   He'd performed his duty, and if anything ever came from Palaver and Ting, it would be on Aja's head, not his.

But if either or both of them were working against the Free States, then they had to be stopped.   But what could he do about it?   Not much.

Or . . . or he could go and do something really stupid like go around Aja to someone who would actually take him seriously.

Chapter 36

Well, if this went poorly, it would not reflect well to his re-enlistment board. Or any future potential employers. If this went well . . . maybe a pat on the back and a support tag in future documentation.

If the risk/reward ratio is that steep, how can I resist?

He felt uncomfortable with what he was about to do and not only because of the possible consequences. Titus had become something of a gym rat to battle stress levels. The enlisted and officers had their own gyms, but shared a pool, and with as many hours as he'd put in the gym, he got to know the workout routines of many of the staff and officers. Including that of Colonel Jeremiah Cannon, the director of G2-30, and Major Aja's boss.

Titus didn't normally swim laps, and he felt out-of-place as he walked into the pool area in his speedos. He took a seat even with the colonel's lane and waited for the man to finish. And waited.

Is this guy swimming to Earth and back?

After eleven more laps, the colonel stopped. Still in the water, and without looking over the edge of the pool, he asked, "This had better be important, Corporal Pohlmeyer."

Titus hurried over, extending a hand. The colonel looked at it with disgust, but he reached up and let Titus give him a boost out of the water.

"Well?"

"Yes, sir," Titus said, gathering his nerve. "Um, if you could just look at this information . . ."

Titus pulled one of the division's secure PAs from where he'd wrapped in a towel. If anything, his scowl was bigger than Major Aja's had been. There was nothing illegal for him to take the PA out of the office spaces, as long as it didn't leave his control, but it was generally considered bad form. Too many military personnel had been kicked out of the service for mishandling the PAs, and as Titus's division head, he would suffer as well if one of his soldiers screwed up the classified.

"What am I looking at, Pohlmeyer?"

Titus had gathered more evidence, despite the Major telling him this line of investigation was over. He hadn't actually ordered Titus to stand down, so technically . . .

"I have uncovered the possibility of an incursion into the MOC."

"What kind of incursion?" the colonel asked as he swiped through the readout.

"I don't know, sir."

"You don't know, and so you thought it your job to come to me with nothing?"

"Not nothing, sir. Communications were flagged, and trying to discover why, I found evidence of a ghost."

"A ghost? You've been watching too many flicks, Corporal. We don't use the term 'ghost.'"

"A fa—"

"I know what you mean, Corporal. This is the Army, not Hollybolly."

He swiped a few more times, then asked, "And what does Major Aja say about this?"

"Major Aja was... reluctant to pursue a matter that didn't pertain specifically to military intelligence, which is why—"

"Just a moment, Corporal." Colonel Cannon raised a finger and poked into Titus's chest. "Are you telling me you've come to me to circumvent the chain of command? That you've gone behind your direct superior's back to try and get me to act on something that he refused to act on."

Titus tried to clear his throat twice before he was able to mumble out, "Yes, sir."

"The command structure upon which our military is built is sacred, Corporal," the colonel hissed, grabbing Titus by the shoulder and turning him around. Two other soldiers looked up at them curiously. "It was built to establish order and efficiency. Break that chain and the entirety of our system is at risk. Undermining a superior is something that I will not abide in my division. You are undermining Major Aja, Corporal. Do you understand that?"

Titus's face flushed, and he just gaped at the colonel.

"Do you understand that?"

"Yes, sir."

"You're done for the day. Go back to Uray and your quarters while I decide what I'm going to do with you."

"Yes, sir," Titus said, reaching for the PA.

"I said you go back to your quarters now. I'll take care of this."

Which was against regs, but he guessed regs were only good for enlisted. Officers could do whatever they damned well pleased. He drew himself into a position of attention, saluted, and left for the enlisted lockers to get dressed.

If he'd been considering re-enlisting, he'd just blown it. Maybe it was time to consider that civilian desk job Rodra had been recruiting him for. If he was going to get treated like shit, he might as well get paid better for it.

Chapter 37

Titus snapped his head up, looking around his small quarters. He had a half-empty bottle in his hands. Three empties were on his desk. He scraped the top of his tongue against his teeth, wondering what had woken him.

Three sharp raps on his door gave him the answer. He struggled to get out of the chair, then took another swig of the now warm beer. Three more raps sounded.

"I'm coming, I'm coming," he yelled, looking at the door display. His heart dropped.

Colonel Cannon was standing outside his door, in full uniform. He looked around the room in panic, then dove for the empty bottles and shoved them behind his desk. He pulled down the edge of his T-shirt, then opened the door.

The colonel gave him a long look, and Titus only then realized he was standing there in his underwear.

"Colonel Cannon, sir!"

"Corporal Pohlmeyer. May I come in?"

Sleepiness drained from him like a well-plumbed sink as he snapped to attention, saluting before he

"Of course, sir" Titus said. Looking at his room. It was a mess, not only with a half-eaten pizza and an empty bottle he'd missed, but spread out over the desk were civilian recruitment brochures.

Any hopes he'd had the colonel would miss them were dashed when he walked over, picked it up, and gave it a look.

"Nice starting salary," he said.

"Yes, sir. Uh . . . what time is it?" he asked, wondering if he'd overslept.

"Zero-four-thirty-six."

"What . . . can I put on some clothes, sir? I'm feeling a little underdressed," Titus said, sweeping a hand down his boxers.

"Forget about your clothes, son. I want to discuss this," he said, pulling out a PA.

Titus knew that was the one the colonel had taken from him. He felt a tiny flash of indignation. It would be his ass that it hadn't been turned in the day before. Then the realization of what the colonel had said sunk in.

"I thought—"

"There are ears everywhere, corporal, even in the PAC pool. Some are sticklers for protocol who might not approve if I listened to a soldier who tried to circumvent the chain of command. Others might simply want to be in the know. As much as I hate it, if I want to continue to serve in the AIC, I do have to play politics from time to time. And that goes doubly so when we're dealing with one of the ministries."

Titus nodded. It made sense, he supposed, but that didn't explain why the colonel was standing in his quarters at zero-dark-thirty in the morning.

"We've been hearing whispers that there is a leak in the MOC. Many of them, in fact. The odd conversation, little titbits where Federation and Brotherhood reveal that they know things about our economy that they shouldn't. Things that cost us. Now, I don't know if whatever you found relates to that or not, but I agree that something is up. All the counterintel assets are looking into it, and this is the first bit of evidence that we've collected. And least that AIC has collected. Maybe some of the others."

"If ISA or ESA have Intel, wouldn't they share it?"

The colonel actually laughed. "I forgot how young you are for a moment. Politics, son. Politics. Knowledge is power."

Titus digested that for a moment, then asked, "With all due respect, sir, why are you here? I mean, in my quarters?"

The colonel smiled and said, "I've been talking to Colonel Jaeger."

Titus stiffened. Most of what he'd done with Colonel Jaeger was off-the-record. Oh, it was somewhere, but not in the Army Personnel Files.

"He seems to think highly of you. I contacted him to find out if you were a soldier who could keep his mouth shut about this while others . . . *investigated*. Instead, he told me you had other talents."

"Sir?"

"Are you interested in some field work, Corporal?"

"I . . ."

He didn't know what to say. He'd accepted that his career was over, but given the opportunity to go back into the field? To go hunting?

"Unless those big salaries are your sirens' calls," the colonel said, pointing to the brochures.

"Oh, no sir. I was just . . . I . . . I thought you were going to shitcan me, sir, for going over Major Aja's head.

"I don't like to waste talent on the bullshit, Corporal. So, we need human assets on the ground. Are you my man?"

Titus paused, taking a deep breath. He had to pretend like he was at least thinking this over as a mature, responsible operative would before answering, even if he was like a racehorse pulling at the bit.

"I'm your man, Colonel."

"Excellent. Come to my office first thing in the morning."

"It *is* morning. Sir."

"Keen observation, Corporal." Colonel Cannon marched past Titus toward the door. "My office at ten hundred." And the door shut behind him.

Chapter 38

There were lots of things Titus was passionate about. The economic and political problems of Kyne and the Free States. Football. His career, and not wanting to end up like his dad, stuck as a low-level provisions manager for one of the local mine-supply companies. He wanted to be someone, to do something great.

Fives was not one of those things on his personal radar. Sure, he'd learned about the game in school, and as he spent more and more time on New Mumbai, it became apparent that the sport was a major part of the local culture, so it became a part of fitting in with the rest. Even so, he was never able to dredge up any real excitement for the sport. He would not dare to mention how slow and boring the game could become for fear of being lynched by those with the "Fiver Fever."

The fact that he wasn't a fan and didn't follow the sport explained why he'd barely heard of the Hornets before.

The Hornets played for Biera, a middle-sized city in the north of the planet, far from most of the rest of the population. It was famous for being dull, where the only thing to do on a weekend was to get stinking drunk. That and root for the local Fiver team. The Hornets. Initially made up of weekend players, where drinking and partying were among the main draws, the team won a B-League championship in their second year. The city went ballistic, and the team became its soul. When the Hornets advanced to the A-league, people thought that it was divine intervention.

Unlike every other team in the A-league, the Hornets were owned by the citizens of the city. They controlled the team and the marketing, and instead of wanting to make the Hornets the fan favorites, flooding the market with jerseys, they liked being unique. They limited merchandising, and they were obnoxious at best, pure assholes at worst, when the team played away games. The team quickly gained a reputation as cheaters and bastards, hated by the rest of the league and fans the planet over, especially since the Hornet's play tended to get them to the divisional rounds every year. Worshiped by the Biera citizens, this was the team that everyone else loved to hate.

It had made acquiring a jersey of the team difficult, considering none of the local stores carried them. He'd had to have one dropped-shipped and had to pay double the retail price.

And since it was brand new, he'd had to go through ridiculous efforts to make it look like it was old and beat-up.

He wondered if the effort was even worth it.

It took him three days of preparation, which he frankly needed because there was a lot that he needed to get down pat. He had to pass as a fan.

Despite that, when he entered Run Rabbit Run, a neighborhood sports bar, he still didn't feel prepared. The bar was packed, thanks to the Fives divisional round match between the Biera Hornets and the North Fork Gryphons.

The bar was dark, barely illuminated by wall lights—all the better to see the many screens that cast their own light into the bar. A holostand took up a good chunk of the floor space, tuned into GallantMart Stadium, where the match was being played.

Wasted money.

As with most sports bars, the fans seemed to like the screens better. The holo showed the entire field, but the screen feeds got up close and personal. They could see the expressions on the face, the spinning of the ball, details lost in the holo.

As he expected, the bar was full of fans, most wearing bright red jerseys with a pale gold and white griffin on the front, which contrasted with his black jersey with the bright yellow hornet on the front. As he made his way to the bar, Titus caught more than a few glares aimed his way, but Titus ignored them as a true Hornet's fan would.

"I'll have a cider," he said with a grin to the bartender.

"Dangerous place to be," the man replied, placing a tall mug under the tap. "Gryphs are down three."

"I won't gloat too much," he said.

"Good idea if you don't want to get blood over your jersey."

"Why do you think we make them black. We're used to it."

He turned to the largest screen to watch the match, cheering loudly every time the Hornets scored or yelling at the umpire when a call went against them. Each time he did, heads swiveled in his direction. They did not look pleased, to say the least.

My target better show up soon. Way things are going, I'm looking at getting lynched.

Before things escalated to that point, another patron in a Hornet jersey entered. Aaron Palaver looked exactly like his ID image, a faceless mid-level government worker, like a million others. His jersey was gold with a black hornet, the reverse of Titus's. A few of the Gryphon fans nodded at him before turning back to the match.

Palaver spent a lot of credits at this bar, and with the Hornets playing, Titus had rolled the dice that the man would show up to watch. This time, he'd bet right.

His target went up to the bar where the bartender poured him a draft without asking what he wanted. "You've got company," he said, pointing at Titus, who was facing the main screen, acting like he was engrossed in the match."

"Hell, I thought I was the only idiot here," Palaver said with a laugh before making his way over to Titus.

"Hornet Pride!" the man said, tapping Titus on the shoulder.

Titus turned around, acted surprised to see him, and said, "Hornet Pride!" before raising his free hand, forefinger extended.

The two touched their fingers, then whipped them away, making a zip sound. The "sting." Titus had practiced this a hundred times to make sure he got it right.

"Didn't expect to see anyone from the Hornet's nest here," Palaver said. "I'm usually the only one here."

"Hell, there's two of them now," a woman on the other side of Titus said. "You're bad enough, Aaron."

"Not my fault if you can't see the light, Ann," Palaver said, raising an eyebrow at Titus.

"Hornet Pride," Titus said.

"Aaron Palaver," he said, holding out his hand. "Good to meet you."

"Callan Barksdale. Good to meet you, Aaron."

"I haven't seen you here before, Callan."

"Just transferred in from Mountain Home. I'm with the MOA R&D. Just started at the Gil Agricultural Research Center."

"A farmer?"

"Not hardly. I work with organics. You know, developing the strains to feed the fabricators."

"Impressive. But if you're from Mountain Home, why are you a Hornet fan?"

Titus shrugged, then lowered his voice and said, "Because the rest of the teams are wimps. Especially the fans," he said even quieter in a conspiratory voice. "Besides, I'm not from Mountain Home. I was born in Goa."

"Wow. No needs to say more."

The Goa Rams, or "Lambs," as they were usually called, had a long history of futile mediocracy, having never made it past the divisional rounds.

"What about you? Why are you part of the Nest?"

"Biera born and raised," Palaver said proudly, pounding his chest?"

"No shit? Really? In that case, the next rounds on me," he said, motioning for the bartender.

Palaver visibly puffed up his chest.

Titus still didn't know what Palaver's game was, but the forensic techs had found some interesting bits of data, more than enough to justify a warrant to bring him in for questioning. But the higher-ups wanted more. If there was some sort of ring within the MOC, then they wanted to use Palaver to work their way in. Getting in good with him was the first step.

The Hornets scored again, and the two cheered, much to the disgust of the rest of the patrons. The two did the sting, and the bartender delivered the second round.

Chapter 39

"You going to eat that?" Palaver asked, eyeing Titus's fries.

Titus shook his head. He wasn't fond of Dempsey's and their "secret" fries programming, but the quickstop fab vending kiosk was one of Palaver's favorite, so Titus didn't complain.

Two weeks after meeting in the bar, the two had spent most of their evenings together. Despite that most of the people at Run Rabbit Run seem to know him, they obviously didn't like him—and not just because he was a Hornet fan. The man was a blowhard, with grand opinions of his self-worth, and his somewhat lame attempts to interject himself into any conversation.

The forensics techs had uncovered more than enough to get a conviction. The man was selling MOC data, with Ting as his intermediary. That much was certain. But they didn't know who Ting was. His "wife" had been an electronic construct, window dressing. His back-story was better filled out, but it was just as much an electronic construct. The difference was that the wife had never existed, while he was a very real person. He—or she--just wasn't Winston Ting.

Titus was running out of time. Colonel Cannon had told him that people were getting anxious to get their hands on Palaver, hoping they could break him. The problem with that was Titus agreed with the colonel—who was only passing on what the forensics techs were telling him—that Palaver didn't know anything. He was simply a collection tool, without ever knowing who was doing the buying. If they were going to find out more, someone had to get in touch with Ting, and that someone was him.

He'd chummed the waters over the last two weeks. Acting as if he was boasting, he let "slip" a few references to some new organics they were developing that would bring down fabrication costs. Despite Major Aja's flippant remarks about algae, this would be valuable information, if it were true. It wasn't as if the real MOA R&D weren't attempting it. All governments and big biofirms were always developing new strains. Any hint at a breakthrough would create a prime target for espionage.

He also had shown a level of disdain for the government, which, coincidently fit in with a large percentage of Hornets fans. They were a contrary lot, by-and-large, that liked to separate themselves from the rest of society. That was their reputation, at least, but as is often the case, many rumors were built over a foundation of of truth.

The final support of this three-legged stool, was carping that he wasn't getting paid enough for his work. A real person with Titus's assumed background would be pulling in a hefty salary, complete with year-end bonuses. Callan Barkesdale, though, had taken a government scholarship for school, and now he owed six years to the government. He was getting paid the same as any two-year tech.

Now, he had to set the hook, or his operation would be pulled and Palaver arrested.

Palaver reached across the table and grabbed a handful of fries, dipping them into the blue cheese sauce glopped onto his tray.

"That's disgusting," Titus said without acting. It really was disgusting.

"You don't know what you're missing, Cal. Try one," he said, holding a soggy fry, now dripping with the sauce.

"You can clog up your arteries if you want. I need to keep mine healthy. Fucking medical bills."

"What? You've got GH. You're covered."

"Not for me. For my mom," he said.

"Oh, yeah. Sorry. How is she?"

"Not good," Titus said.

He wished he could form a tear at will, but he'd failed when he tried to practice it.

"She needs a cloned heart, but her t-cells are wonky, so it has to be a genmodded donor, and you know how expensive that is."

"And Public Health won't cover it?"

"Nope. They do the transplant, but not the genmodding."

"Man, that sucks big time," Palaver said before going off on one of his rambling explanations on genmodding, how it was done, and a hundred other details that were not pertinent to the problem Titus presented.

Titus nodded, just wishing the guy would get to the end of his lecture.

"Four-hundred-thou," he said when Palaver took a breath. "That's what it's going to cost."

That stopped Palaver, who looked surprised, then asked, "Do you have it?"

"No. Not even close. I've cashed in everything I can, and we're still almost two-hundred-thou short."

For once, Palaver was quiet, not saying a word as he stared at Titus.

Come on, take the sparking bait!

"I'd do anything for my ma," he said. "Rob a bank, sell my soul . . ."

"I . . . Cal, there's a possibility that I can help."

"Help? Right. I'm sure you've got two-hundred-kay just sitting around," Titus said as he scowled.

"Not me, but friends. Look," he said, leaning in close and lowering his voice to just above a whisper. "You've got no love lost for our exalted government, right?"

"Right. So?"

"Well, there are people who will pay for information, pay well," he said, stopping to see how Titus was going to take it."Titus leaned back and stared into Palaver's eyes. "You mean like the Federation? The Brotherhood? Stuff to overthrow our government?"

"No, no. You watch too many spy thrillers."

Which was the second time in a month he'd been accused of that.

"I'm not talking about anything to hurt the Free States. More like corporate information."

"I don't have access to anything worth—"

"Sure, you do. You work in MOA's research lab. Didn't you tell me you've made some quantum leaps in organics?"

"Well, yeah, but I'm just a tech. I don't have the big picture."

"Doesn't matter. I mean, if you could smuggle out samples, that might be worth big credits. But anything you know would pay off."

"By who? I may think our government sucks, but it's better than the fucking Feddies. I would never—"

"Shh, keep your voice down. No, not the Feddies. Companies."

"But what we're doing will be licensed to the companies. Free States companies."

Palaver laughed, then started in on a ten-minute lecture on how there were no such things as national companies anymore. They were all multi-galaxals, working together and against each other without regards to governments.

Titus had to wait for an opening, then he jumped back. "So, then why do we even do the research? If it doesn't matter?"

"But it does matter. We need the new tech for humans to survive. It doesn't matter who develops the tech nor who implements it. Humankind benefits.

"I mean, that's what I do at MOC. I make sure that the public at large sees the benefits.

You sell data to a foreign buyer. Don't give me that bullshit.

"Really?"

"That's what I do. I just cut through the red tape to get the information out sooner rather than later. You know the government red tape, am I right?"

"Well, yeah, I guess."

You keep trying to justify what you're doing. Hell, I think you might even believe that crap.

"Look, I hope you don't mind, but I've told some people about you. No names, of course, but just what you might have access to."

The surprise on Titus's face wasn't faked.

He already contacted someone? How? And why didn't we pick that up?

Palaver was under constant surveillance. If what he was saying were true, somebody had dropped the ball.

"So, I can arrange a meeting. Not in person, but let you talk it out, see if there's a match."

Titus took a moment, then asked, "But no foreign governments, right? I'm not a traitor."

"No, of course not. Just business. Free States businesses, too, who are just trying to stay ahead of the curve. You know how long the government takes to trickle stuff down. Meanwhile, Feddies companies come out first and steal the market."

Titus acted like he was thinking about it, and Palaver added, "Come on, just take the meeting. If you don't like it, no harm, no foul."

"Well, I guess that wouldn't hurt," he finally said. "So how will I know—"

"Leave it to your buddy here. I'll get back to you before tomorrow."

Chapter 40

"Before tomorrow" was twenty minutes after the two parted company. An excited Palaver said that his "friends" were very anxious to meet him. To his surprise, this meeting was to be face-to-face at a local 15-Pin Alley. Palaver would take him there but would not be part of the meeting itself.

Titus buzzed the colonel with the news who told him to stand pat and go to the small apartment that was in Callan's name for the last two years. Made him wonder, when he'd been given the access codes if the two-year record had been fabricated, or if the apartment had been rented under Callan's name, just waiting for this identity to be needed.

He waited impatiently until almost 0515 when he received the pick-up message. The "trash" consisted of some dirty shirts he stuffed in a bag in lieu of any real trash, which he took to the recycler chute and dumped in. He reached inside the chute and up, pulling out the package that had been placed there. It took an effort of will to wait until he got inside his apartment to look open it up.

The first thing he grabbed was the PA. He powered it up, and almost immediately, the colonel appeared, in full uniform behind his desk. Sometimes, Titus wondered if he lived there.

"Good work, Corporal," the colonel started. "Go ahead with the meeting. You're going in naked, though."

That caught Titus's attention. "Naked" meant without a backup and without a weapon.

"Your meeting won't be with a handler. It will be with an interviewer, who will make the call if you are legit or not. And they'll be watching the alley, probably since before you received the call. It will just be too risky to send in a tech team now."

"But no weapons. sir?"

"No. You'll be searched and scanned to your component atoms. But don't worry. This is only an initial screening. If you pass, then you'll be connected with a handler and given your first mission."

Easy for you to say.

Titus had been there when things went south, and he'd feel much better if he was armed.

"So, no weapons, no recording, no anything. What am I supposed to do?"

"Charm them, son, of course," he said with a laugh, then, "Sorry about that. No need for jokes. Just be Callan Barksdale. Record everything you can remember as soon as it's done, but you do have one more mission."

"What's that, sir?" he asked not getting a warm and fuzzy.

"You will need to mark whoever's there."

"Sir? Mark?"

"Yes, something new. See the green capsule?"

Titus looked through the packet and spotted a generic-looking green capsule in a clear vacuum-pack. he held it up to the PA.

"That one. That's a DNA marker. Just before you arrive, take the pill and bite down. That will release the DNA particles into your mouth. Breath in and out a few times."

"DNA?" Titus asked apprehensively.

Like many people from the Rim, he had a distrust of DNA meddling, even if it was simply a part of modern life. Blame Hollybolly with their huge library of genmodding gone wrong, resulting in everything from zombies to glow-in-the-dark ogres. All crazy, he knew, but still . . .

"Yes, DNA. With a very short half-life. Less than forty minutes. We don't think your meeting will take that long, but keep that in mind."

"For what, sir?"

"Well, I would think it would be obvious. You need to sneeze or cough on whoever you meet. Once they leave, we'll be able to track them long enough for another operator to tag them. They might not be handlers, but they might be able to lead us to them."

Why haven't I heard of this before? he wondered until, *Duh! Need to know. What other little tricks do we have that I don't know about?*

"So, go to work, meet Palaver, and go to the meeting. Easy-peasy."

Once again, easy for you to say.

The colonel went over a few more things, and at 0523, cut the call off. Titus was on his own until after the meeting.

He wanted to go to the gym to relieve some of the stress, but "Callan" did not exercise and didn't have a gym membership. He could get a day pass, but he didn't want to act anything out of the ordinary in case he was under surveillance. It was difficult to stay in his apartment, then go to the lab at the normal time where he sat in front of a screen where a program took over, simulating the work he was supposedly doing.

Lunch was tasteless, a glob of calories, nothing more, that he struggled to swallow. Somehow, the hours finally went by, and he left work, heading back home to the apartment garage and took out his 11-year-old Jasper. The small three-wheeler was beat up, but it worked. He drove to Palaver's apartment building and called him. Fifteen seconds later, the man was opening the door to get in.

"Nice ride."

Titus shrugged. "You know my job. Did you expect a limo?"

"Sorry. Not fair. You'll be able to afford something better soon. Me, too."

"Are you getting paid for recruiting me?" Titus asked.

"Sure am. They pay for everything. And if you can come through, I'll make more than I get in six months, so don't screw it up" he said without a trace of shame.

"Oh, to make sure you get paid, I'll make sure I don't."

The sarcasm was lost on him.

The Royal Court Bowling Alley was twenty klicks away, across the public magrails instead of along them, which was why Titus was driving. And because of this, it would be easier for the bad guys to see if he was being tailed. He could feel eyes on him, and he had to resist checking the rear camera every 15 seconds.

Titus was nervous—not so Palaver. Now that Titus was part of the family, so-to-speak, he felt free to regale him with his work selling information. Titus would have killed for a recording of it all, but that was OBE—Overcome by Events. He had bigger fish to catch.

One thing of interest was the messages that had first caught Titus's attention. The key had been in the numbers. Reading between the lines of Palaver's chatter, it was evident that he had problems with the convoluted encryption techniques, so with him being a sports nut, the decision had been made to simply use scores, since he was messaging everyone else in the galaxy with them. With a simple code, he was able to use the scores to identify online dropboxes and keys to unlock them.

AIC had been defeated by what were essentially onetime ciphers.

"Just remember," Palaver said, "Let me do the talking. I know these guys."

"I thought you said you'd never met them, except for that first time."

"Well, true. But I understand them. We don't want any trouble, right?"

"You expecting trouble?"

"No. I mean, I don't think there will be any, but these guys play for keeps, so we need to keep our heads about us."

"Well, color me reassured," Titus said. "I have a bat under the seat, just in case."

"I hope we don't need it," he said without his normal tone of confidence.

"Are you keeping something from me? Something I should know?"

"No, not really. I just get the impression that they're feeling the pressure. They keep wanting more from me. That's one of the reasons I brought you in. I need them to know I can produce."

He didn't even seem to realize that he'd just admitted to using Titus.

"Still, if they agreed to work with me, it probably means they want to keep working with you. Maybe even push you up into a position of more trust."

"That or they see me as a loose end that needs some cutting."

"That's what the bat under the seat is for," Titus said, making Palaver chuckle. "Look, I'm guessing you've made them a shit ton of money. They won't want to cut that flow just because they're in some kind of trouble. If anything, they need you now more than ever."

The Jasper puttered into the bowling alley parking lot. As Palaver got out, Titus pulled out the green capsule that had been in his pocket and bit down hard.

****

If they needed Palaver, they didn't show it. He was stopped by a small woman with wickedly-intense eyes and told to go to the bar and get himself a drink. The woman turned to Titus and searched him, her hands probing everywhere—something he would have enjoyed under other circumstances but this time made him feel naked. Which was probably their intent. Keep him off-balance. He was glad he hadn't tried to bring a weapon.

The bowling alley was rocking with music and the sound of pins crashing. This was not a quiet, secluded spot, and Titus wondered how he'd be able to talk to his contact. He felt safer in public, though.

Evil Eyes took his PA, then escorted Titus to Lane 33 where middle-aged man with a beer-belly was bowling. The ball hit the center pin head on, leaving only the eleven and fifteen pins standing. Titus had never bowled before, either ten-pin or fifteen-pin, but he had to assume that getting both of them with the next ball was difficult. As Titus stood behind him, the man took his ball, lined up, and let it fly . . . and the ball went between the two pins. A big "YOU MISSED" and a laughing face flashed on the display over the pins.

He turned and shrugged, motioning for Titus to take a seat. He gave a nod to Evil Eyes, who left them alone. Titus started to speak, but the man held up hand to stop him, reaching over the scoring table to flip a switch. Immediately, all the alley noise stopped, to be replaced with a soft humming.

Now it made sense. Bowling alleys were noisy, raucous places, but even the bowling crowd sometimes wanted to talk. Each lane had a small privacy generator, that continually matched the incoming sound waves and counteracted them. What was left was a small sphere where people could hold a conversation.

"So, Callan Barksdale, you want to work for us?" the man said without any social niceties.

"No, sir," Titus said, and the man frowned.

"Then why are you here?"

"I want to sell to you, if the payment is right. But I work for the Ministry of Agriculture, and I don't need another boss."

The smile crept back over his face, and he asked, "But you do know that we will be the only, shall we say, buyers? And if we ask for something, we expect it to be delivered? That sounds like working for us."

"It might sound like it, sir, but it isn't. I work for myself. If you want something, I'll attempt to get it. But I have access to things that I'm sure will interest you."

"Like what?"

Titus was nervous, and it was showing. That was probably fine since Callan would be nervous as well. This was where he'd either succeed or fail. He cleared his throat and started down the checklist he'd memorized. If the man asked him too many questions about them, he wouldn't be able to answer. He had to hope that the man was not an expert.

He would be an expert. Probably psychologist, which was bad enough, but Titus hoped he was not an agricultural expert.

The list had been provided for him, and it was guaranteed to elicit interest. Some of the items were useless, put in there because Callan wouldn't necessarily know what they might want, but within the static were four or five prime targets. The man's eyes lit up after hearing two of them, so he knew something about the field.

After he finished, the man asked him a dozen seemingly unrelated questions. Some made sense, such as why was he willing to sell information (greed), but others were seemingly random, such as his favorite flick (*The Red Star*). Titus had studied interrogation both in the Army's Intel school and on

Earth with the Feddies, but this didn't fit any of the techniques to which he'd been introduced.

And then, the interview was over. Titus checked the old analog clock on the wall. He'd been there 18 minutes.

The man shut off the privacy generator, and the blast of noise almost broke his eardrums. The man laughed at his reaction. Keeping his mouth closed, he took several deep breaths, a technique that was supposed to bring about a sneeze, but he had nothing.

Evil Eyes stepped up to him, PA extended. Titus took it just as the man started leaving. If a sneeze wasn't going to work, then he'd have to go to plan two. He cleared his throat, bringing up some phlegm, and raised his hand to his mouth— to the side of his mouth, not actually covering it—and coughed onto the man's back. The man spun around, and Titus apologized, wondering if he'd just given himself away. Evil Eyes tensed up, her hand moving to his hip where Titus now recognized the outline of a small handgun.

The man relaxed and said, "You'd better get that cough taken care of. We don't want you to miss any days at work now, do we?"

"Yeah, yeah I will."

As the man turned around to leave, a glistening glob of spit on his back caught the revolving lights of the alley.

Chapter 41

While Titus was tagging his contact, the forensic techs had finally gotten some traction. Every tiny piece of information gave them more and more of the total picture.

The first break came through not from Titus, not from Palaver, but from another leak. The fact that this leak wouldn't have been discovered without Titus's initial findings gave him little comfort. Even less comforting was the fact that Major Aja was getting the credit for it.

One of the contractors, HHF, Inc, was a bidder on the new line of armored personnel carriers. Roundly considered the least qualified by the press, it seemed that it was an afterthought to the process, something to make it look like the favored bidder, Boston Systems, had some competition. The fix was in, true, but not in the way everyone expected. HHF won the bid, which was initially lauded as proof that the bidding system was fair and corruption free.

The techs, who were unravelling the network, pulled some communications that indicated something had been off. Numbers changed, dates changed. More unravelling revealed that the bid was fixed. Several acquisition officers had rigged the data to make HHF seem like the best choice over the other four bidders. That was bad enough, but there had been some heavy insider trading taking place, both short-selling Boston System and buying HHF on margin. "This is some fantastic work, Pohlmeyer."

Economic crimes were normally under the purview of the MOC and MOJ, but as this was an Army contract, it went to AIC, with Major Aja as the action officer. Totally in over his head, he'd simply farmed out the analysis and waited for the results. Then he'd forwarded it to MOJ for action. That was it. And he was the Army's golden boy for the moment.

Meanwhile, Titus was going to the lab every day, waiting for his first request from the bad guys. They still didn't even know who they were. Sometimes, they seemed like simple commercial spies, and at other times, there were the fingerprints of a foreign state. With the Federation, that was one and the same, but there were 58 government groups and independent states, and that left too many with the motive to steal from the Free States.

AIC's win in the HHF case made a blip in the news, then faded from the public consciousness. It was soon business as usual. Titus still met with Palaver, still went to the Hornets' games, he still sat on his desk watching the program simulate work. He wanted to scream with frustration.

Palaver seemed overjoyed to have a fellow conspirator, and he came over almost every night. And he was very free with his exploits. It was as if he wanted Titus to know that he was still the big dog. Titus smiled and listened, then sent up a report after Palaver had left for the night, or in the morning if he'd stayed over.

Titus made his first delivery, and that had been a blip in the boredom. He didn't know what he'd delivered. Probably something real, as it would be tested, but not too valuable. For all he knew, the file had a virus that would take down the operation's computers. If it did, no one told him. He was a field operator, and the less he knew, the less he could reveal if he was snatched up.

He had Colonel Cannon's emergency number, and while he held his PA every couple of days to call him for an update, he resisted.

He had Chinese delivered one evening, not the pizza Palaver wanted. But it was his apartment, and he was paying, so it was his choice. Palaver was late, and Titus let the anger fester inside of him.

Fuck Palaver, the dick, he thought after waiting an hour while the Twice-cooked pork and Misty Mountain Lamb grew cold. He opened the lamb and started eating, turning on the wall display, more as background noise than anything else. That was until a story caught his attention. He put the lamb down and turned up the volume.

There had been more arrests, with the NMBI spokesman announcing that another spy ring had been broken.

Who's getting the credit this time?

This was another financial crime, which hinted at corporate spying, but it still could be foreign states. The spokesman pointed to a white-display where an interlocking chart of people and agencies were delineated. One was a vice-minister in the Bureau of Trade. The display cut to him being led away in handcuffs, proclaiming his innocence.

Tell that to the judge, asshole, he thought with a chuckle.

The display reappeared and the line from the vice-minister led to . . .

"Oh, shit!"

Titus dropped the food on the floor, then stepped to the side of the window, looking out. He didn't see anything suspicious, but that meant nothing. He pulled out his PA, ready to put in the call to the colonel, but he held up. He had to find out for sure, first. Too much time had gone into creating his persona.

He pulled a hoodie out of his drawer and slipped it on, then left the apartment to the elevators. To save energy, the apartment was down to one again, and it went to the first floor before starting back up. It stopped for a moment at five, then eight, then continued on up.

Titus got a bad feeling as he watched it. Of course, it was coming up. He'd summoned it, after all. When it reached the tenth floor, Titus's nerve broke, and he bolted down the hall and back to the emergency exit. He opened the door, knowing that it would send a signal to security. Not that Grace Monti could do much about it other than take his photo and register a complaint. She was in her nineties, and not as spry as she once might have been.

Titus took the stairs three at a time, bounding down the floors, going as fast as he could without falling. He stumbled twice, saving himself by grabbing the railing. Puffing hard, he reached the bottom and pushed out the door to the alley in back of the building.

"Calm down, Titus," he muttered, taking deep breaths, then forcing himself to casually walk down the alley, then out to the main drag.

He didn't look towards the entrance, but he could feel crosshairs on his back.

Titus skipped Fortrand Station, the magrail stop a block away, but walked further, to Baseline Station. He tried to act calm, like a nobody going about his unimportant business. The more he tried, though, the more he knew he stuck out. Eight stations down the line, he got off the train and exited the station on the north side of Gil.

He pulled out his PA, opened the Tuesday's Choice Flick, then kept his eyes glued on it as he walked, but every sense locked on the plasticrete and polyndium building on the south side of the street. Nothing looked different, but he walked past it by a block before crossing Gil and heading back. Nothing looked different as he arrived at the building, so he entered the lobby and started to reach for the buzzer to 516 when something stayed his hand. Pushing the buzzer could alert someone.

Titus had a key, courtesy of too many drunk nights, and he used it to get on the elevator and ride it to the fifth floor. The door opened, and presenting as narrow a target as possible, he looked down the hallway. Nothing.

Got to do it.

He started walking down the hallway, trying to move quietly, when the door opened behind him just as he passed. He jumped and spun, ready to lash out.

An old lady looked up at him in surprise, clutching her purse.

"Sorry, ma'am. You scared me."

"A big young man like you? I scared you? You about gave me a heart attack!"

"I'm sorry, I'm sorry."

"I haven't seen you before," she said, narrowing her eyes. "What are you doing here, sneaking around like a thief."

He glanced down the hall to 516, expecting to see the door open.

"Well?" she demanded.

She had just come out of 506. He thought back, and suddenly, with a clarity to make Agent Greer proud, he saw the directory.

"But I've seen you, Mz. Arbatz. Many times."

"Oh," she said, looking confused.

"And I hope you have a great evening. I'm just going down to see my friend now."

"OK," she said, voice wavering. "You have a good evening, too."

Titus turned and continued down the hall, taking his time. He reached 516, and he looked back. Mz. Arbatz hadn't taken a step, and was watching him. He waved.

He couldn't hear anything inside the apartment, but they were built with noise in mind. He placed his ear against the door and was greeted with silence.

From down the hall, Mz. Arbatz started walking down toward him.

He'd rather take more time, but that was a luxury that Mz. Arbatz just wasn't going to give him. With another wave, he keyed the entrance and slipped inside, shutting the door behind him, freezing with his back against the wall.

The apartment was dark, and he couldn't hear anything. He waited for a full minute, listening, before he moved. The apartment was small: one bedroom, a living room, and a bath. It didn't have a kitchen, only a small fabricator and fridge. He didn't see anything in the living room, so he tip-toed to the bedroom door and pushed it open.

Titus had been in battle, and the smell of a dead human, guts exposed, shit, piss and blood spread, was something no one ever forgot. He knew what he'd see before he turned on the light.

Aaron Palaver sat on the bed, facing him. His torso was ripped open, his entrails spread out in what was almost an artistic pattern. His arms were nailed to the headboard, outstretched in a perverse welcome.

Titus slammed shut the door as half-eaten Misty Mountain Lamb was splattered over the floor. He heaved six times before he could control himself.

Pulling out his PA, he entered a series of eight letters and numbers. As soon as the indicator turned green, he shouted out, "Mission abort. I say again, mission abort. Code four-zero-hotel-niner-six-victor. Extract on my position, flash priority."

Titus's missions as Callan Barskdale was over.

Chapter 42

Titus leaned back in the driver's seat, his eyes staring unfocused on the windshield in front of him. The unbearable waiting that he ended up doing in this job was the worst part of it. Just being asked to sit and stew with his own thoughts as other, more important people were assigned the important missions. He couldn't help wondering if this was because he'd pulled chocks on the Callan Barksdale mission. That he'd panicked.

Aaron Palaver had been killed. That much was certain. What wasn't certain was why, and who'd killed him. At least that was the gist of the report on the incident. There was no doubt in Titus's mind. Palaver had talked. He probably hadn't meant to talk, but the guy just wouldn't shut up, and it had brought down a major spy ring, taking some Free States heavyweights with it. The bad guys weren't stupid, and they'd been able to piece together enough to zero in on Palaver.

Palaver was a traitor. He was annoying. But Titus hoped he hadn't been killed as a result of what he'd passed up the chain. It probably was, however. He'd recognized the company name when he'd seen the news report. He'd passed up information about it two weeks before.

And if Palaver was killed, Titus knew he was next. The civilian agent who'd debriefed him (he still hadn't forgiven Colonel Cannon for letting the ISA run the debrief. He was Army, for God's sake, not a freaking ISA agent) seemed to think he'd jumped the gun, that he'd sacrificed all the time and effort it took to create the Barksdale identity because he was scared. He'd turned to an Army lieutenant colonel who was there and said that was what happened when the Army wouldn't stay in its lane, when they sent amateurs into the field. Titus had wanted to jump out of his chair and punch out the arrogant prick, but he'd held back.

He knew he was next. Palaver had brought him into the fold, and he was a liability. He didn't know if those in the elevator coming up were coming for him, but he didn't know that they weren't. If it wasn't them, it would be them the next time.

His personal PA had been taken and left alive. It never rang again. If he were still in their good graces, they would have contacted him again.

He'd already been replaced in G2-30, so he'd had nowhere to go for two days until he'd gotten his orders. He was now a driver. A fucking driver. Oh, those first two weeks, after he'd gotten over the shock, had been fun. He'd taken defensive driving classes, where he'd been able to push the hovers and cars to their max. He'd spent 20 hours at the range, firing over 30 weapons before he'd settled on his personal sidearms. Drivers were also bodyguards, and they were not limited to Army weapons. Titus had settled on a Springfield Armory .45, not because Lem Rodriguez used one in most of Assassin Hunter flicks, but because the handgun made by the centuries-old company fit him well (although the Lem Rodriguez panache certainly didn't hurt).

He looked down at his shoulder holster at the thought. It sure did look good there.

The problem with the job was the boredom. He'd taken some minor functionaries to and from meetings, jumping to hold the door, closing the door, driving them, listening to their prattle on the phone while they preened that they'd finally reached high enough on the ladder to rate a driver-slash-bodyguard. The last three dipwads had even gotten selfies with Titus, proof that they'd arrived.

The truth was that these were only school fodder. Sure, they were getting the service, but they were there for Titus to practice with. He had to perform fifty hours without a problem before he was a designated driver, ready for his first assignment.

The timer on the dash kept ticking away. He'd been sitting here waiting for three hours and seventeen minutes. The only good thing he could say about that was it was three hours and seventeen minutes closer to finishing his fifty.

His PA kept calling him, but he resisted. He couldn't bring up a commercial site, of course, while on duty. The only reason it was even possible was if his passenger needed something, and he had to find out where the nearest Brazil Blue was so the passenger could get double espresso. But he could still use all the rest of its functions.

Hell, he thought, pulling out the PA. *I'm weak. Live with it.*

He pulled up the other timer, the one he started the minute he picked up the passenger and turned off the minute he'd returned them.

Forty-two hours, twenty-one minutes, and twelve seconds. Another seven hours, thirty-eight minutes, and forty-eight seconds to go.

Chapter 43

He was not happy with his assignment. Not happy at all. He was now the personal driver of Brigadier General Aarav Vihan. He was a supply general, not combat arms, and one rumored to be about to retire. Titus had heard about the type. They barely did any work, and certainly nothing that would attract notice. All they wanted to do was served the required two years at the rank and then retire. Life as a retired general in the Free States was pretty cush. Corporate boards loved to have generals and admirals sitting on them. Two days of meetings a year and a huge paycheck.

If he was going to be a driver, then he wished it was for any number of other flags. General Towbin, for example. Rumor had it that he sometimes had his driver drag race other soldiers at Fort Charax while he opened the window and smack-talked the other drivers. Instead, he gets some doddering pogue.

And there he was, coming out into the loading line, fumbling with some papers. Titus jumped out and opened the door, standing at a modified position of attention. Drivers didn't salute when on duty. They needed to have their hands free in case there was an assault on their principal. As if that was going to happen three floors below ground level at the Pyramid.

"To Camp Uray, sir?" he asked.

"Yes, Corporal. Building 4057."

Titus hit the release request, and a Sergeant First Class waved him off, like a launch officer on the flight deck on an ancient wet-water aircraft carrier.

Titus was driving a Proteon III, a midsized commercial limo with beefed-up armor plating. It was a heavy monster, the twelve hover repellers barely able to keep it off the ground. That made it prone to bottoming out, especially when the road changed elevation—like at the end of the loading ramp where the exit took off for ground level. Titus slowed, to allow the repellers to compensate, then sped up once they were on the incline.

The general kept the partition down as he pulled a Fremont from the cooler. Titus had received the general's brief sheet, and Fremont was his non-alcoholic drink-of-choice. Not that he was limited to non-alcoholics. At the drivers' school, the instructors had story after story of drunk passengers puking in the cooler, enjoying the company of others—usually younger and easy on the eyes. When Titus had signed out the Proteon, he'd wondered how many old—but powerful—farts, had gotten laid in the back seat before.

"Sir?" he asked when the general didn't raise the partition. "Is there anything else?"

"So, you're Corporal Pohlmeyer, right?" he asked. "Sorry I didn't introduce myself properly. Too much on my mind, but that's no excuse."

Titus's mouth dropped open before he realized it. He closed it with a snap. Generals didn't apologize to corporals. Hell was about to freeze over.

"Uh, yes, sir. Corporal Titus Pohlmeyer."

"That's a mouthful," he said with a laugh. "So, what do you want me to call you while we're in the limo?"

"Sir? Call me?"

"Yes. Call you. As in 'Corporal,' 'Corporal Pohlmeyer,' 'Titus,' 'Hey you.' We're going to be spending time together, so what do you prefer?"

This was getting weirder by the minute. Maybe that's why he was on his way out. Not Army enough.

"Um . . . sir, you can call me whatever," he said before a phrase his grandfather used to say came to his mind, and before he could stop it, his traitorous tongue said, ". . . except late for dinner."

The general looked up, eyes wide, then laughed uproariously. "I haven't heard that line since Ethan David, and you're way too young to remember him. Who told you that?"

He did know the name. Ethan David was a comedian of fifty years ago. He was a little disappointed to learn that his grandfather had stolen the line from him.

"My grandfather, sir."

"He must have had had exquisite taste. But you didn't answer me. Is 'Titus' OK? Or is that not respectful?"

A general who worries about disrespecting a corporal? Hell not only froze over, but all molecular action has ceased.

"Titus is fine, sir.

"OK, then Titus it is. So, I'm a little tired of the all the BS today. How much longer to Uray?"

Titus checked the trip comp, which took into account traffic, and said, "Just over twenty-three minutes, sir."

"Well, then Titus, tell me about yourself."

This general's off his rocker.

"You read my records before I was assigned as your driver, right sir? I mean, Sergeant Hallis said you picked me."

"Oh, that? Of course. Lots of dry reading. Went hither, stayed three months. Trained thither for four weeks. Worked under Major So-and-so, five months. Dull stuff and doesn't really tell me anything about *you*."

Titus was confused, not knowing what the general was looking for. "Just what do you want to know, sir?"

"Well, you can start with where you're from."

That was on his records, and he was sure the general knew that. But he'd asked, and the Proteon was doing most of the driving at this point. No reason not to humor him.

"I was born on Kyne, a border planet populated originally by soldiers who fought for our liberation—"

"I know about Kyne. Tell me what I don't know. What was it like growing up there?"

"Well . . . it was good, I guess, sir. I mean, I had a good family life, and Kyne's pretty diverse, not like here—"

He stopped cold. He'd been about to say that New Mumbai was very stratified, especially in the upper levels. But the general came from that social and ethnic class.

"You mean here in New Mumbai, where most of us are bindies. I understand. Go on."

He blanched. "Bindies" was a common nickname for those from the Indian Diaspora, and it was used freely used among themselves, but not so much by others. Did the general think he'd been about to say that?

"Well, sir, it was good, like I said. We had a river running through town, and my sister and I spent a lot of our free time fishing. I even caught the biggest cat pulled out of it one year. Almost as big as me—of course, I was only nine at the time. Uh . . . we had schooling through 12 grades. Oh, lots of festivals. Almost every weekend. Those were pretty fun. What else . . . good weather? We had that. I don't know what else you want to know, sir."

"OK, I'll cut you some slack. What about your parents?"

Titus still wasn't sure what the general was trying to do, but he said, "Uh . . . my father, Axel Pohlmeyer, worked distribution for one of the mine supply companies. Never went to uni. My mother worked for the same company at the reception desk. That's how they met. Both are retired now.

"I've got two sisters. Georgia is the oldest, married and with four kids. Melody is the youngest. She's getting her master's in economics in one of the best universities on Kyne."

"You didn't want to go to uni?"

"No, sir. Not for me. I wanted off the planet."

"That's why you enlisted?"

"No, sir. Well yes."

"Which one is it?"

The tone of the question changed, and Titus looked up again, peering at his passenger, studying the man. The laid-back body language was there, the breezy smile, but now it didn't reach his eyes. They seemed to be studying him, actually interested in the answer he gave. It was a trick right out of an operative's playbook, the one that got answers out of people who thought they were asking the questions. Get someone comfortable, get someone talking, and eventually, something would slip out.

Hell, Titus, the guy's in supply, not Intel. You've spent too much time with the spooks.

"My parents worked dead-end jobs their entire lives, and for what? A pittance in retirement? Don't get me wrong. I love and respect them, but I wanted to do something, to contribute to society. I wanted to make my mark on the galaxy."

"And have you?"

"I don't know, sir. I hope so."

The Proteon beeped for his attention. There was traffic ahead, which required Titus's hands on the wheel, even if the car was still driving itself.

"I'll let you do your job, Titus. Thanks for opening up. I'm going to catch a few minutes of Z's, so wake me up as we approach the gate.

"Yes, sir!"

He looked up in the rear-view mirror as the general leaned back and closed his eyes. A few moments later, he started to snore.

Chapter 44

"Lately, I've been spending more time in this car than at home," the general said, leaning his head back and rubbing his eyes.

"I think you're right, sir."

This wasn't simply lip service. The general was a man on the go, his schedule in flux. Titus, like most soldiers, barely gave a thought to what it took to get the Army what it needed, when it was needed. The only time anyone noticed the supply corps soldiers was when something wasn't there to be issued.

Like many soldiers, Titus had a low opinion of "pogues." Technically, as AIC, he was one, but he'd started out as a combat engineer, and while not infantry, they weren't considered pogues. Now, watching the pace of the general, listening in on his side of conversations (the general never raised the partition in the limo) he was beginning to grasp not only how difficult the job was, but how vital it was to the running of the Army. If an infantry unit screwed up, that only affected them. If a supply unit screwed up, that affected all those soldiers down the supply chain.

Titus wished he was back in the field, but this job wasn't bad, and he'd come to respect the general. If he'd thought that the man was just marking time until retirement, the general had destroyed that assumption with his frenetic pace.

And, he just liked the man. The general treated him as a fellow soldier, not a slave to jump at his every whim and desire. Other than keeping the cooler stocked with Fremonts, there was no personal servitude, and after shooting the shit with other drivers, that was rarely the case. Drivers ended up buying flowers for spouses, taking uniforms to be pressed, picking up presents for grandchildren, or anything else the principal wanted.

The worst thing about the job was the waiting. All day meetings out of the Pyramid meant Titus drove the general to them, then waited all day to drive him back. Titus had never been much of a card or game player, but with all that time, often in the company of other drivers, it helped pass the time. When he was alone, he gravitated to novels, something he found he enjoyed and wondered why he hadn't read much before.

Today had been typical. At 0610, he'd picked up the general at his quarters in "Flagville," the nickname given to the flag officer housing complex, then driven him to a conference at the Winsted Arms on the west side of the capital where he'd given a presentation on Army Acquisitions to a mixed government and civilian audience. The general slipped out before the conference lunch—he hated mass meals like these, calling them "plastifood"—and they'd stopped at Chicago Doggies, a small, hole-in-the-wall that he liked to go to whenever they were in this part of the city.

After their quick lunch, it was back to the Pyramid where he had a meeting with his boss, and at 1345, he picked him up to take him to the Annex for yet one more meeting. He pulled up and started to get out when the general stopped him.

"Wait inside the limo, Titus, then when I call you, bring up my PA."

"Sir? You're PA's right there beside you."

"I am aware of that."

Titus was confused, but his orders were clear. He shrugged and said, "Yes, sir."

And with that, the general opened his door before Titus could get to it and marched to the entrance. Titus stared after him until a Navy MP motioned for him to get the hover out of the passenger drop-off. He drove to Lot R and parked. He could see some of the other drivers he knew, but the general had told him to wait *in* the car.

After nine minutes, the general called, saying, "Corporal Pohlmeyer, I seem to have left my PA on the back seat. Bring it to me, would you? Room Twelve-forty-three. I've got you cleared for the floor."

"Right away, sir,"

He had no idea what was going on. Because of that, he noted everything. It was more difficult because he didn't know what was going on, or what the general wanted for him.

He was scanned in at the front security without question, but on the twelfth floor, he went through a more thorough screening, and he had to surrender his Springfield. He reached the room where he was stopped by an Army MP, who scanned him one more time before he could enter.

Room 1243 was a large conference room. There were at least forty men and women standing around, about half in uniform, half in civilian attire, most back near a table laden with snacks, coffee, and tea. He spotted the general, who was standing in a small group of three civilians and a Navy admiral. Titus made his way around the conference table and approached the group.

"I've got your PA, sir," he said.

"Thank you, Corporal," he said with a big smile on his face. "I swear, I'm getting so forgetful lately. I'd forget my head if it wasn't bolted on."

"Whoever invented this aging crap should reevaluate it, Aarav. Heck, I forgot to put on my shoulder boards last week. Came to the Pyramid looking like a Seaman Recruit," the admiral said, pointing up to the gold-laden, two-star shoulder boards, the insignia of his rank.

The others laughed while Titus bit back a smile. He could imagine security turning back an admiral.

"I'm not sure how long I'll be here, Corporal, so don't go back to the limo. Wait for me in the room across the hall. I've already cleared you for it."

"Yes, sir," Titus said.

"Afraid you've forgotten something else? Need your batboy close?"

"I need all the help I can get, Wanda," he said.

Titus turned and left as one of the other civilians started talking about his latest rejuv treatments. "I was told to wait here?" he asked the door security, who pointed to the room directly across the hall.

Titus thanked him and opened the door. If the conference room had forty people, there were half that many in this room, and none looked like drivers. There were officers, all mid-rank, many who sported the braid of an aide. The civilians didn't wear uniforms, but otherwise were just like the officers, up-and-coming juniors with important bosses.

They all looked up as he came in, but when they took in his age and rank, they immediately dismissed him and turned back to their conversations. They'd classified him as a lackey, not worthy of consideration.

What do you think you are? You're all lackeys.

He wished he'd brought in his latest novel. He was three chapters from the end, and he was anxious to see how the main character was going to get out of the mess she was in. He moved to the back of the room where a much smaller snack table had been set up. He was still burping Chicago Doggies, so he took a Coke and stepped to the side, out of everyone's way.

He caught snippets of conversation. The Galaxy Cup was about to get underway on Hiapo. The Free States had two teams in the field of 64, which wasn't many considering the confederation's population, but with Aday in goal, most people thought the New Mumbai team had a shot of making it to the knock-out rounds. The latest Daughters of the Nova had just been released—Titus made a mental note to go see it this weekend—and one woman was giving a blow-by-blow account. Titus turned away so he wouldn't hear a spoiler. And there was gossip. Lots of gossip.

The gossip ran the gamut from the mundane to the spicy— and of course, Titus drank that in. It sometimes still surprised him that the private lives of the high and mighty weren't that different than anyone else. Well, that wasn't quite accurate. The *desires* and *proclivities* weren't different, but they had more tools in the toolbox to act on them.

"So, when's the old perv doing the deed?" a Navy lieutenant was asking a lieutenant commander, that one with the gold braid of an aide.

"Saturday. At the Thunderbird."

"And you have to go make the payment yourself?"

"Yeah, and in person."

"That sucks big time. I wouldn't want a reservation from there on my financials."

"Tell me about it. But he does this shit all the time."

Who does? Titus edged a little closer, but to the two officers, it was as if he wasn't even in the room. Invisible.

"Is he going to pay you back? He didn't last time, right?" the lieutenant asked.

"Fuck if I know. Last time he gave me a vase."

"You've got to be kidding me. A vase? As in a flower vase?"

"Said he can't pay me back in credits because that would flag his account. He said *my* account, but you know . . ."

"Why the hell do you put up with it? I'd—"

"You'd what? Walk out on the next CNO? Give up on the reaping the rewards for all these years of shit-licking?" the lieutenant commander asked.

"Yeah, sorry. You're right. It's still bullshit."

"At least it's not as bad as what Makiko has to put up with."

"Fuck yeah. I'm surprised she hasn't stuck a .38 in her mouth and eaten a round."

Titus didn't know who the lieutenant commander worked for, or who Makiko was, and he wanted to hear more, but the topic veered to more mundane subjects.

The general had said he wasn't going to stay long at the meeting, and that was why he was waiting in the room, but it was almost four hours and after most of the aides had rejoined their principals before the general stuck his head in the room and retrieved him. The general didn't say much until they'd left the hotel and were back on the road.

"So, what'd you learn?" he asked the moment Titus turned over control back to the limo.

"Sir?"

"You were in a room with a group of up-and-comers who spend most of their time with some powerful people. They know them the best, and like people, they like to talk, often about their principals."

"I don't, sir," he blurted out.

"Really? You've never mentioned me?" he asked, like a father with a five-year-old.

"No, I don't—" he started, before he started thinking. "Yes, sometimes, now that I think about it. But never about anything important."

"An expert can glean a lot of information about someone from seemingly *unimportant* facts. But leave that for now. What did you learn today?"

Was this a test?

Sparking right it was a test. But why?

Not for the first time, he wondered about his boss. He was a supply one-star, which was powerful, but hardly the top of the heap. But he was far busier than most generals, more often than not working 16-hour days (and running Titus into the ground). Titus wasn't an expert, but it seemed to him that often, where he went and who he met were not in the supply sphere.

For a moment, the general reminded him of Agent Greer back on Earth. He shook that off and tried to pull up something of interest that he'd overheard.

"Lots of sports. Galaxy Cup's getting ready to start. The new Daughters of the Nova."

"Good film, but *Lost Hope* was still the best in the series," the general remarked. "But go on."

When did he have time to see it? I drive him everywhere?

"A civilian named Ricardo was worried his boss was going to get sacked. I didn't hear the name, but he's a vice-minister."

"Ricardo is right. Vice-minister Khemu will be out of a job by Friday. Basic incompetence, so not my concern."

What the heck does that mean? He meant to say that, not "his concern."

"Oh, and a lieutenant commander was bitching about his boss, someone he thinks will be the next CNO. The lieutenant commander had to pay for a reservation at Thunderbird, and he doesn't think he'll be getting paid back. I didn't hear where Thunderbird is."

"The Thunderbird is a rather posh hotel favored by the rich and powerful for its exaggerated sense of discretion," he said as he seemed to consider what Titus had just told him.

Titus felt the stirrings of the joy of the hunt, something he hadn't felt for some time. His heart started pounding.

"If this admiral might be the next CNO, then this could be important. I can go on Saturday night to see if I can spot him."

The general waved a dismissive hand, "It's not illegal to take a mistress for a night of banging."

"But, he took money from a subordinate. That is illegal," Titus protested.

"That's Lieutenant Commander Justinou's fault," he said. "And yes, I understand the command dynamic here. But he could refuse, if his moral compass demanded it. No, as far as I know, Vice Admiral Jones is a vain, philandering credit-pincher who takes advantage of his rank. That alone is not on my horizon."

What is going on here? Why would a vice admiral be or not be on a brigadier general's "horizon?"

"What else did you hear?" the general asked, full attention back on Titus.

He strained to pull every detail he could remember, which wasn't much. He'd entered the room without knowing he was supposed to listen.

But Agent Greer had said to always be on the job. Sometimes that was when the biggest break came your way.

By the time he was done, he felt he'd been wrung dry by an ITT master sergeant. He was drained.

"So, what did *you* learn, today?" the general asked.

"That we've got an admiral that likes to screw around on his wife?"

"I'm not looking for some flippant quip here," the general said, frowning. "What did you learn in general."

Shit, control your smart-ass mouth, Titus!

"Uh . . . that people gossip, and that's a good source of information?" he asked.

"And, what about you?"

"Me? Well, that I should keep my eyes and ears open all the time and, uh . . ."

"And do what you've done before. You know how to pick out the most relevant pieces of information. You over-ruled an AI and a major before, and you were right."

That was the first time the general had specifically mentioned any of Titus's previous billets.

"As long as you're my driver, you are my eyes and ears. Keep them open, take in the information, and give me good intel."

"Yes, sir. I will."

"I know you will, son. Jaeger said you could, and I think so, too."

Colonel Jaeger has a hand in this? Why?

"Titus, I changed my mind," the general said, changing the subject. "I'm not going back to the Pyramid. Can you take me to my quarters instead?"

"No problem, sir," he said, telling the limos navcomp to change their destination.

He looked up in the mirror. In the back seat, the general had put his head back and closed his eyes.

This conversation was unearthing more questions than he had answers to. One thing was for certain: There was more to General Vihan than met the eyes.

But what?

Chapter 45

Over the next month, it became obvious that the general was the teacher and Titus the student. Yes, he was a driver, and yes, he was a bodyguard, but his prime mission was to absorb what the general could teach him.

Some of it was intel and spycraft, but more was on a wide variety of subjects ranging from psychology to history to economics and everything in between. They spent one four-hour drive discussing agriculture around the galaxy. Titus didn't have a clue as to why that was important, but he soaked up the general's teaching like a sponge.

Several times, Titus was given small missions, mostly hand-offs to the drivers or aides to other men or women while the principals were in a meeting or cocktail reception. He had no idea what was in the files he passed. He was dying of curiosity, but he never asked. For all he knew, he could be an unwitting accomplice to treason, and he'd considered that more than a few times. But his gut told him that the general was on the good guy side.

He just wished he knew who the good guys were.

Chapter 46

"And she puked all over the back of the limo," Santos Carrerra said. "I can still smell it."

Santos drove for ES17 Wilimina Tyson-Panwar, a rising star in the Ministry of Commerce. An ES17 was the civilian equivalent to a brigadier general, but she was half the age of the military junior flags. She was also an alcoholic who couldn't control her impulses during her free time. Titus suspected that Santos offered her more than his job description required, but this was all old news. The general was very aware of Tyson-Panwar's proclivities.

"That sucks," Titus said, meaning it.

"Not that you'd ever have to face something like that, Titus," Petty Officer Three Lee Meung said. "Not with General Boring."

Titus's initial impulse was to defend the general, but that was exactly the persona he was trying to portray. He just shrugged and accepted the statement as if it was true.

"Now me," Meung said, "Admiral Morecock took me to the Gryphs match . . . in a VIP booth. Did I tell you that?"

"A hundred times!" the other two drivers yelled in unison.

"Ah, you're just jealous. I was in the V . . . I . . . P box, for god's sake. Being waited on like a Bindi billionaire." He switched to a high, affected voice and said, "Would you like another drink, sir? Would you like another plate of marsala, sir?"

"Can I give you a blow job, sir?" Santos said in the same voice.

"Eat me," Meung said. "You just wish you were there, too. But your principals suck with a capital S."

"Drivers, As and Bs may pick up your principals now. Cs, wait until I release you," the dispatcher announced.

"That's us, sucka," Santos said. "Hope you get out of here before dark, Titus!"

"Yeah, and I hope Wilimina doesn't puke in your ride, too!" Titus retorted while the other two got up and joined the mass of drivers leaving.

Santos gave him the finger, and Titus picked up his bookpad, flashing up the history book the general had recommended, an account of a United States Marine who was on the USS Philadelphia when it was captured by the Pasha of Tripoli back in 1803, Old Reckoning. As usual, he didn't know why the general thought he should read it, but it was pretty interesting.

Titus had rediscovered reading since joining the Army, but he'd mostly read fiction. Driving for the general, he'd started reading more non-fiction, and that had opened up new worlds for him. He found himself questioning things more, not simply accepting what he was told as he used to.

He immersed himself in the account and was surprised when the C-drivers were called to pick up their principals. It had seemed like he'd started reading only a few minutes ago, but almost an hour had passed.

This conference was at a mountain-top resort 105 klicks from the Pyramid. From the front of the resort, the distant lights of Vishnu lit the horizon. Titus pulled the Proteon into the queue, then slowly crept forward along the narrow entrance. The resort was grandiose, but it was not designed for a hundred vehicles to be there at the same time.

The principals were not helping things along. Titus watched as they started for their rides, only to stop and talk to others who were catching their rides as well. Titus had an almost overwhelming desire to get on the horn and not releasing it until they all got in their limos and got out of the way.

He finally made it to the front of the queue where a black-dressed young woman asked his principal's name.

"Brigadier General Vihan."

She entered that into her pad, then said, "Go ahead and pull up into slot F."

He eased past the other cars, but he never reached the slot. The general was anxiously waiting, and as soon as he saw

Titus, he stepped out to meet him. Titus didn't have a chance to open the door; the general opened it and clambered inside.

"Let's get the fuck out of here, Titus," he said in a tired voice.

"You OK, sir?" Titus asked as he pulled ahead.

"Yes. Just tired."

He looked more than just tired. He looked spent.

"To your quarters, sir?"

"No, to the annex. I've got more work to do."

"Yes, sir." He entered the annex address, but kept control of the car. The road down the mountain to the expressway was winding and small, and he felt better being in control.

He looked in the rearview mirror. The general's eyes were closed.

They rode in silence for the next hour, but Titus kept checking on the general. The man hadn't moved. Sometimes, Titus forgot that despite his drive and seemingly unflagging energy, the general wasn't a young man, but in times like these, that became clear.

Sparking hell. I'm not going to let him work anymore tonight.

"General? Sir?"

The general stirred, then opened his eyes. "What?"

"Begging your pardon, and I hate to suggest this—"

"But you're going to, anyway, right? So why bother to say that?"

"Well, yes, sir. I think you need to go to your quarters. With all due respect, you're not really in shape to do anything productive. Go home, get a good night's sleep, and I'll be there to pick you up at zero-dark-thirty, if you want. Or, say, zero-eight-hundred?"

"'With all due respect' you say? In enlisted talk, that means listen up, you knucklehead, right?"

Titus chuckled, then said, "I cannot confirm nor deny that, sir."

"Where are we now?" he asked, rubbing his forehead.

"Three clicks from the cut-off. I can take that, then have you back in twenty minutes. Or, we can go to the annex, fight the Friday night traffic, and you can spend two hours getting five minutes worth of work done."

"Hell, is it Friday?"

The annex was situated in Fox Heights, which had enjoyed a revival over the last few years and was now one of the city's hottest entertainment districts. It was packed every Friday and Saturday night.

"I promised General Kelly I'd meet with him there."

"You can call him, sir. Reschedule."

The general sat silently for a moment, and then said, "I probably could use a little shuteye." He pulled out his PA, connected to General Kelly, and said, "Sir, General Vihan here. I was wondering if we can put off the meeting tonight. Truth be told, I've been running ragged and I'm . . . oh, OK. Great, sir. On Monday? . . . Yes, sir, I'll see you then. Have a great night."

"The general's tired, I gather?"

"He's already home. Forgot about the meeting."

"So, you're free of all obligations, and the cut-off is coming up. Your quarters?"

"What the hell. Yeah, home, Titus."

Titus knew he was getting protective of the man, but this was the right thing to do. He went into manual mode and took the exit. The Banas Parkway was more of a small road, but it led through green spaces around the outskirts to the city. With no traffic lights or circles, it would be a straight shot through the hills, coming out into the city proper just over two klicks from Flagville. In the daytime, it was lovely and peaceful. At night, with no lights, it could seem like he was driving through a tunnel with huge, centuries-old banyans lining the way.

Urban legend had it that the banyans were not part of the original terraforming, but the first settlers just wanted a taste of home, and they sacrificed a portion of their weight allowances to bring the saplings, each passenger bringing one. Now, the forest was a planetary treasure.

And it was very dark. Titus slowed down. He had the forward sensors running, of course, but there was a herd of axis deer in the park and adjacent green spaces that had a habit of sitting at the side of the road, then panicking and dashing in front of vehicles when they got close.

"Thanks, Titus," the general said as they drove through the banyans.

"No problem, sir," he said, looking up at him in the mirror.

The front sensor alarm sounded, and Titus started to slow down when his lights illuminated . . .

"Get down, General!" Titus shouted, slamming the limo into reverse and stepping on the power to perform a J-turn.

Instead of a deer in his headlights, a man had stepped out into the road, a missile launcher on his shoulder.

Titus just started his J-turn when the man fired, a gout of flame lighting the night as the missile covered the distance in a second and slammed into the front right side of the Proteon where it shot out stream of superheated plasma that destroyed the powerblock compartment in a microsecond, slamming the heavy limo onto the road. The limo's passenger compartment armor shell held, but the Proteon was dead-in-the-water.

"Are you OK, sir?" Titus asked.

"I'm with you, son."

Rounds started pinging on the windshield, tiny stars appearing where each one hit.

"Fleet control, Mayday, Mayday. We are under attack by unknown assailants along the Banas Parkway. Vehicle is disabled. I repeat disabled," he passed on the emergency net. Powered by a standalone battery inside the cab, it wouldn't be affected by the powerblock being taken out. Except the LED confirmation remained a stubborn red. He tried it again, but it still remained red. The transmit LED was green, but it wasn't getting to FC.

Which meant they were being jammed. The missile was one thing, but with the jamming, Titus knew this wasn't a simply hijacking or robbery. This was an assassination attempt.

"My Mayday didn't get through. I think they're jamming us," he said, turning around to face the general.

"What do we do?" the general said, his voice almost steady with just a hint of wavering to show he was nervous.

"I need to see what's happening."

He reached for and pulled on the night-vision goggles and looked out through the windshield. Twenty meters ahead, the missileman was pulling another missile from a pack at the side of the road and fitting it into the launcher. Flashes of fire sparkled among the trees. With the armor, those rounds were harmless, but they were being fired to keep the two of them pinned for the more powerful weapons. Titus and the general had survived the first missile, but at some point, they'd be rooted out.

But the Proteon, while dead, still had a few surprises. Titus flipped the emergency circuit, and the dash came to life again. The right front beamer was dead, but the left front was still operational, charging up from the emergency cells. The problem was that it was such an energy hog that they might only get two shots from the plasma gun—and since it could not be aimed across the limo, Titus had to hope someone approached from that side.

He had the right rear Stapleton, though. It fired a linked .35 caliber jacketed round, which only needed the minimal power to activate the trigger.

Ahead of him, the missileman had locked in the new missile and was synching the control. Titus and the general only had seconds left before he'd fire.

Titus jammed his thumb over and over on the Stapleton's release. Under full power, the weapon could be deployed in a second. Under emergency power, the cover slowly receded and the stubby barrel raised.

"Come on, baby. Hurry!" Titus said, trying to will it to speed up.

The missileman didn't seem to be in a hurry. The two of them were trapped, after all. He stared at the control for a moment before he nodded, then moved several steps to his left, presumably for a better angle directly into the cab. The Stapleton was fully deployed, but it had to be aimed. Titus set the crosshairs on the missileman's center-of-mass, then waited, nerves screaming, as the Stapleton's aiming point started to swing to the crosshairs. Too slowly.

The missileman had on NVDs as well, and with the missile on his shoulders, he took a moment to smile broadly and give Titus a thumbs up.

Big sparking mistake, buddy!

That short delay was enough. The two points hadn't exactly met yet, but the instant the Stapleton's aiming point reach the missileman's extended elbow, Titus fired, walking the gun in. Whether that first round hit or not, it made the missileman jerk away, dropping the missile. The next round, or maybe the one after that hit, and he dropped.

"Did you get him?" the general asked, trying to control his fear.

"Yes, sir. Dropped the sucker."

"So, now what?"

"They can't get us with small arms, sir. FC is going to know we disappeared, and they'll scramble. We've got to hold out maybe five minutes?"

"They can't get us in here?"

Titus lowered the aim of the Stapleton into the missile pack, then fired a ten-round burst. The pack blew apart as the rounds chewed up the missiles. He then raised the aim and fired into the trees, just to remind those out there that they were still armed and dangerous.

"Not unless they have something bigger. Protocol is for us to remain in place," he said. "Don't worry, this is a strong cage.

"You do have your supermans on, though, right, sir?"

"Uh . . . not exactly."

"Shit, sir. Why the hell not?"

"Supermans" was the nickname for a thin two-piece body suit, worn under clothing, that offered a degree of protection against shrapnel and some small arms. After Admiral Gil had been killed a month ago, the Supreme Command had ordered that all flag officer wear the armor when out and about. That was already the SOP for bodyguards such as Titus, but many of the flags balked.

"They make me itch. I thought it would be OK. Besides, I'm just a one-star. A nobody."

Itch or dead, sir? Which one? And I really doubt that you're a nobody.

Titus had two more sets of supermans in the trunk of the limo, but he couldn't very well just go saunter out and get them.

"Well, hopefully you won't need them," he said before he reached under the dash pulled a Big Yancy out from under it and passed it back to the general. From the second slot, he pulled a Windmoeller SST and checked the magazine.

The general powered the Big Yancy up with sure hands. It was a short-barreled weapon designed for close-in fighting aboard a ship with a max effective range of about twenty meters, but within those 20 meters, it was a killer.

"Let the bastards come," he said, his voice steadier.

There was a thud hitting the roof, different from the pings of small arm. Titus looked up, but couldn't see any damage.

"Don't know that that was, but we look fine—" he started to say when a brilliant light erupted beside the Proteon, sparks shooting into the air. The windows couldn't dim fast enough to compensate.

Titus whipped off his NVDs before his sight was ruined.

"They're trying to burn us out," the general said as he scooted to the window to look out. "That's an incendiary!"

As an engineer, Titus was very familiar with the various incendiary devices used my military services. They were small, but put out an amazing amount of heat, enough to destroy artillery pieces to keep them from being captured or burn their way into a bunker. They were not considered weapons, but just last month, a Feddie Marine had used one to take out an armored pirate during a ship rescue. The armor protecting the cap was top-of-the-line, but it couldn't stand up to an incendiary grenade. Depending on the make and model, it might take a few seconds, but it would burn through.

"Get ready, sir. We may need to make a break for it. Run to the limo's seven o'clock and don't stop. Keep trying to get out the Mayday."

"And what will you be doing?"

"I'll try and hold them off long enough to give you a chance to break away."

The general nodded, not bothering to go through the facade of protesting. Titus's job was that of a bodyguard, not the other way around. General Vihan had to be protected, and if there was any truth to the vague notions that had been running through Titus's head over the last couple of months, the general was far more important than his current billet would make him.

There was another thud on the roof. Both men froze, looking up. Titus was just about to relax when a brilliant light appeared on all sides of them. The inside of the roof started to glow.

"Now, now, now!" Titus shouted, vaulting over the center console and opening the general's door. He dove out, then pulled on the general, yanking him to the ground outside just as the grenade fell through the roof. Radiant heat almost singed his face.

Incoming fire increased as rounds impacted on the burning limo. Titus stood up and sprayed the trees, telling the general, "Get ready."

He ducked back down, then pointed in the limo's eight o'clock. "Try and keep the limo between you and the firing. If they're using scopes, the fire will work against them."

The general nodded, gripping his Big Yancy.

"OK. One . . . two . . . three!" he shouted as he popped back up, shooting through the black billowing smoke into the trees. He doubted that he's hit anyone, or even came close, but he hoped that whoever was out there would focus on him.

He heard the general get up and start running, then a single, sharp report, different from the rest of the incoming fire. That was followed by a grunt and a thud.

"Shit," he yelled, realizing immediately what had happened. The assailants had placed a sniper who had patiently waited while others tried to take them out first with missiles, and when that failed, with an incendiary grenade. The sniper was the third line, and Titus had let them be flushed like rabbits.

Titus bolted to the general, who was trying to get to his feet. He grabbed the general under his arms, then dragged him away. He felt two rounds hit him, but his superman protected him. Not with the third time. There was the crack, then the sniper's round struck him in the back on his right scapula. A superman was useful, but it couldn't stand up to whatever the sniper was using.

Titus stumbled, dropping the general.

Come on, Titus. Just push through it.

He fired a burst with his Windmoeller in the general direction in which he thought the sniper was, then dropped it. He needed his left arm to carry the general. With a grunt, he hoisted the general to his shoulder like a sack of rice, then bolted to the trees.

To his utter amazement, he made it. He ran another fifty meters before the shock of being shot set in. A wave of dizziness swept over him, and he fell, dropping the general.

"Are you with me, sir?"

"I'm here. I don't know how long, though," the general whispered.

Titus straightened the general out, then gave him a quick once over. He'd been hit high in the left side of the chest, the round going through him and out his lower right side, a gaping, fist-sized exit wound. He was surprised that the man was still conscious.

"Don't worry sir," he said, pulling a pressure pad out of his medkit and plastering the exit wound. "You'll pull through."

"I hope so," he said before breaking out int a coughing fit, blood black in moonlight. "But, I can't be captured, son."

"I'm here to make sure that doesn't happen."

A steel hand gripped his upper arm. "No, you don't understand. I *cannot* be captured."

"Sir—" he started to say before shouting reached them. Just getting into the woods was not going to stop their assailants.

"This isn't some Hollybolly flick, son. You can hold them all off. If . . . when things get dire, do it," he said, nodding at the Springfield in his shoulder holster.

"Permanently?"

"Permanently."

A supply general might be a useful prize for kidnappers, senior enough to hit the media and be worth something. He wouldn't have any information, however, of use to a foreign power. The fact that he'd just ordered Titus to shoot him in the head, making resurrection impossible, hinted at much more.

The assailants, though, had tried to kill him, but with a body shot, not a head shot. This could be a terrorist attack, but the way the general was still gripping his arm, there could be many more layers to that.

"Roger that, sir," he said as the general closed his eyes and relaxed his grip as whatever was driving him faded. "But let's see if we can avoid all of that."

The shouting was getting closer as they tried to cut off the two of them. Or maybe they were shouting to herd them. The obvious route to escape led directly down the hill where the outskirts of the city were probably 700 or 800 meters away. Titus didn't like taking the obvious way.

"Can you hold on if I get you to my shoulder?"

"Like a baby possum, son."

Titus picked the general up, and with his help, got him to his right shoulder. Pain was radiating from where he was shot, and having the general draped over him made things worse. But he needed his left hand free.

His NVDs had been lost in the confusion, but he had his ears. He listened for a moment, and between the shouts and sounds of bodies moving through the forest, he thought he had a decent-enough picture of the situation. At least six assassins were moving toward them, with the only opening downhill. Something told him, however, that they'd left a surprise in that direction.

He locked onto a voice to his left, drew his Springfield with his left hand, and with the general holding on, charged. Only 25 meters into the charge, he burst upon the surprised assailant, who got off one un-aimed shot before Titus double-tapped him, one in the chest, one in the head. He didn't stop but vaulted over the body and kept running. Voices shouted out behind him as he cut over and back to the Banas Highway, then turned and ran *away* from the city, not toward it. He hoped that would buy him some time.

After only 200 meters, however, he started to flag. He wasn't ever the best athlete around, he'd been shot, and the general was freaking heavy, now just a dead weight. Titus dropped the general once, then managed to get moving again at a slow trot. As soon as the assailants realized where he was going, they'd be able to run him down. He considered just getting off the highway and try and hide, but he was pretty sure that they'd have the basic scanners and he'd light up a temperature scan like a Christmas tree.

Titus was blowing so hard that he missed the first call. He caught the second, though.

"Victor-delta-one-three-six, what is your situation."

"Transport Control, we are about 600 meters from our vehicle along Banas away from the city," he said. "My principal has been shot and is in serious condition. I need an immediate medevac."

"Roger that. This is Alpha-four. We've got the quick reaction team enroute. ETA on your pos in four minutes. Will have Fitzgerald Emergency standing by for your principal. Keep this line open."

Alpha-four was the Army central watch, the round-the-clock nerve center at the Pyramid. This had quickly gone beyond Transport Control.

Titus strained his ears for signs of pursuit, but he was breathing so hard that he couldn't be sure. He was at his limits, though. He had to turn over the general's survival to the reaction force. With a grunt, he lowered the general to the ground. His principal was still alive, but barely. Titus had seen his fair share of injuries and death in battle, and he was surprised the general still had even the tiniest grasp of life. And since he hadn't had to follow the general's orders and blow out his brains, even if he passed now, he should be a good candidate for resurrection.

A crack in the forest below startled Titus, and he drew his Springfield again. Instead of pointing it down into the forest, he held it against the general's temple, his finger tight on the trigger. If someone took him out, he hoped his finger would contract and fire the round into the general's brain.

That was how the reaction force found him three minutes later, unresponsive. A PFC gingerly pushed the barrel of his Springfield aside, then medics loaded both in the Stork and whisked them away while the rest of the force tried to track down the assailants.

They never found them.

Epilogue

Titus reached for his bravos, then recoiled as the pain lanced through him. After a month-and-a-half of regen and therapy, he'd have thought he'd learned by now. His supermans might not have stopped the heavy .330 round that the unseen sniper had fired at him, but they'd slowed it down enough so that his scapula hadn't shattered into a hundred pieces. Once the round was removed, he had a fairly benign regen and therapy—but he'd still been shot, and it would take several months to fully recover.

He switched arms and brought down the uniform, which he hadn't worn since the assassination attempt. His uniform of the day since then had been sweats and zip-up hoodie, but since he was requesting leave, and since he was using the regen doc's letter saying he was fit enough to travel, he wanted to present as normal an appearance as possible.

He checked his ribbons and insignia, then gingerly put on the blouse. He'd grit his teeth and fake it if he had to. With no work other than rehabilitation, he was going bat-shit crazy, and if that was his fate, he'd rather do that on Kyne at his sister's graduation. No Pohlmeyer had ever graduated from uni, and Titus was busting with pride that Melody had broken that not-so-great streak.

Looking . . . presentable, if not sharp, he left the barracks and made his way to the battalion office. Unlike most battalions—no cohorts, Titus kept having to remind himself-- where the officers and SNCOs knew every soldier in the unit, the Headquarters *Cohort* was merely provided admin support for hundreds of soldiers who worked at Army HQ. The commander had no control over the soldiers in the century, and he didn't see them on a daily basis.

Titus entered the personnel office and said he wanted to put in for leave. The clerk didn't know Titus from a hole in the ground, but there were procedures in place. The PFC pulled up his records, then asked for the Medical Century's approval of the request, which he handed over. Two minutes later, he had his leave approved and in hand.

As he started to leave, the PFC said, "Corporal, the sergeant's cutting score came in about an hour ago. Congratulations. You made it."

"Really? he asked, surprised. He knew he should be getting close, but for some unknown reason, he hadn't been paying it much heed. He wanted to be a sergeant, of course, but unlike when he'd made corporal, he hadn't been checking the message logs every day.

"That's what it says. You'll probably pin it on . . . let me check . . . I'd say the first of September."

"Well, thanks," he said, suddenly feeling in a much better mood. Getting his leave approved. Finding out he'd made the cutting score for sergeant. It had been a pretty good day.

His leave didn't officially start until midnight, so he had an entire day to kill, and no one to kill it with. Unless he headed back to the hospital. He'd become casual friends with several other rehabbing soldiers there, and he could at least share the good news with them.

His PA buzzed, but the calling number ID was blocked. He was tempted to ignore it, but he was in such a good mood that he answered.

"I see you got your leave approved," Colonel Jaeger said.

Shit, is he keeping that close a watch on me?

Titus was not in J3, and he would not be up for reassignment until he was released from the Medial Century with a clean bill of health. The colonel had contacted him a few times to monitor his progress, but the therapists and doctors were like guard dogs, making sure old units didn't try and get wounded soldiers to "just come in for an hour. You're the only one who knows blah, blah, blah."

"Yes, sir. Going home to see my sister graduate. I leave at zero-three-twenty."

"You must be pretty proud," he said, but without feeling. That was just the social thing to say.

"Look, I need to talk to you before you leave. Where're you at now?"

Technically, it was hands off of him, but the colonel would still be a colonel when he was back on full duty, so he said, "I'm at battalion. I mean, cohort. I'm about to head up to the hospital—"

"Great. Meet me at the general's room in thirty."

Titus knew who the general was. While General Vihan was supply and the colonel was AIC, it had become clear to Titus that there was a connection between the two. He had ideas on what that might be, but he didn't want to assume anything.

He'd probably have stopped by the general's room anyway, so he agreed.

General Vihan had died on the way to the hospital from the ambush. He'd been rushed into the zombie ward, where he'd undergone an immediate resurrection. With no brain trauma and the short amount of time he'd been biologically dead, the resurrection had been rather routine. Titus knew none of this at the time, being unconscious from his own wounds and loss of blood.

While the resurrection had worked out well, it had been the regen that caused all the problems. His body had a severe reaction to the regen drugs, and he'd been on the brink of dying again three or four times. The reaction had also been serious enough that he'd had brain damage.

The doctors had struggled to save the man, and they'd only just managed to keep him on this side of the River Styx. With such a serious reaction to regen, he was no longer a candidate for more. He was alive, albeit with brain damage, and he'd have to go through healing the old-fashioned way.

Titus skipped the therapy ward when he arrived at the hospital. He'd catch the boys later after he was done with the colonel. He took the elevator to the top floor. A Navy MP manned a post there, and he signed Titus in, not bothering to ask for his ID. This wasn't the first time Titus and come to visit.

Ward V was for VIPs. Some were on active duty, most were retired. This was where admirals and generals came to heal or to die. Compared to the lower floors, such as where the therapy for lower ranks took place, the ward looked like a high-end spa.

"Hey, Titus," a weak voice called out of a room as he passed it. "You coming to see me today?"

"Sure will, Admiral. Just let me check on the general first."

Admiral Sochi Khan had been the CNO forty years before, and he'd run for president, being beat by a miniscule 40,000 votes. He'd been brought to Fitzsimmons nine months ago, and he'd probably never leave alive. He'd cornered Titus a month ago, on his first visit to the general, and to Titus's surprise, he rather enjoyed the old man's company. Now, each time he came to visit General Vihan, he'd stop by and play a game of chess with the admiral.

Maybe someday I'll actually beat him.

The nurses at the station looked up as he walked by, then ignored him. They knew where he was going.

Titus rapped on the door frame of the general's room, then walked in. Colonel Jaeger was already there, and he stood up, hand out to shake. Titus didn't know what the colonel wanted, and to be honest, he was a bit wary. He shook the hand, then waited.

Instead of speaking, the colonel took out a small cone, placed it on the tray beside the general, then activated it. A small pressure wave washed over Titus. He didn't have to be told. All three were in a sphere of silence, essentially free from eavesdroppers.

"Ajun, if you will," the general said.

Colonel Jaeger stepped back, out of the sphere.

"How are you doing, sir?" Titus asked.

"Shitty, like always. The docs say it'll be a year at best before I can be discharged."

"And . . . ?

"It comes and goes. Sometimes I forget things. Other times . . . well, it's like someone poured concrete into my brain housing group."

"Will you get better?"

"That's the question, isn't it, son."

The general had taken more and more to calling Titus "son." Titus rather liked that. He'd become very fond of the man, general or not.

"I should be . . . what's the word? You know, when you can do things?"

"Functional?"

"Yeah, functional," he said frustration evident in his voice. "I should be functional, meaning I won't need someone to wipe my ass or make sure I don't wander away. How much more, no one knows."

He took a deep breath, then stared off into space for a moment.

"But enough about that. First, Ajun says you made the cutting score for sergeant. Congratulations, son."

"Thank you, sir."

"I'm sorry we couldn't have sped that up. You've deserved it, and anywhere else, you'd have been meritoriously promoted. But in our line of work . . ."

Our line of work? Supply?

But Titus didn't blink. He knew the general was not just a supply officer. What else still eluded him, though.

"We have to keep a low profile, sir."

"Yes. We do, even if our work is vital."

"What is our work, sir?" he asked, emboldened by the sphere of silence and the direction of the conversation.

"Have you given thought on what you want to do when you are back on full duty?" he asked, deflecting the question. "You can't be the driver for an old fart who's restricted to his bed, after all."

"I haven't given it much thought, sir. The needs of the Army, I guess."

"And you'll excel wherever that is, I know. But, most jobs for you would be a tremendous waste of resources, but I think I have a job that might interest you more. Suit you more."

"You know, sir, that's pretty similar to the speech Colonel Jaeger fed me when he was recruiting me for AIC."

"That's probably because I told Captain Jaeger something pretty similar to that, and that, in turn, was pretty similar to what I was told back when I was a lieutenant many years ago."

Titus had expected some revelation, but not that.

"Recruited for what, sir? I don't understand."

"I know you don't, son. I was recruited into the Shield Society."

"I've never heard of that, sir."

"That's not surprising. We've kept it that way. We're a small group of, shall we say, *influential* persons from varied government ministries and businesses whose goal is to keep humanity safe. Safe from outside attack, and safe from tearing itself apart."

"You are part of one of those cabals who work against the government?" Titus said, recoiling.

"Oh, come on, lad. You know me better than that, I hope. Almost all of us are Free States citizens. I would never work against our government, but I use my influence, such as it may be, to nudge and steer us away from conflict and to cooperation."

The general was getting excited, and his mind seemed clearer. "I serve the Confederation of Free States, but I also serve humanity. We are more and more divided. Pirates roam the Far Reaches almost at will. Religious crackpot groups like the Soldiers of God spew hate and death, trying to bring about Armageddon. The Federation sinks in a morass of decay and corruption, and the Brotherhood takes away more and more basic human freedoms. If we can't right the ship of humanity, we might tear ourselves apart."

Titus tried to digest what the general had said. It was hard to take in. Some group in the shadows that worked for the good of humanity? That sounded like a Hollybolly fantasy.

There had been other such groups in history, but none had lasted. Most had fallen into corruption themselves. Was this the same thing?

"What do you expect of me, sir? I mean, what would I be doing?"

"Whatever you are called upon to do, son. If you accept, you'll stay in the Army, with your AIC job, whatever that may be. You'll be fed operations from time to time. You'll be given access to resources you've never dreamed of. It's for a higher cause than any government could give you.

"But before you commit, you won't get any glory. Very few will know what you've done. We don't make waves, for good or bad. You've seen how I'm treated. Most people think I only got to where I am because of my family connections. Anything you do through the Shields will be in the shadows, away from any cameras or spotlights. No glory, just commitment. Not to some government or agency or another but to the entirety of the human race."

Titus looked up, still trying to read the general's face, still trying to understand just what the man was saying. "I honestly can't tell if you're serious or not, sir."

"Rest assured that I am. We would have groomed you longer, but the gods are capricious when they play their games. I no longer have the ability to fulfill my duties. Colonel Jaeger will be stepping up to my place. Others will step up, but that will leave a gap in the operators' ranks. We both think you are the man to fill that gap."

"Was this the reason you asked me to shoot you in the head when we were ambushed?"

"I know too much. If they were trying to capture me, I could not let that knowledge fall into their hands."

"Who were they?"

"We don't know. Maybe they were targeting me for who I really am. Maybe they were terrorists who just wanted a high profile kill. Good Lord, we've got enough of them running around. It wouldn't take a genius to know that at least one of us returning from the meeting would take the cut-off."

"Could it have been the government, sir? Our government?"

"Yes. It could have. I am not working against the Free States, but there are some within the government who give more fealty to the almighty credit than to the citizens. We want to stamp out corruption, and some would find that a threat."

At least he didn't lie about that.

"And if I say no? If I walk out of here, what will happen? Is the colonel there to clean things up if I say no?"

A hurt look came over the general, and he said, "No, Titus! If you walk out, then that is your choice."

"And if I turn you in as traitors?"

The hurt look grew deeper. "Then we've misjudged you."

Titus was sorry he'd hurt the general, but this was something pretty big to have thrown in his lap. He had to know what he was getting into.

Hell, "getting into?" I guess my mind is already made up.

Titus was not a traitor, and he would not work against his people. But he'd already been fighting to root out corruption, he'd already been working as an agent for good. If the general was being forthright, then this was simply a cell within the larger effort to serve not only the Free States, but humanity. Goodness knows there was enough evil in human space to keep someone busy for a lifetime trying to stamp it out.

The key assumption was that the general was telling the truth. Was he an agent for good or evil? The man had been willing to die to protect his cause, which was to his credit. Evil men rarely would sacrifice themselves for a cause. But this was beyond that one action. Titus had known the man for four months, but in that time, he thought he'd been able to judge the temper of his steel. And Titus was sure his blade was true.

If he was being hoodwinked into something, he could always take action later. But for now, he was onboard.

"I am your man, General. I'm your man."

Thank you for reading *Soldier,* and I hope you enjoyed it. As always, I also welcome a review on Amazon, Goodreads, or any other outlet.

If you would like updates on new books releases, news, or special offers, please consider signing up for my mailing list. Your email will not be sold, rented, or in any other way disseminated. If you are interested, please sign up at the link below:

http://eepurl.com/bnFSHH

Other Books by Jonathan Brazee

Agent of the Confederation
Soldier
Spy (coming 2019
Puppet Master (coming 2019)

The United Federation Marine Corps
Recruit
Sergeant
Lieutenant
Captain
Major
Lieutenant Colonel
Colonel
Commandant

Coda

An Accidental War (A Ryck Lysander short story published in BOB's Bar: Tales of the Multiverse)

Rebel
(Set in the UFMC universe.)

Ghost Marines
Integration (2018 Dragon Award Finalist)
Unification
Fusion (coming soon)

The Return of the Marines Trilogy
The Few
The Proud
The Marines

The Al Anbar Chronicles: First Marine Expeditionary Force--Iraq
Prisoner of Fallujah
Combat Corpsman
Sniper

Werewolf of Marines
Werewolf of Marines: Semper Lycanus
Werewolf of Marines: Patria Lycanus
Werewolf of Marines: Pax Lycanus

To the Shores of Tripoli

Wererat

Darwin's Quest: The Search for the Ultimate Survivor

Venus: A Paleolithic Short Story

Secession

Duty

Semper Fidelis

Checkmate (Published in *The Expanding Universe 4*)

Non-Fiction

Exercise for a Longer Life

<u>Author Website</u>
<u>http://www.jonathanbrazee.com</u>

Twitter
@jonathanbrazee

www.ingramcontent.com/pod-product-compliance
Lightning Source LLC
Chambersburg PA
CBHW061543170626
46811CB00001B/64